Towards
the
Within

REECE WILLIS

D1534187

Published by Worldworx Publishing 2018

www.worldworx.com

A catalogue record for this book
is available from the British Library

ISBN: 978-1-9164301-2-9

This novel is a work of fiction. Names, characters, places and
incidents are either the product of the author's imagination or, if
real, are used fictitiously.

For more information on Reece Willis visit
www.reecewillis.com

For Catherine,
who was there every step of the way

1

I was surprised by how quiet it was. It wasn't that I was anticipating seeing a man-eating tiger or a herd of stampeding elephants as soon as we arrived, but I expected more than this. Buildings worn grey and nicotine beige, loomed as if they'd topple at any moment. One already had judging by the pile of rubble that sat at the side of the road where our cab had come to an abrupt stop ten minutes ago. This wasn't how I had imagined India to be.

The disagreement between Aiden and the driver was impacting on the otherwise peaceful street. From the few that were beginning to crowd, I noticed a small girl, her pink dress smeared in dirt just like her face. She looked on in wonder at the two men yelling at one another, while a gentleman – her father I presumed – set up his rickety stall for the day.

'You're out of your mind if you think I'm paying you six hundred rupees. I keep telling you, we've already pre-paid.' Aiden had no intention of backing down.

Neither did the driver, 'And I am telling you I am not pre-pay taxi. You are taking wrong taxi and you are a thief.'

'Thief? You're the thief. You take us from pillar to post, stopping off at your friends and relatives trying to sell us this and that, and you still want us to give you money? It's taken ages to get from the airport.'

'But you are saying you are wanting hotel, I am showing you

four hotel,' the driver exclaimed, holding up four fingers to emphasise his point.

'Not the one we asked for though, eh? And when do carpet dealers, souvenir shops and travel agents count as hotels?'

It was time to mediate, 'Guys, guys, take it easy, I'm sure this can be all worked out.'

'Yes, if you are paying me my money.' The driver took his stand at the back of the car to prohibit access to our luggage.

I'd already unstapled some notes from the stack of dirty rupees we'd exchanged at the airport. Leafing out six leathery one-hundred bills, I gave him the fare. He waggled his head, clicked the latch and lifted our backpacks and guitar cases from the car.

Aiden was by now red faced and livid, 'Have you taken leave of your senses, Sam?'

'Look, we can stand here all day and argue, or we can check into that, um, nice hotel over there, get a shower, something to eat and some rest. It's your call.' He sneered at the cabbie who had already started the engine and was backing up. 'Come on mate, let's get you inside.'

I'd only known Aiden for a few months. He'd wander into the music shop where I worked and tinker about on a guitar or two. He was different from everyone else. There was a certain charm in the way he carried himself; a sense of panache. His well-spoken English accent commanded immediate attention and he was a huge hit with the ladies. An itching restlessness hung over him however, as if he wanted more out of life.

One Friday afternoon as I was closing, he asked, 'If you could go anywhere in the world, where would it be?'

I recalled memories of being a boy, hunting my parents loft for buried treasure and coming across old black and white pictures that had faded with time. Lavish palaces, domed mosques, snake charmers and all sorts of strange and interesting faces were captured forever in the room above me. I spent endless nights lying awake, staring up at those intriguing lands, imagining that one day I would go there and see all these sights for myself.

My father didn't speak of his time serving in India during the

Second World War. He didn't speak to me much at all. I could tell there was something of those years that haunted him though, if only by the way the photographs had been tucked away, not once retrieved from their dark corner. I know this because I didn't get into trouble for messing with them, which can only be because he never found out. Whatever it was that had disturbed his mind remained his secret.

'India,' I answered.

'Yeah, India sounds good,' Aiden nodded and left it at that.

The following morning, I awoke to an urgent banging at my front door. 'Prepare yourself for three months in India,' he said, beaming on the threshold. 'I've just put a deposit down. We leave in one month.'

So here we were, Paharganj, the backpacking hub of New Delhi, climbing a pristine marble staircase leading to our room. A shower, jam on toast and a cup of tea later, we collapsed until lunchtime.

Muffled noises brought me to. Curiosity of what the outside world was doing got the better of me. Aiden didn't stir as I padded across the cold tiles to the balcony. On first inspection, everything seemed as it did seven hours ago, but as I slid the glass across I soon realised I'd been lulled into a false sense of security. The intense, suffocating heat was accompanied by an overwhelming aroma, the components of which I tried to identify: wood smoke, garbage, burnt diesel, spiced cooking and cow dung I could easily pick out; quite a contrast to the delicate scent of jasmine that had welcomed us in the hotel lobby.

My sense of smell wasn't the only thing enjoying a workout; my ears were assaulted with the clamour of people talking and shouting, engines running and squealing, horns blasting – all of which seemed to echo for miles across the mass of flat concrete rooftops ahead of me. The sleepy street had transformed into utter chaos. Motorised and peddled rickshaws competed with cars and scooters to avoid a river of oblivious pedestrians. A couple of stray dogs fed from the edge of a mound of rubbish that was being monopolised by a huge white bull. Sitting cross-legged next to the garbage, a man fried something gnarled and greasy in a large blackened pan, while his neighbour hammered away at a worn leather boot. In front of them both, two skinny workmen in white vests smashed a hole into the concrete with pickaxes. I swished the door shut behind me, relieved by the whir of the air-conditioning unit.

'Who was it then?' Was he talking to me? I couldn't be sure. He looked asleep. 'Yeah, I know, didn't I pass it to him when I bought the chocolate? Ha ha, yeah, we used to call him Froggy.'

'Aiden.' He groaned and turned his head. I increased the volume, 'Aiden.'

'Huh? Oh, Sam, what's up?' He looked around, unsure of his surroundings, still immersed in his dream.

'I thought we might go out and do some sightseeing,' I picked up the guide book and thumbed to the page marked, The Qutub Minar. 'India's tallest minaret was constructed in 1192 and stands as a tower of victory to Muslim rule, celebrating the fall of the last Hindu Kingdom in Delhi.'

'Spare me the details mate, I've just woken up.' He rubbed his eyes and took a swig from the half cup of cold tea he'd left earlier, dribbling it back upon realising the temperature, 'Eww, what was I thinking?'

'I really don't know.' I changed into the most inconspicuous shirt and trousers I could find. 'So, who's Froggy?' I asked.

'What?'

'Never mind.'

Whilst Aiden got ready I waited in reception. 'Yes sir, acha, of course sir, and again, I am very sorry sir,' said the manager, the telephone wedged between his cheek and shoulder. His unfaltering smile went down with the receiver and he wiped the sweat from his brow. I caught his peripheral and his tired, smiling face switched on again, 'Ah hello sir, I had not seen you there. How are you finding your stay?'

'Yeah, good thanks. We're going out in a minute, have you got a business card so we know where to come back to?'

'Of course, sir, a business card is not a problem.' He presented a white card with a little red logo, address and contact details below. 'You are situated in Arakashan Road, sir.' He waggled his head.

'Thanks. What does the head-wag thing mean?' I asked. He tilted his head to one side, trying to understand what I'd just said. I attempted a demonstration, though I found my head-wagging skills rather robotic.

'Ah, yes sir, it mean many thing, you will see.'

'What about acha?'

He looked at his watch and sighed, 'Acha mean okay or I understand or I agree, or maybe I understand or maybe I agree, or maybe I do not agree at all, but seem to agree for the sake of customer satisfaction.'

'Acha.' I raised my eyebrows and glanced to the ceiling in confusion.

'Ha, now you are learning a little Hindi. Very good, sir.' He stretched his smile as far as his patience would allow. 'Now, if you will be excusing me sir, I really must be going.'

I was left alone in the cocoon of marble and incense, the doorway to the rest of India ahead of me. To say I was apprehensive about stepping outside was an understatement. It had slipped my mind to inform Aiden of my discovery on the balcony, and as he flip-flopped down the stairs in knee length shorts, a Hawaiian shirt with sleeves rolled-up to the elbows, sunglasses and a wide brimmed straw hat, I didn't have the heart to tell him.

'Just to confirm, you haven't read any of the guidebook?' I asked.

He looked over my shoulder, sniffing out the new smells, twitching to get a better look, 'I thought you'd read enough for the both of us.'

'Only what I read on the plane. You've had hold of it most of the time, I haven't had the chance.'

He side-stepped me and confidently walked towards the door only to lunge back from the wall of heat with disbelief. He looked over his shoulder, 'Have you seen it out there?'

I joined him at the threshold, 'I have. Are you ready?'

I walked out on my own. Aiden still hovered at the door, 'What's it like?' he called out.

There were a lot of people, all staring. What I'd seen on the balcony was now eye level and I was the centre of attention. I looked over to the hotel for support, 'Aiden, come on.'

He stepped down as if entering a swimming pool for the first time, gingerly treading water and wading out to my position of safety. He would have made it if it weren't for the collision with the boy on the oversized bike who wobbled but masterfully regained his balance. The boy rode on laughing, leaving Aiden unimpressed, 'Did you see that? He tried to kill me.'

'You're all right though, yeah?' I didn't hear his answer. I, like Aiden, stood rooted not knowing what to do next. A naked toddler squatted before us, squirted out what looked like toffee ice cream and ran off, nearly straying in front of a passing car. I scanned for any distraught parents but saw none. At the foot of the rubbish pile, a dog sniffed the air and tracked the scent to the child's waste. It seized the dessert opportunity and slurped the path clean whilst Aiden and I looked on in horror.

'Let's just start walking, we're bound to find a bus stop or something,' I said, diverting our attention. We turned left for no apparent reason and said nothing to each other. We were too preoccupied finding ways of moving around parked cars and avoiding the waves of people from every angle. There was nothing that resembled a bus stop and there were no buses. Oddly enough, there were no backpackers either.

'Have you got the guidebook?' We'd come to a standstill.

Aiden patted himself down, 'Does it look like I've got the guidebook?'

'What do we do then? We can't just wander aimlessly.'

The buzz of a tin bee hovering beside us saved us from ourselves, 'Auto-rickshaw you like?' said a voice from within. I coaxed Aiden into the back and squeezed in beside him.

'Qutub Minar,' I said, thinking my pronunciation was perfect, but the driver's face suggested otherwise, lifting from a frown to a smile several times before a light flicked on behind his eyes. He tilted his head from side to side and said, 'Acha,' which made me wonder if I'd been understood at all.

Throttling forward, we darted in and out of the crowds and saw life from a relatively safe distance. At the top of the street the driver pushed aside a cycle-rickshaw and turned into the gridlock of the main road. Behind us, the angry grill of a single deck bus growled in neutral, while ahead, the back of an orange goods carrier with a happy blue font of 'Horn Please' filled the cab with exhaust fumes. One wrong move from either neighbour would obliterate us.

We edged our way forward accompanied by a chorus of blaring horns and revving engines while a policeman stood fruitlessly directing traffic from a concrete podium; shouting, blowing his whistle, slamming car bonnets and the sides of trucks with a bamboo cane. Presented with an opportunity to pop the bottleneck, the driver put his foot down and accelerated into a wide avenue lined with slender palm trees as we did our best to absorb this new world around us.

Vehicles of all sizes hurtled towards us from all sides, narrowly missing us at the last second. Our driver wasn't any different. Keen and fearless to veer on the wrong side of the road, he overtook whenever opportunity presented itself, singing to himself as we held the steel railing, life dependent.

On the approach to a set of traffic lights we relaxed into a line of cars. A man no older than me appeared at my side of the rickshaw with an upturned palm thrust forward. His far away eyes were set deep within the sockets of a skull shrink-wrapped in broken skin. I reached into my pocket and took the first note my hand touched; a fifty, which he gently took and held to his forehead in gratitude.

Aiden and I observed our surroundings, saying nothing to each other until the Qutub Minar towered into view. We were welcomed by a gathering of souvenir touts all gunning for our attention, blurring our vision with postcards, trinkets and joss sticks. I bought a book of postcards in hope it would disperse the struggle, but it only intensified the rush. Squeezing through the pandemonium into the main entrance, we came into a clearing of well-tended gardens where our eyes were drawn to the cylindrical brick tower.

Intricate bands of Arabic calligraphy worked their way to the tapered summit.

'The sandstone inscriptions you see are verses from the Quran.' I turned to see a middle-aged man with a salt and pepper beard, white kufi cap and an immaculately pressed kurta.

'Thanks mate, but we don't need a tour guide,' Aiden snapped and walked off.

The gentleman frowned, 'I am not a tour guide, though I am not blaming your friend for thinking otherwise. I come here now and then to find a little peace from the city.'

'Sorry about Aiden, it's our first day in India.'

'Which country are you from?'

'England.'

'I thought you are all leaving in 1947,' he chuckled, thrilled with his timing. 'Apologies for my humour, my wife say it will get me into a good deal of trouble one day. Speaking of my wife, if I do not return home soon for my afternoon meal, there will be no marriage to be speaking of.' He shook my hand energetically and bowed his head, 'Salam Alaikum. Peace be upon you.'

I found Aiden slouched against a wall smoking a cigarette, 'Made a new friend I see,' he said, smirking.

'He wasn't a tour guide.'

'Whatever, I'm boiling sitting here, let's go.'

We wandered the ruins of the funerary buildings, stopping momentarily to observe an ancient iron pillar protruding from the patchwork of paving, but by now the sun was burning our fair skin so we took shade beneath a straw canopy. A young man appeared with a tray of soft drinks, looking much like an usher ready to sell interval refreshments. The short sleeves of his worn grey t-shirt hung loose and redundant, his neck having to bear the full weight of the tray with the help of some rope that was tied each side through a couple of crudely drilled holes. An additional piece of string was also making use of the one to his left, on the end of which was a bottle opener. I helped myself to two bottles of cola, removed the caps and placed the money on the tray. Listening to the throngs of Indian holidaymakers echoing the monuments, we sat back for a few relaxing moments savouring the taste of the sweet fizzy pop.

I suggested to Aiden we get something to eat at a nice hotel and restaurant I'd seen earlier in Arakashan Road. We returned the empty bottles on our way back to the gates and jumped into one of the many auto-rickshaws poised for tourists like us.

Doused in chilled air as soon as we entered, the reception offered a welcome relief from the heat outside. We were directed through a set of glass doors into the restaurant and shown to our seats. The air conditioning didn't extend to this part of the building, but the ceiling fans provided a comfortable temperature. As Aiden sat down I noticed a sign above him that read "DO NOT BEFRIEND STRANGERS". It had been printed on old-school computer paper and tacked on to the wall. I wondered what had prompted the need for such a motto and felt a little uneasy of my surroundings. We each ordered a vegetable biryani and a sweet lassi.

There were only two other people in the restaurant: a bald European man in his mid-thirties with oval spectacles and denim dungarees, and an Indian lady in her early forties, who had just paid her bill and was preparing to leave. As she opened the door, a sparrow flew past her, headed for the dining area. The man called out to the waiter to switch off the overhead fans and as they slowed to a stop, he clambered over the furniture to prevent the bird coming to any harm. He came over to where we were seated and asked if he could use a chair at our table to stand on. Using a rolled-up newspaper he tried to entice the sparrow from a ledge above Aiden's head. As he did so he accidentally tore the banner. The noise was enough to startle the bird into flight again. This time it made for the open door and flew to its freedom.

Ruben introduced himself to us and we gestured for him to take a seat. We learnt he was Italian, living in Lisbon and had been working as an investigative journalist in Delhi for the last two months. He spoke about recent bombings across the capital in the run up to elections, 'Thirteen people were killed in a blast in Lajpat Nagar Central Market only a few days ago. This area, including New Delhi Railway Station, has also been threatened.' I thought

9

about the rubble where a building once stood near our hotel. 'Anyway, enough of all of this, how are you finding Delhi?' he said, quickly changing the subject.

Aiden wiped a white ring of lassi from his lips, 'Interesting to say the least.'

'It's a bit hectic, huh? This is my eighth visit to India and Delhi still baffles me. I'm travelling north to Manali in a few days to escape to the mountains. Delhi is great, but it can swallow you up all too soon if you're not careful.'

Late afternoon seeped into early evening as we talked at length about what brought us here and listened to Ruben's adventures in India. Any insecurity we might have experienced earlier had now dissolved.

'We should think about getting back to our hotel,' said Aiden, to which I nodded in agreement. As I stood up I looked directly ahead of me. With all the earlier commotion and being fully engaged in conversation for the last couple of hours I hadn't noticed. Ruben and Aiden were sat next to each other below the sign that now read "BEFRIEND STRANGERS".

With an air of confidence lent by our new friend we walked back to our hotel. By the rubble, the man was packing away his stall for the day as the little girl found curiosity in a small cardboard box. She held it above her head and shook it free of invisible contents, giggling at the prospect of her new hat.

2

Below me the street was wide awake; the cobbler repaired a bamboo cane that was supporting the tarpaulin over his pitch, while one of the food sellers scoured a black pan, readying it for future customers. The hole that I'd seen created yesterday was now home to a telegraph pole, fixed firmly in place with cement. A man dangled precariously from the top, supported by a slither of leather around his waist. He was trying to connect wires through a loop and was seemingly unfazed by the fizzles, bangs and flashes that occurred as he poked and prodded with a pair of pliers.

A lady stooped over the pile of garbage, picking for discarded plastic bottles which she placed in a large canvas sack over her shoulder. Over to the right, the man on the stall was preparing dark leathery leaves with a white paste. Small silver foil sachets decorated the frame and the word Paan was painted on a sign that hung to an angle one side of the cart. The little girl was nowhere to be seen. To the left, a woman poured water from a copper vessel onto her infants, washing the soap from their glistening skin as they laughed and screamed with excitement. The river of people and traffic continued to flow, but the familiarity made everything less imposing.

I slipped past Aiden's sleeping bundle and went downstairs to order some breakfast. The manager was glued to the TV reporting of continuing violence in the region of Jammu and Kashmir. The footage showed huddled police firing tear gas from a street corner at a group of angry protesters.

'Very bad, not good at all,' he mumbled to himself. He addressed me as I came into view, 'Ah, good morning sir, how can I help?'

'Two plates of jam on toast and two teas please.'

He scribbled the order on a pad, 'Will that be all, sir?'

'What's the word for water?'

'Pani, sir.'

'And two bottles of pani please.'

'Very good, sir. Your Hindi skills are quite remarkable.'

Aiden woke to the waiter clinking cups and plates onto the glass table. Slumped into a chair with a slice of toast in hand, he said, 'I really fancy a joint, don't you?'

'I'm not that bothered to be honest, I'm high enough on all the diesel fumes.'

He inspected a mark on his cup, scratching it away with his thumbnail, 'But wouldn't it be cool to have a couple of spliffs? It must be amazing to hear those sounds outside when you're a bit stoned.'

'I'd rather keep my wits about me,' I crunched the last of my toast, washing it down with a large mouthful of tea.

'I suppose you're right.' He sighed and stared at the floor, 'I've been drinking and smoking pretty much non-stop for the last year now. Life can seem a bit shit without it.'

I hoped to distract him from his thoughts, 'I forgot to ask, what did your girlfriend say when you told her you were going to India?'

He laughed, 'I said that I was on a secret mission for Her Majesty's Government and if I didn't get captured or killed, I'll be back in her arms in three months.'

I tried to imagine the sincerity on his face as he told her, 'So Mr Bond, your job at the pizza place was all a cover up? You're pure evil, mate. Did she really fall for that?'

He pointed to his freshly adopted expression of innocence, 'Look at this face, what do you think?'

We agreed to visit the tomb of the second Moghul Emperor,

Humayun. A cycle-rickshaw rider rang his bell as we departed the hotel and we hopped in and hoped for the best. He stood heavy on the pedals, pushing off slowly, but soon gathered momentum. At the junction at the top of the street we veered alongside a silver bus chugging thick grey smoke from its exhaust. An old man leant from one of the windows and spat a large amount of red liquid down the side of the panelling.

'That looks like blood. Do you think he's okay?' I shouted over to the rickshaw driver.

He looked over to where I pointed, 'Paan, he is chewing paan – betel nut. You not have paan in your country?'

'No, what is it?'

'Paan like caffeine, very popular. Made in betel leaf, mix with areca nut paste. Chew, then spit. If brave, then swallow. Make you spit red.'

'There's a guy near our hotel who sells paan in small packets too.'

'This paan masala, quick hit, also make breath smell fresh.'

'Do you like paan?'

'No Sir. It does no good, rot teeth, maybe give cancer.'

The rickshaw rider said he'd wait for us while we had a look around the tomb. The main structure dominated the centre of a Charbagh, commanding our immediate attention. Rising palms threw lines of shadow across tall sandstone arcs inlaid with elaborate patterns. Minarets and small pavilions surrounded a white dome surmounted by a brass crescent finial pointing high in the clear blue sky. It was easy to forget we were still in Delhi as we explored the serene grounds, taking in each striking angle with every step as mynah birds squawked in the clusters of neem trees.

A dozen or more wires now flowed from the top of the telegraph pole outside our hotel, leading to various points either side of the road. Where there were buildings there were wires. Tangled cables ran overhead or hung vertically across façades, creeping like vines.

Neither of us had ever been anywhere like India before. A trip across the sea to Europe was the furthest we'd ventured. Now we realised just how out of our depth we were, having hardly prepared or researched before we arrived. With little idea of where to go or what to do next, it dawned on us how stupid we'd been. Over tea on the balcony we discussed our underestimations and turned to the guide book for advice, but it was filled with so much information, it only served to compound our confusion.

'The Taj Mahal,' I said. It was the first thing that always sprung to mind when I thought of India. 'What if we go to Agra next and see the Taj Mahal?' It was a way of getting us moving I thought.

'I suppose,' Aiden replied. He leant over the railing to glare down at the street. 'The history and buildings are all right and stuff, but I'm more into the idea of twisting alleyways and spice filled bazaars; to get a taste of the culture and people.' He glanced at me and then looked down again, 'I didn't think it would be like this, I mean, this difficult.'

'We're not used to it yet that's all. It's going to take a little time for us to adjust and settle in.' At that point I couldn't see how, but offered assurance nonetheless. 'I think there's a travel agent on the way to the restaurant at the top of the street. We'll ask about Agra and see how we go from there.'

A sandwich board with the words Rajasthani Tours and a list of destinations stood outside the travel agency. I looked through the glass at posters of palaces, camels and red turbaned men that hung upon the walls. The door squeaked as I pushed it open, alerting the attention of the shopkeeper who rose from his desk, 'Ah my friends come in, please take a seat. How can I help you?'

'We'd like...' I began.

'You would like chai? No problems. Yes, come take a seat.' He guided us around two chairs to the front of his desk, then opened the door and barked, 'Chai,' to someone outside and put three fingers up. He came back to his seat and pulled it towards the table, tucking his round belly behind. 'Okay, you are wishing to go to? I have many good deal on today, very good price, just for you, as you are from where?'

Aiden seemed twitchy, uncomfortable with the eagerness of our host, 'The UK.'

'Ah, you are very lucky. Today I have special offers for peoples from the UK only,' he waggled and beamed.

The door nudged open. A boy holding two glasses of tea and a third between his arms squeezed through. He put the drinks on the desk and shook his wrists, blowing them as he left.

'Maybe an exciting tour of the Great Thar Desert and many of its exotic palaces, yes, that is what you need,' the agent continued.

Aiden leaned forward, 'Agra, we want to go to Agra.'

The shopkeeper leant back, 'I am afraid this is not possible.' He rested his arms behind his head, 'Agra, you see, has been flooded. There is no access to the city at this time. But it is not a problem for you, you can go to Jaipur instead. Yes, very good luxury coach. You are seeing beautiful Pink City and Palace of Winds. You will like very much.'

'Flooded? The whole city, even the Taj Mahal?' I tried to envisage the scene.

'Yes, very unfortunate, very dangerous indeed. There has been big cholera outbreak.'

'Jaipur doesn't sound so bad,' Aiden said upon reflection.

Rs750 lighter, we were booked on a coach leaving the next day at 8am. A nervous excitement filled me as we walked to the restaurant. Aiden felt the same. The pink city, home to the palace of winds; our journey was about to begin.

Ruben sat in a shaded corner, nose deep in an Italian broadsheet. On his table was a camera with an impressive lens, a notepad and a cup of black coffee. Aiden peered over the newspaper, 'Hello mate.'

He folded it away, took off his glasses and rubbed his eyes and the top of his nose, 'Guys, sit down. What have you been up to?'

'We've had a mad day,' Aiden animated. 'We saw two really bad traffic accidents on the way to a street market. One guy died. Then we got into a tussle with a rickshaw driver and he dropped us in the middle of nowhere. I managed to get us through the streets to a market though.' I kept silent, intrigued by the outcome. 'We were buying a shirt from this Sikh guy and he started arguing with me over the price. He ended up throwing hot tea over me.'

'Quite the eventful day then,' Ruben smiled as he looked through his glasses at arm's length, catching the light and removing a speck of dust before returning them to his face. I couldn't be sure, but it struck me that Ruben wasn't fooled.

Unsure of what Aiden was doing, I changed the subject before he had chance to continue, 'Are you still going to Manali?'

'Yes, it's getting far too hot in Delhi. I'm looking forward to chilling in the mountains and listening to the rivers again.' Ruben checked his trouser pockets and sighed, 'I've left my wallet in my room. Can you guys look after my things for ten minutes while I go back and get it?'

Aiden stood, 'I'll come with you. I could do with some fresh air. Sam, wait here, we'll be back in a minute.' As soon as they left, the waiter brought the three coffees I'd ordered. I browsed the newspaper while sipping my drink. When I had finished with both, the guys hadn't returned so I started inspecting Ruben's camera and then drank the other two coffees. An hour had gone by and I didn't know whether to be worried or if I should go looking for them. Convincing myself they would be back soon I ordered a lassi and a greasy samosa. When the waiter brought them to me I tried engaging in conversation, but his English was limited to the contents of the menu, so I sat watching the comings and goings of the restaurant.

By eight o'clock they returned. Ruben called over to the waiter and ordered more coffee. He apologised and thanked me for looking after his stuff. Aiden sat down with a thump, 'On the way back from Ruben's hotel, I thought I'd stop at ours for my cigarettes. The manager said that if we planned to check out tomorrow, we would need to do so at 6am. Our bus to Jaipur doesn't leave until eight, so we would've been stuck with our luggage on the streets for two hours.' He drew on a cigarette, blowing smoke into the fan, 'Ruben told the manager he was being unreasonable, but the manager said as we'd checked in at 6am originally, that was the time we would have to leave.' I was about to suggest we could wait in the restaurant for a couple of hours and have breakfast, but Aiden was eager to continue, 'Ruben suggested we take it up with the police, so we went to Paharganj police station and the guy in charge came back with us and gave the manager a right bollocking. We now check out at 11am.' I pictured the poor manager reaching for a noose behind the counter as they left.

'Some other great news,' There was more? Aiden was on a roll, 'We're going to Manali with Ruben. I've booked us on the same coach. How cool is that?'

'Aren't we going to Jaipur?'

'I thought it would be better to travel with Ruben first. He said he'd be happy to show us around and sort out a hotel for us. We're going to get a firmer hold on this trip if we start it with an experienced traveller.'

It made sense. I looked to Ruben, 'Are you sure you don't mind?'

He waved away my question, 'Of course not, it's my pleasure.'

It was half past eleven by the time Aiden and I got back. The reception area was frosty, no false smiles from the manager this evening. Heads down, we slipped up the stairs and vanished out of sight. The silence of the street was dispelled by the occasional dog bark and distant vehicle. We leant upon the balcony rails under the flickering amber of a street lamp.

'Why did you lie about our day to Ruben earlier?' I asked.

He averted my eyes, focusing on the man who slept under the paan stall, cradling his daughter in his protective arms, 'I wanted to make our day sound more exciting than it was. He's a journalist and travels all over the world in the thick of it. Us, what do we do? Sit in a restaurant and prance around crappy buildings all day.'

'But we're not journalists, we're just tourists. I'm sure Ruben wouldn't have thought any less of us if he knew the truth.'

'Look, does any of this matter? I've bagged us a trip to Manali, which you agreed was a good idea. Let's just get some sleep.'

It was early, it must have been. Though I was half expecting the usual medley of sounds, there were none. I crept onto the balcony, lit a cigarette and stretched. The sky was in its last phase of sunrise from blood orange to pastel pink. Some way up the street I saw two men talking to an open sewer hole. A slimy arm rose out splashing a handful of wet dirt onto the concrete and then retracted like a snake. The same thing happened four or five times until the owner of the arm emerged, wearing the same thick muck and gasping for air. The teenager bent over, coughed and spat out dark brown gunk as one of his colleagues slapped his back. Sewage clearing – Paharganj style.

Aiden was in high spirits, thrilled at the prospect of going to Manali with Ruben, so much so that he offered to buy me breakfast. At our regular restaurant, we ordered omelettes and a half set of tea. We were due to leave for Manali at seven the following morning. The bus was to depart near Ruben's hotel and Aiden thought it would be a good idea to stay there so everything ran smoothly, booking us a night's stay for one hundred rupees less than our current hotel.

He finished his tea and went to the wash room. Twenty minutes elapsed and I began to wonder what had happened to him. I couldn't see him anywhere. I approached a passing waiter, 'Excuse me, have you seen my friend? He looks a bit like me.'

'Oh yes, yes, I am thinking this way please.'

I was ushered over to the hotel lobby where two men were talking on a red couch; one was a middle-aged westerner with glasses, cropped white hair and beard and the other was Aiden, who glanced up as I approached, 'Oh, hi Sam, this is Don. Don, this is Sam. Don's from Texas.'

We exchanged greetings and I sat beside them. Don, I discovered, was on a spiritual journey throughout Asia. He'd left Thailand last week and was heading to Sri Lanka in a few weeks to study Buddhism for six months. His wife had lost a battle with leukaemia a few months earlier and unable to cope with regular life on his own, Don left his home in Austin to travel indefinitely.

'I don't mean to be rude, but we should think about packing if we're to leave the hotel before eleven.'

'Yeah, of course,' replied Aiden. 'We'll maybe see you later.' He reached out his hand to Don, who reciprocated with a firm handshake.

With our loaded backpacks and guitars in hand, we passed the paan cart and rubble. A little way along we found our new lodgings; not as nice as our previous hotel, but adequate for our needs. The beds were hard and there was no sit-down western toilet, instead, a ceramic hole in the floor shaped like a keyhole; beside it, a blue plastic jug and above, a tap. There was no window or balcony, but thankfully there was a shower and air-conditioning.

We'd noticed Ruben had a shoulder bag for day to day items and Aiden suggested we go out and find two similar for ourselves. An auto-rickshaw ride later and we arrived at a small street market where stalls sold everything from exotic fruits and fresh vegetables to bootleg videos and electrical goods. Searching around, all we could find were two small rucksacks with brightly printed images on. One had a motorbike, which Aiden instantly laid claim to, leaving me the one with multi-coloured balloons.

As we were about to leave an elderly man sidled up beside us. Although he said very little, it was evident he was in need. He held the ulcerated stumps at the end of his wrists towards me in request for money. I stopped and gave him twenty rupees. Nodding his thanks, he left me to catch up with Aiden who smiled all knowingly, 'You're far too soft with these people. If you keep giving your money away like that, you'll be the one begging before too long.' I understood what he was saying, but it was hard to just walk on by. 'Anyway,' he added, 'half of these guys will be part of a begging ring and it's the guy at the top that makes all the money.' If that was the case, then maybe the guy would get an easier time from his boss today.

At the hotel, I took a shower and heard Aiden call through the door, 'I'll be back in a minute. I'm going downstairs to get some drinks.' When I came out ten minutes later, he hadn't returned. Another thirty minutes passed, still no sign. One hour turned into two and I was losing patience with his disappearing acts. I searched the hotel and looked out of the doorway to the street, but he was nowhere to be seen. On the third hour, I thought about having a walk outside. I put my hand on the door handle, only to have it turned from the other side. A breezy Aiden ambled in.

'Where have you been?' I asked. 'You said you were only going to get some drinks.'

He sprawled on the bed and put his hands behind his head, 'The hotel didn't have any so I went out for a walk and bumped into Ruben. We went to a place that sold fruit juice and sat watching the world go by. He asked after you by the way.'

'You could have come back and told me, I was getting worried something bad might have happened.'

'Yeah, sorry. I walked too far to come back.' He got up and went to the bathroom, 'It's so hot out there, I'm gonna take a shower.'

The door closed behind him and the shower sprinkled on.

Half an hour later he came out, laid down and fell asleep. Unsure what else to do, I updated my journal, read a little about Manali in the guidebook and ended up falling asleep myself. When I woke, Aiden had gone. There was a note on his bed, 'Gone to restaurant. See you there.'

In the restaurant, I found Aiden with Don and Ruben, the three of them gathered around a table talking. Ruben pulled out a chair and invited me to join them, but Aiden was quick to intervene, 'Oh Sam, I was just about to suggest we all go out for a walk.'

'It's getting late and we have to be up early for the bus,' Ruben said, looking tired. Aiden persisted and out of politeness, Don and Ruben eventually agreed.

Walking into the night, we turned left onto the main road. All around was still, aside from the odd passing vehicle or the occasional rustle of a street dweller bedding down for the night. Ruben and I spoke about photography as we walked in the shadow of the other two. I only had a small compact camera and I told Ruben how much I liked his Canon SLR. 'Maybe you could return one day with a better camera,' he said. 'You can capture some amazing sights in India.'

Lost in conversation, Ruben and I weren't paying attention to where Aiden was taking us. It was only when we saw the road narrowing into an alleyway that we realised we must have strayed from the main road into a series of back streets. We came to a stop at a dead end and gathered under the haunting glow of a street lamp. Tied nearby, a horse shining in sweat stood with its snout covered in a grubby feed bag. The creature was so skinny it looked as if a thin layer of brown velvet had been draped over its skeleton. Ruben was about to suggest an alternative route, when Aiden spotted an alley to the right of an apartment block and dashed off, shouting, 'This way guys, follow me.'

Ruben took chase, calling after him, 'Aiden wait, I know this area, it can be quite dangerous this time of night. I'm sure I know a safer way back.'

Don and I tried to keep up, but we lost them in a series of tight bends. We continued walking a darkening street until something thudded into my lower back and I stumbled to the ground. I looked up and saw the face of a young Indian man staring down at me as he walked past.

Don was quick to my side and helped me to my feet, 'Are you okay, Sam?'

I checked my back for any blood, worried that I'd been stabbed, 'Yeah, I'm okay I think. What happened? Are you all right?'

'Yes, I'm fine.' He pointed to the man I'd seen, 'That guy came up behind us and punched you.' Don looked left and right, 'We need to get away from here. There's some men coming this way and they don't look too friend...' A small rock slammed into his right cheek causing him to fall back into a pile of refuse. I pulled him up as he held his face.

'Shit, Don, are you alright?' Are you okay to walk?' He put his arm around my shoulder as I assisted him, desperately shuffling and looking for a way out. Behind us three men drew closer.

The path we took led to an open square with a road ahead and two lanes leading off either side. We stopped, wondering which way to turn. The man who assaulted me reappeared from a doorway and pushed an abandoned steel cart in front of us to block our way forward. Without the aid of street lighting we could hardly see a thing. I turned to the left and then to the right, only to discover we'd been flanked on all sides. Fear shot through me and my legs began to tremble. The four men closed in, backing us up against the cart.

'Money now or we will kill you,' one of them said. From the back of his trousers he produced a rusted carving knife and held it against my throat. I squinted, inhaling his stale sweat and alcohol breath on my face. Don offered his wallet without hesitation. It was snatched away by one of the others.

'Now you,' the man said, and backed off slightly, still pointing the blade to my throat. 'Hand over your money or I will cut you open.'

My hands pushed into my pocket, and as I was about to lift out my wallet, I heard a shout from somewhere in the darkness ahead, 'Hey, leave them alone, the police are right behind us.'

The men turned, looked at each other, said something and sprinted out of view to the lane left of us.

'Are you guys okay?' Ruben asked as Aiden came running up beside him.

'Yeah, I think so. Where did you two go?' I didn't care for the answer; I was just glad they were here.

Ruben scanned the shadows, 'There's no time to talk. We should leave now. They might come back with some friends. Follow me.'

Keeping close to Ruben, we checked over our shoulders every few minutes in case we were being followed. We continued at a steady pace through the maze of lanes and eventually reached the safety of the main road again. Ruben suggested we take refuge in New Delhi Railway Station for a while, giving us chance to cool down and get our heads together.

'Did you really call the police?' I asked Ruben.

'No, I only said that to scare them off.'

'Shouldn't we go to the police station and report them anyway?'

'Did you get a good look at their faces?'

Don and I looked at each other, 'Not really, it was too dark,' I replied.

'That's all the police will be interested in. Without a description, it would be hopeless. I am still happy to go, but bear in mind, we could be in there for hours.'

'I think I've had enough for one night, how about you?' Don turned to me and I agreed.

Ruben inspected his face, 'Are you hurt badly? We can try and find a doctor.'

'I'll be fine, nothing a little ice and sleep won't sort out. At least they didn't damage my glasses. There wasn't much money in my wallet, so that's good.'

Under the low bridge near the station, with used needles at their feet, heroin addicts congregated and glanced up at us with deceased eyes as we passed by.

'Were you scared?' Aiden asked.

'Of course I was bloody scared. What happened to you?' Adrenaline still consumed me and my patience with him was wearing thin.

'I don't know. I got lost. Luckily, Ruben found me and then we found you.'

Inside the foyer of the railway station, a dozen or so people snoozed beside their belongings as they awaited a train. Shuffling to a stop at Ruben's feet, a crippled beggar looked up at him. Ruben placed a note in the man's shirt pocket and he pulled himself away using his hands inside worn sandals as a replacement for his lifeless legs. We sauntered along the platform and mused about the last couple of hours until we thought it was safe enough to leave.

We escorted Don back to his hotel and headed back to ours.

'Goodnight guys. See you at 6.30,' Ruben said and closed his door.

3

'Sam, wake up.' I opened my eyes to see Aiden's face hovering over me in the dark. He nudged me, 'Sam, are you awake?'

'I am now.' My lower back throbbed, my mouth was dry and my stomach was gurgling. 'What time is it?'

'Huh? Oh, hold on.' He leant over to the bedside cabinet, '3.30. I really need to talk to you about Ruben.'

'Can't this wait until later?' I turned away, unable to resist the hold sleep had over me.

'Don't you think it's strange how we met him?' Begrudgingly I slipped back. 'Remember the Do Not Befriend Strangers banner in the restaurant when we first met Ruben, and how he tore away the Do Not part? What if he did that on purpose?'

'You woke me up for that, seriously?' He got up and switched on the light. 'Bloody hell mate, are you kidding me?' I shielded my eyes with my arm to cover the fluorescent sting, 'What's got into you?'

'I remembered something someone told me before I left England. I'd completely forgotten until now. He said, "Watch out for the Thuggees." I asked him what he meant and he explained that Thuggees are a group of assassins that travel across India befriending tourists and gaining their confidence, only to hang them when they least expect it. They then rob them and bury the bodies, all in the honour of Kali, the Hindu goddess of death. What if Ruben is a Thuggee?'

As bizarre as it sounded, he had my attention. I sat up, 'Ruben seems a decent enough guy and he certainly doesn't strike me as a crazed serial killer. On the contrary, he comes across quite normal. I really like him.'

'Yeah, he does seem like a nice guy, but what if it's all been a cover up?' Aiden began pacing the confines of the room. 'He appeared to know his way around the area you and Don were attacked in like the back of his hand.'

'He probably knows his way around because of his job. Anyway, it was you that suggested we take a walk at night, and it was you that led the way. If you're saying we were set up, how is that possible?'

'Before you came to the restaurant yesterday evening, Ruben was saying how great Delhi is at night, especially for photography. He said we should go out for a walk one evening. I just chose the night.'

'You don't think it's all a coincidence? I just don't pick up any bad vibes from him.' I took a sip of flat cola and lit a cigarette.

'What if I'm right though? What if last night was a failed attempt at murdering us? What if we get to Manali and there are more of them waiting there for us?' He sat down on the end of the bed, 'I'm not travelling with him. I'm not going to risk my life over this, Sam.'

It was all sounding rather sinister. The prospect of being murdered decreased my confidence in travelling with Ruben. Despite being unconvinced by what Aiden was saying, there was a slim chance he was right and he was adamant about not going to Manali. We made the decision to get our things together and check-out of the hotel before Ruben woke up. We'd find another hotel and go to Jaipur or Agra as originally planned. I scribbled a note on the back of a postcard I had bought from the Qutub Minar:

Dear Ruben,

Thanks so much for everything. Unfortunately, we have changed our plans and will not be travelling to Manali after all. It's been a pleasure knowing you. Good luck on your travels and keep safe.

Best regards,
Sam and Aiden

I didn't tell Aiden about the note. I let him lead the way down the stairwell and past Ruben's room. When he was out of sight, I slid the card underneath the door and caught up with him in reception. The clock on the wall read 05.27am.

The backpacks were heavier than I remembered, even with the disbursement of contents in the rucksacks strapped to our chests, and our guitars felt cumbersome by our sides. Arakashan Road was quiet, which was to be expected at that time of the morning, but in our current mindset it felt eerily so. We were scared; that at any moment we might bump into the assailants from last night or that Ruben might appear from the shadows. Aiden had spooked me and by the time we approached the top of the road, I was a quivering wreck.

'Yes, come, rickshaw,' a gruff voice shouted from our left and I'm sure I squealed with fright.

We'd never ridden in an auto with our entire luggage before. It was an infeasible idea. Fortunately, one of the many skills a rickshaw driver possessed was to make the seemingly impossible possible. Within seconds we were cemented into place, unable to breathe, but nonetheless the driver was a genius.

Delhi was waking, opening its eyes in a soft haze, a mist that made everything silhouette at a distance. Ghostly shapes emerged on the roadside. Food vendors echoed their morning pitch, beggars lurked in shadows for sparkles of hope, people soaped away the night heat from their bodies, cows and stray dogs scoured the earth for whatever they could find. The city gradually came to life as the unforgiving sun announced another day.

We were shown to a guest house where a young man introduced us to a room where cobwebs hung from the ceiling and cracks split the panes in the windows. The bed sheets were stained a dirty yellow with spots of blood speckling the pillows and swastikas decorated the walls, which gave us the final thumbs up to leave.

My fingers frantically turned the pages of the guidebook, 'Ah, here.' I pointed to a line of text, 'The Government Tourist Office in Janpath. They're bound to help.'

The driver leant over the metal bar that separated the cab from where we sat, 'Government Tourist Office open at 10.30, it now 6.15. I know other tourist office open, I take you.'

Ten minutes later we were delivered to Ajanta Tours, a shop set back from the road on a gravel driveway. Plastered on the windows were pictures of white cars and posters of the Taj Mahal. Our driver enthusiastically ushered us through the door and the owner sprang to attention, 'Hello, my friends. Please take a seat, lift the weight from your feet, have some chai. What is your country?'

Turning down the offer of tea, Aiden got straight to the point, 'Can you help us find a hotel or a bus to Jaipur?'

'I cannot help you with a hotel, but I can offer very best in luxury cars for all your travelling needs,' he grinned, confident he was on the cusp of a sale. 'Excellent Hindustan Ambassador, very good air-cool, very nice car, only seventy dollars a day with driver.' As far from our budget as we were from home, we thanked him and left.

Our driver propelled us from one hotel to another, unofficial tourist office after unofficial tourist office in a bid to gain as much commission as possible. He must have fared well, despite our lack of interest in his choices. It was all too familiar and a fruitless pursuit. We paid him the three hundred rupees he demanded and alighted.

Apart from the odd vehicle soaring past every now and then, the road we stood in was deserted. The guidebook maps and information may have been correct, but there were no street signs and it was impossible at ground level to figure out where we were or where to go. To the best of our knowledge we were somewhere near Janpath, but the government tourist office was a long way from opening.

A motorcycle rumbled alongside us and the rider called out, 'Boys, you must leave this area at once. Find yourselves a hotel away from here. Government elections, bomb blasts, you are prime targets for terrorists.'

Our need to find accommodation had escalated and I couldn't

help wondering if we would have been better travelling with Ruben after all. On spotting a hotel up ahead we looked at each other in relief, but as we neared, the manager appeared waving his arms, 'I am sorry, but you cannot stay here. It is too unsafe. Please, let me pay for a rickshaw to take you somewhere else.' Aiden declined the offer, stating he didn't want another tour of the city's downtrodden hotels.

We weren't used to pacing such a long way with this much weight and the further we walked, the hotter it became. We were both fit but agreed what we were carrying was far too heavy. Stopping beneath a bridge to cool down, we took off our packs and slouched against the wall as traffic echoed around the curve of the underside of the bridge, beeping even more at the sight of us. The guitars weighed next to nothing, the rucksacks the same. It didn't take long for Aiden to find out what the problem was: two steel support bars hidden in pockets on the inside of our backpacks. He ditched them on the roadside, making our luggage that much lighter.

'We're going to have to find a hotel soon, we can't go on like this. I'm getting really thirsty,' I said. 'Let me have a look at the guidebook a minute, I want to show you something.'

I opened the book on the floor and turned to the section entitled, Travel Away from Delhi, and pointed out the rail fares. Aiden studied the words and raised his eyebrows when he saw that a train to Agra cost sixty-two rupees, 'Why didn't you tell me this before? All this bloody screwing around and you didn't think to mention it?'

'I automatically assumed you knew what you were doing. I mean, you're quite happy to arrange all our travel plans and cancel them at the last minute. Anyway, I only got my hands on the guidebook yesterday; I never had a chance to tell you. You've either been absent or otherwise engaged in conversation with somebody else. You've had hold of the guidebook most of the time, why didn't you tell me about the trains?'

'I haven't been reading it.'

'Why doesn't that surprise me?'

'Oh, shut up.'

'You want rickshaw?' a gentle voice drifted above us. We glanced up and saw the face of a grinning man in his forties standing alongside an auto-rickshaw.

'No, you're all right thanks, mate,' Aiden replied without looking up. 'We've had nothing but trouble from the likes of you this morning. I'm sure you would charge us the earth and take us to the moon and back.'

'Oh no, sir, I am Mr Lim, very honest and reasonable man. I can take you to good hotel or tourist office.'

We looked at each other and laughed. Considering our present situation, we didn't have much of a choice. 'Shall we start again?' I asked Aiden.

Mr Lim was true to his word and did everything within his capabilities to find us a decent hotel, including asking various people along the way. 'Okay, I am finding you good place, I think. We will go there now,' he said.

We turned a corner and I noticed a paan cart near a pile of rubble. I nudged Aiden, 'Did you see that?'

'See what? Hey, that looks like the place we bought our Jaipur tickets from.' It was. We'd landed up exactly where we had started, in Arakashan Road.

'I am finding you excellent hotel,' Mr Lim said proudly as we stopped outside the hotel adjacent to the restaurant we'd eaten in so many times over the last few days.

At the reception desk, I paid Rs395 for a night's stay if only for the familiarity of our surroundings. I went outside to see Mr Lim who was talking with another rickshaw driver. He refused the two hundred rupees I offered, insisting on only fifty, 'Please, as I say, I am Mr Lim, honest and reasonable man.' He heaved our luggage into the hotel and shook our hands. With a head waggle and cheek to cheek grin, he said, 'Now my friends, you are happy?'

'Yes, thank you,' I replied.

'Then if my friends are happy, then Mr Lim is also happy.' He left with our faith restored that not all rickshaw drivers were the same after all.

The hotel was the best we'd stayed in so far. The beds were neatly made with fresh linen and the room was a refreshing temperature. There was also an immaculate bathroom and western toilet, which I took immediate advantage of. When I came out, showered and shaved, I found the room empty and supposed that Aiden had done another of his disappearing acts, but he came in a few minutes later with a bottle of sparkling orange in each hand. I couldn't have been happier.

4

The monotonous ringing of the alarm clock woke me six hours later. It had just gone 4pm. If we were to make any progress onwards from Delhi we should do so sooner rather than later. Aiden was flat out, despite my best efforts to wake him. I thought about how the morning started and a plan materialised in my head. Knocking the inside of the door, I opened it and said, 'Ruben, how did you find us? Why have you got an axe in your hand?'

Aiden shot to his feet, wrestling the bed sheets and fell onto my bed only to find me in fits of laughter at the end. 'Oh, very funny,' he snapped and stormed off into the bathroom.

On the way to New Delhi Railway Station we did our best to pass through the crowds, but our progress was temporarily hindered by a brown bull wandering aimlessly, forcing pedestrians and vehicles alike to manoeuvre around it. On approach to the underside of the bridge near the station courtyard, we avoided the junkies and a huddle of children inhaling deeply from paper bags.

The foyer heaved with commuters, chatter reverberating around the high ceilings. Pushed and shoved, we attempted to make sense of the confusion around us and the signage, which was mostly in Hindi. A man in a smart brown uniform with a red band and a dangling gold tag on his arm stepped down from a stairway, 'I am official railway assistant,' he said, pointing to his shiny medallion. 'You are looking lost; you are wanting assistance?'

Aiden wiped away the falling sweat, 'Can you tell us where we can buy tickets to Jaipur or Agra?'

'Main ticket office closed for today,' he answered and started walking away. 'Please, follow me. I will take you to other ticket office across street.'

Thankful to be away from the crowds, we tailed him across the road to a building advertising luxury coach trips. Another ticket office indeed, but not the kind we would have hoped for. The crafty tout slinked away into the traffic, bound for the station in search of more unsuspecting tourists no doubt.

'Welcome, my friends,' a salesman boomed with confidence, beckoning us into his shop. 'Come inside, which country are you from?'

'England,' Aiden said sharply, tiring of the question. 'Is Agra still flooded?'

'Agra? Flooded? There has been no flooding in Agra,' his smile was temporarily broken by a look of bewilderment. He regained his patter, 'Agra is very dry and very good for luxury coach tour.'

I turned to Aiden unsurprised by the answer, 'Find out some prices for us, I'm going outside for a cigarette.' When I returned, Aiden had bought two tickets to Agra leaving tomorrow morning. I said nothing and handed him my half of the fare.

'How much to Varanasi, mate?' A young western traveller stood in the doorway, more out than in. His accent was British and he was heavily tanned.

'For you, sir, special price of one thousand rupees.'

'That's a bit steep. Okay, cheers.' He was about to leave when Aiden called out and introduced himself. Glen and his four friends, who were waiting outside, were from the south of England. They'd been in India for two months and looked as if they had come straight out of a hippy festival. The group had spent half their time on the beaches of Goa before travelling north to Manali. Glen and Alan – whose hair and beard were so bushy it made him look like a yeti – were toying with the idea of visiting Varanasi, but money and time were both short as they were all due to fly home in a few days.

Without warning Aiden offered to pay for a room in our hotel for a night, which they gratefully accepted. 'Their knowledge will be invaluable,' Aiden said, 'I'm sure they'll have a ton of information to share with us.' That I didn't doubt, but Aiden's impulsiveness concerned me.

Paul asked how much we'd spent so far and on what. 'You've spent far too much,' he said, arriving at the hotel. 'India is so cheap to travel. You've just got to know where to look and how much to pay. This place is far too expensive for a start. We'll find a cheaper place tomorrow and you can see how we do things in India.'

Glen collected the key and we followed them up the stairs. I reminded Aiden we were booked to go to Agra tomorrow, but my words fell on deaf ears until we were in the room and the guys were unpacking, 'You can go to Agra if you want, but I'm hanging around with these guys. I want to be better prepared for what's out there.' I couldn't argue. We were as unprepared as it could get and at the rate we were spending money we'd be going home within a month.

None of us had eaten for a while so I suggested the hotel's restaurant, but upon inspection of the menu Justin concluded it was far too pricey. We went out again and followed the same route to the railway station. Just past where we'd bought our coach tickets earlier we stopped. Glen held out his arm to the right, much like a magician pulling a rabbit from a hat and presented a long bustling road. 'This, my friends, is the Main Bazaar.'

Hawkers shouted their wares: gold, silver, electronics, the very best claims in fashion and the sweet charms of confectionery prepared before our very eyes. There were restaurants and hotels in abundance as well as travel agents galore. Everywhere you looked something was happening. All this was right on our doorstep the whole time.

'If you can't find what you want here, somebody will know someone who can,' Glen said as we struggled to keep up. Our new friends floated through the crowds effortlessly, gliding by rickshaws, animals and touts until they came to rest outside an eatery wafting burnt kerosene and a fusion of aromatic spices.

'We'll try this place.' Jack pulled his blond hair into a ponytail, scratched his goatee and motioned me inside, 'After you, mate.'

The restaurant was filled with long tables and benches. Apart from a western couple sat in the corner, it was only locals that occupied the area. A waiter made eye contact and sailed over, arms filled with steel dishes of food, 'More seat upside, come.' He closed in behind us and guided us up the stairs where we were met by another man who showed us to a table.

'How much for thali and chai?' Alan asked.

The waiter grinned, 'Thali fifty rupees, chai fifteen rupees. How many are you like?'

'Slow down, mate. Thali ten rupees, chai three rupees,' Alan retained eye contact.

The waiter retained his grin, 'Thali fifteen, chai six.'

The guys leaned in, whispered, nodded and returned with backs straightened, assertive and confident, 'Thali twelve, chai four.'

The waiter stood firm and the guys motioned to leave. 'Okay, Okay, thali twelve, chai five.'

Aiden and I were amazed. Within minutes the tea was served in small glasses and the thali – which was new to us – was presented on shiny steel plates with circular indentations brimming with vegetable curries, pickles, rice and on the side, flat round chapatis.

'Eat as much as you like, mate,' Jack said, tearing off some bread and scooping up some food with it. 'There's plenty more where that came from.'

It was still early evening and Aiden and I were invited to hang out in their room. Jack flicked through the channels on the TV and landing on a Hindi movie, he said, 'The Indians love their films, big business over here. If you're unlucky enough to book a coach with a television, you'll have to sit through loads of films blaring out at full volume for most of the journey.' He flicked again, resting on the American coastguard drama, Baywatch. 'The Indian men are particularly fond of Baywatch.' Jack tilted his head as Pamela Anderson, clad in a red bikini, came bouncing into frame, 'And who can blame them?'

Justin reached into his backpack and withdrew a velvet

drawstring pouch. From inside the bag, he removed a black conical pipe, a stained rag, a half empty packet of cigarettes and a dark brown substance wrapped in plastic, which I soon realised was hashish. 'All right if we have a smoke?' he asked and used the piece of material to clean the inside of the chillum. Aiden's eyes lit up like it was Christmas morning. 'This stuff is bloody lovely,' declared Justin as he peeled back the plastic from the brown finger of hashish. 'It's called charas and it's cheap. One tola – 12.5 grams – costs around three hundred roops in Manali. It's growing all over the place up there.'

He blended the hash and tobacco carefully and then guided the mixture into the wider end of the pipe, padding it down with his thumb. With the chillum held upright he steered the flame of his lighter into the pipe and chuffed to entice the heat. He then inhaled, very deeply, waiting for a few seconds before lifting his head and triumphantly blowing out a cloud of smoke. He leant forward and offered it up for the taking. Aiden was quick to accept and embraced it as if it were a long-lost friend. After fogging the room so thick we momentarily lost sight of each other, he passed it to Glen, who then passed it to me.

I'd seen how it was done a few times now and was confident I could imitate. I held the pipe between my fingers, puffed and inhaled deeply. My eyes widened as my lungs registered the burn. My cheeks filled with returning smoke and when I couldn't hold it any longer, I spluttered in all directions, eyes watering and coughing uncontrollably much to everyone's amusement.

'You'll soon get the hang of it,' Alan said, as he lit a chillum of his own and passed it on. 'The Manali locals rub the marijuana leaves and the resin sticks to their hands. They rub for a day and make about eight or nine grams. The faster they roll, the weaker the substance. You get the best stuff when they rub slowly and they make two or three grams a day. That's when you get Manali Cream, and that gentlemen, is what you're smoking right now.'

Aiden was in his element. I, on the other hand took longer to adapt, but as Alan had suggested, I did eventually relax into it and the coughing receded. Somewhere, outside of the euphoria, I heard

Aiden ask, 'Has anyone heard of the Thuggees?'

'What's that, like a rock band or something?' Paul asked.

'No. They're these dudes who worship Kali and rob and kill travellers.'

The others glanced at each other, none the wiser.

Jack's eyes grasped a memory, 'Hold on, I think I know what you're talking about. Yeah, I read about them a couple of years ago in the library. They did kill a lot of people, you're right; over two million travellers in fact. Pretty sure they haven't been around for about a hundred and fifty years though.'

'Trust you to know that,' Glen laughed. 'Anything related to Indian history and Jack's got an answer. We were thinking of getting a useless-facts jar for him to put ten roops in every time he spouts his boring shit. Just think guys, if we'd done that, we'd have been living it up tonight in a palace with a kinky harem.'

Aiden chose not to pursue the subject any further, 'So, is Manali as good as they say?'

Paul tapped the contents of his chillum into the ashtray, 'That and more, mate. It's so laid back. You'd love it. Peace, love and Jelly Babies, bro. Goa's amazing too. Mind blowing beaches with bowing palm trees and golden sands and the most awesome parties I've ever been to. Man, I miss those beaches,' he looked up longingly as if Goa was right there.

I slept well that night, but before I drifted off, I thought of Ruben and how we could have been in Manali, glad my intuition about him was right.

5

It was mid-morning and we were in the Main Bazaar again in search of cheaper accommodation. The haphazard buildings were mostly two and three storey businesses showing signs of age and structural damage. Above shops, bright signage sprawled the cracked discoloured concrete: boards advertising handicrafts, books, clothing, doctors, hotels and restaurants, telephone and travel services. Fresh faced travellers were surrounded by salesmen or shocked into parting with their money by disfigured beggars; young ladies struggled with unwanted attention from groups of men who crowded, placing their hands here, there and everywhere. I felt grateful of the invisible safety cord attached to our new friends.

Glen brought the group to a stop outside a hotel and disappeared inside to find out a price. 'Too much,' he said as he reappeared. 'How about one person stays with the luggage, while the others split up into two groups? It should speed things up a bit.' Aiden volunteered my services as watchman.

Left alone on the corner of an alleyway, I piled the luggage against a wall. I turned to find three men staring; not touting nor talking nor smiling, just staring, watching my every move. I became anxious, worried that they might be the same guys that assaulted Don and I. Surely, they wouldn't be brave enough to rob me in broad daylight, would they? Someone tapped my shoulder, 'You okay, mate?' It was Jack.

'Yeah, I guess. You made me jump.' My eyes were still set on my potential assailants.

'Sorry about that. We found a good hotel. The others will be along shortly.'

'What are these guys staring at?' I muttered under my breath.

'Who, these guys?' Jack turned to the three men and held his hands at chest level, palms pressed together, fingers pointing up and bowed his head slightly, 'Namaste, aap kaise hain?' he asked. The young men waggled their heads and smiled. They mirrored Jack's hands and said 'Namaste' back to us. They told us they were very well and thanked him for asking. They enquired as to which country we were from and how we were finding India; what we did for a living, what our fathers did for a living. Aiden and the others turned up and attention was soon drawn to them.

'Nine times out of ten, people in India mean you no harm when they stare. They're only interested in you and your life.' Jack heaved his backpack over his shoulders, 'It's strange coming from a country like ours. If you stare at someone in England, it's seen as rude. Here, it is nothing more than curiosity.'

'So, I guess namaste is some kind of greeting then?'

'Namaste, namaskar, yeah, like hello or welcome – a salutation. It goes a long way in India. As does the word baksheesh.' Glen and Paul chuckled as Jack continued, 'Baksheesh can mean tipping or a donation or even bribing. That word might come in handy one day.'

With our gear strapped up, we walked further down the Main Bazaar and turned right into a passageway and right again into our new hotel. Aiden and I paid for the room and with our passports registered, our bags were escorted up the stairs by a cheery young chap who only communicated in waggles, gestures and smiles. He showed us to our room and left content with a small tip. There were two double beds. I'd share mine with Jack, Glen would share his with Aiden. The others were happy to sleep on the floor using thin foam mattresses unrolled from their backpacks.

'That thali yesterday was great,' Aiden said. 'It'd be nice if we could go out and get some more for lunch.'

'I'd love to get some lassi too. Do you guys know where we can get...'

'I wasn't talking to you, Sam,' interrupted Aiden. 'Anyway, didn't you say you were going to buy us all some drinks? Toddle off then.'

I swallowed my embarrassment and smiled, 'You're right. Where are my manners? I'll be back in a minute.'

I slipped out of the room as our friends sat in silence. With my back to the door, I let out a sigh, glad to be away from the uncomfortable atmosphere. I was about to go downstairs and order when the young man that carried our bags, came up the steps. I tilted an imaginary bottle to my lips and he beckoned me to follow him, leading me up a flight of stairs to an open rooftop. There, with his back to us, stood a chubby man cooking on a stove against a blackened wall. The young porter tugged on the cook's vest and he turned around with a beaming smile, 'Ah hello, my friend. My name is Harish. Welcome please. What can I be doing for you on this fine day?'

The jolly man in his late twenties offered me a chair by a swaying electric fan.

'Could I get seven soft drinks please?' I asked.

'Of course.' He opened the refrigerator, 'What you like? We have Pepsi and Thums up, Mirinda, Citra and Limca.'

'Okay. I only know Pepsi. What are the others?'

'Limca is lemon-lime, Thums Up is cola, Citra is orange,' he twisted a bottle to read the label, 'and this Mirinda is orange too.'

'I'll have four Pepsis and one of each of the others, please. Can I sit and drink one up here?' I wasn't ready to go back to the room just yet.

'Why not? Please, sit and enjoy sunshine and drink.'

He asked my name and country, 'It is a pleasure to be meeting you Mr Sam. This is Nitin,' he pointed to the young man who brought me up here. I was then introduced to two other teenagers washing and drying dishes in the corner, 'Anil is on left, Rajeev is on right.' They were unable to hear the introductions above the clatter. 'You would like to see more of Delhi? Come.' I followed Harish up a bamboo ladder to another level which overlooked the rooftops of Paharganj for as far as I could see. Kites darted the sky, people hung washing, tended to flowerpots or relaxed and read a book. I even caught a glimpse of a game of cricket being played.

'I am thinking you are in room number twelve,' Harish said, sipping his tea from a plain china cup.

'That's right. Why, are we a bit noisy?'

'Oh no, Mr Sam, nothing like that. I am thinking that some of you must be sleeping on floor.'

'Only three of us, but they're okay with it, they're hardy travellers.'

'Oh, if they are being happy, that is good.' Harish looked across the city and then to the sky, 'You and friends must come to roof tonight. I am feeling big storm in my bones, air too thick. I am hoping to see all of Delhi light up this evening.'

'Thanks Harish, that sounds cool. I'll tell the others.'

Nitin assisted me with the drinks to the room and went back upstairs. I opened the door and was immediately engulfed by smoke. Everyone was thankful for the drinks except Aiden, who refused any of the choices. I sat on the floor and Alan passed me a chillum. I smoked a little and another was passed from Glen. I coughed, but not as much as before. And then it hit me; the same feeling as last night, only deeper, heavier. My heart rate increased, my mouth became dry, voices echoed and merged. I was sleepy, nauseous and dizzy. I closed my eyes, dropped my head and tried to slow the spinning carousel. When I opened my eyes again, waiting for the room to refocus, Aiden came into clarity. His stare was fixed upon me, intense and steely. I looked away as he addressed the others, 'Let's get something to eat then.'

The sounds outside were louder, the sun hotter, the sights more chaotic and the smells more overpowering. I kept close to the others. Faces stared and scared me, my heart hammered in my head. Aiden glanced over and smiled, seeing the discomfort in my face and fear in my eyes. I relaxed only when we took our seats in the thali house. Parathas were served – fried unleavened bread packed with chopped potatoes and cumin. I couldn't eat much. It wasn't something I would usually choose and my stomach was on the delicate side. Instead, I sipped chai from a glass and stared out to the street below. My thoughts were shattered by Aiden's voice, 'We're going shopping. You go back to the hotel, Sam. You don't look well.'

'He looks all right to me,' Justin said as he paid his bill. 'You can come with us if you want, mate.'

The thought of Aiden's increasingly odd behaviour did nothing to entice me. I thanked him but said I would go back to the hotel.

Jack stood and stretched, 'I'm gonna stay behind too, catch forty winks.'

In the hotel room, Jack made up a chillum, 'Has India got any easier by hanging out with us?'

'Yeah, I think it has. It's interesting to see how you guys interact with the locals. It's teaching us a lot.'

'We were just like you two when we first arrived in Delhi, didn't have a Scooby Doo, mate.' He passed the pipe, 'Got proper ripped off. But we soon learnt and bit by bit things got better.'

'India's got a steep learning curve, eh?'

'You're not wrong, mate. So, what's up with Aiden then? He seems a bit off with you.' Jack took the chillum from me and prepared for another round.

'I'm not really sure. We were the best of friends before we came out here, but since we arrived he's become increasingly hostile, especially when we're around other people. At first, I put it down to the lack of a smoke or a beer. But since he's had a smoke, he's got worse if anything.'

'This place can do funny things to people. It can bring out the best and the worst in folk. Aiden's a little insecure I think and perhaps India isn't what he thought it'd be. He's probably trying to prove himself in front of us.'

It felt good to have someone neutral seeing things from an outside perspective and gave me hope that Aiden was simply adjusting and we'd be back to normal again soon. Jack smoked the last of the chillum and leant back against the wall, 'Have you got an alarm of some sort? My watch drowned in Goa.' I pointed to my clock. 'I don't know about you, but I'm knackered with this heat. Set the alarm for three and if you like, we'll pop out later to Connaught Place.'

A nasty throbbing in my head woke me before the alarm did. The ringing of the clock a few minutes later only intensified the pain. Jack awoke and noticed my head held in my hands, 'You okay, mate?'

'I've woken up with a splitting headache.'

'I haven't seen you drink much today and when I have, it's been either fizzy drinks or tea. You should always carry a bottle of water around with you. This heat can be a real killer; you need to keep hydrated. You won't last long if you don't.' He went to his backpack, found a small medicine bottle and threw it over to me and handed me an unopened bottle of water, 'Take two of those pills and sip some of this water. Give yourself twenty minutes and you'll be as right as rain. Don't rely on the tablets though, keep those fluids up.'

The Main Bazaar was dense, even more so than usual. We could hardly move. Hooters were honking, bells were ringing, the air swelled with thousands of excited voices. Somewhere a trumpet played hopelessly out of tune, cymbals crashed and a base drum boomed. Jack and I squeezed our way to the end of the street and were carried by the crowd onto the main road at the mercy of a procession. The root of all the excitement seemed to emanate from an elaborate god adorned with orange garlands and gold necklaces that was carried on the shoulders of four men. There was no interest in our faces now, all eyes were focused on the cynosure. Pilgrims chanted, threw petals and placed offerings at the idol's feet. The more we tried to break away, the more we were entangled in the human jungle. It was becoming impossible to breathe with so many sweating bodies pressed up against us. As the road widened and the ceremony dispersed, we took the opportunity to slip the net.

We sat on a wall and took a minute to compose ourselves. Thankful of Jack's advice, I sipped from the bottle of water I'd brought with me. 'See mate, I told you the water would come in handy,' he said and drank from his own. 'You never know what's going to happen in India from one moment to the next. It was a bit intense, huh?'

'I thought we were never going to get out. It was quite exciting though.'

'You get quite a few religious festivals in India. They can be a lot of fun, but can be dangerous too, hundreds die each year from stampedes.' I could well believe it. I'd never felt such claustrophobia. 'Watch from a distance if you can.' He pointed to a group of men across the road, 'There's some rickshaw wallahs over there. Shall we grab one?'

We began walking. 'Okay, but what's a wallah?'

'A wallah is a person who provides a service, for example: paan wallah, chai wallah, dhobi wallah and in this case, rickshaw wallah.'

'And what about these skirts I see guys wearing?' I pointed at two rickshaw wallahs.

Jack chuckled, 'That's a lungi, mate. I've got one. Wore it all the time in Goa. It beats trousers in this heat.'

A cycle-rickshaw wallah fanned himself with a newspaper as he spoke to his colleagues. He was quick to dismiss them when he saw us. He tapped the back seat of his tricycle, 'Yes, come.'

Jack put his arm across me to prevent me from boarding, 'How much to Connaught Place?'

'One hundred rupees.'

Jack giggled, 'Don't make me laugh.' He nudged me, 'Come on Sam, we can do better than this.' We started to walk away.

The wallah tagged along behind us, 'Okay, how much you pay?'

'Ten rupees,' Jack said without turning.

The driver chuckled, 'Now you are making me laugh, sahib.' He skirted around to the front of us and stopped us in our tracks, 'Sixty rupees, and I am giving you very best offer.'

Jack raised, 'Twelve.'

'Okay, forty rupees. Come.' He walked back the way he came.

'Twenty and we're right behind you.'

'Okay, okay, twenty, come.'

We settled in and pulled away. 'You're really good at this,' I said to Jack.

'Don't tell me, let me guess, you've never agreed a price before you've set off? How have you guys got any money left?' he laughed. 'Always agree a cost before you set off. Be fair and don't rip them off, but don't let them rip you off either. Start low and meet them at a reasonable price. It's good to know roughly how far away things are, so you can judge the distance in accordance to the fare.'

'What's Connaught Place?' I asked.

'It's one of the most vibrant commercial districts in Delhi. It was built in the early 1900s by the British and is constructed into three circles. The outer and inner circles contain residential properties, businesses and retail establishments and the central section is made up of parkland where anybody can enjoy a picnic, read a book or even play a spot of cricket. The Indians love their cricket.'

'Cricket you like?' The rickshaw wallah called out above the noise of the traffic.

'Yes mate,' Jack yelled back. 'England to win, eh?'

The wallah laughed, 'Never against India, my friend.'

The brakes of the rickshaw squealed to a halt and we paid the agreed fare. Jack led the way around the outer avenue lined with large white columns where people sold a variety of goods on the pavements. Men grumbled over games of chess while wives gossiped in the background. Children played hide and seek around parked cars with frustrated security guards. High fashion stores and luxury brands tempted passing socialites and the cream of the city. We stopped outside a Wimpy burger restaurant. Jack opened the door, 'Milkshake?'

There were no actual beef burgers on the menu. 'The cow is sacred in India, Hindus don't eat beef,' Jack reminded me. Instead, we settled for spicy bean burgers and strawberry shakes. We took our meal into the central park area and laid back, relaxing on the trimmed lawn. It was at last beginning to feel like a vacation.

An auto ride in the fading light brought us back to the hotel where Aiden and the others were talking over a few chillums in our room. 'What have you guys been up to?' Jack asked, receiving a smoke.

'Old Delhi, Chandni Chowk,' Paul replied. 'Went shopping, bought a few chillums for the loved ones back home. What about you guys?'

'Grabbed a couple of burgers and sat out in the park at Connaught Place,' Jack passed the chillum to me. 'Did you get caught up in that procession earlier in Paharganj?'

'Can't say we did, mate. Were there a lot of people?'

As Jack was about to answer, the lights went out and the air-cooler died.

'Bloody power cuts,' Glen said. 'No use going out, won't be able to see a thing on the streets. Just have to sit it out here and hope it doesn't go on too long. I'm already sweating like mad.'

'I know where we could go,' I said as I fumbled for the door handle. 'Guys, follow me.' Intrigued, everyone stood except Aiden, who remained seated. 'Aren't you coming?'

His face radiated in an orange glow as he drew on a cigarette, 'No, I'm fine here.'

Glen went over and reached out his hand, 'Come on mate, I want to talk to you both about something.' Aiden reluctantly got up and followed behind.

Up on the roof, working by dim torchlight, Harish stopped what he was doing and invited us to sit, 'Please come, I will be making chai for us all,' he said and put Nitin and Rajeev to work.

I introduced my friends, 'And finally, Aiden.' Aiden turned his back without acknowledgement and looked over the edge of the roof in silence much to my chagrin.

We settled down and Glen addressed Aiden and me, 'We were having a chat about where you two should go next and came up with Naini Tal. It's a little hill station town with a beautiful lake tucked away in the Kumaon foothills. It's about three hundred kilometres east of here. It'll give you guys a chance to relax away from the bustle of Delhi.'

'Sounds good,' I said.

'Yeah, I suppose,' Aiden added.

'Right then, that's that sorted. We'll search around for some tickets tomorrow,' Glen concluded.

Nitin approached Aiden and tapped him on the shoulder, 'Get your bloody hands off me,' Aiden blasted and shoved him aside so hard he nearly lost his balance. None of us quite understood what had just happened.

'Christ, what's got into you, Aiden?' Jack barked and walked over to Nitin. 'Are you alright, mate?' Nitin waggled his head and smiled. He placed his fingers to his lips to gesture an invisible cigarette. 'Of course, no worries,' Jack said and handed him his pack. Nitin removed two; one he lit, the other he propped behind his ear for later.

Harish pointed a torch at a bamboo ladder, inviting us to make ourselves comfortable on the higher level. We sat down as Nitin and Rajeev served the tea. Harish, the only one standing, looked out to the city, 'Yes, very good time with no power. Much dark, very good time indeed.'

Paharganj was shrouded in darkness, less a few glimmers of temporary lighting and vehicle headlights. In the streets below, voices interspersed with the sounds of beeping and dogs barking. Aiden stood to leave, 'I'd rather be in our room than stuck up here. There's not much point sitting around in the dark doing nothing. It's all a bit shit if you ask me.' He stepped down to the top rung of the ladder and as he did so a crack of distant thunder startled him and made him lose his footing. Nitin, who was closest, shot to his feet and grabbed hold of Aiden's arm as he was about to fall. Regaining himself, he mumbled something to Nitin in the way of thanks and sat down again, silently watching silver veins strobe the city skyline in the distance.

6

Recurring gurgling and vicious cramps in my stomach had me tossing and turning as I searched for sleep. I tiptoed over Alan and Paul to the bathroom and closed the door behind me as quietly as I could. I knelt on all fours with my head hung over the latrine. The stench crept up into my nostrils, reaching inside and yanking out everything I'd consumed in the last twenty-four hours. Exhausted and drenched in sweat, I fell to one side in a shivering heap.

After what seemed like hours, but couldn't have been more than five minutes, I used the sink as leverage and pulled myself up to catch my reflection in the mirror. I looked haggard, just as I felt. I splashed water on my face and filled the bucket to wash the toilet, but a sharp pain in my stomach had me winded with an unstoppable engagement to the keyhole again, this time due south. Afterwards, I sat shaking with my back to the tiled wall. When certain nothing was left, I showered and crumpled into bed.

The next time I woke I found the room empty aside from Jack sorting through items from his backpack. He glanced up as I got out of bed, 'Hello mate, sleep well?' he asked.

I gave him a run-down of the night's bathroom events, 'I've been feeling a bit odd for a couple of days now, but nothing near as bad as last night.'

'Sounds like you've got a touch of Delhi Belly, and where better to get it, eh?' He laughed and put the last of his things into the top of his pack, paused for a moment as if searching his memory and then clipped the top shut. 'What did you eat before we came along?'

'Vegetable curries, omelettes, jam on toast, club sandwiches.' I felt queasy just at the thought of it all.

'In those club sandwiches, was there any meat? And those lassis you're so fond of, any ice?'

'Ice in the lassi and ham in the sandwiches.'

'Mystery solved then.' He opened a side pocket of his backpack and found a half empty strip of red pills, 'Take two and we'll get some more when we're out.' I washed the tablets down with some water. 'Try your best to avoid eating meat. Refrigeration and sanitation are not high on the agenda in a lot of places. Also, watch what you drink. Ice is usually frozen from local water and our western stomachs aren't up to the challenge. Keep your hands clean and fingernails short, and whatever you do, don't bite them. Doing all this will help, but you can't do everything. You will get ill and you will get used to it. Most common is diarrhoea, it wipes out thousands in India each year. Just keep drinking water to replace lost fluids.' He bent down and looked under the bed and then under the other bed, 'Also, only eat in clean places where there's a lot of other people eating, especially locals.' He looked around the room mystified.

'You lost something?' I asked.

'A bottle of Indian Bagpiper whiskey I bought for my dad a couple of weeks ago, I'm sure I packed it. Either the other guys are winding me up or I left it at the last hotel. Not like me to leave things behind, especially something like that. Oh well, shall we head out for a bit?'

Jack took me to a hole-in-the-wall chemist along the Main Bazaar where I bought some red pills from a man who sat boxed in with shelves of pharmaceutical paraphernalia. I was surprised at how easy it all was and pondered the alternative had we not met our new friends. If Aiden or I fell ill, the only thing we would have successfully done was panic.

'They should keep you going for a few days. If you're still unwell after that, you should think about seeing a doctor,' Jack advised me.

I popped the pills over breakfast in the thali house which was sweltering despite the overhead fans. The overwhelming heat was the thing I'd struggled with the most since arriving in Delhi. Today felt like the hottest day so far. I mentioned as much to Jack. 'It's warm all right mate,' he said. 'Harish told me this morning it could climb to one hundred and ten Fahrenheit today.' It was hard to comprehend such a temperature being so used to unpredictable British summers that came along a little too often.

Outside, we flagged down a cycle-rickshaw. Jack instructed the wallah to take us to the Red Fort in Old Delhi.

'The Red Fort was constructed in the mid seventeenth century by the fifth Moghul Emperor Shah Jahan,' Jack said. 'It housed the emperors of the Moghul dynasty for nearly two hundred years.'

Our progress was slow as we emerged into a built-up area where narrow lanes and avenues swarmed with people, hand-drawn carts, cattle and heavy traffic. Dark, cramped alleyways were illuminated by shops selling glittering gold and silver, enamels and colourful carpets, bright saris and salwar kameez and a variety of garlands and turbans for weddings and festivals.

'This is the walled city of Old Delhi,' Jack shouted above the din. 'It was also built by Shah Jahan who shifted the Moghul capital from Agra. See that over there?' Jack pointed to the far end of the street to a sandstone building with three white domes and tall minarets either side, 'That's the Jama Masjid, India's largest mosque, again, built by Shah Jahan.'

'This Shah Jahan guy sounded pretty powerful,' I said to Jack as we broke away from the crowds, travelling freely alongside the impenetrable vermilion walls of the fort.

'Absolutely mate. There are some amazing buildings all over northern India that were built under Moghul reign. The most incredible of course is the Taj Mahal. You've got to try and see it if you get a chance.'

Stretching out for as far as the eye could see, the fortress walls, punctuated every so often with bastions and turrets, seemed to go on for miles. We drew to a halt outside Lahore Gate which dwarfed all those that walked beneath its grand archway. Jack handled the souvenir salesman with ease, laughing and joking, making it look all too easy. Through the gateway, we ambled along a small bazaar selling handmade handicrafts and sparkling jewellery and came out into a spacious courtyard with gardens and avenues filled with ornate fountains, lavish stone pavilions and halls of public and private audience. Beneath a tree, we took shade and relaxed for a while sharing stories of our lives in England.

I found out that Jack was a primary school supply teacher. He loved his job and enjoyed coming back from a trip and furnishing the imagination of the children with his tales.

'I wouldn't swap it for the world. The kids' faces light up when I tell them about my travels.'

A honeymooning Indian couple sheepishly approached us and asked if we would take their photograph. They also asked if they could take a picture of Jack and I to show their family of the new friends they made from England. It was endearing to say the least.

No sooner had we left the fort, we were surrounded by three young boys calling after us, 'Rupee, rupee, school pen, school pen.'

From his pocket, Jack pulled a handful of coins and gave them to the boys, 'Here you go lads, knock yourself out,' he chuckled. 'Come on mate, let's grab that auto over there or we'll be here all day. They'll follow us all the way back to the hotel.'

We entered the room to a haze of charas which made me feel stoned within minutes. We talked of our afternoon and smoked a few chillums and soon, I felt my eyes dropping and my head accepting the comfort of my pillow. It was dark when I woke and the room was empty. The need to visit the bathroom came on instantly. Delhi belly or not, whatever it was had me hugging and squatting the keyhole again and again. The pain in my stomach was becoming unbearable and I left the bathroom staggering and clutching the door frame with weakness.

Hoping to find the others, I went to the rooftop. Harish was sat on an upturned bucket cooling by the fan. He was smoking a thin brown leafed cigarette called a beedi whilst Nitin busied himself at the stove. In his usual professional and charming manner, Harish stood and offered me his seat, along with a cup of his lovely chai. I asked if he had seen my friends. He hadn't.

'Very, very hot,' he said tilting his hand left and right. 'Despite storm, still no rain fall on Paharganj. Everyone in Delhi is waiting for birth of this year's monsoon. Soon I am hoping much rain will come and save us from this dreadful heat. Then, I will be most happy. You join us for dinner? I am making very nice dish.'

I happily accepted the offer. Nitin grinned and mimed a cigarette. I gave him two. I talked to him in English and he tried to converse with me in Hindi, but neither of us could understand one another. I tucked in to Harish's vegetable curry despite my nausea, amazed at how easily it went down, mopping the plate clean as Harish and Nitin musically rolled off conversation to each other.

Harish turned to me, 'Oh, Mr Sam, please forgive us. Hindi must sound very strange to your ears. Nitin is finding English very odd too. Please tell us, how are we sounding to you?'

'How are you sounding? I guess it sounds like you're speaking extremely fast.' I tried to replicate how I heard them, 'Berigiaweregerafalawalla. Something like that I guess.'

Harish's smile fell and his mouth dropped open. Rice dropped from his fingers and the two them stared at me in what seemed an everlasting silence. A new sickness stabbed away at my stomach, one of dread that I might have offended them in some way. Harish confirmed my fears, 'You have just insulted my family and call Nitin's uncle, son of smelly goat.'

I was mortified, 'I'm so sorry, I really didn't know what I was saying.'

Nitin looked at Harish, eyebrow cocked. Harish whispered something to him and Nitin sprayed rice everywhere with laughter, then rolled onto his back, nearly choking. Harish placed his hand on my shoulder and chuckled much to my relief, 'Mr Sam, please be forgiving me, I am only having joke with you.'

'Harigedoeywahdoeywah,' Nitin giggled, tears now streaming his face.

'What did he say?' I asked Harish.

'I am not having any idea. Nitin is telling me he is speaking

51

English Hindi.'

I had numerous encounters with the bathroom throughout the night and decided to spend the next day in the room to recuperate. It seemed the most sensible thing to do given that I wasn't getting any better.

It was Aiden's twentieth birthday and he was in high spirits. I gave him a card from me and one from his mother that she left in my care before we left. Things between us were good again.

'I got the tickets to Naini Tal. Glen found a great place, 175 rupees each. How are you feeling?' I answered that I was starting to feel better. He offered me a cigarette but I declined with a hand wave and smile.

'I'll get you the fare money,' I said, reaching for my backpack.

'No, it's on me mate, all paid for.' He sat on the end of the bed and lit up.

'Cheers, that's really good of you.' I leant back against the wall to line myself up with the air-conditioning unit. 'It's been good today, just like old times again.'

'Yeah, sorry about all that. The last few days have all been a bit strange for me. I think I've found it hard to adjust.'

I'd been acting out the part accepting this new life and hadn't given a thought to how Aiden must have been dealing with it all.

The next morning, Jack and I left the others asleep while we slipped out for breakfast. I was feeling much better. The five guys were flying home that evening and Aiden and I would be on our own. I mentioned how we were getting along again.

'Yeah, we had a few gentle words with him,' Jack said. 'He realised he was being out of order towards you, hence the apology.'

'Whatever you said, it did the trick, thanks.'

Jack went in search of another bottle of whisky for his father and I changed some money in the bank. The room was empty when I returned. Scattered across the floor was all my stuff, but no sign of my backpack. I picked everything up and stacked it neatly on the bed and sat trying to figure out what had happened. I didn't have to wait too long before Aiden returned with the answer.

'Do you know what happened to my backpack?' I asked.

'Stored it,' he replied.

'Stored it? But why? And where?'

'In storage lockers, two rupees a day. I took the cash from your money-belt along with the fair to Naini Tal while you were out earlier.'

'Why did you do that? What am I supposed to do now? Where will I put all my stuff? This is a joke, right?' He ignored my barrage of questions. 'How am I supposed to travel India with just this?' I pointed to the pathetic rucksack, 'It has bloody balloons on it. It doesn't look like it's going to last another day.'

Walking towards the door, he paused and looked over his shoulder at me, 'I'm not getting into this now. You'll see it's for the best in the long run. We leave for Naini Tal tonight, make sure you're packed and ready.' Before I had time to respond or even mention the gift of the bus ticket, he added, 'And one other thing, as you and Jack have been spending so much time together, I told the others you didn't like them.' With that, he slammed the door behind him.

This was utter madness. Had he taken complete leave of his senses? I recalled his words and actions over and over. It felt like a bad dream, a side effect from the pills maybe or too much charas still lingering in my head, but I could only wish that was the case as I stared at my pile of clothes and the irritating coloured balloons. Once I repacked my belongings into the bulging rucksack, I realised how much I'd have to leave behind: a sleeping bag, a pair of jeans, two pairs of trousers, three shirts, a light sweater and jacket. I'd paid over one hundred pounds for that backpack, it was perfect for the trip. I would have rather lightened that than use the nasty nylon replacement. At least the backpacks could be retrieved later, which was some consolation.

I settled the bill with Harish and offered a one-hundred-rupee tip which at first, he flatly refused. I insisted, 'You guys have been so good to us and I've had a great time on the roof. Please accept and then maybe when we return to Delhi you can look after us again.' Humbly, he took the money and we shook hands goodbye.

'Just about to get some drinks, do you want one?' Paul asked as I approached our room.

'Yeah, thanks.' I walked with him to reception. 'You know I like you guys, right?'

He cocked his eyebrow, 'Uh yeah, what's on your mind Sam?' He placed the order and as we waited I explained what Aiden had said. 'Don't worry yourself, mate. We know you wouldn't have said anything like that. We deliberately paired you up with Jack because we knew you would have more in common with him. He's really into his buildings and history, and all that boring stuff, like you.' Taking the bottles, we ascended the stairs. 'We thought Aiden might be a bit of a handful, and he was, he disappeared eight times on us. We visited the same places as you and Jack, the only difference was keeping up with Aiden.' We paused at the door and I thanked him for everything. 'It was our pleasure mate, we had a really good time. Now tell me something, is Aiden really on three months leave from the SAS?'

I smiled, 'No, but let's pretend I didn't tell you that.'

He winked, 'Your secret's safe with me.'

Aiden was friendly enough as we all enjoyed our last chillum session together. I spent the afternoon and evening observing the special bond between the five friends. They'd taught us so much and I was thankful that Aiden grabbed Glen's attention at the tourist office.

Geared up with our ridiculous rucksacks, we said our last goodbyes to the guys as night fell on Paharganj. At 9pm, we boarded a modern coach and took to our seats. I tried to engage in conversation with Aiden, but all I received was short, sharp answers. For the most part he ignored me. His eyes were heavy and when he stood, he staggered. There was also a strong smell of alcohol on his breath. From his rucksack, he removed a small vial of pills and a bottle of Bagpiper whisky, half full.

My heart sank, 'Where did you get that whisky?' I asked. He ignored me, so I asked again.

'Jack gave it to me,' he lied.

'After all they did for us, how could you steal from them? That was a gift for Jack's dad.'

'Yeah, well it's a gift for me now,' he snapped. He showed no remorse, but instead laughed as he knocked back a couple of Valiums with several large gulps of whisky. He'd been smoking copious amounts of charas all day and his behaviour was erratic. 'Bring it on,' he yelled to the bewildered faces sharing the coach and swung the Bagpiper above his head.

The bus roared to life and joined a busy highway bound for Naini Tal. I gripped the handrail and my eyes widened with fear as we flew towards blinding headlights, overtaking at ridiculous speeds. Terrified of the roller coaster ride from hell, I looked to my left and saw the devil himself staring wildly back at me.

7

A chain of mountains emerged from behind a veil of mist, the sun peeking over the summits, illuminating the landscape below. The open windows let in a cool breeze, brushing my cheek and carrying away the staleness of a night spent in the confines of the bus. Everyone was quiet. I looked around at the other passengers, many of whom were still in blissful slumber before turning back to see us pass a giant's staircase of maize terraces and a turquoise lake. Closing my eyes, I absorbed an overdue feeling of serenity.

Sunlight flooded the coach and the central walkway where Aiden lay, his head resting on a folded shirt that bore evidence of his night-time drooling. Dried vomit stained his clothes and he was missing a boot. I was assisted in moving him back to his seat where he sat slumped, snoring and grunting, the dry cracked blood on the left side of his face a heavy reminder of the last seven hours.

The driver expertly steered the vehicle around the tight bends that snaked up the hillside, pausing every so often to allow other vehicles the opportunity to pass. As the coach ascended a steep hill, a group of men armed with ropes and straps looped around their shoulders gave chase. The brakes let out a sigh, the doors swished open and the engine spluttered to a stop. I shook Aiden to wake him as the porters flocked the doorway shouting, 'Yes, yes, I take your luggage.'

'Where are we?' Aiden came to and wiped the sleep from his

eyes and dribble from his chin. He looked down at his lap where he'd wet himself, looked to the ceiling and back to his lap, 'How did that happen?'

I helped him to his feet, 'Come on, we need to get off.'

He followed me to the exit, not taking too kindly to the porters as he stepped down from the vehicle. 'Piss off you bloody idiots, can't you see I can manage perfectly well by myself? Hey, is that my shoe? Why have you numpties tied up my shoe?'

I made numerous apologies on Aiden's behalf while he untied his boot from the ladder attached to the back of the bus. Luckily these good people were incredibly gracious. We started walking without saying a word to each other. It was an uncomfortable silence that didn't belong amid the scenery surrounding us. To our left was a spectacular lake nestled amongst snowless mountains, glinting under the sun's early morning rays. Brightly painted boats moored along the shore would no doubt later be carrying visitors on a scenic excursion across the water. Were we still in India? It was hard to believe. It was more reminiscent of the Lake District in England than what we'd become accustomed to over the last week. Aiden and I arrived at a small café opening its shutters to greet the morning and took a seat at one of the tables outside. I ordered two rounds of tea and toast; a small start at soaking up the evening's sins.

'Do you remember any of last night?' I asked.

'Do you?' Aiden placed his feet on the table, rested his hands behind his head and leant back in his chair.

'Oh yes, I remember.' How could I forget?

'Well go on then, you're obviously dying to tell me.'

'Where shall I start? How about the empty bottle of Bagpiper you threw from the bus window or you dancing on the seat while swinging your shirt in the air shouting "I'm the King of the world"?'

'Yeah, that sounds familiar,' Aiden smirked.

'Later we pulled over to a rest stop and deciding you didn't want your meal, you hurled the plate like a Frisbee and hit a dog. You threw up over a waiter and stormed off, tripped over your untied shoelaces and hit your head on the corner of the table.'

'You lost me now, mate,' Aiden began eating a slice of toast, but ended up just pulling it apart and spreading the fragments around his plate.

'You took off your boot, threw it at the bus and then hurled a string of insults at a nice man who tried to help you.' His dismissive attitude started to anger me and I could hear my voice tremble. 'After throwing up again, you proceeded to the back of the bus to tie your boot to the ladder. You then climbed onto the roof and started singing at the top of your voice, The Good Ship Lollipop.'

Aiden nearly choked on his tea with laughter, 'Good boy, didn't I do well? Got any headache tablets?'

'No. It took all my efforts to calm you down, apologise to the other passengers and convince the driver you were in a fit state to travel. Finally, you collapsed in the walkway, mumbled something about the SAS and passed out.'

'Chill mate. Why are you so worked up?'

I rose from my chair, 'For goodness sake Aiden, can't you see how irresponsible you are?'

'You sound like my mother. Surely you can see the funny side?'

'There is no funny side. You could've got us into serious trouble. I don't know how much more of this I can take.' Exhausted from lack of sleep and Aiden's antics, my patience was being stretched to the limit.

'You wouldn't last five minutes here without me. So, stop your whining and drink your tea.'

'Is that so? Well, you know what? I think I would be better off without you.'

'Go your own way then, see how far you get.'

'Fine, I will.' I picked up my rucksack and stormed away from the table, but my dramatic exit was hampered as one of the bag straps caught on the chair. As I pulled it and attempted to hoist it over my shoulders it ripped and a large hole appeared, causing the contents to spill out on to the ground. Hands shaking, I tried to gather everything together, including myself.

This was ridiculous, he was right, I couldn't travel by myself.

What was I thinking? I turned to sort it all out only to find Aiden gone; just an empty glass and chair as a reminder of his presence. I looked along the road, but he was nowhere to be seen. I attempted to figure out where I would've gone if I was Aiden and realised I'd never been able to work out what went through that crazy head of his. I had no idea where he was. The hills had so many paths leading to so many buildings. I scanned the maze of lanes tucked into the tall trees but saw no sign of him. With an armful of my belongings clutched to my chest, I concluded it would be more prudent to search for him later.

8

There were no obvious hotel signs, no rickshaws, not even a wandering cow or a passing beggar. Of the few cars that went by, none resembled a taxi and the occasional pedestrian I encountered didn't speak any English. My stomach was in knots and my arms and pockets were bulging with my stuff. I stopped to catch my breath and gain a sense of my surroundings. A set of stone steps ahead of me led up into the hills. I started to climb and at the midway point found a guest house overlooking the lake. Without attempting to haggle I handed over two hundred and seventy rupees. The hotel keeper helped me with my things and left me in the room with my guitar and a pile of clothes, my useless rucksack slung into the corner.

There were two windows: one at the front with a partially obscured view of the lake and one small frosted window at the back next to the bathroom. An old wooden chair proved useful as I sorted through my belongings, which left the slightly hard, but comfortable bed clear for me to relax. I assumed Aiden would turn up again, maybe at the café or where we left the bus. But what if he didn't? He had taken the guidebook and had forced me to strip back to the point I had very few clothes and useful items with me. This time yesterday I was surrounded by so many friendly people that could help me, but now I felt the harsh reality of being alone and I didn't have a clue what to do. It was an all too familiar feeling.

When I was fifteen I went to a party where I met a girl called Sandra. We began talking and found we had a lot in common. She loved the idea of working and travelling abroad. Escaping to another country appealed to me too and over the next few days we decided to throw caution to the wind and begin our adventure in Ostend. I had stayed there many times with my grandparents so I knew the town well and I had a friend who lived and worked there. Our plan was to find work and earn enough money to travel on to another country.

I skipped school and we jumped a train to Dover where we took the next available ferry to Belgium. As soon as we got there, things went downhill very quickly. The friend I knew had moved to another part of town and suddenly the idea of tracking him down became an unrealistic task. That left us with plan B, my grandparents' house, but my mum had of course already been in touch and they were not pleased with what I had done to say the least. My grandfather turned us away and ordered me to go home.

With next to no money and out of ideas, Sandra and I rolled into a huge argument and she left. I wandered the streets for three hours trying to think of a way I could still make this adventure work, but in the end, I admitted defeat and returned to the ferry terminal where I managed to persuade the harbour master to arrange travel for me back to England. Upon arriving in Dover, I was met by the authorities and put in a jail cell for eight hours. The following morning a social worker took me to a children's home, which is where I stayed for the next nine months. All my expedition had achieved was to give my father the excuse he needed to have me placed into care. My dream of travelling the world was over.

It had been a long night on the bus and I needed some rest and a shower before I went out looking for Aiden again. Like the air around me, the water was cold and I came out shivering. I took two red pills to curb the nausea that still lingered and lay down on the bed. After dozing for a couple of hours I felt able to venture outside. My plan was to retrace my steps and look for Aiden as well as try and find a place that sold backpacks.

Locking the door behind me, I descended the steps leading to the main road. There was no trace of Aiden at the café or where the bus had stopped. I felt a light tap on my shoulder and my heart soared, but my hopes diminished as I turned to find an elderly Indian gentleman in a beige woolly hat, maroon trousers and matching cardigan, grinning back at me.

'Sir, you are looking lost. My name is Mr Shah, I live long time in Naini Tal.'

'Hello Mr Shah, I'm Sam.'

'Very nice to be meeting you, Mr Sam. I am knowing Naini Tal very good. Please walk with me.' I was suspicious given my time in Delhi, but desperate too. We ambled along the road and he informed me of the area, 'Tal is lake, two-mile circumference. Has seven mountain above. Tallest is Naina, over 2600 metres high. When Shiva's wife Parvati die, he drag her body across country and parts of body fall away. Lake said to be eye of Parvati. This end is Tallital, north end is Mallital.' Although Mr Shah's facts were interesting, I still had to find Aiden and a backpack. Right now, I needed some answers.

'Pardon me, Mr Shah, but could you help me please?'

We stopped, 'Yes, of course. How I help?' Rubbing the bristles of his short white beard, he smiled a toothless grin.

'Have you seen anyone looking like me recently?'

'No, only you,' he chuckled.

'Then maybe you could tell me where I could buy a backpack?' I asked as we resumed our stroll.

'Backback?' he replied. I mimed the motions of lifting a backpack over my shoulders. 'Bag, ah yes, you mean bag.' We came to a stop at the café where I left Aiden and Mr Shah pointed north along the road, 'Follow road topside, there you find many shop. You will get good bag. Now, stay for chai.'

'You've been very helpful Mr Shah, thanks for the offer, but I really must get going. It's been a pleasure meeting you.'

I turned to leave, 'Mr Sam, take boat ride before leaving Naini Tal. Very enjoyable. It bring you much luck. Goodbye, Mr Sam,' he said and returned the way we came.

All I could find as I browsed the shops was a fake leather holdall, not ideal, but an improvement on what I currently possessed. I made the purchase and then looked for a bookshop, but the only one I found didn't sell guidebooks. Back at the hotel I sat in the chair and considered my options. Should I fly home? Should I carry on alone? Where would I go? Manali? Agra? The thought of travelling by myself was daunting; I never imagined the trip without Aiden. I lit a cigarette, dropped my head and sighed.

The sound of loud coughing, clearing of the throat and spitting brought me out of my thoughts. I tried to close the open window by the bathroom, but it was jammed. It was now late afternoon and warmer than it had been earlier. Instead of listening to the same repetitive noises, I decided to take Mr Shah's advice and go on a boat trip. I walked the length of the road until I came across a line of moored paddle boats and a group of eight men talking amongst themselves. As soon as they latched eyes onto me, they surrounded me with shouts of, 'Best ride with me,' and 'This boat cheapest price.' Shoving each other to gain my business, two pushed their way forward. After a minute or so of yelling and jostling, I told them I would decide by the toss of a coin. From my pocket, I removed a fifty paise coin: heads – the older man with the heavy beard; tails – the young man with a hint of a moustache.

I rested the silver on the side of my index finger and placed my thumbnail beneath. The loud chatter around me subsided, all attention now on my hand. The coin flipped into the air, peaked, and upon its descent I swiped it to the top of my hand with a clap. The crowd moved in closer, bending forward over the covered coin. I paused and slowly revealed the answer. The older man let out a whoop of delight and threw his arms into the air, much to the younger man's disappointment.

I was ushered into a Venetian styled boat where I took a seat on the wooden bench. In the background voices were raised and an argument broke out between the young man and one of his colleagues. Fists flew in all directions and the young man walked away with a bloodied nose and battered pride – all this because of my fare? I felt awful for the guy as I was paddled out by the smiling winner. It was out of peak season and there were no other tourists around, so I guessed times must have been tough.

Despite the shaky start, Mr Shah was right; this was just what I needed. Conversation with the boatman was stunted due to his lack of English so instead I used the quiet to contemplate my situation. I was tempted to stay in Naini Tal for a few days after which time Aiden would hopefully have got his head together and we could then reconnect and continue our trip. I almost forgot my worries as I relaxed into the sound of the oars dipping in and being pulled against the cool blue water. The beautiful jade hills soared above, densely studded in places with quaint villas and hotels. The vista was nothing short of spectacular and I could understand why Indian honeymooners chose Naini Tal as a romantic getaway.

The ride finally came to an end just as the sun dipped behind a mountain. I found it sad that I had nobody to share the memories of the afternoon with and I went looking for somewhere to make a telephone call.

'Hello?'

'Hi mum, it's Sam. How's things?'

'Sam, how are you? I'm fine, don't you worry about me. Are you still in Delhi?' Hearing my mother's voice upset me as I felt the pull of homesickness.

'I'm okay, well sort of, I'm not with Aiden any more. We had an argument. I'm now in a place called Naini Tal, east of Delhi. I haven't seen him for about twelve hours now.'

'Oh darling, what are you going to do? Please come home where you're safe.'

Suddenly it all caught up with me. Tears filled my eyes and I looked away from the staring shopkeeper. For a moment, I considered her offer, but then declined, 'I'm going to try and do this on my own.' I could hardly believe what I was saying and with so much resolution. 'I have to give this all I've got, mum. If I leave now, I'll probably never return and will always be left wondering.'

'Okay, you know you can always come home.'

'I know. Listen, I've got to go now, this is costing me a small fortune. I'll call again when I can.' I wiped my cheeks clear of tears in preparation of returning the receiver back to the shop owner.

'Take good care of yourself.'

'I will. Bye mum.'

'Goodbye sweetheart.'

The line fell silent. I looked up, gob-smacked at the cost. As I exhaled smoke from cigarette into the night sky, I gave a description of Aiden to the shopkeeper and asked if he'd seen him.

'Yes, I am thinking I know him, very bad man. He took Gold Flake cigarettes without paying, afternoon time. He called me very bad names. Are you knowing him?' I wish I never asked.

'Yes, I'm afraid so. Please accept my apologies, allow me to reimburse you.' I gave him the money and quickly moved on in search of something to eat. Maybe it would be a good idea to stop enquiring after Aiden.

Beside an empty restaurant was a tourist office. Inside, boards advertised travel around northern India. Apart from Delhi, I didn't recognise any of the destinations, except for one – the Jim Corbett National Park which I'd seen in the guidebook. The price and the exciting pictures of snarling tigers was enough to convince me to buy a day excursion leaving tomorrow. Next door in the restaurant I took a seat at a grimy table. There was nobody in there apart from me, the waiter and the cook. Jack's advice about empty restaurants echoed in my head, 'If there's nobody eating in these places, you've got to ask yourself why.' I was feeling ill; I was tired and I didn't have the energy to hunt for somewhere else. I settled back and placed an order of plain rice. If I kept it simple, there'd be less chance of becoming sicker than I already was.

Taking a mouthful of the rice, I swallowed, but it instantly returned the way it came. Panicked, I held my hand over my mouth as my eyes darted around for some sign of a bathroom. The waiter saw my dilemma and pointed to the back of the room. I made a dash behind a curtain, found a sink and hurled. Taking a moment to compose myself, I splashed my face with cold water, but I only wish I went straight back to my table as I stared at the shit covered latrine, which to my horror was just a metre away from the shared kitchen. Flies were everywhere, crawling all over a large bowl of rice, no doubt the same as I'd eaten. I paid the bill and left in haste for my hotel.

I fell to the bed and lay in darkness with my head swimming and my stomach churning. The pressure of my money belts wasn't helping matters. I got up, switched on the light and removed them, placing them on the bed. I had three ways of carrying money: a red nylon pocket wallet to carry everyday money (usually five hundred rupees or less); a denim money belt that contained the rest of my Indian notes, and a waterproof money belt that held my passport, emergency address details, travellers' cheques and the airport tax for my return journey to England. I counted the notes, then unzipped the waterproof money belt and removed the items. There were no travellers' cheques. I searched my luggage, the room, my pockets – nothing. I'd always had my money belts with me, apart from yesterday when I went out with Jack, where they were tucked away in my backpack. Aiden must have taken the cheques when he took the money for the storage lockers and bus tickets. What was I going to do now?

The hotel manager was watching cricket on a black and white television set as I approached the counter, 'Excuse me, is there an American Express office nearby?'

His body turned in the swivel chair and a few seconds later his head followed, his eyes reluctant to leave the screen, 'American Express, that will be doing nicely,' he giggled, mimicking the TV advert.

'Thanks for that. Is there an office nearby?' I asked again, not in the mood for humour.

'No near here, you must go Delhi. There you will find office.' His eyes returned to the screen and I thanked him, mortified by his answer. I returned to my room as he shouted obscenities at the television. The thought of returning to Delhi so soon didn't thrill me at all, but I'd think about that tomorrow. I had had enough for one day and wanted nothing more than a few hours' sleep.

9

My arms flapped frantically against the freezing water desperate to keep me afloat. A sail boat glided by, sending me deep beneath the waves. Just when my lungs couldn't take any more I surfaced, splashing the lake in sheer panic. I looked around for some sign of hope and spotted a figure in the moonlight of the water's edge. The blurry face came into focus and my spirits soared, 'Jack, is that you? Thank god. Please Jack, help me.'

'Bloody hell, mate, I can't leave you alone for five minutes, can I? Hang tight, I'll go and get some help.' He turned and disappeared into the hills.

Somebody else was walking slowly along the road. He paused and scanned the lake, 'Mr Sam, is that you? Lake is bring you luck, yes? If no boat, great swim you are having.' The hunched figure was accompanied by a dog who pawed the lake at a bobbing tennis ball. The man waved his stick, but resumed walking, fading into the darkness.

'No, wait, Mr Shah come back.' My mind was in turmoil, my heart fit to burst. Every single muscle worked overtime to keep my head from going under.

Jack reappeared clutching a red lifebuoy, 'Sam, don't worry, I've brought the best, mate.' Two figures emerged running in slow motion; Pamela Anderson dressed in a red sari and beside her, wearing a red turban and lungi, was David Hasselhoff.

I heard coughing and spitting and looked around for someone else in the water. It got louder and louder and the lake disappeared. My eyes opened and I was in my room, sprawled across the bed. The coughing continued. It was dark. I fumbled around for my watch and saw it was 6.06am. Marching over to the window, I tried to close it, but couldn't. It must have been raining last night, the handle was wet and my hands slipped. I fell back, landing in a heap on the floor. Good morning Naini Tal.

Still feeling angry over what Aiden had done, I charged towards the travel agents unable to believe what I was about to do. The shop assistant was happy to take my money for a coach ticket back to New Delhi departing that evening. 'Thanks a lot Aiden,' I mumbled as I left.

It was an hour before the bus left for Corbett. I decided to grab some breakfast at the restaurant around the corner on recommendation by the shopkeeper. A masala omelette and a couple of glasses of chai made me feel slightly human again. I spent the rest of the time admiring the scenery and trying to calm my agitated thoughts. Naini Tal was quite different from Delhi. It was spacious and clean, quiet with not too many touts or beggars. There wasn't a sense of urgency from the town folk that emanated in the big city.

It took just under two hours to reach Ramnagar; the small town that acted as a gateway to the National Park. We were driven slowly into the reserve, shards of light beaming through a canopy of sisu trees. The tour guide stood at the front of the bus and began speaking in Hindi, before translating into English, 'You are now in Jim Corbett National Park. Here you see many species of bird and deer, include barking deer, hog dear, sambar and chital. Also, see in park, langur monkey, rhesus monkey, peacock, wild boar, monitor lizard, crocodile, elephant, panther, jackal and tiger. Park built in 1936 by British man Jim Corbett who was very great hunter of many tiger. Later, Mr Corbett found he have interest in studying tiger and became photographer of endangered animal and set up this reserve. In India tiger population very low. Here, tiger protected from hunting.'

The land opened, revealing tall grasses and a herd of deer grazing in the sunshine, which turned out to be the highlight of the tour and the extent of wildlife we encountered along the two-hour ride before we broke for lunch. The canteen was heaving with people ordering food. I didn't recognise any of the dishes on offer but overheard two gentlemen in the queue beside me order dhal and rice. I politely interrupted to enquire about their food and was asked if I would like to join them at their table. One of the men engaged in conversation with me while his friend simply stared and ignored me any time I tried to talk to him. They were from the city of Lucknow, south east of Delhi and were successful cotton fabric manufacturers. When asked which country I was from, the silent man pushed his chair back and left the table. The remaining man gestured to the waiter for some chai, 'Please be excusing my friend, I am afraid he is not liking the British very much.'

'Oh, why's that?' I asked as I attempted to finish the spicy lentil dhal.

'When British rule India, they did many good thing; they build schools, bridges, roads and a wonderful railway network. These things make life easier for British, but they did many bad things to Indians. Most British treated Indian people with no respect, like dirt. Indian people were not allowed to visit certain places in their own country. Signs would be hung saying things such as, No Spitting, No Dogs and No Indians. They degraded and physically assaulted many Indian people. I am afraid my friend still holds grudge against the British. You see, his family were treated extremely badly by Britishers.'

Feeling very conspicuous as the only white face in the crowd, I apologised on behalf of my country. When the tea was served, I took the opportunity to change the subject and pointed to a painted sign upon the wall, 'The Swastika behind you, I saw one in a guest house in Delhi, is it something to do with the Nazis?'

He chuckled, 'No my friend, this dates to Indus civilisation. It is used in Indian religions such as Hinduism, Jainism and Buddhism. Translated it means higher self; being good to yourself and those you encounter. The Nazi Swastika is reversed and means much different thing: fascism, hatred and white supremacy. In fact, exactly what the British fought against in World War Two. How ironic the British Empire was guilty of the same, invading almost a quarter of the Earth's total land mass and ruling over one-fifth of the world's population. Thank god for the great Mahatma Gandhi who stood up to British oppression and defined India as the great independent nation we know today.'

I sensed he was of the same opinion as his colleague, only more open and friendlier about it. I steered the topic of conversation to the National Park and we both agreed the landscape was most enjoyable, however the lack of wildlife was disappointing. I said goodbye, bought a packet of biscuits and a bottle of water and went outside to take refuge from the baking sun under a mango tree. An elephant was tethered to the ground nearby, there for the benefit of tourists who lined up to have their picture taken one after the other.

We were taken back the way we came, seeing even less than before. Despite not sighting a tiger, I had enjoyed the day. Clouds rolled in, playing hide and seek with the sun as fine rain began to fall in Mallital. A rainbow emerged over a Ferris wheel emitting shrieks of joy from its passengers. I soaked up the cool spray, watching the raindrops pockmark the lake, before returning to the hotel.

Loud Indian music filled the room as I entered and I made another futile attempt at closing the window. I decided to leave early and returned my key at reception before descending the wide concrete steps in the dark. The only illumination came from the moon and I could see its reflection shimmering on the lake. This morning's dream flooded back and I kept a wide berth of the water as I headed towards Mallital. There I settled against a wall to stare out at the lake.

When 8.30pm arrived, I boarded the bus and took a window seat next to a Nepalese man. He introduced himself as Prakash and was travelling to Delhi to see his family after holidaying in Naini Tal. Light conversation was exchanged while waiting for the bus to depart, which was forty-five minutes behind schedule. At an appropriate opportunity, I placed my earphones in and drifted away to Mike Oldfield's Incantations. My mind wandered, as it often did. Aiden had at least been a good distraction, but now I was consumed by my own thoughts. In between interruptions of the occasional klaxon I drifted back, sometimes rocked gently to sleep by the bus as it made its way along the uneven road.

Four hours had passed when the coach stopped at a roadside café and everyone departed. Everyone except Prakash and me. Arms and legs splayed, Prakash was fast asleep in his chair blocking my exit from the vehicle. Any attempts at waking him were unsuccessful. He had positioned himself in such a way that it was an impossible hurdle to overcome. A boy I recognised as a passenger from the bus stood outside smiling at me. I asked if he would get me a Coke if I gave him the change from twenty rupees. He came back with an ice-cold bottle, which he also returned for me once empty before the driver started the engine again.

Prakash was letting out some ghastly gassy smells. I tried to avoid the pungent aroma by only breathing through my mouth, but there were times it became unbearable. How could one man produce so much of a stench? He was no fun to sleep beside either. When I dosed off, I'd be awoken with shouting, kicking and elbowing. The several times I gently moved him away only made him worse as his sleep assaults took on heightened levels of violence. I was exhausted. My limbs were stiff after being sandwiched between him and the window and the smells only added to my sickness. The morning light and returning heat gave some comfort that the journey would soon end. Small villages and white washed temples interspersed with endless fields stretched far off into the horizon.

Prakash awoke and declared what a good sleep he'd had just as the driver called, 'Dilli, Dilli, Dilli.'

10

After Naini Tal, returning to Delhi was a huge smack in the face. I had no idea whereabouts I'd been dropped off and I'd forgotten how daunting the city was. It was 6am. Litter danced the dirty street over and around the dishevelled homeless that slept on a mattress of concrete. A scrawny dog pattered past a beggar with appalling disfigurements who stumbled in search of his next source of income. Everything that society had disregarded was revealed, brutal, harsh and on full view. It humbled me, making my problems seem insignificant and left me to wonder if I should be here at all. It was a grim reminder of how far I was from home.

My thoughts were broken by the long buzzing of an approaching auto-rickshaw. The driver, in his early thirties with swept back shiny black hair and a well-trimmed moustache, leant over and beckoned me to the back seat, 'Hello my friend. Please come and take a ride in the best auto in all Delhi.'

'The best auto in all Delhi?' I replied, his energy elevating my sombre mood.

'The best in all India, my friend. I am the great Rahul, rider of rickshaw, guardian of the morning traveller.' He pointed to the sky as he waggled his head.

I let out a chuckle, not something I had done of late. I enquired to the cost to Paharganj and was given a price of one hundred rupees. I took a gamble and brought him down by half.

'Haha, you are not new to India I see. Fifty rupees, a very fair offer sir, I accept. Please take seat, I promise very safe drive.' Rahul did drive safely, keeping his eye closely on the road. After ten minutes, he pulled over to a chai stall, 'Morning chai; my treat?'

After such a tiring night, the chai was very welcome as was the uplifting conversation with Rahul. He considered himself blessed to have a good job, a loving wife and two beautiful children. 'What more could a man ask for?' he said as the skin from the chai hung loosely from his top lip.

I'd not missed the heat. My shirt clung to my back with sweat as Rahul brought the auto to a stop. At first, I was sure he had taken me to the wrong place as everywhere looked so unfamiliar. It was only seeing New Delhi Railway Station that confirmed that we were indeed in Paharganj.

Unfurnished by the crowds, buildings were more exposed, making the Main Bazaar appear completely different to how I remembered. I left Rahul and worked my way down a street that I was convinced was the route to the hotel, only it turned out to be a dead end. Twenty-five minutes went by of more dead ends before I found the correct street. Midway I caught sight of the blue banner hanging between buildings advertising the hotel next to mine. I turned right and right again. A man I didn't recognise stood behind the counter as I crossed the threshold. The balding moustached gentleman approaching fifty gave me a cold stare, grunted something and handed me a key as I paid for a night's stay. At the top of the first set of steps I stopped and looked to the door on the right. Vivid memories flashed past of the last few days, so much had changed since I last stayed here.

'Berageehayadowana,' I heard chuckling from behind.

'Hey Nitin, how are you?' My words were met with a puzzled expression. I tried again, 'Caraywahderyoodoo.' He laughed, tugging at my shirt sleeve as he pointed to the ceiling. 'The roof? Okay,' I replied.

Sitting on the rooftop with his head down and a towel around his neck was Harish, 'Mr Sam,' he said, looking up, pleased to see me. 'So soon come back. I thought maybe we not see you again.

Take chair, sit with me. How are you being, my friend?'

'I'm fine thanks, and you?' Nitin sat between us and accepted a couple of cigarettes.

'I am being okay also,' Harish replied. 'I am still looking forward to rain of monsoon. You are on your own, what of your friends?'

'The others have gone their separate ways, just me now.'

'Ah, I see. Please, I am going to have good shave. You will like, come.' A little strange I thought, why would he want me to watch him shave? Harish instructed Nitin, Anil and Rajeev to hold the fort while we were gone and told Nitin to take my luggage to my room. 'When we return, if like, Anil take any clothes to dhobi wallah,' he suggested as we went down the stairs.

'Dhobi wallah?'

'Wash clothes, laundry man, five rupees a piece.' I was a little cautious about someone taking away my belongings, but my clothes did need a good wash.

Ambling along the Main Bazaar, Harish enquired about my time away and I asked about the new hotel receptionist. 'Ashoka, ah yes, I have given him job. He can be difficult at times, very stubborn man, but he friend of father.'

'So, you run the hotel?'

'Yes, it is my hotel. I am being passed down from father who still has small hand in affairs.'

He opened a glass door and ushered me into a barber shop. There, four chairs faced four mirrors, one of which was occupied by a gentleman who was having his moustache trimmed.

'Mr Sam, please be seated, I am buying you nice shave, good relax.' I was pleasantly surprised by Harish's offer. It had been a while since I'd last shaved.

This was a whole new experience and one that was a trifle concerning. With my bristles brushed with shaving cream, a menacing cut-throat razor was unsheathed. A new blade was set and the barber glided the razor along a leather strop, preparing it for my worried face. He pulled my skin taunt, my eyes widened and he shaved a clean stripe, washing the stubbly foam beneath a running tap. The process was repeated and completed without a single drop of blood spilt. My face and neck were cleaned of excess foam and then slapped with moisturiser and massaged thoroughly. My skin felt invigorated. But wait, there was more? The barber's fingers gently ran through my hair, 'Head massage?' he asked.

'Why not?' I replied and relaxed into the chair.

His fingers became heavy, pushing hard along my head, feeling as if I was being scalped rather than massaged. Then the kneading began, digging knuckles into my skull, excruciating jabs of pain driving through my head. I opened one eye to see Harish in the mirror lying back blissfully in his chair, receiving the same torture, but seeming to enjoy it. When the barber was one hundred percent sure my head was bruised enough, I clambered from the chair and thanked him. Harish paid the bill and opened the door for me, 'You see Mr Sam, very good relax. I am always enjoying good shave and massage.'

Laughing as we entered the hotel, Ashoka threw us a stern look and mumbled something in Hindi under his breath which straightened Harish's face in an instant. He turned to me and smiled, 'Mr Sam, please be excusing me, I am having to talk with Ashoka.' I made my way up the stairs as a heated exchange of words echoed behind me.

I was startled by a knock at the door, 'Hello, I am now taking clothes to dhobi.' Anil stood with outstretched arms in wait for my laundry. I gathered my items, passed them to him and he left. After a quick shower, I decided it was time to get some rest and I eased into a relaxing slumber.

A loud series of knocks yanked me from a deep sleep, 'Mr Sam, I am bringing you your things,' a muffled voice said. I opened the door to find Harish standing with a neat stack of my clothes. I was impressed at how clean, dry and pressed everything was, and how little time it had taken. 'Mr Sam, I am wishing for you to meet very good guest. Mr Sean is long time visitor to hotel, very good man. He too, is also coming from UK.'

Harish's smile was infectious and I couldn't help but raise a wide grin in return, 'Okay, give me two minutes and I'll be right with you.'

I met him outside of the room and we went downstairs to another room right of the reception area. Harish knocked the door and a westerner in his mid-thirties with cropped brown hair answered.

'Mr Sean, please, this is Mr Sam I tell you about,' Harish said, rather proud of himself.

'Hi Sam, come in and have a seat,' the man laughed. 'Thanks Harish, look after yourself, mate.'

Harish closed the door and Sean sat opposite me on the edge of the bed. 'Sorry about that. Harish does that from time to time. Whenever another person from England stays here, he automatically assumes we must be related and leaves the poor buggers at my door. Anyway, I'm Sean. How're you doing?' I reached out to shake his hand. 'So, what brings you to India?'

I filled him in on recent events including Aiden's obstreperous behaviour. I also shared my plans of buying a ticket tomorrow for either Manali or Agra.

'That mate of yours sounds like a right one. You're better off without him if you ask me.' He quarter filled a glass from a bottle of whiskey and motioned towards an empty glass on the table beside me, 'Have one yourself, mate. I always bring a bottle of Bells with me, not keen on the Indian stuff, bit set in my ways like that.'

I paused for a moment, looking at the bottle, the bottle staring back at me and politely declined, 'No, you're alright, thanks anyway.'

'That's odd not seeing any wildlife in Corbett, what entrance did you take?'

'Ramnagar,' I replied.

'Well, there's your problem. I thought it was strange you saw next to nothing. You won't see much via Ramnagar, full of tourist buses. No, you need to enter the Dhikala end. You can stay in the dormitories for three nights for about fifteen rupees a night. I'm sure there's a small entrance fee too, but nothing too expensive. It's lovely out there. You'll get the chance to go on safari and see all sorts. I promise you won't be disappointed. I've not travelled the road, but I'm pretty sure you can easily get to Manali from Corbett.

If not, go to Rishikesh and then grab a bus to Manali from there. Easy.'

He scribbled away some town names in the back of my journal. It was something to bear in mind if I couldn't get tickets to my other chosen destinations. He suggested we go out and eat, 'I know a lovely little pizza place in the Main Bazaar if you're up for it.' I could handle pizza, I thought.

We passed Ashoka who gave us a frown and turned his back to us. 'Right miserable git, that one,' Sean said as we entered the Main Bazaar. 'Harish employed him as the hotel manager. From what I can make out, Ashoka wants to discourage foreigners from staying. Harish wants the opposite and I think they're struggling to reach an agreement. Hey, I have to pick something up from this place. Could you give me a hand?'

Sean walked into an open fronted shop, shelves stacked with colourful folded material. He spoke to the owner and came out struggling with two holdalls full of patterned bed sheets. He handed one to me, 'Thanks mate, dinner's on me. I ordered these sheets earlier; they'll make a tidy profit back home.'

We clutched the bags with both hands and heaved them up some steps to an open-air restaurant. The muggy evening heat was occasionally lifted by a slight breeze as we ate good cheese and tomato pizzas whilst enjoying the night lights over Paharganj. Sean informed me I would need to report the theft of the travellers' cheques to the police first, get a docket issued and take it to the American Express office in Connaught Place. He returned to the topic of Corbett and the more he talked, the more attractive it began to sound. I was sold on the idea by the time we left the restaurant and bought a ticket back to Naini Tal for tomorrow.

As we neared the hotel, a barefoot elderly Indian man dressed in an orange robe approached us. His forehead was painted with white stripes and his hair was long and matted. In his hand was a tin cup. Sean dropped in a few coins. The man put his hands together in a prayer motion and walked on. I'd seen men dressed like this before around Delhi and at times found them quite fascinating, though a little intimidating. The strange hair, painted faces and gold trident they carried always grabbed my attention. I found out more from Sean, 'Sadhus are wandering Hindu monks who follow a strict spiritual path to enlightenment. They usually reside in caves, forests and temples and rely on alms to live. Sadhu basically means good one or holy man and most Hindus believe that sadhus positively affect their karma.' Sean picked up his bag and we walked the alleyway to the hotel.

'So, what exactly does karma mean?' I asked.

He laughed, 'You ask a lot of questions. Karma is a cycle of cause and effect. For instance, what you did yesterday will affect what you do today, what you do today will affect what happens to you tomorrow; and so it goes on. Basically, if you're bad today, it will come around and bite you on the ass at some point in the future. There is no escaping karma. Whatever is thrown at you in life, always handle it with dignity and honesty, and be good to your fellow man. I'm inclined to go along with it all myself. I feel like I've gained a lot from adopting it into my life.'

I left Sean at his door and thanked him for a nice evening. He was flying home in the early hours and I wished him a safe journey.

I wasn't sure how to get to Paharganj Police Station, so I hailed a cycle rickshaw. From the bright morning sun, I stepped into a large dimly lit room. In the right-hand corner behind a desk was a man in a khaki uniform and beret. I asked him if I could report a theft. He didn't look up but continued writing without answering me. I asked again and was ignored again. I sat down next to the desk and he stopped what he was doing to look up at me. I stood, asked again, but he returned to his writing.

Maybe I wasn't being polite enough, 'Namaste,' I said. 'Please can you help me?'

'No English,' he snapped, his eyes not leaving his writing pad. This was going to make things difficult.

As I returned to my seat to ponder for a moment, a lady walked in and spoke to the officer in Hindi, I presumed. When she concluded her affairs, I asked if she would be so kind as to translate for me. They conversed for a couple of minutes and the policeman looked at me and then disappeared into a room behind the desk. The lady told me she'd relayed the information.

I sat for a further hour getting nowhere fast. People came and went and I tried to report the theft to two other officers, but they told me I had to talk to the original officer I had attempted to report it to earlier, but he'd left the station half an hour ago. Nobody seemed the slightest bit bothered that I was sitting here twiddling my thumbs. The room became increasingly hot as the sun heated the building. The original officer later returned and I tried once again to speak to him, but to no avail. A colleague joined him and they talked in between looking at me and laughing, before they walked off down a corridor. If it wasn't for my desperate situation, I would have left hours ago. Without my travellers' cheques, my time in India would be shortened considerably.

The unhelpful policeman came back and sat at his desk and Jack's words came into my head. 'Baksheesh!' I blurted out. Had I really just attempted to bribe a police officer? Surely, I hadn't been that stupid. Apparently, I had. He stopped what he was doing and threw me a stare that locked me up in an Indian prison for the rest of my life.

'Are you trying to bribe me?' All this time he could speak perfectly good English?

'Um, well, um, uh, no,' my voice trembled. 'I was just offering a gesture of goodwill for your time.'

He picked up a tough bamboo lathi and pointed it at me, 'I am a good officer. I do not take bribes. Come with me at once.' I followed him into a small room with a desk and chair either side. He instructed me to sit and left the room with my fate in his hands. Twenty minutes later, with paperwork under his arm, he returned and sat opposite me.

'What are you wanting?' To be returned to my country safely. To not be attacked by a psychopath in the middle of the night in a dingy cell. I froze and said nothing. 'Why are you here?' he asked the pale shaking foreigner.

'To report a theft,' I answered and quickly added, 'Please accept my apologies if I caused any offence. I sometimes get Hindi words mixed up.' I was riddled with fear and he could see it.

'You should have reported theft as soon as you arrived.' I did! 'When is this theft taking place?' Relieved he'd overlooked the baksheesh mishap, I explained the missing cheques and stated that I simply wished to receive a document to take to the American Express office. 'As cheques were missing in Naini Tal, you need to go there and report to police, it is not possible here.' My spirits declined ever further. Go all the way to Naini Tal and back to Delhi again?

'They were taken in Delhi,' I exclaimed. 'I discovered them missing in Naini Tal. Please sir, is there nothing you can do?' What could I do to escape this city?

He slid a form across the table and looked me in the eye, 'Write answers on paper. You understand this is very time consuming?' I held his stare and confirmed the hidden meaning by a nod of the head.

The officer passed a pen and I filled out my details on the theft report. He stamped a small rectangular document, ripped it from the book and handed it to me. I was just about to take it when he pulled it back and with the other hand, rubbed his fingers and thumb together.

''How much?' I asked, not really wishing to know the answer.

'One thousand rupees.' He frowned as I showed my wallet with only five hundred rupees in. 'Give money now, bring the rest tomorrow.' He leant forward as I handed him the cash, 'If you do not come, I will find you.' I got up and he pointed to the door, 'Cello.' My look of concern turned to puzzlement. Cello? He raised his voice and waved his hand at the door, 'Cello. Go, go!'

'Oh right, of course,' I said, as he followed behind me.

He ushered me to the main entrance and as I was about to leave, he placed a firm hand on my shoulder and whispered in my ear, 'Tomorrow.' With that, he slapped my back and lifted his voice in a jolly manner, 'Thank you for using our services. Have a good day, sir.'

I was glad to be out of there and feel the scorching Delhi sunshine on my skin, hear all the noises and view the chaotic traffic on the road where I stood. Not so glad however to see the mangled taxi parked outside the police station with a blood stained steering wheel crumpled into the seat where a driver once sat. I rode an auto to Connaught Place where I found the appropriate office within the Amex building. It took another hour to receive my new cheques leaving me no time to go in search of a guidebook. I still had to get something to eat, pack and get to the coach pick up point. I said my goodbyes to Harish and his team and returned to Connaught Place for 7.30pm.

Once seated on the bus, the conductor came along and requested an extra fifty rupees luggage fee. He told me he could not guarantee the safety of my bag and guitar if I didn't pay. Fifty rupees lighter, I sat back in my seat and awaited departure. An hour later and the coach still hadn't moved. The conductor came to my seat again and this time demanded one hundred rupees for air-conditioning. I explained I didn't need air-conditioning, but he told me it was compulsory. I noticed I was the only westerner on board, and the only one who had to pay these ridiculous charges. Hoping it would be an end to being fleeced, I gave in and paid. The air-con didn't work and the driving was hair-raising. The exact same stench that Prakash produced on the road down to Delhi returned. I asked the lady beside me if she could smell the same. She said it was the smell of raw sewage from outside. So, it wasn't Prakash after all.

After another gruelling journey, the swirling roads of Naini Tal came into view and the porters began their morning chase. I flexed my biceps upon leaving the vehicle, telling them with a smile I could manage by myself. At the summit of the hill, I was surprised to see a familiar face.

'Hello stranger,' I said as he viewed the lake.

He smiled a warm toothless grin, 'Namaste Mr Sam. I am enjoying very much beauty of Naini Tal. Come, we go for chai.'

We commenced the slow pace to the café and Mr Shah picked the same table where Aiden and I sat when we first arrived. He took the same seat as Aiden opposite me.

He drank his tea, 'Mr Sam, how are you liking Naini Tal? Lake is bring you luck, yes?'

I thought of the weird dream in which I was drowning, 'Yes, it's been lovely here Mr Shah, the boat ride was wonderful.'

'If no boat, great swim you are having.' He looked at me with a knowing smile. 'Mr Sam, you are learning much from India, not everything what it seem, eh?' He chuckled, slowly stood and grabbed his walking stick hanging from the table. Stepping to the roadside, he turned before leaving, 'Go your own way Mr Sam, see how far you get.' Speechless and numbed by his words, I drank my chai, paid the bill and walked with my head in a daze to Mallital. On Sean's advice, I'd decided to revisit the Corbett National Park, properly this time. I stole one last look at the tear drop lake, knowing this is where my journey alone would truly begin.

11

Wherever I turned everything looked the same, nothing to distinguish my route only daunting stares tracking my every move as I tried to navigate my way to the bus station. I'd been dropped in the middle of Ramnagar where the communication barrier was shut tight. The accumulating crowd offered no assistance only hand-covered giggles at my misfortunes. I wondered if I was the first white face they had seen, so interested were they in my journey around their town. Perhaps they couldn't fathom why I was wandering around in circles in the blistering midday sun. If only one of them could have understood the two words 'bus' and 'Dhikala' to point me in the right direction. 'Come on Sam, it's a small town, you can you find your way out of this,' I said to myself. I wished that were true, but I was utterly useless.

Met with yet another dead end, the shadow of people behind me stopped. A goat walked to where I stood, urinated in front of me and trotted off. From somewhere nearby I heard the familiar blast of a musical horn and I was filled with hope. I parted the group of locals and began to jog along the streets until I came to a main road. Looking right I saw a beaten up old bus and breathed a sigh of relief. I picked up pace, running as fast as I could and came alongside the vehicle. My fingers grasped the doorway and I pulled myself in, gasping air and dripping sweat onto the floor.

'Dhikala?' I panted on the verge of collapse.

'Naini Tal,' the driver replied with a frown.

I turned to alight the bus but misjudged the steps. While the bus picked up pace, instead of making a quick exit back on to the street, I twisted my ankle and fell to the ground.

'Ooh, that looks nasty. Are you all right?' A figure stood in front of me eclipsing the bright sunlight. She crouched down and I could just make out her face, sweet and kind. Smiling, she took a sip from the bottle of Fanta held loosely in her hand. 'Shall we get that cut sorted out before it gets infected?' I looked down at my knee and saw the result of my fall. With her help, I got to my feet and hobbled around the corner of a building where she sat me in the shade next to a man in his late teens with short brown hair, stubble and spectacles.

'David, be a dear and retrieve some iodine and antibacterial ointment from my pack, oh and a small bandage.'

'Yes of course.' He fished the items from the rucksack by his feet.

'Oh, silly me, we will need some water too. Would you like to finish my drink? I've only just started it.' She held the bottle of Fanta towards me, 'Hold on, let me get you a new straw.'

Reaching over to her rucksack she removed a bottle of water and a packet of straws. I took the drink and as I put the straw to my mouth I realised how thirsty I was. In no time at all I was slurping the last drops.

David returned with a towel, laid it on the floor and placed the items down.

'Now, let's get this cleaned up then. This is going to sting a little,' she said. Squeezing her hands into a pair of disposable medical gloves, she pulled up the left leg of my knee length shorts, washed away the excess grit and blood and dried my leg with an antiseptic wipe. She then applied the iodine and I yelped pathetically. 'Oh honestly, you men are so dramatic. David is exactly the same.'

'Ah, but what would you do without us hunters and gatherers?' David replied.

She chuckled, 'How long have you got?'

'Thanks so much, that was really kind of you,' I said as a bandage was set. 'I'm Sam, by the way.'

'It's nice to meet you, Sam. I'm Imogen and David is my brother. We're twins.'

'So how come you guys are in Ramnagar? I mean it's a bit out of the way, isn't it?'

David looked over from repacking his things, 'We're on our way to the Dhikala dormitories in Corbett National Park.'

'I was hoping to do the same, but after I arrived from Naini Tal I went looking for the place to pick up the Dhikala bus and got hopelessly lost.'

'Well, lucky Imogen found you. You're in the right place now and the bus should be along any minute.'

David fastened his backpack and Imogen came around the corner from returning her bottle. She pulled her pack onto her shoulders as a bus came into view, 'There's our bus now. Do you need a hand getting on?'

'No, I should be fine, thanks.'

I followed the pair to the bus and sat in front of them with my holdall on my lap and guitar between my legs.

Imogen took her long auburn hair from a pony tail and let it fall to her slim shoulders, 'How wonderful you're coming with us, Sam. Today you must rest though and then tomorrow we can go and find some tigers together. We came last year and had a lovely time. Dhikala is only about fifty kilometres from here, so it shouldn't take long.'

From our conversations, I discovered they were both studying at Bath University in England and were coming to the end of their two week visit to India. As we spoke, a young Indian boy poked his head between the twins from the seat behind. 'My name is Dinesh. What are your names and countries please?' David pointed to himself, Imogen and I and answered the boy's questions. 'It is very nice to be meeting with you. I am speaking very good English, yes?' he asked with a wide grin.

'Yes,' Imogen replied, 'Very good indeed, Dinesh. Where did you learn such fine English?'

'I am learning from school and also, I am learning from my father. I am hoping to one day be a doctor. Are you going to Jim

Corbett Park also?'

'Yes, we are. We're very much looking forward to it. How old are you Dinesh?' Imogen took a packet of boiled sweets from the pocket of her rucksack and handed one to us all.

Dinesh tackled the candy with his tongue, 'I am eleven years of age, but soon I am being twelve. My father is owner of two textile companies. I have come to park with just my mother and brother at this time. I am looking for very big tiger.'

The bus drew up at a small building and we alighted, taking our things inside. I paid the entrance fee and to stay for three nights, which came to only 275 rupees. Another bus soon pulled up and took us on a short journey into the park itself, leaving us with a magnificent view of flat grasslands leading to a stunning backdrop of the lesser Himalayas. Only bird song could be heard, no traffic or crowds. Never had I seen such a large area of open space. Imogen broke my trance as she stood beside me, 'Simply amazing, isn't it?'

'Truly. It's all so beautiful. I'm expecting to wake at any moment.'

'Yes, you're right, a beautiful dream, one that I have dreamt for a year. Now I'm here again, living the reality in all its glory. Shall we go to the dormitories?'

We met David at the doorway. Inside the small shaded room were four, three-tiered simple bunk beds without linen. We laid claim to our unit: me on top, David in the middle and Imogen on the bottom.

'Are you hungry Sam?' David asked. 'The cafeteria here isn't too bad at all.'

A pathway led from the dormitories to the restaurant. On route, we met Dinesh and his family. 'We are staying in log cabins. Tomorrow morning, I am taking elephant ride with my brother Deepak. We will be looking for many tiger.' We smiled at Dinesh's enthusiasm as we entered the cafeteria.

The clattering of dishes and cutlery shattered the silence of the world outside. The twins and I found three empty seats at a table and chose dahi aloo, a Punjabi dish of potatoes simmered in curd sauce, complemented with hot naan bread. David and Imogen had pre-booked a jeep into the jungle the following morning and asked if I would like to share. I confirmed my place immediately.

'If it's okay with you two, I'm going to read in the dorm.' David veered right towards the dormitories, leaving Imogen and I looking out to the warm apricot of early sunset.

'Shall we sit down, Sam?' Relaxing at a wooden slatted table we breathed in the pure evening air. Above us, sitting on the branch of an old withered tree, a black faced langur monkey pruned its silver fur. Ahead, the sky reddened, lending the horizon of peaks a deep russet tone and the land a sandy beige.

I climbed down from the top bunk and fumbled around in the dark to get dressed. A blast of cold water in the insect infested showers woke me fully before I met the others. We positioned ourselves in the Jeep and entered a dense sal forest with the morning sun rising over the hills behind us. The driver took it easy as an occasional deer ambled across the road. The air was filled with the sound of wildlife greeting the morning; birds, monkeys and barking deer, all making their presence known. It was as if we'd ventured into another world, observers of a wild kingdom where humans had no place. Slowing down, we were asked by the driver for our silence as he pointed to a large clearing on our left. Ten or so metres away, a herd of wild elephant and their young passed, trumpeting and breaking fallen branches as they stomped by.

David carried a list of birds and delightfully ticked off peacocks, woodpeckers, kingfishers, parakeets and eagles as he sighted each one. Briefly stopping at the edge of a cliff, our guide revealed two motionless fish-eating gharial crocodiles on the banks of the Ramnagar River below. One had its long, thin jaws wide open, while the other balanced a white bird on its back. Imogen, who was seated to my right, leant over and placed her hand on my leg, 'Sam, can you see them? Here, use our binoculars to take a closer look.' They made even more of a spectacular sight magnified.

Without any signs of a tiger, we were returned to the dorms and I spent the rest of the morning relaxing with the twins and updating my journal. As the midday sun worked its way around the mountains into early afternoon I decided to stretch my legs. Five minutes into my stroll I heard Dinesh call out, 'Mr Sam, this is my brother Deepak, may we be joining you?' Deepak looked maybe two years younger than Dinesh and slightly slimmer.

'Of course,' I replied.

A short way along a dirt track we discovered a watch tower and observed five elephants bathing in the shallow water of the river and being cleaned by their respective keepers. We climbed down the ladder to investigate and as we approached, I asked one of the mahouts if we would be allowed to join them. He was more than happy and invited us in.

'Dinesh, you go ahead with Deepak, I'll be back in a few minutes.' I ran the way I came, back to the table where David was slouched snoring and Imogen was reading a book. 'You guys, come quick, I promise you won't be disappointed.' Curious of the excitement in my voice, they jogged beside me to the river.

'Oh, my word, how splendid,' Imogen said as she saw Dinesh and Deepak splashing each other. 'Thank you so much for coming to get us, Sam.' She kissed me gently on the cheek, making me blush, and ran off to the river bank, throwing her socks and sandals to one side.

I waded in knee deep to join them and was handed a flat rough stone the size of my palm to scrub an elephant with. The mahout showed me the correct way to rub, instructing me to be firm on the elephant's tough grey skin to avoid the danger of tickling him. As I scrubbed, I noticed patches of depigmentation on the elephant's ears and bristles of hair on his back, chin and about the wrinkles of his beautiful wise eyes. I was warned not to stand too close to his feet and to keep clear of his whipping tail.

An hour later and the elephants stood slowly, leaving their bath one by one. The last blew an impressive jet of water from its trunk before climbing the muddy bank. I took a final photograph of the mahouts and their grand elephants standing in a line with the river and mountains behind.

'That was incredible, Sam, thanks,' David said, as the five of us made our way towards the dormitories. 'A wonderful tale to tell our grandchildren.'

'You've got to find someone who'll put up with you first, so you could be in for a long wait,' Imogen teased, nudging him in the arm.

After changing out of our wet clothes we set out again, this time for a ride on the back of an elephant in search of an elusive tiger. It was the same elephant I washed earlier. We climbed aboard the wooden howdah, which had a red cushion in the centre and a foot platform either side. As the elephant strode forward we heard a shout from behind, 'Please be waiting for me, I am still wanting to find tiger.' Dinesh's little legs ran as fast as they could to catch up with us. He was lifted onto the howdah the same way we were; holding the creature's ears and raised by the trunk. He climbed into the arms of the mahout and was seated next to David.

We moved off through the long grass avoiding tall termite mounds as birds of varying colours flew in the early evening sky. Steadily we rocked from side to side looking out to the rich grasslands. An hour passed, the sun began its descent and we turned to go back without the slightest glimpse of striped fur. It was hard not to be disappointed, but as we came to terms with not seeing a tiger the elephant was brought to a halt and the mahout whispered, 'Tiger.' Our stomachs filled with butterflies as our eyes scanned the grass. 'There!' the mahout pointed.

We followed his finger to the most majestic of tigers; a beautiful female, lying still and keeping a cautious eye on us. We were told to keep as quiet as possible which was difficult for Dinesh who struggled to contain his delight. Excited myself, I leant out to take a photograph and my foot slipped from the platform, sending me lurching forward. The tiger jumped to her feet, snarling and showing her sharp teeth. Imogen grabbed the top of my shirt just in time and wrenched me back to the cushion.

'Phew, you gave me a real fright there. Now that's two you owe me,' she said.

Still shaking, I put the camera away, hiding my embarrassment under the cloak of the darkening sky.

After a hearty meal, David, Imogen and I stood talking whilst admiring a gecko on a rock. We were joined by a smartly dressed

Indian man, 'Pardon me, but I couldn't help but notice your guitar when you arrived yesterday, do you play?'

'Yes, why do you ask?' I replied.

'I also play and have brought my guitar with me. Would you like a jam sir?' The gecko made a quick escape.

'Sure. Why not?'

Retrieving our instruments, we improvised to an accompaniment of birdsong and an audience of friends until the evening ended.

While the others slept, I slipped outside for a cigarette. On the pathway, illuminated by the moth filled light above me, a hairy black warthog stopped in its tracks, glowing eyes fixed upon the night intruder with suspicion. I looked back with respect and apprehension of its unpredictable nature as well as being conscious of where the door was should I need to make a quick escape. An owl hooted breaking the silence and the hog walked on, grunting, probably laughing at my inferiority.

The twins and I agreed to take another elephant ride at six in the morning but when we arrived there was only one space left. With my support, David convinced Imogen to go, agreeing to meet her when she returned. The restaurant was empty apart from the cook who served our fried eggs and toast. My stomach was still on the delicate side and the now familiar pains were returning, though I managed what I could.

'What are your plans after Corbett?' David asked as he tucked in.

'Manali with any luck. I was told I might be able to get a bus from Dhikala.'

David peered over his glasses at me, 'I'm pretty sure there's not a bus direct to Manali from here. Dhikala is within the park itself – only one way in, one way out. You'll need to go back to Ramnagar.'

Returning to Ramnagar didn't sound so bad, 'Do you know if it's a direct route?'

'Manali is quite a way, it could take you three to four days with a lot of bus rides and overnight stays. It's that or back to Delhi and direct to Manali that way. We could've helped you out from Ramnagar, but we leave this afternoon.' He stopped eating, 'Are you okay? You look a bit pale.'

I was stunned into silence and sat back as I digested his words. Spending the best part of a week on buses was bad enough, but all the way back to Delhi was worse. Imogen came in a short while later and sat beside me. I asked her how her trip went, 'We saw an amusing group of monkeys and some deer, but no tigers. You look like you've seen a ghost, Sam. What's wrong?'

David answered on my behalf, 'I think I may have delivered some bad news about Sam's onward travel plans.'

'Oh, that's so typical of you, David. Can you not think before you speak? What did you tell him?' David didn't answer but looked down at the breadcrumbs on his plate. 'David, what did you say?'

I was quick to let him off the hook, 'It's fine, honestly. I've planned my journey a little wrong that's all. He was being rather helpful actually.'

'Oh, well that's something I guess. Did you know he once told our grandmother he didn't like her new hat and went into great detail as to why? She didn't leave the house for a week after that.'

David lifted his head to meet Imogen's eyes, 'Oh please, not that again. You always do this. Every time there are other people around you take great pleasure in telling stupid stories about how I did this and how I did that.'

'Guys, guys,' I interrupted. 'You're leaving soon, let's not bicker, eh?'

'Yes, you're right,' Imogen smiled and placed her hand on my arm. When she thought I wasn't looking she poked her tongue out at David who did the same back.

While the twins awaited their ride from the park, Imogen handed me three 35mm camera films, 'Take these, we're not going to need them now. You make the most of them and show us the pictures of your trip one day.' She leant forward and kissed me softly on the lips, 'Take care Sam, I'll never forget you.'

I gave David a manly handshake and wished them a safe trip. They left, waving from the bus until it was swallowed into the darkness of the forest. With my head down I walked away, kicking the dirt, not really knowing what to do next. They were such nice people and I'd enjoyed their company. Under different circumstances I thought maybe Imogen and I could have been more than friends. But for now, I was back on my own.

Wandering the riverside, I saw an elephant in the distance, howdah full, riding into the jungle and I smiled at my misadventure with the tiger. I climbed the watchtower and soaked up the endless view of the bare mountains in the early afternoon sun. A rhesus monkey sitting beneath a tree eating fruit from its tiny hands looked around and then up at me. Tilting to the right it raised its left arm in an arc and scratched its short red fur. It then straightened up and threw the fruit stone to one side.

'Mr Sam, is that you?' The monkey let out a high-pitched screech and scuttled away on all fours, rustling fallen leaves as it entered the cover of the jungle. 'Mr Sam, it is Dinesh and Deepak. The elephants are back.'

Sure enough, plodding into the water were the five elephants we washed yesterday. 'Come,' a mahout shouted and waved us in.

We splashed water on the elephants and began scrubbing. I reached down, took a handful of water and soaked Dinesh. His face lit up with a fit of giggles, 'You will be getting it now Mr Sam,' and he splashed me back.

Deepak shouted with glee, 'Now I am getting you wet,' and threw water at Dinesh.

'Stop what you are doing right now,' a voice boomed from behind us. We froze before slowly turning around. Towering above us on a hillside by the riverbank was a man dressed in a peaked cap and a khaki uniform. 'You are to be leaving river at once and reporting with me to park keeper's station immediately.'

It was reminiscent of being summoned to the headmaster's office, an all-too-familiar occurrence. Dinesh and Deepak were sent to their mother. I was marched into a room adjacent to the canteen.

'Sir, you cannot go into Ramnagar River,' said the park keeper. 'Elephants are very hazardous to health and river is frequented by crocodiles. You and your friends cannot play water games in there.

There is a sign close by that clearly states, Ramnagar River is inhabited by crocodiles. Swimming is prohibited. Survivors will be prosecuted.'

'I'm sorry. Thanks for telling me, I had no idea.' I was glad he hadn't caught us washing the elephants.

'I will not be prosecuting on this occasion, but I will be fining you one hundred rupees.'

In the canteen, I sat at a busy table alone, not wishing to interact with anyone. Outside, one or two nightjars could be heard singing from afar and insects gathered wherever they could find light. I sat at a wooden table beneath an old tree and looked up at the empty branches. Ahead, the sky was dark blue with the black mountains beneath. Beside me was an empty chair and my heart wished my departed friends were still there.

After a breakfast of Bourbon biscuits, I went in search of the mahouts. I found them talking by their herd and gave them one hundred and fifty rupees to split between them, thanking them for the great time we had. I didn't want to visit the next place. My shoulders dropped and I let out a sigh as I entered the park keeper's office. Nobody could stay longer than three nights in Dhikala and my time was up. The same gentleman from last night was there, 'Good morning sir,' he smiled. 'How can I be helping you?'

'I would like to pay my exit fee please.' I handed over seventy-five rupees.

'Ah, many face I have seen like yours at this point. Jim Corbett Park is very enchanting, no?'

'It is that.'

We chatted for a few minutes as I told him of the things I did during my stay, leaving out an elephant bath or two. 'Why not join me for chai with my colleagues,' he said, rising from his chair. We walked to a building opposite and inside there were nine men dressed in similar uniforms sitting at a long table, laughing and talking over cups of tea. The keeper introduced me, 'Hello my friends, this is, er, your name sir?' I whispered my name, 'Thank you, this is Mr Sam.'

There was light laughter amongst the men and one of them said aloud, 'Yes, the great crocodile splasher.' The laughter increased.

'My friend, please, pay no attention to them. They are hearing small story and making big joke about silly foreigner, I mean you, I mean somebody that looks nothing like you, sir.' I chuckled and patted him on the shoulder in reassurance.

12

The mountains drifted out of view and the road opened to reveal small shacks on the roadside and growing numbers of people. We had arrived back in Ramnagar. Dinesh and Deepak were first to leave the vehicle with their mother who threw me a scornful stare. The boys ran ahead of her and banged on the side of the bus, 'Mr Sam,' Dinesh shouted, jumping up and down at the window, 'Thank you so much, Mr Sam. We have wonderful time. I saw very big tiger and wash very big elepha…' He turned to see his mother heading in his direction. He widened his grin and waved at me before replacing the happy face with a look of shame as his guardian shooed him away. Throwing a smile over his shoulder one last time, he winked and turned his head back to face the ground. I continued to look out the window until the family had melted into the crowd and then I moved into the aisle so I too could leave the bus.

The midday sun held no mercy and beat hard upon my head and neck. I went in search of the shaded area where I first met David and Imogen. In the back of my journal were the city names Sean had written: Rishikesh and Dehra Dun. I repacked the book and looked around, Rishikesh it was then. 'Be brave and confident,' I muttered and hurled myself into the chaotic arms of Ramnagar once again.

The first corner I turned I saw a parked bus, the front

concertinaed a quarter of the way in, diminishing the little confidence I'd raised. Further along a shabby tourist office offered a glimmer of hope and I struggled through the doorway with my holdall and guitar. The jovial salesman informed me that there were no buses from Ramnagar to Rishikesh and suggested instead that I take one to Naini Tal or Corbett National Park. He was on the verge of spilling out a convincing sales pitch, but I saved him the trouble. Outside in the heat again I felt defeated. A man passed by, stopped and walked back to me, 'You are looking lost, Sir. Are you needing help?'

'Thanks, I'm trying to get to Rishikesh, but apparently, it's not possible from Ramnagar.'

'My friend, you must not believe everything you are told. Some people will tell you certain things to suit their own agenda. Please, follow this road on right side and after few minutes you will find local bus parking. There you can get bus to town of Kashipur, maybe fifty kilometres away, then to Rishikesh.'

I thanked him and sure enough, after walking two hundred yards or so, on the opposite side of a busy road was a bus station of sorts. Getting across to it was not going to be easy. Timing would be critical. A bus hurtled towards me from the right and then a truck from the left. A car from the left and then another, and then one from the right. A lorry approached from the left and was overtaken by a car. It whizzed past dictating to anything in its path to get out of the way for it had no intention of slowing down. 'Beep, beep. Beep, beep," was all I could hear above the engines. I spotted a gap and took my chance. I didn't pause to think, I just ran as quickly as I could and despite one near miss I made it to safety.

At the end of a lane of dust covered buses a group of people were gathered. I asked them for directions for the bus to Kashipur but was met with vacant stares and misdirection. 'Kashipur, Kashipur, Kashipur,' someone shouted and a bus moved away. The conductor leant from the doorway yelling the town name over and over. I ran and climbed aboard as it pulled out on to the road. Squeezed between a young boy and an elderly man, I stood holding a handrail for two hours as the bus filled up more with each stop. I held great respect for those who manoeuvred around me and my baggage; effortlessly finding an available nook or cranny that I was sure didn't exist.

Kashipur was like Ramnagar but on a larger scale. The bus left me by the roadside and once again I had to find transport to my next destination. I wondered why the drop-off points were not at the bus stations in these towns, it would have made things so much easier. Searching for another bus was not my idea of fun and as I walked along with no clue as to whether I was even heading in the right direction, traffic skimmed dangerously close. I was beginning to feel sick again. Feverish chills clawed at my muscles and every sight, sound and smell threatened the act of vomiting.

Asking for directions was pointless. It was the familiar story of blank faces or quizzical looks. If there was a point to this whole trip it was lost to me. I couldn't expect a David or Imogen to be around every corner and without them everything felt like an endless struggle. Cows, dogs and hairy black pigs roamed freely around me. Corrugated iron shacks and plastic sheeted homes held together with bamboo poles fringed the roadside. I looked left and right in hope of spotting something that resembled a bus station but saw nothing. A crippled man pulled himself along on a makeshift skateboard using his one useful arm, the other missing at the shoulder. 'Baba, baba, baksheesh baba,' he cried. His disfigurements made me look away in shock as I gave him a few coins. He rolled off and I stared down at my fully working legs with a new-found appreciation.

There were no smiling faces, no jolly rickshaw wallahs and no gleeful children running up and asking which country I was from, just the glum faces of people in a rush to get to their destinations. If only I could get to mine. A long strange looking auto-rickshaw with eight seats drew up beside me. The driver said he was willing to take me to the bus station, but I would have to cover the cost of four passengers. I couldn't take the risk of him taking me all over town hiking up the fare even further, so I walked on. Of the few businesses I did see, they appeared only to cater for local needs – open fronted motor repair shops with tyres stacked outside;

stonemasons – workers chipping and chiselling away at marble and sandstone slabs; sculptors – rows of white gods awaiting decoration. Kashipur was certainly not built for tourism.

Passing a line of these shops, my path ahead was blocked by several stacks of rubbish piled high against a wall. The overwhelming stench engulfed me immediately. I looked to the road to see if I could cross but the level of traffic made Ramnagar look like a sleepy village on a Sunday afternoon. My only option was to zig-zag my way around the rubbish, briefly stepping into the road and darting back in as quickly as possible. When the opportunity came, I made my first move. Once I was amongst the garbage I was consumed by the smell and could hardly breathe. I shut my eyes and began to feel strangely comforted as memories swirled. That familiar stench: putrid and sweet, warm with the heat of summer. Nobody was around and the treasures others rejected were mine for the taking. My fingers trawled through the egg shells, soiled nappies, cold sauces and carcasses; searching for a discarded gem. Bingo! Smooth plastic. An Action Man minus one arm. A real toy; not another broken key ring or old air freshener for my secret home-made space station, but a real toy, from a toy shop. I could hide it somewhere so he wouldn't find it.

Flies swarmed all around, buzzing louder and louder, landing on my face, crawling in my ears and up my nose. I opened my eyes and walled in by waste I saw the Kashipur traffic speeding past. Maggots were slithering in and out of the crevasses of the rotting waste and I then looked down to my hand. There was no precious toy in my grip, instead a decomposing rat, its ribcage exposed and with grubs crawling the chest cavity. I wiped my hand vigorously on my trousers. In panic, I stepped out into the road as a truck thundered past.

I had to think fast, but my mind was in a spin. Sweat stung my eyes and blurred my vision. I couldn't stay here. My only option was to chance the chaotic road. As I tried to compose myself I heard a loud bang followed by the sound of tortured metal and screeching tyres. The ground beneath me shook and vehicles slowed to a stop. I stepped into the road and out into the stationary traffic. To my left was an extended auto-rickshaw and three cars crumpled into each other. Spectators gathered and I could hear screaming and shouting. Soaked in sweat I took advantage of the awful situation and squeezed between car bumpers to reach the other side and an alleyway between two buildings.

Batting at the flies I was convinced still encircled me I made my way along the pathway and fell against a closed shop front. On the other side of the main road, a young boy now occupied the space between the rubbish piles. Picking through, he ate the little he could find, seemingly unconcerned by the roadside carnage, flies, germs and the stench. I pushed my way through the crowds and turned a corner to find a chai wallah under the shade of an umbrella attached to his cart.

'Come, welcome, have chai,' he beckoned in a gravelled voice. A green patch was positioned over his right eye and his teeth were betel nut red. 'You are looking like you are having very bad day, sir.' He offered me his chair, but as I went to sit down I stumbled and collapsed to the floor.

'Sir, are you being okay sir? Sir?'

The chai wallah's voice sounded distant. When I opened my eyes fully his concerned face was in front of mine. On seeing I was okay his expression changed to one of relief. I sat up with a yelp as pain charged through my shoulder and down my right arm where I'd landed. He offered me a drink of water, 'Look sir, it is sealed cap. See?' His smile widened as he opened the condensated bottle and handed it to me. The icy water slipped through my system, temporarily relieving me from the heat. After a few moments of regaining my breath, rubbing my shoulder and waiting for my head to clear, I asked if he knew how I could get to Rishikesh. 'No sir,' he replied, much to my dismay. 'But please, be waiting here.'

On his return from talking to someone across the street, he said, 'It is not possible to go direct to Rishikesh from here. First you must go Moradabad from bus stand near end of road.' He pointed along the street and then poured me a glass of chai, which I sipped cautiously, not wanting to further upset my stomach. When I'd finished, I thanked him and slid some notes under my empty glass.

Following his directions, I found the bus stand and the correct bus almost straight away. On board, I slouched in a seat with my head against the window as we moved away. I stared out at the endless cycle of farmland and small towns, drifting in and out of consciousness. Three hours later the conductor yelled, 'Moradabad, Moradabad, Moradabad.'

Here we go again.

Roads were wider, buildings taller and there were more people than in the previous towns. Along a main road, a line of urinals came into view. A couple of men standing with their backs to the traffic were using them. In desperate need of a toilet myself, I braved an available latrine around the corner with less staring faces from car windows. Hideous as it was, I carefully placed my feet in the lesser of the shit smeared spots.

By the time I found a line of buses, I was in no mood for the trail of kids shouting their stationery demands and I snapped at them to go away. Not that they took any notice and continued to follow me until I boarded a bus, at last to Rishikesh. Every muscle in my body was aching and the bones in my lower back were fed up from being knocked about by uncomfortable seats on what felt like endless bus rides. I'd lost count how many times I felt like I was going to pass out or nearly throw up on the person in front of me. At the beginning of the journey I asked the driver how far it was to Rishikesh and how long it would take. He told me, 'Maybe two hundred kilometres north and maybe four hours of driving.' Then laughed and waggled his head, 'But we are running on Indian time sir, so maybe much longer.'

An hour after the estimated four hours, the bus engine went quiet and we drifted to a stop. It was only when the driver attempted to start the vehicle over and over that I knew something was wrong. After some tinkering around the engine area and a few clangs of tools, the conductor came back on board. Something was said and passengers groaned. Then he came over to me, 'What to do? Bus is no longer working. Please find other bus to Rishikesh from bus stand near railway station. Take ticket, explain what happen, pay no more.'

'This is not Rishikesh?' I slurred, now feeling as if I'd drunk a gallon of vodka.

'No sir, not Rishikesh, but look,' he grinned and pointed to a wide rushing river, 'The beautiful Ganga of Haridwar.'

Sightseeing was the last thing on my mind, but I appreciated the cool night air. I stopped on a long bridge that spanned the river. On the left bank, an illuminated Hindu temple and the city reflected shimmering colours in the water creating a sparkling wonderland.

I trudged into the town to chiming bells, alien voices singing and chanting. A religious festival was taking place and as I walked the streets the buildings and people blurred, trailed and rippled. There were no signs in English, but I made it to the bus station. Stood in a dark corner beneath a shelter I exhaled a heavy sigh and waited for a bus to arrive. Rain tapped on the metal roof above and a dirty cow beside me stared into space.

Sounds and sights flitted through my mind: a tear drop lake, rotting food, an elephant ride, buzzing flies, shouting and singing, splashing crocodiles, laughter, a dead rat, horns blasting, the Good Ship Lollipop, crawling maggots, twisted metal, a black faced silver monkey, a disfigured beggar, an old withered tree, a reassuring hand reaching through the darkness, a bottle of Fanta and the innocent face of an angel. Tears of exhaustion flooded my eyes and streamed my dirty face. A dark silent emptiness suffocated any attempt at sobbing; the weight of the world far too heavy for my shattered heart to carry it another step. Sleep spindles cast strong threads and heaved at my conscious resistance, promising a comfortable pillow wherever I lay my head. I tried to focus on the slow-motion chaos around me. Somewhere beyond the maelstrom was a stretching groan, 'Reeeeeesheeeeeekessshhhh, Reeeeeesheeeeeekesh, Rishikesh.'

13

Through the clatter of clanging, trickling, chinking and chopping, I heard voices – English from what I could make out. Young. Male.

'Have you asked her?'

'I haven't got around to it yet?'

'Haven't got around to it? Ha, too afraid you mean.'

I lay with my eyes closed. My body was unresponsive. All I could do was listen until the darkness became silent.

'Where have you been?' A new voice woke me again. He sounded older than the other two. As my eyelids lifted I could see patches of blood, expanding and branching out across a white canvas. The pulsating blur moved in sync with my breathing. I was mesmerised. I began to take deeper breaths to gain a sense of my surroundings and focused on a minute red spider crawling across the floor. Or maybe it was an ant. I caught sight of another one and another and realised the red invasion was hundreds of these tiny insects navigating their way from one side of the room to the other.

'Why aren't those tables ready?'

'I...'

'Don't bother me with your excuses, I don't want to know. This is your last warning.'

'But...'

'I'll be back in one hour. I want to see everything done by then.'

Footsteps marched and gradually faded.

'You've been gone for ages. He was going crazy, yelling at me for letting you out of my sight.'

'Yeah, sorry about that. Anyway, do you like them? I just bought them in town.'

'A pair of jeans? So what? You think she's going to suddenly like you because you've got a new pair of jeans. They look expensive.'

'I saved my wages. I think she'll like them. One day we'll leave this place and travel the world.'

I pulled myself up and rested against the bed. The room was pristine, almost clinical, marred only by the miniature guests still conducting whatever business it was that occupied them. There was a table with a television set and in the corner, a red couch. It resembled a private hospital room.

I stumbled into the bathroom just in time. Diarrhoea and vomit were about to make their first visit of the day. Thankfully there wasn't too much and I turned my attention to the shower. Only icy needles came out, which stung my skin. Glimpses of yesterday came back and I started to connect the dots from Dhikala to Haridwar, but from there, I kept drawing blanks. I had no idea where I was or how I got here. As I towelled myself dry I saw my reflection in the mirror and hardly recognised myself, hidden behind a sallow complexion and sunken eyes.

The young voices returned from the room next door, which I guessed was a kitchen. They were mumbling so I couldn't hear what they were saying. The older man interrupted their conversation and they fell completely silent. I couldn't make out what he was saying either, but I seized the opportunity to find out where I was. As I opened the door, an Indian man in his late forties appeared before me.

'Excuse me.' I paused as I mulled over the question I was about to ask in my head, realising how weird it might sound. 'Where am I?'

He smiled professionally, but judging by his frown, he didn't fully understand.

I tried a different question, 'Am I in hospital?'

'You need doctor, sir?'

I did, however that wasn't the answer I was looking for. Through a doorway to the left was a kitchen where two young Indian men were working; one preparing food, the other washing plates. These must have been the guys I'd overheard.

'Could I speak to one of these two please?' I asked, pointing at the kitchen.

'They are not speaking any English, sir. I am only person here who can speak English.'

'Are you sure? I heard them speaking English earlier.'

'This is not possible, sir,' he replied.

'But I heard them, they were speaking very good English.' He called to the young men and spoke to them in Hindi. They stared at me as if I was mad. I looked to the left and spotted a folded pair of blue jeans on top of a shelf, 'The jeans,' I animated. 'You were talking about a girl and the jeans.'

They looked to the older man, clueless of what I said.

'I am very sorry, sir, you must be mistaken. As I say, they do not know English. Sometimes I think they do not understand Hindi either,' he locked on to them with a look that would have shattered a block of ice. They were quick to stare at their feet.

'Will that be all, sir?' he asked, restless to be elsewhere.

'I'm in Rishikesh, right? This is a hotel in Rishikesh?'

'Yes, sir, hotel in Rishikesh. Rickshaw driver bring you last night.'

Before I had a chance to report the insects, he was gone. I attempted to talk to the kitchen staff in English, but they just smiled and waggled their heads. Retreating to my room I closed the door and sat on the bed as the talking resumed from the kitchen; the same two voices I heard earlier, but this time in incomprehensible Hindi.

In the hotel's restaurant, I poked at a masala omelette, while trying to coax my memory into delivering me to Rishikesh. Gradually scenes materialised. I remembered leaving a bus and a kind rickshaw wallah helping me find a hotel. He only charged me ten rupees. It felt like we were driving around forever. He must have brought me here. I mused over this morning and the staff who were speaking English. How would I have known about the jeans if I couldn't understand them? My head was a mess. Nothing made sense any more.

The omelette wasn't getting any smaller. Breakfast could be a struggle at the best of times, but feeling so nauseous, it was an even bigger ordeal than usual. I'd eaten nothing since the biscuits yesterday morning and knew I should eat something. I thought about Aiden and wondered what he was up to. He probably had the sense to go to Manali via Delhi. At that moment, I wished for the chance of his companionship again, however annoying it might be. The thought of another day alone without a clue of what I was doing was depressing.

At the reception, the manager directed me to the bus station on the other side of the river via the Lakshman Jhula Bridge. I waved down the first ride I saw which happened to be one of those odd extended rickshaws, like the ones I'd seen in Kashipur and Moradabad. There was something quite sinister about these vehicles, resembling a huge black goat's skull on wheels. On board was a newly married couple on honeymoon from Malta. They were happy to share the cost, of what I discovered, was called a tempo.

Rishikesh, they said, was a great place to practice yoga. There was an abundance of ashrams with long stay options should I wish to find my inner self. For a moment, I considered if staying in one would be good for me, but dusted the idea away, too intent on where I really wanted to get to. After negotiating the traffic and potholes, the tempo stopped at the Lakshman Jhula footbridge. There, the driver left me with further directions to the bus stand before chugging away in a thick cloud of exhaust smoke.

Running parallel to the river, a line of flora covered hills provided a backdrop to the iron suspension footbridge which I was somewhat apprehensive about crossing. Half way across I stopped and looked out to the flowing emerald Ganges coursing a winding path through the hills. To my right, a red and white Hindu temple rose like a wedding cake from the river bank.

A confident rhesus monkey jumped up and sat half a metre away from me. Clinging to the wire cables, he shot me a glance and then looked out to the river. For a fleeting moment, we shared the same view before he jumped down again and padded past me on all fours. I caught myself smiling; reminded of the monkey I observed from the watchtower in Corbett.

Working through the directions the tempo driver had given me wasn't so easy. The streets didn't tally up with his suggested route and I found myself at the bottom of a slope with steps leading down to a temple complex. On each step sat a sadhu, silver bowl at his feet for donations. As I descended, each one called out for alms. I chose the last of the holy men on the bottom step. He wore orange robes, had round spectacles and a long pointed white beard. He leant forward and painted an orange stripe with his finger in the middle of my forehead as I rose from dropping a five rupee note in his tin. 'Tilak blessing,' he said. 'Acts as third eye. Enables you to see truth beyond appearances.'

The stomach cramps resurfaced as I went away. I knew it wouldn't be long before I needed to be sick again, so I picked up pace, passed a wall of colourful Hindu gods encased within glass cabinets and found a pathway leading from the complex. I arrived at an open pedestrianised area of temples awash with bright oranges, yellows and reds. There, a group of westerners were engaged in conversation outside an ashram. I overheard them talking of what it was to be enlightened and how others in this world had no idea how it felt to touch the hand of God as they did. I wondered which of the millions of Gods in this country they were referring to.

When an appropriate opportunity presented itself, I asked for further directions and was advised to walk the river's edge, taking a pathway further along that should lead me to the bus terminal.

Their attire matched the reds and oranges of the temples and was vivid, loose fitting and relaxed, almost too relaxed like the tone of their voices. The one who gave me directions spoke so softly I doubted her authenticity. She seemed to be patronising me for my lack of understanding of what it was to be at one with mother earth;

as if I was too low to reach the dizzy heights of her enlightenment. With her hair wrapped tightly within a scarf, I saw more beyond her eyes than she would have liked to have revealed. She, just like me, was lost in this world, but had found a haven in the den of this ashram.

I strolled along the pebble shoreline for fifteen minutes without any sign of a way into town. Weak and fed up, I perched on a boulder with a view of the river and hills. I shaded my eyes from the sun with my hand and searched the river bank for anything that resembled a pathway or trail. In the distance a break in the trees showed steps leading to buildings above. The smell of wood smoke, cooking meat and incense hung in the air. It was coming from a pile of burning timber further down the river, maintained by three men. Hoping some of the food was for sale, I drew nearer. Jack may have cautioned me of the dangers of street food, especially when it came to meat, but the aroma had awakened my appetite and was hard to resist. When I was a stone's throw away, I came to an abrupt stop. My much-welcomed hunger switched to disgust as I caught sight of two human feet protruding from the pyre, charred, flames licking the blackened toes. Shocked and disturbed by the cremation I recoiled and left them in peace.

At the top of the stairs, a man with brown dreadlocks and a scruffy beard was fiddling with the front wheel of his motorbike. Unable to shake the macabre scene from my mind, I asked him if it was normal for people to be cremated in the open like that. I mean it wasn't something you would see along the banks of the River Thames.

'It's all good dude,' he said in an American accent. He placed a hand on my shoulder in reassurance and gazed below to the river, 'For Hindus, the Ganges acts as a vehicle of ascent from earth to heaven. It's the ultimate carriage for ashes of the dead to go forward into the afterlife and for the spirit to be granted with instant salvation. Sounds like the perfect way to go if you ask me, my brother.'

'Oh right, thanks,' I said and pondered on his words. Looking around, none the wiser of where I was going, I asked if he knew how to get to the bus station.

'I sure do buddy. You're right on top of it.' He pointed along the road directly in front of us, 'You want to head up there and take a right at the intersection. You can't miss it.'

'Thanks. Take care on your bike, eh?' I shook his hand, relieved I didn't have much further to walk.

The area surrounding the ticket booth was heaving with people. I joined a long queue and waited for what seemed like hours shuffling in line every few minutes until my turn arrived.

'One ticket to Manali please,' I said.

Soon I could relax, put my feet up and all would be well.

'No Manali. Next.'

'Hold on, no bus to Manali? What, today or one doesn't leave from here at all?'

'There are no buses to Manali from here. Please move aside. Next!'

I couldn't believe it. I scanned the road for any other travellers, but there were none. I suddenly remembered Sean had written another place in my journal in Delhi. Maybe I needed to get a bus to a place called Dehra Dun first. Joining the back of the queue again, I shuffled my way eventually to the front.

'One ticket to Derra Dun, please.'

The man behind the glass tilted his head, 'Where?'

'Derra Dun,' I said.

'There are no buses to Derra Dun.'

'Derra Dun,' is all I could say. Exasperated, I repeated it again and again, 'Please, Derra Dun.'

He was now becoming quite frustrated, 'Next!'

The man next in line tapped me on the shoulder as I left the queue, 'Sir, please, are you meaning Dehera Doon? I think this is maybe where you are wanting to go.'

I took a moment to take in what he was saying and on realising my mistake replied, 'Yes, thank you. That's where I want to go.'

As I turned around my face fell at the length of the queue.

'Please,' the gentleman said and gestured me in front. 'Be my guest.'

The teller was far from impressed to see me again. 'Yes,' he sighed, no doubt awaiting another destination he couldn't serve.

'Dehera Doon,' I triumphantly exclaimed, pronouncing more O's in the Doon that was necessary.

'Ah, Dehera Doon. One ticket to Dehera Doon.'

Issuing me with a ticket for a bus that left in twenty minutes, he pointed to the bay where I could pick it up.

The final embers of the sun highlighted the peaks of the rugged hills, leaving the indigo fade of night to arrive. Looming the opposite horizon were dark thunder clouds menacing the sky. A hostility resonated amongst the townsfolk of Dehra Dun as they budged past me and there was unease in the air, which I found intimidating, almost threatening. I made my way from hotel to hotel looking for somewhere to bed down for the night, but at each place I tried I was met with short blunt responses of 'No vacancies.' Half an hour went by of fruitless searching until I came to a dilapidated building with a worn sign advertising accommodation. The reception area was in darkness apart from an empty desk to welcome my arrival. I peeked through the doorway leading to the hotel's restaurant. It looked as if it hadn't been used in years; dust covered the tables and chairs, and cobwebs hung from the ceilings and windows. Fractured light filtered in from the darkening sky, barely illuminating the interior.

'Yes,' a voice said from behind me making me start. I turned to see a tall man standing in front of me. His features were hard – chiselled chin and cheek bones, thin moustache and eyes fixed on me as if I were his prey.

'I'm looking for a room,' I said, averting his stare.

'We have one room available. Five hundred rupees.'

'Two hundred and fifty?'

'Five hundred.' He didn't return my smile but moved closer where I caught wind of stale tobacco and rotten fish on his breath.

Rain began to pour as the storm closed in. As unwelcoming as it was here, it seemed the lesser of two evils. I peeled back some notes and handed them to him along with my passport.

'Any chance I could get something to eat?'

'Restaurant is closed. Power is out.' He reached around behind him, pulled a key from a hook and waved his arm at me to move, 'I will take you to your room.'

As I followed him, light returned and the fans stirred to life.

'Perhaps I could get something to eat now?'

He stopped and sharply turned to face me. With gritted teeth, he motioned me back down the hallway to the restaurant, 'Wait in there, I will see what I can find.'

I'd been waiting for some time and was looking at my luggage. The fake leather holdall had frayed at the zip and was opening either side. I didn't hear him return and shot up out of my seat as cutlery banged down on the table's surface followed by a plate of unappetising food.

Swimming in greasy brown liquid were unidentifiable dark shapes bobbing around a slimy hard-boiled egg that occupied the centre. 'Eat,' he said and sat before me, never taking his eyes from me, watching me reluctantly slurp each spoonful.

The spiciness was savage and burnt the inside of my mouth and throat but did little to disguise the rancid taste of the egg. I called it a day as soon as I thought I'd consumed enough to be considered polite and eagerly reached for the Coke bottle to wash the slop down and put a more pleasant taste in my mouth, but even that wasn't right; strangely sour instead of sweet.

'You get a lot of power cuts here then?' I asked, thinking I might start a conversation.

'Town has been without regular electricity and water for two weeks, many government problem.'

'That must be really difficult for business,' I continued, but the conversation was over. My plate was taken to the kitchen through a set of double doors.

He reappeared moments later, 'Cello.' I picked up my stuff and followed him to a flight of stairs, then up to a sheltered corridor with a row of bolted and padlocked doors on the left. At the last door, we stopped and he slid back the bolt.

'Your room.'

14

The interior was in complete darkness. I stepped inside fumbling for the light switch and found it just as the door slammed shut behind me. I froze. My bag and guitar slid free from my grasp, landing carelessly on the floor. With systematic precision, my eyes worked their way around the room. Everything was the same; the beige carpet, the white wood-chip wallpaper, the small oak cabinet next to the steel framed bed. Even down to the white sheets and pillow accented by a thin chocolate coloured blanket. Along the left wall was an oak wardrobe, an empty bookshelf and a wooden suit valet stand. The ceiling fan and the doorway to the bathroom were the only differences. Fear consumed my whole body, ignoring any passing thought that this was a simple coincidence.

I didn't want to be here and with a sudden surge of energy I grabbed my things and turned for the door. I rattled it and tugged with all my strength, but of course it wasn't going to open. Like my neighbours' doors all the way along the corridor, it had been locked from the other side. I started to bang the door and yell, but all I received in return was grazed knuckles and a hoarse throat.

As I turned to face the bed, the lights went out and the fan slowed to a stop: another power outage. Rain drummed at the windows and flashes of light alternated with the rumbling of thunder. I fished around in my holdall for my pocket torch, found it and flicked the switch, only to find it was already in the on position and the batteries were dead. I sat on the bed. A metallic creak sent a shiver down my spine. With my back against the wall, I listened to the rain and watched the room reappear and disappear with each episode of lightning. Immersed in this replica of my bedroom as a young boy, it was hard not to think about my past and what had brought me to this point.

My earliest memories were of bright sunlight and vivid colours; everything dusted in a golden haze. All around were towering silhouettes and stretching shadows; smiling faces. It never rained, except for a few days in autumn when I remember going to the park and jumping in puddles and fallen leaves of crimson, ochre and bronze. Bedtime stories told of a horde of goblins armoured with rusty shields and swords or the troll under the bridge, which kept me awake and alert of what may be beneath my bed should I dare look. Knowing my mother was close by I soon fell asleep, securely navigated into adventurous dreams.

On Saturday mornings Mum took me to Croydon, where we'd pick out a new toy or book, then share a pepperoni pizza for lunch. Sometimes we'd go to the cinema once I was old enough. The first movie we saw together on the big screen was Grease, the next one Superman. I ran out of the auditorium that day believing I was invincible. My imagination also led me to think what a great dad Christopher Reeve would make. He was the kind of handsome man my Mum should be with. Afterwards we came home and watched The Muppet Show followed by Doctor Who while huddled together on the sofa, my Mum protecting me when I got too scared of the Daleks.

Some weekends were spent with my grandparents. I'd eat sugared butter biscuits and watch Heidi and Different Strokes on TV while my grandmother prepared dinner. Time would tick away with excitement as I waited patiently for my grandfather to come home from work. The moment he walked through the door I'd launch into a barrage of hugs before he could even get his coat off. We would play together all evening until I dosed off to sleep in his arms. He would then take me upstairs into the spare room, tuck me safely into bed and my grandmother would read me a story.

The first four years of my life I lived in a ground floor flat in Penge, a suburb of London. I would hear the heavy footsteps of Big Daddy, the famous British wrestler, who made regular visits to the guy above us. We then moved to a three-bedroom basement apartment nearby where we stayed for the next few years and that's when I met Gordon. A year older than me, Gordon was as much like an older brother as a best friend. We'd go with our Mums to Crystal Palace Park and feed the animals at the petting zoo or go on a boat ride or just run around like lunatics on the grass.

It wasn't too long before Gordon moved to the other side of London and I never saw him again. By this time my great grandmother had moved in with us, who was a lot of fun. She would visit my shop every day and purchase her plastic groceries and items I had grabbed and lined up from the kitchen; then sit down and watch the many musical concerts I would stage with my kid's guitar, red electric keyboard and small drum kit with worn cheap plastic skins ripped and battered by the continual playing. In the afternoon, she would have a nap and I would play with my other toys. There were stretchy plastic figures, Weebles that wobbled but never fell down and a miniature tree-house with rooms neatly appointed with furniture, a garden swing and a family of four complete with faithful dog. It was my books I loved the most though. Tales of travel and adventure, mystical creatures and magical powers transported me to the most exciting lands imaginable. I could go anywhere, be anyone, any time.

It was still so hot despite the storm. Water trickled along guttering and vehicles could be heard splashing through deep puddles in the street below. The ceiling fan came alive again as light returned to the room. I got up and shook the door in hope it might have somehow unlocked, but it hadn't. Another bout of chronic diarrhoea and vomiting took me to the bathroom. I had no idea where it was all coming from. No sooner had I dried myself from a shower, I was sweating and shivering again. I slumped back on the bed exhausted, held my stomach and stared out to the bookshelf and valet stand.

Callum would turn up every now and then at the ground floor flat my mum and I lived in. A giant with flared jeans and long sideburns, he didn't say a single word to me. I was always sent to my room to read or play, which I didn't mind so much. Sometimes the two of them would go out for a couple of hours and leave me home alone.

One night, thunder and lightning cracked outside. Terrified, I raced from the apartment to see the old lady who lived above but tripped on some concrete steps and was knocked out. When I regained consciousness, the old girl was nursing the cuts on my head and shoulder. My mother returned late that evening and apologised for leaving me on my own. She then delivered the news that we would be moving to a new apartment. We were going to live with Callum.

I was enrolled into a new school where I made friends easily and even met my first girlfriend, Rachel. For a while we were inseparable until one day I chose to hang out with her cool older brother instead of watching her in the school play. Small things can carry such importance, especially when you're eight years old, and Rachel saw my lack of loyalty to her as reason enough to dump me.

At home, there were plenty of children of a similar age in the surrounding flats. Richard and Robert were brothers, originally from Nigeria, but brought up in England. I got along with Richard the most. Unlike his brother, who preferred staying indoors and working on science projects, Richard was a little bit rebellious and for the first time in my life I had a friend I could be mischievous with. We were never seriously troublesome, except for one occasion when we were caught throwing stones at a neighbour's stained glass window. My Mum was so disappointed in me but promised not to tell Callum if I swore never to do it again.

Days later, an unbelievable pain in the right side of my pelvis erupted without warning. Mum found me crying in agony behind the sofa and rushed me straight to hospital where I was diagnosed with a ruptured appendix. Gerry Raffety's Baker Street played on the radio and there was a real Dalek donated by the BBC in the ward, which scared the life out of me.

Most of the other children received gifts in hospital, a new toy to keep their spirits up or at the very least some sweets and comics. On the few occasions my Mum visited me she came empty handed. Our outings to Croydon on a Saturday were now a thing of the past and I couldn't remember the last time she treated me to anything new. She never stayed for long. Callum always accompanied her but in usual fashion didn't speak to me. While she carried out her duty of checking how I was and if there was anything I needed (Were the nurses looking after me? Was I in any pain?), Callum sat there in silence. Soon after arriving, as was politely possible, they left.

When the weekend shopping trips came to an end so too did any visits to the cinema. Apparently paying for cinema tickets was a waste of money when Callum could pick up all the latest releases from a guy at work. Except the video tapes he brought home were never suitable for a young lad so I never got to watch any of them. The television programmes I used to watch were also replaced by endless game shows, American crime dramas and sport. I could no longer curl up with my Mum, Callum vocalised that boys needed to learn to be independent and that I had been clinging on to the apron strings for far too long. He now occupied the seat next to my Mother and I was often sent to my room. When I was lucky enough to be allowed to sit on the floor in front of them it was on the proviso that I was quiet and didn't disturb their TV viewing.

One day, we drove to a house in the country to pick up a Labrador Whippet cross breed, called Kelly, from a lady who had rescued her and provided foster care awaiting a permanent home. On the shelf was a badge with a 47 in the centre, red numbers, yellow flames trailing to the circular enamelled edge.

'Can I have that badge, please?' I asked mesmerised.

'Of course,' the lady replied with a gentle smile.

Immediately I detected a change in the air, something in the room had gone sour. An evident heavy silence on the return journey was broken by the screech of halting tyres. Callum grabbed the badge from my hand and hurled it across a dark field. The words that followed were stern, laced with anger and disappointment at how I had had the audacity to ask and should now be taught a lesson for the embarrassment caused.

Something wonderful came out of that day though. Kelly bonded with me immediately and was an amazing, loyal companion. Her friendship gave me a sense of security and I cherished the warmth and love she gave. A few months later Kelly was given away because Callum said I was becoming too reliant on her.

I hadn't noticed the cockroach's arrival on the wall above the bedside cabinet, nor the dark figure standing outside the window strobed by a background of relentless lightning. The insect's antennae were wavering, as if searching the air for my exact location while the silhouette's intimidating presence outside, stood motionless looking in. A series of loud bangs coincided with cracks of thunder. At first, I thought it was the manager realising his error in locking me in, but my inner voice told me different, something wasn't right. The door knocked again and shook violently.

'I can't open the door, it's locked from the outside,' I shouted. The bolt slid back. Why I decided to open the door, I wasn't sure. Every fibre in my body told me not to, but I did, to a man roughly my age. From his right cheek, through his lips and down to his chin was a deep scar. His hair was jet, curled and oily, his clothes shabby and his frame skinny.

Despite me asking how I could help, he said nothing at first, but stared straight through me, finally slurring a reply in a thick Indian accent, 'Currency. See your currency.'

I didn't understand. Why did he want to see my currency?

He became forceful, repeating and raising his voice, stepping forward through the doorway. I put out my hand to try and prevent him from coming any further, 'Hey, wait a minute, back up,' but he slapped it away and pushed past me.

Locating my luggage, he bent forward, ripped away the zip – the last thing holding my bag together – and grabbed my clothes, throwing them in all directions.

Severe dizziness had me leaning to the wall for support. 'For God's sake,' I shouted. 'I can give you five hundred rupees, have my wallet, take it it's yours.'

'Dollars?' he spat.

'No, only rupees,' I replied, clinging to the last particles of consciousness.

Nausea welled as daggers of light pierced my eyes before I succumbed to darkness.

'On your feet, boy!' I knew that voice only too well and what would follow if I wasn't at the end of my bed in a few seconds. He didn't have to look round. He knew I'd be standing to attention, arms tight to my side, back straight, chin up, head facing forward.

Slowly he hovered, scanning the room for the slightest discrepancy, wiping his finger for dust on the bookshelf, accounting the drawers for balled socks lined side by side, shoe polish and brushes in the correct order. On to the wardrobe, creaking open the doors, checking the spotless mirror, inspecting the clothes, ironed and folded in appropriate order. And then to the suit stand – every morning would be the same, every morning he would discover something unsatisfactory. This morning was no different, however many times I'd gone through my final checks the night before. He would always find something not to his liking.

He scrutinized my shoes, holding them at eye level, catching the light, commenting on my inability to produce a mirror shine. I was reminded for the millionth time how I would make a useless pile of shit soldier. I scanned the room, mentally working through my check list. Everything seemed in place, except not quite. At first, I couldn't figure out what it was. He commented on an invisible crease on the collar of my school shirt. Then I spotted it – the jeans folded on the top of the bookshelf. How could have I been so stupid? I must have fallen asleep last night before I managed to hide them. I embarked on a rescue attempt even though in my heart I knew it was a futile mission.

'Stop what you are doing right now.'

I did as I was told and stood motionless with one foot in front of the other as if I was trying to re-enact the famous crossing of Abbey Road by The Beatles.

'I saw them the minute I walked into the room,' he barked, still with his back to me.

This was the first time he'd worn his army uniform around the house. Dressed in impeccable khaki, with a peaked cap on his head and a stick held under his arm, he marched out of the room, but I knew it wasn't over. Thumping back up the stairs armed with a pair of scissors, he stormed straight over to the jeans and shredded the denim to rags. Then, as he always did, he smashed everything to pieces. He threw my clothes everywhere and tore up my school books and homework.

The usual lecture followed. I would have to pay for the damages by washing cars and doing more newspaper rounds. When I wasn't working or at school, however, I would be confined to my room with nothing to keep me occupied. I was grounded from any other activities because of my disobedience until further notice. He left, breathing heavily from exhaustion, the smell of rage and sweat clinging to the air.

Before me was the aftermath of a cyclone: splintered wood, tattered homework, clothing strewn and glass smashed. All my belongings, the few that I had, were damaged. It wasn't the first time I faced such destruction and I knew I would have another late-night cleaning it all up ready for the following morning's inspection. But for now, I had to concentrate on not being late for my paper round. I had to be at the shop to fill my bag at 6am, ready to make my deliveries in time for the daily news to be read over breakfast.

Afterwards I would come home and try and salvage what I could of my homework, get dressed in my ill-fitting school clothes (because despite having grown out of them, there "was still plenty of wear left in them yet") and jump on my rusty bike, only to be a punchbag at break times at the hands of school bullies. Before leaving my room, I looked around once more and briefly closed my eyes, pretending for just a few seconds that all of this was a dream.

My eyes opened slowly and I could make out the fan on the ceiling above me and a bright light. It took me a while to realise I was still in Dehra Dun. I had no idea what the time was or how long I'd been unconscious. Pain pounded at my head, the slightest movement increasing the intensity. I was on the floor, lying on my back, between the valet stand and bedside cabinet, my head at an awkward angle against the wall. I leant forward to check for any injuries. There were none apart from the sore bump on the back of my head. It was the tickling on my fingertips that was my immediate concern. A cockroach was scaling my hand. I yelped, throwing it into the air, springing to my feet with an energy that surprised me. The creature turned from its back and scuttled under the bed.

The room was a mess. The entire contents of my luggage were strewn all over. Nothing was missing from what I could see and there was no sign of anyone. The door was locked again from the outside.

I looked around the room, remembering the seven long years I spent here. My only joy came from the school library books I stashed between the mattress and the springs in my bed – my imagination, my only form of companionship. I counted myself lucky he never discovered this hiding place.

I'd had enough of this room. I'd had enough of India all together, of being sick and getting nowhere fast. I came here to forget, to find a certain peace and happiness and a freedom to breathe. Instead I felt stifled and confronted by every step. India had defeated me, had broken and bruised me and left me in the gutter. Adventure was one thing, but I no longer felt human. I was a physical wreck and wanted out. In the morning, I'd try and find a bus back to New Delhi and take the first plane back to England.

I updated my journal to keep my mind free of my past and as I came to the end, I hesitated. After everything I'd been through to get here, I couldn't believe I was giving up. I felt sad my adventure was over, but the pull of home was too strong. With my mind made up, my sore eyes closed and I slipped into a broken sleep.

15

Standing beneath cold jets of water, I leant against the wall, glad the fever was lifting and I was starting to feel moderately well again. I had another long day ahead of me. There was still a part of me that wanted to try for Manali, but the likelihood of yet more disappointment outweighed any of the positives.

The rain had stopped. Pale light warmed to sunrise. Through the front door, I heard a passing vehicle or two. I inched the bolt across, lifted the handle and pulled, expecting resistance, but there was none and the door opened. The balcony was empty, no sign of any staff or my evening visitor, just a row of doors and drying puddles.

I'd tied a belt tight around my bag, but it wasn't looking good; clothes poked out at all angles and things fell out from loose ends. I closed the door and as I did, I noticed the room number: 26. This was the same number of the apartment I lived in when I was younger. My decision to return to England was cemented there and then. This was all too weird.

A film of white dust covered the empty reception area. I returned the key to the counter, glad to leave. It was just after six. Shutters were pulled down and the road was lifeless apart from a stray dog snoozing under a wooden cart alongside an old man, also asleep, with a crutch by his side. It wasn't long before I saw parked buses and a queue of eight or nine people at a ticket kiosk. Four of the people were western: two guys and two girls in their mid-twenties. I joined the back of the queue and asked one of the guys in front if he knew if a bus left for Delhi from here.

'Yes, it will be leaving in about ten minutes,' he replied in a German accent. His brown hair was shoulder length. His jaw was strong, like his physique, and his eyes were kind – light blue – with a softness that matched his smile. 'Have you been in Dehra Dun long?' he asked.

'Only for one night.'

I looked over the heads of the queue and then to my watch.

'Can I get your ticket for you?' he asked. 'Maybe it would save you some time.'

'Thanks, that'd be great.' I gave him three hundred rupees.

'It shouldn't cost this much. I will bring you change.'

His friend had a slimmer frame, wavy dark brown hair hanging loose below his shoulders. 'You at the end of your trip, huh?' he asked, in what sounded like an American accent.

'Yes and no. I had intended to spend a little over three months in India, but it's kind of got the better of me. I've only managed seventeen days.' I half smiled and disconnected eye contact, looking over at the bus that was about to leave for Delhi.

'Why? India is amazing. This is no good, you must stay,' the German said.

'Don't get me wrong, I've enjoyed some of it. Naini Tal was nice, Corbett was great, even a few places in Delhi were cool, but getting everywhere is a nightmare and I'm as sick as a dog.'

'Yes, you look it.' I admired his honesty. 'How did you end up in Dehra Dun?'

I gave them a brief rundown of the last couple of weeks as the queue dissolved and we shuffled forward.

The two girls, who I assumed the German and American were with, sounded Australian. They bought a ticket each to Shimla.

'Take your luggage and I will bring you your ticket,' the German said and pointed to the parked buses.

'Oh, okay.'

Feeling unsettled about leaving him with my cash, I neared the buses, keeping the best view of the kiosk as I could. The girls boarded a bus behind me as the guys came over. The German handed me a bus ticket, 'Here is your ticket.'

I thanked him, took my change and said goodbye. I turned to leave and looked at the ticket. It read Dehra Dun to Shimla. He'd obviously made a mistake and given me his ticket.

He was lifting his backpack up to the American on the roof of the bus, 'Excuse me,' I called out. 'It appears I have your ticket.'

'No, you have your ticket,' he replied, without looking around.

'But I think you're mistaken. My ticket says Dehra Dun to Shimla, not Dehra Dun to Delhi.'

'Yes, this is correct.' He turned to me as his friend climbed down to join him, 'Please do not give up on India, it is an amazing country. I ask you to give her one last chance and do what you came to Dehra Dun to do, to see Manali. If you really do not like Manali, then I will pay your full bus fare back to Delhi.'

Time wasn't on my side. The final calls for Delhi were made and the last of the passengers boarded the bus. A slight crack had appeared in my plans, but the light that shone through was enough to sway my decision.

'Okay,' I said as I followed them to my seat.

Daniella and Harper – the two girls they were with – sat two rows in front. The German and American sat side by side to my right. I sat next to an elderly Indian gentleman who seemed overdressed for the climate. Upon his head was a woollen hat and below, a face that held a thousand wrinkles and a million tales to tell.

'I'm Sam.'

The German, nearest me, sorted through his shoulder bag, 'I am Kurt and this is Tyler.' Tyler raised a hand from his Lonely Planet.

'You're from Germany?'

'Austria. Tyler is from Canada.'

I'd not only got the nationalities of Kurt and Tyler wrong, but also the girls' who were from New Zealand. Kurt and Tyler met in Pushkar in Rajasthan and from there they travelled to Delhi where they met the girls.

Kurt laid a couple of slices of bread on a serviette, took a can from his bag and opened it with a utility knife. He flipped the lid to reveal processed cheese, dug the knife in, scooped out a chunk and began spreading. Slapping on the top slice of bread, he offered it to me. 'Eat. You look like you have not been eating properly and you need to keep your strength up.' It looked enticing considering the options I'd been presented with over the last week.

I never thought a cheese sandwich could taste so good and by the time I got to the end I was presented with another and a small bottle of water to wash it down with, to which Kurt had added some rehydration powder.

Aside from a passing gust of diesel, the air blowing through the top of the windows was fresh and clean. From the gateway of the lesser Himalayas we ascended the hills through the Doon Valley and my mood shifted. A weight dropped from my shoulders and lifted from my heart and a sense of security steadily resumed.

'It is maybe three hundred kilometres to Shimla,' Kurt said. 'Do you have a guidebook?' I shook my head. From his bag, he produced a dog-eared Lonely Planet, 'Here, you can have this one. It is from the last time I visited India. I have a newer copy in my backpack.' I opened it randomly and scanned the pages.

On a bridge beside a large waterfall we made way for a convoy of orange goods carriers. I followed the eyes of the other passengers to the valley dropping away below. Half way down, a bus was upended, its wheels pointing to the sky. It was completely flattened. The roof had smashed in to the point the window frames had disappeared. The idea of it being full to the brim with passengers was sickening. I looked away and grabbed the handrail a little tighter as the wheels of our bus moved off, teetering the edge of the road, sending dust and rocks over the side.

The guys had fallen asleep and although I too was tired, I was kept awake by the content of the book. There were so many amazing places, the photos alone captivated me. I discovered my route to Dehra Dun would have probably been a lot easier if I'd taken a bus back to Naini Tal from Corbett after all. From Naini Tal there were direct buses to Rishikesh and Dehra Dun. Looking back, although it was tough, I was happy with the way I went. I was fed up with backtracking on myself and revisiting the same place time and time again. It felt as if I was never getting anywhere. Plus, if I'd taken a different route, I might never have met my new friends who in the matter of a couple of hours, I felt like I'd known forever.

In the shadow of the forested Shivalik Hills, somewhere on the road from the town of Nahan, we rested and drank chai. The girls were sitting at a separate table from us and were engrossed in conversation. Tyler mopped up some dhal with a roti, while Kurt ate a banana from his bag.

'You are not eating Sam, why is this?' Kurt asked. I explained my appetite dilemma, telling him my stomach hadn't accustomed to Indian food yet and I found it a struggle to eat anything that wasn't western. 'It sounds like you have not found the right food yet,' he said. 'Maybe we will find something more to your tastes in Shimla.'

Tyler finished the last of his meal, sat back and lit a cigarette, 'Looks like you need to get a backpack too.'

'Definitely, I'll be wearing all of my clothes at this rate.'

Ever higher we corkscrewed the mountains; dense pine forests, maize terraces and orchards at our sides. For the first time since Corbett, I relaxed. I was rehydrated and although my stomach was still in a touch and go state, the discomfort fell to the back of my mind. I was happy again.

Signs of life appeared. A donkey heaved a wooden cart of bricks; legs buckling beneath the weight but spurred on nonetheless by its owner. Auto-rickshaws buzzed to and fro and porters – shoulders abound with ropes – gave chase. One got lucky, grabbed the ladder at the back of the bus and hitched a ride the rest of the way. He smiled at me through the window, no doubt his sights set on my departure.

The road led us into Shimla, perched upon a mountainside 2398 metres above sea level, and built upon by the British who once used the hill station town as a base to escape the plains in the unforgiving summer. It had taken us just over seven hours to get here and Kurt, Tyler and I were exhausted. We decided to stay the night, while the girls pressed on to Manali, having no interest in staying a moment longer.

Stepping down from the bus we were immediately set upon by the luggage carriers. They were handled effortlessly by the two guys with the use of comical banter. Tyler left us and queued in line for tickets for tomorrow morning's journey to Manali whilst Kurt and I looked out at the breath-taking clouds slowly rolling over a Himalayan wonderland. Behind us, as below, the hills were dotted with hundreds of pale blue, yellow and white properties.

The illusion of this enchanting city was somewhat broken as I caught sight of beggars and the homeless gathered beneath a bridge. Their faces were withdrawn, no doubt tired of the life that had been dealt to them, with each hour melting into the next searching for another way to make it to the end of the day.

Kurt caught my attention, 'I came here last year. I know of a good hotel close by. We will settle into our rooms and go out again later for something to eat.'

Despite our attempts at suggesting somewhere else, Kurt was insistent on finding the place where he stayed previously. After half an hour of traipsing from street to street we found it, only to be told that there were no vacancies. Instead we walked up a steep incline and followed a sign for another hotel. There was one room left, a double, with a view of a valley of shaded hills stretching out to the horizon. To the right of the window, a deodar tree occupied two infant rhesus monkeys that played and screeched in the late afternoon sun. The room was small and the three of us had to share a double bed. Hardly enough room for ourselves, mind about our luggage, we unpacked lightly. Tyler suggested that we go in search of a new backpack for me.

Outside in the crisp evening air we ambled along the lower bazaar and there, amongst the bustling vibrancy of hotels, restaurants, souvenir and fashion shops, we found a stall selling just the thing: a small, but sturdy recognised brand. Tyler haggled playfully and got the price down from five hundred to three hundred rupees.

From the main trunk of the road, we took one of the many twisting branches leading off and climbed some narrow steps between two buildings to the Mall. A long thoroughfare flanked by rows of half-timbered Victorian buildings, it resembled more of a Swiss-English village than an Indian town. The area was pedestrianised and people strolled leisurely, walking without a care in the world. I caught sight of men holding hands. Kurt said it is considered a common demonstration of friendship in India between men.

On the western shoulder of Jakhu Hill known as The Ridge, a cream coloured nineteenth century neo-gothic church dominated the eastern end. With an incredible view of the majestic foothills and jagged peaks of the Pir Panjal and Great Himalayan ranges, we took advantage of the sunset as it exposed vivid mauves and pinks across the reddening sky.

A restaurant nearby advertised western food of pizzas, burgers and suchlike. We were welcomed by a teenaged boy playing an acoustic guitar in the corner and an older man who came to our service.

When the Strawberry milkshakes and Margherita pizzas arrived, the boy stopped playing, 'Where are my manners? Please forgive me,' he said. I asked how long he'd been playing, 'Since I was very young. My father taught me to play and I have not stopped since.' His father, the man that served us, waggled his head and smiled as we looked over.

'Maybe you would like to listen to some western music?' He wandered off around the back of the counter. Suddenly, Soundgarden belted through the speakers before it was turned down a notch. 'Is this to your liking?' he asked and we nodded our approval.

Apart from the boy and his father we had the place to ourselves. I leant back and let out a huge sigh of relief, over the moon I was here with these people.

In the hallway of the hotel a group of young Indian men were shouting and laughing. As soon as they saw us, they surrounded us. The usual questions were served and we smiled as we replied with answers that had been given so many times before. We were offered beer and biscuits and invited to their room where they were having a small party of sorts. One guy brought a transistor radio with him and tuned into a station playing Bollywood hits. The guys were college friends from Bikaner in Rajasthan and were holidaying in the cool climate of Shimla. A couple of them began to dance and asked if we would join them. Tyler and I attempted a Bollywood dance under instruction, but soon sat down laughing and out of breath.

Kurt was next to be called upon, 'I do not dance well,' he said. 'But I can show you some Tae Kwon Do.'

Their faces lit with excitement and one eager student was first up to learn a kick. Kurt stepped back to prepare himself. The young man stepped forward just as Kurt launched a kick that connected with his chin and sent him flying across the room.

'Oh, my God,' Kurt apologised frantically, and helped him to his feet.

'It is not a problem,' he replied grinning and slightly disorientated. 'Please, show me again, I will keep clear this time.'

For a few hours, we hung around laughing and joking, but got an early night, ready for the next leg of our journey first thing in the morning. Just before I went to sleep, I slipped out into the night for a cigarette and absorbed the sprinkled lights of the town. I said a silent thank you to the sky that my new friends found me when they did. I was a world away from where I was this morning.

16

A mad rush ensued as we repacked our things and burst through the doors into the morning streets of Shimla. We'd overslept and had just minutes before the bus left for Manali. Kurt was fast. His powerful legs and strong physique soared ahead of Tyler and me as we raced down a hill, weaving in and out of a group of porters who stooped under the weight of all manner of objects.

'Go ahead, hold the bus for us,' Tyler shouted to Kurt who hadn't seeped a drop of sweat. My legs stumbled, burning with muscular stress. Only one road stood between us and Kurt waving from the bus doorway. Pressing forward, we used every reserve of energy. A few more metres and we'd be there. Just then a group of uniformed school children appeared. Their faces filled with terror as two red faced, sweat drenched lunatics came hurtling towards them. With our eyes focused on the goal we had to think fast. Shifting our weight from one foot to another we darted into the available spaces and outmanoeuvred our opponents giving us a clear path ahead. But it was too late. The bus was already pushing its way into the traffic.

'Stop!' Kurt yelled, but the driver had other intentions.

Tyler and I managed to catch up with the vehicle, running alongside it, but not quite making the doorway as it gathered speed. Kurt stood on the steps with his arm out, ready to grab the hand of whoever got close enough.

'For God's sake, man, stop,' I heard him shout to the driver.

I pushed hard but felt so weak and was losing the race. My legs couldn't take another step and gave in. Where I had failed, Tyler succeeded and made contact with Kurt who hoisted him in. All I could make out were the faces of Kurt and Tyler looking helplessly from the windows. Game over.

Panting, I watched the back of the bus almost disappear into the distance. But then it seemed to slow down. Without hesitation, I was off again, charging along the road. Ahead I saw it being held up by congestion. 'Wait, I'm coming!' I screamed. Racing alongside the bus once more I banged on the metal panelling. I kept pace as an orange truck blasted its horn dangerously close to my left. It sped up and veered in front of the bus causing the driver to slam on his brakes. This was my one opportunity.

I grabbed the doorway and Kurt shouted, 'Give me that stupid guitar.' He took it from me and I reached out for the handrail and pulled myself in.

'Man, that was a close one,' Tyler said as I took to my seat. 'The guy's crazy.'

Crazy was one word to describe him. Another was drunk. In the first four hours of the journey, eight people threw up from the windows, including Tyler. The driver accelerated and hit his breaks repeatedly and was taking insane risks. He overtook carelessly and threw us into the path of oncoming traffic, causing complete chaos on the roads. Kurt had had enough. He launched from his seat and marched to the cab. 'What the hell are you doing? You are going to get us all killed. Pull over. I can drive this bus better than you.' But his words went ignored.

A short while later we arrived at the first rest-stop and were flung forward in our seats as the driver pressed heavily on the brake and came to an abrupt stop. The basic, open-aired restaurant was much the same as the other dhabas I'd encountered – small seating area, even smaller cooking area and toilet – but this one served thali as well as the usual dhal and rice and I polished it off in no time. Kurt was on to his second helping as Tyler and I sat back for a cigarette. We were in mid-conversation when one of the other passengers informed us that the bus could be delayed for several hours while we waited for a driver to replace the one that was snoring behind the steering wheel.

'This is unfortunate, but for the best I think,' Kurt said. 'Manali is about three hundred kilometres from Shimla and slow going for the last quarter of the trip through the Kullu Valley. We need a driver who is alert. It may take seven hours or more to reach.'

We ordered more tea and talked. Already the scenery was nothing short of spectacular and I couldn't wait to see the Kullu Valley. Kurt asked what I knew of Manali and I answered with what I'd been told and the excitement in the voices of those who had described it. He said it was all true.

We took our seats back on the bus which finally moved away with a sober driver now at the helm. The hard seats may have taken their toll on our backs, but the view made up for any aches and pains.

I was in awe of the Kullu Valley – a picture perfect utopia of fertile jaded hills rising high above a fast-flowing river. The landscape rolled out scenes of ever-changing rice paddies, orchards and enchanting cedar forests. As the vehicle's tyres balanced precariously on the edge of the road, I did my best to ignore the several hundred metre drops staring up at the window.

'The river you see is the Beas,' Tyler said. 'It's the same river that flows through Manali. It rises from the Himalayas in Himachal Pradesh and courses its way south to the state of Punjab.'

Steadily, the hills turned into mountains, lightly dusted with snow. White veins sloped through pined woodland and melted into the rushing water beneath. I was taken aback at just how big the mountains were. I had never felt so small. My friends laughed at how my jaw dropped by the scenes that were unfolding around every bend. I said that I'd never seen real mountains before, only in books. They both found this surprising and amusing, each coming from countries that are home to great ranges.

Light rain descended from the heavy clouds that hung over the peaks as we followed the river into the town dwarfed by mountains on all sides. It was like an illustration from a fairy tale. At last I'd made it; to the place on everyone's lips, to the place I'd longed to find, but thought I would never see.

Kurt led the way along dark forest trails as he searched for a guest house he stayed in last time he visited Manali. We climbed a steep hill, crossed a bridge, walked in and out of the woods and encountered several dead ends, before Kurt admitted we were lost. Tyler teased him about his navigational skills and decided to take charge. Leading us along a path we came out by the Beas and propped on a hillside was a rickety guest house overlooking the river.

The room consisted of one double and one single bed. I took the single. The toilets and showers were outside and shared by other guests. Delighted I had something special to write about I took out my journal and began to update it as cold air blew through the window with the river thundering below. Once we settled in, we took a stroll to a restaurant on the edge of town and ate macaroni cheese. At last it felt like a real holiday. I felt safe, happy and with the help of Kurt's antibiotics and magic water, I was starting to feel well again.

On the communal veranda, I stretched my arms to the slightly clouded sky and rubbed the sleep from my eyes. To my right and left were overlapping snow tipped mountains that spread out for miles. Ahead, a dense deodar forest with the tallest trees I'd ever seen. Leaning on the hand rail I breathed in the fresh air and listened to bird song and the music of the river. A week ago, I was on my way to Dhikala for three nights. It felt as if a year had gone by since then. I stared in to the white water crashing over the rocks and compared my time spent in India with life at home. The last six months had slipped by so quickly with no stand-out memories I could recall. It was all just one giant medley of mundane living. I realised that a life doing the same thing, day in, day out, without a variety of memories to bookmark my days, was a short one.

Already I felt at one with my surroundings. Although the usual darkness lingered in the back of my mind, I felt a sense of harmony and security residing within. I took the splintered wooden steps down to the river and sat on a boulder with my thoughts. A voice called from behind, 'Good morning Sam, how are you feeling?' I turned to see Kurt on the veranda.

'Yeah, great thanks. And you?'

He stretched and yawned, 'Very good, my friend. It is wonderful to be here again. Not too hot, not too cold, perfect in every way.'

Tyler came up beside him, 'Hey Sam, how you doin'?'

'Couldn't be better. Sleep well?' I asked, as I scrambled up the bank to the base of the steps.

'Better than ever. I thought the noise of the river would keep me awake, but it had the opposite effect and sent me straight to sleep.'

We went for breakfast at a place called the Moondance Café in Old Manali, just up the hill from us. Parked in the seating area outside we slurped banana porridge and sipped chai. I was about to settle the bill when I was surprised to see a familiar face enter the dining area. He hadn't seen me so I crept up behind to surprise him.

'Hello stranger,' I said.

Ruben's eyes lit up through his oval spectacles as he turned to face me, 'Sam, wow, it's so good to see you again.' He grabbed me into a tight hug. 'How are you, my friend? Where's Aiden?' I explained in brief as he joined us at our table. 'Ah, I was afraid that might happen. Aiden was what you'd call a loose cannon. I am sure he can look after himself though.'

'How have you been?' I asked.

'Good. I've enjoyed my time here, as I knew I would, but I'm leaving to go back to Delhi today. I'll miss this place.' I introduced him to Kurt and Tyler and we talked as if we were all old friends. When the time came to leave, Ruben embraced me again, 'Take care of yourself, Sam, I wish you the very best of luck. Enjoy India and she will reward you plenty.' I treasured the moment, so glad that our paths had crossed once more.

Tyler went off on his own to sort through his luggage at the guest house, whilst Kurt and I headed into town. At the top of The Mall – the main road lined with shops, restaurants and hotels – a sadhu asked for a donation. In one hand, he held a golden trident, and in the other, a walking stick with a silver bowl dangling from his wrist for the collection of alms. I dropped in a few rupees. He tilted his head and smiled thanks. As he left, two girls in their early twenties approached us. One was lightly tanned with long, wavy blonde hair and was first to speak. Immediately I detected an English accent as she asked if we knew of anywhere decent they could stay.

'The guest house we are in is okay,' said Kurt. 'A little expensive maybe, but the rooms are clean and comfortable,' he continued, though his attention was drawn to the girl with olive skin and shiny black hair.

'Is it far?'

'No, it is not far. I need to change some money, but if you would like to wait a few minutes, we can show you the way.'

The girls and I waited outside the bank until Kurt reappeared. Sophie was a nurse from London and had met Neria in Kathmandu while travelling in Nepal. Instantly hitting it off, they decided to stay together and had been in India for two weeks prior to arriving in Manali. Neria was from Israel and had embarked on a year-long trip to discover the world as soon as she had finished National Service. When we reached the guest house we found Tyler sat on the veranda smoking a beedi.

'Hey guys,' he said, pausing as we approached, clearly distracted by our new companions.

'This is Sophie,' I said, introducing the pretty blonde girl, 'and this is Neria. They were looking for somewhere to stay.'

Tyler leant forward and shook their hands, 'Nice to meet you. You're in luck, our old room is free now, I've just switched it for a larger one. I'll show you to reception so you can get booked in.'

'We're going back into town now. Would you like to come with us?' Kurt asked, but his words were unheard as Tyler and the girls disappeared downstairs.

The Mall was relaxed, no touting and we weren't stared at in fascination, probably due to the number of western travellers around. We passed a vegetable market, then turned into a small square where Kurt brought us to a stop outside a post office.

'I need to collect a letter from a friend. You see that shop?' He pointed to the corner, 'Have a look around, I'm sure you'll like what you see. I'll meet you there in a few minutes.'

The small shop was packed with handicrafts and clothing: Hindu and Tibetan artefacts, spiritual works of art, t-shirts, sweaters, jewellery and trinkets. Behind a glass counter stood a stocky Tibetan man. He greeted me with a smile, 'Hello my friend. Please, look around. It cost nothing to browse.'

I did just that – at t-shirts embroidered with Tibetan script and the eyes of Buddha; at silver bracelets and rings; at cotton and woollen bags from Nepal dyed with a rainbow of colours. What struck me the most though, was a small red statue of Ganesh, the elephant headed Hindu god.

'Ah, you like?' the shopkeeper asked, noticing my curiosity. 'This is made of soapstone, very good quality.'

'Very expensive too, I imagine.'

'It is not so much. If my prices were high, then you will not come back to buy more. Also, you see, I have three other shop to contend with nearby, all selling similar thing. If my price too high and my service not so good, you will buy from my competitor, no?' He lifted the ornament from the cabinet and placed it on top of the glass, shining a side-lamp to highlight the detail. 'Ganesh is very good protection for traveller.'

I was completely caught up with his sales patter and a heartbeat away from purchasing when Kurt walked in. 'Tah-shi de-leh, Tashi, are you keeping well?'

'Kurt, is that you? Haha so long, my friend, so good to see you again. Yes, I am very well, business a little slow, but all is good.' The two embraced. 'Oh, yes, my apologies sir,' the shopkeeper turned his attention back to me. 'I will be with you in a moment, Kurt. First I must look after this customer.'

'I just saw this, it's really nice.' I showed Kurt the figurine.

'You are knowing one another?' asked Tashi. 'How wonderful, this is a good day to have good friends. Please, now I give you the very best price.' And so it was sold, along with a multi-coloured striped shoulder bag for my day to day use.

In the warmth of the afternoon sun, Kurt and I retraced our route along the Mall. Taking a series of ascending bends, we were gifted with spectacular alpine views furnished with orchards, forests and timber framed dwellings. I was slipping into this new phase of my journey with ease, but there was a part of me that thought something might go wrong at any minute. Ever since I was young, I prepared for the worst and in many ways, it was a habit that had served me well. The downside of such self-preservation is that inevitably I had become accustomed to never truly embracing happiness; anticipating that any joy is momentary, with pain or upset following close behind. I enjoyed life in my own way, but I was in a constant state of being on guard.

Auto-rickshaws passed by, choking and struggling with the rising roads or gliding down free and easy without the engine running. As I was about to ask for a breather, Kurt turned into the entrance of a forest, dense with lofty cedar. We took a break and I cranked my neck up at the pine sheltered sky. In the cool, dark shade, I shuffled from foot to foot, drawing the sun's rays as they pierced the canopy of needles.

An ancient temple raised on a stone plinth appeared as we walked further into the woods. This was the Hadimba Temple. Built in 1553, it was the oldest Hindu temple in Manali. A triple-tiered roof crowned by a brass cone sheltered the whitewashed stonework of the sanctuary. Ibex horns surmounted the entrance, wooden carvings of deities, elephants and crocodiles adorned the façade and supporting pillars, and a brass bell hung above the doorway to announce one's arrival to the goddess Hadimba.

At the base of the steps a western girl in her early twenties danced around us and hummed cheerfully to herself. She stopped to kiss Kurt on the forehead before skipping her way into the forest. We looked at each other, quite perplexed by the occurrence.

When we returned to the guest house we found Sophie and Neria deep in conversation with Tyler on the veranda. Ordering a round of chais we joined them. Tyler had been telling the girls about his interest in photography, in black and white portraits particularly. He explained how he liked to capture the very best in people and had a collection of over two thousand pictures that sometimes would be displayed in galleries and were also framed for sale. India was an absolute dream for him where his art was concerned. So many different and interesting people and he saw a piece of magic in each one.

Later we all went out for dinner at the same restaurant where the three of us had eaten the previous night. We continued to get to know each other, in between general chatter and laughter. We all laughed a lot. I'm not sure what was so funny, but I remember at one point I felt physically exhausted. It was nearing 3am when we eventually hit our beds and I can't remember anything beyond pulling the sheet up and over me and feeling an ache in my cheeks. The consequence of an entire evening spent smiling.

17

It was midday when Kurt, Tyler and I met with the girls again. Last night we had all agreed to go in search of cheaper and more satisfactory accommodation. We stopped off at the Moondance Café for a late breakfast where Tyler saw a friend he'd met in Rajasthan. Sophie and Neria went to order for us, which gave Kurt an opportunity to speak of his interest in Neria.

'She is very beautiful don't you think?'

'I guess, not really my type to be honest.' I replied, browsing the pages of my Lonely Planet.

'Not your type? Are you blind? She's incredible.'

'I think you share that soft spot with Tyler,' I laughed. 'Sophie is very sweet though.'

'Oh yes, Sophie is very nice, but Neria, oh Neria.'

'Oh, Neria what?' Kurt had been too engrossed in his thoughts of Neria to realise she'd come up behind him with a mango lassi in each hand.

'Um, ah, I was just writing a song about all of us in Manali,' he blurted.

'Fair enough,' she cocked an eyebrow and turned to help Sophie who was struggling with more glasses of lassi.

'Writing a song about all of us in Manali?' I teased. 'Really?' He looked off into the mountains and said nothing as I chuckled.

The girls sat down at the table and as the porridge was served,

Tyler joined us, 'My friend Floyd said there is a place just outside Vashisht that rents motorbikes. Do you ride, Sam?'

'No.'

'No problems, you can always double up with one of us. Me and Kurt will collect them after breakfast and meet you back here.'

About an hour later I heard rumbling motorcycles approaching the café. On the roadside were two smart looking Royal Enfields – stars of sunlight catching their shiny petrol tanks and chrome handle bars.

Tyler was first to speak, 'We've landed ourselves a great house in Dhungri near the Hadimba forest. There was a boy at the motorcycle shop who said his uncle is letting the place out for a month. It's a steal at two thousand rupees.'

Kurt continued, 'It is a bargain enough for the three of us, but if we ask the girls to move in, it will be cheaper still.'

They couldn't contain their excitement. It did sound amazing, almost too good to be true. Sophie and Neria needed little convincing. Neria hitched a lift with Tyler, and Sophie and I caught up with them by auto-rickshaw a few minutes later. Along a grassy path, set high within an apple orchard, we laid eyes on our new home – a large timber house, pale blue and white with exceptional views of overlapping mountains overlooking the town and river below.

Inside was spacious and completely empty. By the entrance was a kitchen with a sink, and a bathroom with a keyhole toilet and wash basin. No sign of a shower. Kurt pointed out of the window to an oval tin tub. It looked like we'd be bathing and washing our clothes in cold water outside from now on. The living area was flanked by four doors either side and at the end a wall was halved by long windows flooding daylight into the room.

There was one more bedroom below which was accessed from the outside, which Neria quickly laid claim to. Sophie chose the room neighbouring Kurt and I took the smallest room alongside Tyler's. I may have chosen the smallest, but it had the best view of the valley. I was spoilt by two walls of windows. All our beds were basic to say the least; each a single charpoy with canvas meshing.

Surprisingly, they were quite comfortable.

Kurt and I decided to leave the others to settle in and head into town to pick some things up for the house. It made sense to take the Enfield, except I'd never ridden before and was nervous to say the least. Despite my fears, I pasted a half confident expression on my face and mounted the seat behind Kurt. My apprehension soon turned to exhilaration as I held tight, a blur of pines rushing by. The hairpins we descended were a whole new experience to me as Kurt soon found out. How was I to know you're supposed to lean into the bends? In my own wisdom, desperate not to fall off, I did exactly the opposite and nearly got us into all kinds of trouble. He yelled back at me, 'Lean!' and following his lead I started to get the hang of it.

After buying some supplies we stopped by the guest house to pack the rest of our belongings before making our way back to the house. Tyler was quick to come and tell us about a full moon party that was taking place that evening somewhere in the mountains. 'I'm pretty sure the directions I was given are solid. It's an all-nighter, and from what I've been told it's gonna be awesome.'

The five of us got ready and left for Old Manali in a couple of autos or tuk-tuks as Tyler called them. We stopped for a bite to eat at the Moondance Café before following a path into the forest by torchlight. The dull thumping of trance music signified we were getting closer. Just as well, as after forty minutes of walking, we were beginning to think Tyler had been duped. Ahead of us we could see a clearing and could just make out the silhouettes of people dancing, strobed lighting electrifying the forest as if the trees were alive and dancing too. Although we were still a quarter of a mile away, the atmosphere was charged and tingles of excitement shivered down my spine. I was the last in the single file line making our way to the venue and as my friends marched on in front of me my attention was caught by the movement of shadows in the woods to my right. It was sure to be an animal lurking and I carried on walking, but then I heard a quiet whining sound. I stood still and peered into the trees. I could just make out the figures of three men and then I heard the whining again. Kurt noticed I was no longer behind him and came to check on me. He shone his torch in the direction of my gaze, illuminating a group of Indian men. They shifted, revealing a western girl in her twenties slouched on the forest floor, sobbing into her hands.

Concerned for her well-being, we made our way to her and asked if she was okay. Already the men were backing away. The girl didn't make much sense but as we got closer we could smell alcohol. It haunted her breath as she spoke random words at us, all the time rocking, forward and back, forward and back. She looked up and I thought I recognised her face, but I couldn't place her. There were a lot of travellers in Manali and it was very likely that I had seen her at the Mall or in one of the restaurants.

'How much have you had to drink?' Kurt asked as she fell to one side crying.

It was a while before an answer came, 'How much have you had to drink?' she mimicked. She stood, swayed and then burped loud enough to compete with the music. 'Vodka. Drank vodka. Some.'

'How much is "some"?' I suspected it was a lot but wanted confirmation from her if possible.

Giggling to herself she asked, 'Have you got a joint?'

'No.' Kurt replied.

'Oh, you're such a party poop,' was all she could say before she toppled back down to the floor.

I turned to Kurt, 'Listen mate, she can't stay here. God knows what could happen to her. I'll get her back into town and try and find out where she's staying.' My attention switched back to the girl, 'I'm going to get you to safety, okay?' I said slowly and clearly.

'Okay,' she responded with a dazed grin. Suddenly her cheeks bulged, her eyes widened with surprise and projectile vomit narrowly missed us.

Kurt stepped away from the foul-smelling chunks of undigested food that sat swimming in their own creamy pool on the grass, 'I am not sure you will find the party again on your own.'

'It's fine. I think it's for the best. I can't leave her here.' Kurt helped me put her arm across my shoulder and I walked her back with the sound of music gradually disappearing behind us. By the time we reached the Moondance Café I'd just about managed to get the address of where she was staying. Rather, she'd handed me her hotel key and I'd found out the name from the fob.

It was becoming increasingly difficult to keep her upright. She was drifting in and out of consciousness and because of the lateness of the hour, finding a rickshaw was impossible. At the top of the Mall I woke the sleeping driver of a taxi who was willing to take us to Vashisht where her hotel was situated. On route the cab stopped several times to allow her to narrowly miss the seats and vomit on the roadside. She was asleep when we arrived outside the hotel and the driver and I struggled with her to reach the door to her room. He nodded his head in Indian fashion and drove away with speed, no doubt thankful to rid himself of us and return to his dreams.

I laid her down on the bed on her side with the room's waste paper basket close by should she feel the need to eject more of her stomach contents. I sat on a chair browsing her guidebook, glancing up every so often to check on her. She slept through, snoring and grunting indecipherable words. There was only cause for alarm once when she rolled onto her back and panicked me by nearly choking on her own sick. I leapt from my chair and rolled her back over. With confidence that she was once again okay, I cleaned up the mess and sat waiting until she fell asleep once more. When the first light of dawn arrived, I propped some pillows behind her back and left her soundly asleep.

Outside the hotel was a hut selling refreshments. I took a moment to contemplate the evening over a bottle of lychee juice, with thoughts of the alternative had we not found her.

Once I caught an auto home, I sat on the porch smoking a cigarette and looking out to the mountains as the burning orange of sunrise emerged. Neria and Tyler were the first to return, holding hands, sheepishly smiling at me like teenagers who'd been caught out. I beamed back at their flushed faces and asked them how the party went. Amazing, I was told, the best they'd ever been to. Leaving them all loved up and staring into each other's eyes, I went to my room and collapsed onto my bed.

'Hey, Sam, do you want to get something to eat?' I paused with my reply, trying to focus on the face of the clock. It was a quarter past three.

'Uh, yeah, I guess I'm hungry. Give me a minute, I'll be right with you.'

It was at the Green Forest Café – past the Hadimba Temple, along a pathway and into another wood – where Kurt and I had lunch. It was as if it were the world's best kept secret, magically tucked away in the shadow of the tall pines. The only other diners were locals and they paid us no attention whatsoever. Kurt ordered ten momos: a type of dumpling filled with meat or vegetables, which is either steamed or fried. Kurt chose the steamed vegetable variety and requested two glasses of sweet lassi to wash them down. It was a meal I could certainly get used to. In fact, we found room for six more once the first ten were devoured. I relaxed into my chair feeling full and quite content, listening to the fresh breeze whispering through the trees.

Back at the house we picked up the bike. Kurt fancied a beer and knew of a place along the Mall. Up some stairs and in a room heaving with local men talking, laughing and a few slurring, we spotted a couple of free places at a table and gestured to the guys to ask if we could join them. Kurt ordered a cold bottle of the local brew and I settled happily for a Limca. A few rounds later and Kurt was somewhat tipsy. We took the option of a rickshaw ride home. There were only auto-rickshaws in Manali and even they sometimes had trouble managing the steep slopes, as ours did that evening. On reflection, we probably would have been better off walking.

By the time we got home it was dark. There were no lights on and the door was locked. Searching his pockets, Kurt realised he'd left the key in his room. Around the side of the house we noticed his bedroom window was slightly open. Grabbing a charpoy from inside the garage, we positioned it up against the side of the house and I steadied him as he climbed up and grabbed the ledge. With one final push he was in. He unlocked the front door and let me in and as I lit a candle, a small table and a half wooden tree trunk were revealed in the flickering light. Slightly uncomfortable, but long enough to seat three or four people, the wooden bench and table began to make the house feel like a home.

Neria, Sophie and Tyler returned a little while later and told us they'd found the table in the garage and the wood not far from the house.

'I've just bought these too,' said Tyler, producing a pair of mini-speakers from his bag. 'Thought they would enhance the ambience.' As he spoke he was already hooking up the speakers to his portable CD player. Sophie lit a tall candle and placed it on the table, around which we now all gathered. Kurt and I sat on the floor, while the others huddled together on the log. The music started, an album called 'Chants and Dances of the Native American' by Sacred Spirit. It was perfect. We laughed and joked, talked about our journeys and our lives. Kurt spoke of his love of his home – the city of Vienna – detailing the romantic opera houses and imperial palaces, the beautiful Danube and how the city at night was surely the inspiration for many a fairy tale. Vienna of course had its downsides – the café culture with its creamy coffees and delicious pastries meant gaining a few pounds was inevitable.

Sophie couldn't help interrupting, sharing with us her love for Nepal. She had been won over by the palaces and temples of Kathmandu's Durbar Square as soon as she arrived.

'That reminds me,' she said and walked off towards her bedroom. She wasn't gone long, returning with a huge smile on her face, as she proudly held up her prized possession. 'My didgeridoo! I bought it in Nepal. Hey, let's play something. Sam, you've got a guitar, right?'

What followed was a strange concoction and not one I thought any serious musicians would rush to emulate. Kurt provided the percussion by tapping an upturned cardboard box. With the basics covered Sophie and I took it in turns to play the lead and Neria chipped in now and then with her two-spoon-cymbals. Tyler then conjured up a kazoo from who knows where, which he was very good at, and our band was complete. Somehow it all worked so well.

18

The motorcycle was still around the back of the drinking house, propped up on its kickstand where we'd left it the night before. We gave the owner twenty rupees for taking care of it and rode into Vashisht to have the faulty horn repaired. On a sharp bend, not far from our destination, the tyres slipped on a patch of oil and the bike veered off the road, clattering down a hillside, sending us both tumbling with it. Unscathed we brushed ourselves down and checked for any damage to the bike. Thankfully there was none, having landed mainly on the grassy bank. We couldn't believe our luck. Kurt kicked the Enfield back into life and we continued with our eyes peeled for any further hazards.

Alongside the motorcycle shop there was a café and the perfect place to have breakfast while we waited for the bike to be repaired. Kurt suggested I try curd, 'It is very good for a bad stomach.' The sound of it didn't appeal at all, but when it arrived, sweetened with sugar, I was surprised just how good it tasted; like a thick natural yoghurt.

While Kurt spoke to the mechanic an Indian man approached me as I was lapping up the last of the curd. Through his left wrist was a long carving knife with bloodied bandages hanging down. Taken aback I gave him a few rupees which he gestured for the spectacle alone. Whether he'd inflicted the injury on himself or obtained it in some bizarre attack or accident, I didn't know, it was just nice to see the back of him. Before he left though, I asked for a photo. I was sure nobody back home would have believed me if I didn't have the evidence at hand. Kurt grinned, seeing my look of surprise and simply said, 'That's India for you.'

It was late afternoon by the time we reached the house and it was Neria and Kurt's turn to cook. We had thought it a good idea to devise a rota early on. While they busied themselves in the kitchen preparing the evening meal, I sat chatting with Sophie, Tyler and a friend of Neria's. Rutger was in his twenties and from Holland; tall, nearing bald, rugged features but with a bright smile. Kurt came from the kitchen looking quite distressed, 'I have forgotten to pick up cooking oil today. Neria reminded me earlier, but it completely slipped my mind. I think all the grocery stores are now closed.'

'Shall I see if any of our neighbours have any?' I offered, not that there were any houses particularly close to us.

I ventured out anyway and tried to navigate my way in the fading light. Twenty minutes passed and I came to a little timber home nestled away in the woods. A middle-aged gentleman with a woolly hat, sleeveless sweater and maroon shirt beneath answered the door. Greeting me with 'Namaste', he invited me into a large living area, where a lady of equal age, I presumed his wife, sat in the corner darning a blanket.

'Do you have any cooking oil, please?' I asked, hoping he would understand, but he didn't. His wife, who wore woollen garments and silver jewellery, waggled her head and went to the kitchen area to prepare chai. Had she thought I asked for tea maybe? I couldn't be sure, but they were both so nice and offered a comfy cushion for me to sit on, making me feel incredibly welcome. I didn't have the heart to decline.

Looking around the basic space, there was very little, but it seemed they had everything they needed: a mattress on the ground where they slept, a small kitchen area and a tin bath. They appeared content, happy to be with each other and thankful for what they had rather than wishing for things they didn't.

I pictured Kurt working himself into a frenzy in the kitchen and thought I should make a move. Spotting a frying pan hanging from the low ceiling, I pointed to it and mimed, holding my clasped hand out and making the sound of sizzling. They cocked their heads and then the gentleman realised my request. He pulled the pan from its hook and offered it to me. I took it from him and poured an invisible bottle of oil and circled my finger around. He laughed, re-hung the pan and picked up a rectangular bottle half full of oil from a shelf. I offered him some money, but he shook his head and pushed the bottle into my hands. I thanked him and in return he placed his hands together and smiled. I was about to leave when I saw the face of a small boy appear from the top of the wooden stairs. He stared in awe at the stranger in his home. I smiled and waved. He giggled and then disappeared into the comfort of the shadows. Thanking the couple again, I motioned with my camera for a photo. They happily obliged and then I left them at the doorway as they waved goodbye.

When I entered the kitchen, bottle in hand, Kurt laughed, 'I am impressed. Thank you. We have been preparing as much as we can, so we will eat soon.'

We sat down to our meal; a simple vegetable stir fry with noodles. It was not something I would have chosen to eat in England where my diet shamefully relied too heavily on convenience food, including regular visits to McDonald's and Pizza Hut. It had taken me a while to adjust, but now I was enjoying the home cooked meal made fresh by my friends.

As the evening swept by, we sat on the wooden floorboards playing Blackjack, the only card game I knew, and one we had to teach Neria how to play. I took a moment to observe the people around me and wondered how much of my personality had been crafted by those I had encountered in my past. Layers of paranoia and fear, melancholy and distrust building up over time affecting how I interacted with each new person I met. Already I felt the warmth and kindness of this new unit unburdening me from the dark coat upon my soul, allowing a brighter and happier me to break through. Little could they have known how much they had already changed my life. Oblivious to my thoughts, they laid their cards down one by one.

Life in Manali was panning out well. It very quickly felt like home and it was hard to believe that only a short time ago I was so desperate and alone that I was ready to give up on India. If it hadn't been for Kurt, there's no doubt in my mind that I would be back in England. Instead I was here, sharing a house with four new acquaintances with whom I had never felt more accepted. We didn't necessarily do very much, it was a small town and there were limited things to do, but that was part of the charm. Some days we would simply hang out as a group, while other times we would break off and explore the surroundings either individually or in pairs. It was amazing to feel so free, to wake each morning and spontaneously decide on the day's agenda. For the first time in my life I had no restrictions, no one telling me what to do. I was master of my own destiny and that applied to my four new friends as well.

Early one morning I was woken by the sound of local people talking outside. Looking out to the orchard I saw three ladies and a man picking apples and collecting them in coned wicker baskets strapped to their backs. They were dressed very similarly to the family who had given me the cooking oil. When they'd finished, they separated, walking down the hill via a maze of pathways I hadn't noticed before. The others were still asleep so I ventured out on my own to explore these trails, starting with the nearest to my bedroom window.

After a while I came out to an area that was full of tents and small shacks. From a distance, I observed the community of men dressed in colourful turbans and lungis and women wearing red and gold saris washing their clothes, looking after infants or watching small television sets from inside their makeshift homes. They didn't appear to be from this area, looking more as if they had come from a more southerly state. Close to the camp was a single storey building with an open doorway and as I passed by, I noticed shelves stacked with books and an elderly gentleman sitting behind a counter lost in a novel. I poked my head around the doorway and asked if the books were for sale.

'Yes, come in, my friend,' he said. 'These books are second hand, mostly sold or donated by travellers like yourself, though we do have a selection of new items too.'

I browsed the shelves and my eye caught sight of a book about Phoolan Devi, the Bandit Queen – a modern day Robin Hood. From a life of poverty, cruelty and hardship, she delivered justice to rape victims, robbed the rich to give to the poor and was later imprisoned for her actions. Due to continuous popular support and media controversy she was released and elected to the Indian Parliament.

I picked it up and at the counter I spotted a brand-new Bartholomew fold-away map of the Indian Sub-Continent. Thinking it would be a nice idea to mark my trip so far, I added it to my purchase along with a fine nib black pen. I asked the gentleman about the people in the tents. He said it was a Rajasthani refugee camp, growing by the day.

I had a quiet breakfast in the Moondance Café reading my book and enjoying a cup of hot chocolate. I missed coffee so much and was yet to find that perfect cup in India. Tyler had told me about Manu Temple supposedly a short walk from the café. I packed away my things and recommenced my walkabout. In Old Manali it looked as if nothing had changed for hundreds of years; old wooden and mud built properties with cattle grazing in the yards, men sat smoking pipes and ladies in hand woven clothing gossiping the day away. Life here, as for most of Manali, was so laid back. There was none of the hostility of people back home rushing to work and not caring who they bumped into to get there. People here moved at a snail's pace, smiled and laughed, and seemed to go about their business with happiness in their hearts.

The temple came into sight after a short walk along a muddy path. According to Hindu philosophy, Manu was said to be the first king of the earth and the building was the only temple in India dedicated to the sage. Timber framed, it had two layers of roofing with a tower at the centre ascending to a smaller roof. Swept with pine to their snowy summits, the view of the mountains from the temple was spectacular. I was lucky to arrive on such a beautiful day with a rich blue sky and eiderdown clouds passing overhead. It didn't take long to look around and after a while I returned the way I came.

I decided not to go home just yet, but rather discover more of the town centre. Where Kurt and I first met Neria and Sophie in the Mall I stopped to observe all the different kinds of people. There were western backpackers, Kashmiris and Tibetans, nomad shepherds and Kullu folk; the men in woollen jumpers with pillbox caps, the women in home spun garments with silver jewellery and conical baskets upon their backs. There were Indian holiday makers; men in kurtas or light cotton shirts and trousers, women in colourful saris or salwar kameez.

A little way along from the post office, I stopped outside a Tibetan Monastery and was approached immediately by a smiling teenaged monk in scarlet robes, 'Please come in,' he said, and I followed him through the gates. 'This Gadhan Thekchhokling Gompa. Built in 1969 and all good peoples are welcome to come and look around. Where you from?'

'England,' I replied.

'Ah England, you are very long way from home. Please, spin prayer wheel for wisdom and thoughts of peoples you miss.' He took me along a row of cylindrical golden prayer wheels set into a wall and span the first, gesturing me to do the same. 'You say mantra: Om Mani Padme Hum, it mean, Hail to the Jewel in the Lotus.' I followed his actions, spinning the wheels and reciting the words in unison. At the end, with a wooden beaded mala wrapped around his fingers, he placed both his hands together and bowed slightly, to which I mirrored his actions.

'Please also see Himalayan Nyingmapa Gompa near bazaar,' he said. 'I go now, but please you stay and enjoy peace of gompa.' I thanked him for his time and he bowed again and disappeared through an ornate wooden doorway.

This had been my favourite temple in Manali. The white square building with a bright yellow corrugated-iron pagoda roof was decorated with blue fascias above the yellow windows. There was an impressive entrance painted with dragons and elaborate swirling patterns. Inside was a towering golden statue of a seated Buddha with finely painted features. Walking through the courtyard to leave I passed a tall stupa and large oval stones engraved with colourful Tibetan scripture piled against a wall. I found the Himalayan Nyingmapa Gompa nearby which was very much like the previous gompa, but on a smaller scale.

Around the corner, I returned to the post office, past the Moc Restaurant and stopped at a shop selling cassette tapes. I took a chance and bought, The Elements – Earth by Vanraj Bhatia. Giving some change to a couple of beggars – a middle-aged lady with a mild form of leprosy and an elderly man with a short white beard whose right hand was missing – I continued my way home.

I put in my earphones and listened to the atmospheric sounds of sitars and tabla drums all the way back to the house. Outside Tyler greeted me at the door. He stood smoking a joint, 'When in Rome,' he said, coughing and squinting as the breeze blew smoke into his face.

He passed the spliff to me. 'You're a bit of dark horse, Tyler, I had no idea you smoked charas,' I said.

'You're a fine one to talk,' he laughed. 'I don't usually smoke it, but I fancied some and asked Sophie to pick it up for me.'

'Sophie smokes it too?' I passed it back to him just as Sophie arrived at the doorway, joint in mouth and lighter in hand. 'Busted,' I laughed. She laughed too and tilted her head to one side to avoid setting her hair on fire as she lit the spliff.

'We better head out soon if we're gonna get what we need for dinner,' she said, from behind a cloud of smoke. It was mine and Sophie's turn to cook.

'What we having then?' asked Tyler.

'You'll have to wait and see,' Sophie replied and then turned to flash me a smile.

At the top of the Mall there was a street to the left with stalls filled with fruits and vegetables, which is where we picked up our daily supplies. Sophie found a cardboard box in the garage and brought it with her to carry our shopping. She said that the Indian government was trying to enforce a strict ban on plastic bags for the sake of the environment. With our box filled with vegetables from the market, we went in search of somewhere that sold a jar of the chocolate malted drink Bournvita. We stopped at every place on route that sold clothing or jewellery and whilst I waited outside with the groceries, Sophie indulged herself with the many items that caught her eye. She smiled guiltily each time she came out with her hands filled.

Next door to the shop that sold the Bournvita was a butchery, but unlike any I'd seen in England. The butcher sat in an open wooden framed window hacking away at a carcass while flies settled and buzzed around the meat. It was the mountain of rotting goat's heads below the window that left me quite stunned. Aside from the crawling flies, the skulls were quite enough to keep me from the thought of eating meat. Sophie however seemed quite unfazed by it all. I think travelling around for so long had hardened her to such sights.

Neria and Rutger were leaving the house in search of another party as we returned. They assured us they would be back in time for dinner with the location of the venue so that we could all go together. Six hours later, there was still no sign of them and we were becoming worried that something bad might have happened. Rain spattered against the house, heavy and unrelenting while the wind howled and danced through the orchard. I suggested they may have taken shelter at Rutger's hotel, which didn't seem to go down too well with Tyler. By midnight we retired to our rooms, still none the wiser as to their whereabouts.

I heard a knock at my door. It was Sophie. She was smiling sweetly and said, 'Do you fancy coming into my room for a chat? We could have some Bournvita.'

I wasn't that tired and saw no reason to refuse the invitation, especially when the alternative was staring at the enormous insects that were accumulating at my windows, hypnotised by the light. She went off to make the hot chocolate and brought back two steaming cups, which we nursed for ages as we talked about our lives prior to India. I told her about my ex-girlfriend, Saskia, and how at times I still missed her. I also told her about a course we attended together studying aromatherapy, reflexology and massage. Realising I had been rambling on a bit, I paused to ask her, 'And you? Was there anybody special before you came out here?'

Her expression changed from a relaxed, carefree look to one of surprise. She stumbled before she answered, 'There was someone.' She looked down at the hem of her trouser leg and fiddled with a frayed thread, 'But like you and Saskia, it didn't quite work out between us.'

She seemed reluctant to talk, but I pursued nonetheless, 'You didn't get along too well then?'

'We got on very well,' she looked up and then back to the thread. 'Until I told him I was pregnant.'

'You have a child?'

'No. I lost it after three months.'

'Oh, I'm really sorry. Do you still see him?'

'No, he shot through the minute he found out I was expecting, left me a handwritten note saying he wasn't ready to be a father.' Her eyes weighed with sadness, but she raised a smile, false, but enough to tell me this part of the conversation was over. 'So, you're really good at massage?' She reached over to her backpack and withdrew a small bottle of massage oil. 'Would you mind?'

Before I could say anything, she was removing her blouse and laying down on her front. I perched on the bed next to her and undid her bra, which she then completely removed while I was rubbing a small amount of oil between my palms. Gently I slid my hands along the contours of her back and shoulders for a few minutes and then began kneading the taught muscles. The stress and worry she had gone through had certainly taken its toll. I carried on for about half an hour and then stood up to look for something to wipe my hands on.

'I think I should leave it there,' I said. 'It's not good to do too much in the first session.'

'Stay the night with me,' she said softly, but assertively as she sat up and faced me.

I was taken aback by her proposition and fumbled for an

appropriate answer. She was undeniably very attractive and as I stood looking at her I couldn't help but steal the odd glance at her half naked body. For a moment, she held my gaze, then lifted her arms and began untying her hair, which up until that point had been pulled back into a high ponytail. She took her time all the while showing off her perfectly proportioned curves. It would have been easy to stay and I'm sure many in the same situation wouldn't have hesitated, but as we made eye contact again I realised this wasn't what I wanted. I had been so touched by the friendships made in Manali and that meant more to me than anything. After tonight I knew nothing more would develop with Sophie and so it would be wrong to stay with her. Using the excuse, I had come over tired, I smiled meekly, said goodnight and left for my room.

19

Mid-morning Neria returned with Rutger, hand in hand. It appeared they were now an item. Tyler's face was awash with disappointment, but he accepted the fact they were now together graciously. I was surprised by Neria; I hadn't expected her to be so casual with her affections nor to show such a lack of consideration for Tyler's feelings.

The six of us had breakfast at the Dhungri German Bakery, which was awkward. Aside from the obvious tension around Tyler and Neria, Sophie and I were in a very different place with each other now. No matter how hard I tried to converse with her she wouldn't entertain any interaction with me. At best I was met with short, sharp answers, but where she could get away with it, she simply chose to ignore me. I hadn't meant to upset her. I had only tried to be decent, but she wasn't taking rejection well. I hoped it was a temporary set-back and that once the dust had settled we could return to normal again.

Ahead of me in the corner of the restaurant, I noticed an old man, staring longingly into a glass of chai. I shivered at the sight of him. He looked remarkably like my grandfather. There were a few times when I was younger when I spotted him sitting outside a bar in Ostend, glass of wine or beer nestled in his hand. I never approached him. I just observed from a distance and carried on with my day. My friends' voices became muted and I looked at the stranger not saying a word. Suddenly feeling sick and insecure I made my excuses to the group and caught a rickshaw into town. I decided to phone my mum. It took a few rings before there was any answer and I nearly hung up. Just before doing so I heard a quiet, slightly confused response. 'Hello?'

'Hi mum, it's me. Are you okay?'

'Huh, oh, Sam, it's good to hear from you. What time is it?'

Having forgotten about the time difference, I realised she must still be in bed. 'Sorry Mum, it's early, I'll call back later.'

'No, no, don't do that. It's okay. Are you still in Nunny Till?'

I smiled, 'No, I've left Naini Tal now. I've met some really nice people and I'm sharing a house with them in a town called Manali, in the mountains.'

'Oh, that's nice dear. Your old boss called. The new manager isn't working out and you can have your job back if you return as soon as possible. You'll even get a pay rise.'

'No, you're all right, thanks. Right now, I can't even imagine working in England again. In fact, this is the first time I've thought about my job since I left.'

'Oh okay, I'll let them know.'

'Listen mum, I'm running out of money, I'll phone you again soon.'

'Okay darling, take care. I love you.'

'You too.'

I walked slowly, not caring where the road took me. I hoped the trail I found leading into the top of Dhungri forest would swallow me up, and to an extent the density of the wood did just that.

'Hello mister.' Three Tibetan boys had crept up and were now standing dirty faced in front of me. 'Take picture, take picture,' they called out.

One climbed on to the other's shoulders, stood and somehow assisted the third boy as he scrambled up on to the second boy's shoulders. For a few moments, they balanced, arms out, looking like a strange totem pole until they came crashing down to the grass in a fit of giggles. I couldn't help but laugh along with them. Somehow this beautiful country had a way of frustrating the life out of me but could also warm my heart like nothing else.

'Baksheesh,' they said, holding out their hands. I laughed and gave each of them five rupees each before they ran off chuckling.

Back at the house, I found Kurt and Tyler in the living area. Neria and Sophie were both in their rooms packing. Neria had lost her travellers cheques so the two of them were heading to Delhi to try and replace them. They hoped to return in a couple of days.

'We need to return the bikes today,' said Kurt. 'Tyler and I were going to go out for one last ride. Do you want to join us?'

'Yeah Okay. Where are we going?'

'Naggar Castle is worth a visit,' replied Tyler. 'It's not too far.'

Perched upon a hill, Naggar Castle overlooked the forested mountains of the Kullu Valley. The timber and stone castle was built in the early seventeenth century by the King of Himachal, Raja Jagat Singh. It was now a hotel and a quaint little café within the grounds was the perfect place for us to relax for a couple of hours. We sat quietly for the first half an hour, each of us staring out at the mountains that loom over the little villages below. I was the first to break the silence by asking the guys what they knew about the Tibetan folk in Manali. They told me that many towns throughout northern India were places of exile for Tibetans following the invasion of their country by China. India had granted sanctuary to Tibetans so they may continue their culture undisturbed. 'It is most common to find Tibetans in mountainous regions such as Himachal Pradesh, Ladakh and Sikkim,' said Kurt.

'There are refugee camps in Delhi and other larger Indian cities too,' added Tyler.

Kurt then continued to explain how the fourteenth Dalai Lama took refuge in Dharamsala, three hundred kilometres west of Manali, in 1959.

'It was there that the government of Tibet in Exile was set up to rehabilitate Tibetan refugees and restore freedom and happiness in Tibet.'

'I think the girls plan to go to Dharamsala next. How about you, Kurt?' I asked, already knowing that this was the end of Tyler's trip and he was heading home when we all left Manali.

'Leh I think; I would like to see Leh again. It is beautiful and the road up there is out of this world. Why don't you come with me? I am sure you would love it.'

Honoured by Kurt's offer and delighted to continue my trip with a friend rather than on my own, I answered instinctively without hesitation.

'Definitely. It sounds amazing.'

I set about making morning Bournvita for everyone and left a glass at Kurt's door with a knock. Tyler's door was ajar. He placed the book he was reading down and invited me in. I sat on a blue cushion on the floor opposite him as he took a dark varnished wooden box from beneath his bed. Inside was a chillum, a brown rag and a circular flattened disc of charas. He prepared a smoke and passed it on.

'You've come fully prepared,' I laughed, pointing at the box.

'For everything,' he replied, taking the pipe from me.

I asked him what he was doing before India. 'I lived in Japan for five years. Went out there with fifty dollars in my pocket and a camera over my shoulder and made money taking people's portraits.'

'Wow, that's pretty impressive. Not sure if I'd have the guts to do that.' I took a sip of my drink, allowing the steam to soften my skin.

'You're here, aren't you? Not many people would have the guts to just pack up their lives and do what you've done so far.'

I considered his words for a moment, 'More luck than bravery I think. Who knows where I would have been had I not met you and Kurt.'

'Hey man, don't be so hard on yourself. You're a lot stronger than you think; you just have to believe in yourself a bit more.' He went about making another chillum and opened the window to relieve the room of incense and charas smoke. 'So, you're going to Leh? If you get a chance, you should visit the south too. There's a place called Hampi, it's like something out of the Flintstones; incredible rock boulders, awesome place. And Goa, you've got to go to Goa. Find Arambol Beach, it's so quiet with hardly any tourists; white sands and fishing boats, so idyllic. Watch out for smoking pot in Goa though, plain clothes cops pose as dealers and target travellers. Harsh, dude.'

Kurt came in waving the smoke away with his hand, 'Hey guys, breakfast at Pete's?'

'Sure,' I said, offering the chillum to him. 'Who's Pete?'

'I do not smoke, thank you. Pete is Pete, you will see.' Kurt looked over at Tyler and they smiled knowingly at each other.

At the bottom of the hill, just before the Mall, an alleyway led off to the right between two buildings. Above a doorway next to a wall with a huge spiral of colours, hung a sign announcing, Pete's Café. In a shaded area of the café an old Indian man with a long grey beard and wild straggly hair was playing chess with a westerner. On seeing us he excused himself and walked over to where we were standing. Draped over his skinny frame was a tweed blazer with a tie dyed t-shirt beneath, 'Hello, my friends, please take seat. What can I get you gentlemen?' he asked in a husky voice.

'Hi Pete, how are you? Three bowls of porridge please, one chai and two bhang lassis,' Tyler requested, and looked to us in confirmation.

'I am okay, thank you. It is good to see you again. I have met you both before, on different time though. But you, you are new to my eyes,' Pete said, holding out his hand to me.

'Sam, nice to meet you,' I replied, extending my hand.

He withdrew his without shaking, placed his thumb on his nose and waggled his fingers and then placed his hands together in a namaste. He let out a hearty laugh followed by severe coughing. 'My health not as good as once was,' he said, trying to recompose himself.

We took a seat in the garden. Breakfast was served and I noticed the lassi had strange particles in it, 'Tyler, what is this stuff?' I asked, eyeing the liquid with suspicion.

'Try it and tell me,' he replied, grinning mischievously. I'd seen this type of grin before. Kids at school gave me the same grin right before I was led into something I would later regret. However, on this occasion Tyler was drinking the lassi too. I took a good long gulp. There was something very familiar about it. I analysed the after taste, trying to determine the answer.

Whatever it was kicked in fast. It was as if I'd left my body temporarily and was watching us from a distance. A sense of wellbeing consumed me, followed by slight nausea. Pins and needles cramped my head and I had to steady myself against the table as I came back down to earth.

'Got any ideas yet?' I could just make out Tyler's voice, but it was muffled.

'You are liking my bhang lassi then?' Pete laughed, exposing the only two teeth on his bottom gum. I made a circle with my thumb and forefinger.

Tyler and Kurt returned from paying the bill. This was the moment I dreaded – getting up. It wouldn't have been a problem had my legs felt like they were still there, but they seemed to have taken a complete leave of absence. Kurt laughed, helping me out of my chair, 'See, you will drink Pete's bhang lassi.'

I had to sit on a wall to catch my breath with a perfume of fresh marijuana filling my nose. A little time passed, although it felt like a lifetime, and I began to regain my senses. My friends escorted me out into the street.

'Check out that trailing rickshaw, guys.' My attention quickly turned to a passing sadhu who looked puzzled by my close inspection of his fabulous beard. Kurt was quick to apologise and gave a hefty donation.

'Come on, dude,' Tyler laughed. I ambled back up the hill, staring at anything and everything while Kurt and Tyler did their very best to stay in time with me. We came to a tree set back from the road with ibex horns and knives sticking into it and many more metallic objects such as swords and tridents strewn at the base.

'Uh guys, someone really hates that tree,' I remarked, transfixed.

Kurt laughed, 'This tree is dedicated to Ghatokach, the son of Hadimba and Bhima. These are offerings made by villagers.'

I noticed something else on my left I hadn't noticed before; a small temple perched on a large boulder amongst the apple trees.

Bhang lassi may have made me the most stoned I'd ever felt, but my perception was now top notch. I was led away into Dhungri Forest where Kurt and Tyler sat me on some rocks while they paid their respects to Hadimba at the temple. When they returned I was lying on the floor gazing up at the trees muttering, 'Heavy leaves, man.'

Apart from an afternoon visit to the Green Forest Café where I consumed ten vegetable momos to myself, I spent most the day back at the house flat on my back in my room listening to music. Later in the evening, by which time I'd made a full recovery, I was introduced to a friend of Tyler's. Floyd was from Germany and had been having problems with his back. 'A little bird told me you are really good at massage. I mentioned it to Floyd and he asked if you wouldn't mind,' Tyler said.

'Of course not, lovely to meet you Floyd,' I said.

'I've been climbing recently and have pulled a few muscles I think.'

After a forty-minute session in Tyler's room Floyd stood, stretched and thanked me over and over. 'That feels amazing, my friend, you've done wonders. Please take this.' He gave me two hundred rupees.

'Oh no, please, don't worry about it. Any friend of Tyler's is a friend of mine.'

He insisted, 'Please, it would make me feel better if you accepted. And then, if I have any problems in the future, I can call on you again.'

After Floyd left, Tyler came to see me, 'You can make some serious money out here. You've got real talent. Use it.'

Over the next few days Kurt, Tyler and I spent quite a lot of time around the house. We meditated and learnt some Tae Kwon Do from Kurt, although he found Tyler and I very frustrating, not taking it seriously and squawking like Bruce Lee. Tyler taught us some yoga which we practised in the orchards. One morning I mentioned I was becoming quite concerned about my finances, saying I wasn't sure how much time I would have left in India.

Tyler reinforced the idea that I should charge for my massage services. 'Put some posters up around Leh. There are so many trekkers there, you should do well.' I held it in mind, not having a better alternative in sight.

'Sam, you have not been to the actual town of Vashisht yet, have you?' Kurt asked.

'I've been close to it when we took the bikes back and when I took the girl back to her hotel from the party, but never into the village itself, no.'

'Then today we will go. Tyler, are you coming too?'

'Na, you guys go ahead. I've got laundry to do and I've got to go to the post office.'

Kurt and I took an auto to The Mall where he picked up three bottles of beer before taking the same rickshaw to Vashisht. The ancient village reminded me very much of Old Manali. A grassy pathway led us into an avenue of aged timber buildings and newer white concrete hotels and restaurants. Opposite an ornate wooden temple, we had lunch.

Kurt took me away from the village on what became a very rewarding hike. Gigantic rock faces with powerful waterfalls gushing down to the Beas to our right and on our left, a horizon of snow fringed mountains. We climbed into the hills to overlook the Himalayas and were casually walking along when Kurt suddenly grabbed me by the shoulder and ordered me to stop where I was and keep still. He pointed a few inches away at a section of scaly skin moving stealthily through the undergrowth. 'Snake,' he whispered. 'Maybe a cobra or viper, either way it may be extremely dangerous. They are very fast and very agile, so stay still and let it pass.' I didn't need to be told twice. I was totally fixed to the spot, eyeing the reptile with caution. It slithered away and when we were sure it was gone we made tracks from the area.

We found a place where the bough of a tree made a good seat to relax, providing a perfect view of the valley. Kurt withdrew a bottle of beer from his shoulder bag and offered it to me. 'Not for me, thanks mate,' I said, and pulled out a bottle of water. There we sat for a good couple of hours, chatting about life, our travels, Manali and the friends we had made.

'So, are you ready to fly home?' he asked.

The question came out of the blue and caught me by surprise, 'England? Not for a while yet I hope. Why do you ask?'

'So, Manali is everything you wished for? I will not have to buy your ticket back to Delhi then?'

I cottoned on, 'Ha ha, no. You were so right about this place, thank you. Since I've been here I've thought about little else but the moment I'm in, absorbing every minute with hardly a thought about the past or future.'

'Ah yes, we can only live in this moment and try to make the most of it. You never know what fate has in store around each corner.'

The more Kurt drank, the more relaxed he became, and the more philosophical his conversation, 'We are all one you know, all connected somehow in the fabric of time. By chance strangers may unconsciously know each other's past and dictate their destiny.'

'What?' I laughed as he took to standing, swaying and looking out to a veil of mist hovering the peaks.

'Even the clouds evaporate and regenerate over us, following us through life, witnessing our presence and journey on this earth.' He rambled some more, making less and less sense and by the end of the third bottle, he stumbled back into the seat of the bough. 'My, this beer is stronger than I thought.' He readjusted himself, 'I have a little headache, I'm just going to close my eyes for a moment.'

He looked like a child asleep, curled in the foetal position, but the snoring that emanated from him could have been that of an elephant. It gave me time to think about what he said and how I came to be here with him now. I looked back to Dehra Dun and the hotel room and thought once again about my youth. I felt a sudden pang of anger towards my stepfather. All the years of being alone in my room while I saw the rest of the world go on as normal around me. While I was restricted to one measly meal a day – no breakfast or lunch – he ate like a king. While he spent money on new cars, kitted out the home with all the latest mod cons, and even bought himself a speedboat, I was left with nothing. No toys or books, no TV set nor a radio. After endless days of intense bullying at school, black and bruised, all my father did was turn away as if I didn't exist. Better to be out of sight and out of mind, than a problem to deal with.

Pulling myself back to the here and now, I gazed ahead to the light and shade swaying across the surface of the mountains. I glanced over to Kurt, my friend, my brother. The angst dissolved into sorrow, slipped below the surface, and like oil and water, security floated above the darkness.

I let him be for an hour or so. When he awoke, bleary eyed, he smiled and said, 'Let's get something to eat. It is an hour's walk back to the village and the sun is lowering. We would never find our way back down again in the dark.'

We climbed down from the tree and as we did so a small white dog appeared from the undergrowth. The little fellow accompanied us back to Vashisht. 'I've seen so many dogs in a bad way in India,' I said. 'It's so sad to see them in such a sorry state.' I stopped to make a fuss of him.

'Yes, very sad indeed. These feral dogs are known as pi dogs. Some can be friendly, but others can be hostile. Most are riddled with fleas, scabies and mange, and some even have rabies. This one looks fine though. We shall call him Springer for the spring in his step.' Kurt, as I, was quite taken by him. When we reached the village, the pooch stopped, looked at us as if to say goodbye, and trotted off the way he came. On a rooftop overlooking the hills we took our evening meal. The sun set and the peaks shaded, creating scenes of absolute serenity.

20

Neria and Sophie arrived back from Delhi with new travellers' cheques.

'How did the police go?' I enquired.

'Lucky I reported it with the Manali police first otherwise I'm sure it would have been a completely different story altogether,' Neria replied.

'We spoke to a couple of guys earlier in the Mall,' Sophie said. 'There's a full moon party tonight a couple of miles outside Vashisht. You guys are up for it, right?' She was directing this more towards Kurt and Tyler than me, but we all confirmed our places anyway. I had been mistaken for thinking a little time and distance would have washed any awkwardness away between Sophie and me. She was still as frosty as she had been before she left for Delhi. I could understand her being upset and embarrassed the morning after I had rejected her, but I'd thought she was mature enough to have gotten over it by now.

Two rickshaws took us into Vashisht where we walked along the same pathway out of the village Kurt and I travelled a few days prior. An hour on and the five of us diverted away from the road, crossed a suspension bridge and into a dark forest. Dance music filtered through the trees and little by little a large area of light appeared, figures dancing in time to the beat. A guy at the gate took one hundred rupees each from us and issued a small brown card with Full Moon Party, Manali – 6pm-9am written upon it and with what looked like a red thumbprint stamped in the centre.

The music was loud, very loud, and the atmosphere was amazing. Everybody was smiling, open and friendly; fused together by this moment in time under the light of the full moon. Through strobed lighting Tyler approached me in staccato movements and passed me a joint, 'This party's totally awesome, man,' he shouted above the thumping bass.

'Totally,' I yelled back, nodding my head up and down.

'Kurt looks like he's getting into it.'

I looked over to where Kurt was pulling some crazy moves on the dance floor and even attempting break dancing.

We joined him, Neria and Sophie, plus Rutger and Floyd. Although I was not so hot at dancing myself, I really didn't care, I was having the time of my life. I had no idea where I got the energy from and at 5.30, when dawn arrived, I stood speechless as the silhouettes of three soaring mountains surrounding us gradually came into view. As the light revealed further detail I realised just how close we were to the base of the mountain on our right. It felt so near that I could almost touch the jagged lanes of snow. Small clusters of pine forests dotted the green slopes and an eagle glided above. I was utterly spellbound.

The clock struck nine and the music came to a stop. Everybody let out a huge cheer and applauded the talent of the Japanese DJ crew who packed away their turntables while some of us hung around on a wall with our backs to a small lake. An Israeli guy next to me took a deep toke of his chillum, held it to his head and said aloud, 'Boom Shiva,' and passed it along to me. I inhaled and passed it along the line. An Australian guy with blond dreadlocks and a goatee played a set of bongos, a Korean girl played flute and Sophie launched into her didgeridoo. Everything seemed so surreal.

Over to my far right was a Japanese girl. Her complexion was smooth, almost pure white. Had she sat completely still, I could have mistaken her for a porcelain doll. She turned to catch me looking at her and my stomach filled with butterflies. I plucked up the courage to sit next to her, 'Hi, I'm Sam. Did you enjoy the party?'

She smiled, bowed her head slightly, 'Konichi wa, I am Harumi. Yes, I have a wonderful time. And Sam, how have you found the entertainment this evening?'

'Amazing, the best party I've ever been to. The music was fantastic and the scenery... wow!' She placed a cigarette to her lips. I leaned in and lit it, holding her gaze for a moment. She smiled again, rose and said, 'I go now. Nice to have met you, Sam.'

Kurt caught my attention and nodded over to where Harumi was now hand in hand with the head DJ. I guess she was his girl.

Kurt, Tyler and I left the venue, walking ten yards or so ahead of the three Japanese DJs and two girls that made up the full moon crew. At the end of the long footbridge Tyler began to bob up and down, sending waves along the wooden planks. In unison, the full moon crew did the same. This went on for a few minutes until Tyler slowed the pace to a stop and to applause from us all. They caught up with us and asked if we would like to share breakfast with them in Vashisht.

Breakfast was a mix of steamed rice, soup and rolled omelettes. We sat on the floor at a low table at the apartment the crew had hired for their stay. I noticed the head DJ's front teeth were filed into sharp points – strange I thought, but also kind of cool. After an hour or so the three of us excused ourselves, thanking them kindly for their hospitality.

At our house, we talked about the night for a while until the call of our beds couldn't be ignored any longer. It was late afternoon and none of us had slept for over thirty hours. I closed my eyes to visions of the most beautiful place on earth and the sounds of trance filled my head as I gently slid into a comfortable slumber.

It was 8am the following morning when I awoke again. I couldn't believe how long I'd slept. Impressed by the scenery yesterday Kurt and I decided to walk the same route again hoping to find the party venue, this time armed with a camera.

The weather was warm with a light breeze and the sky blue and cloudless. After a hearty breakfast at the Green Forest Café we hailed an auto into Vashisht. We walked the length of the village and at the end I noticed a wooden doorway with intricate carved circles around the frame. I stopped to take a photo as two pi dogs came along for some attention. One was cream coloured. His brown companion was slightly larger in size. Kurt had a packet of biscuits and fed one to each of them which they gobbled up in no time. They had a soft nature and seemed to like us (or our biscuits) as they accompanied us on our stroll.

The vista was as stunning as it had been the day before; boulders painted with coloured Tibetan script, neck cranking waterfalls cascading and crashing, maize terraces and marijuana fields set against a background of crisp alpine scenery. Around every bend was something new and exciting. The serenity was soon shattered however by the approach of a main road. Trucks and cars roared past, scaring the life out of our little friends. We managed to cross safely but were then confronted by four ferocious dogs defending their territory. Our brown companion scarpered the way we came, narrowly avoiding an auto-rickshaw as he darted across the road. The cream coloured dog was left to deal with the aggressors by himself.

'Kurt, I'm going to grab our friend. You scare the other dogs away,' I shouted above the barking and traffic. I picked up our dog and Kurt ran towards the others, arms waving above his head and yelling at them. Kurt was not a small guy by any means and it was enough to send them scampering in all directions. He came over from the chase and gave our friend a good stroke, him licking us in return. I placed him on the ground and he trotted beside us, looking up from time to time with what appeared to be a smile on his face. We gave him the name Tic-Tac.

Kurt agreed to walk ahead with Tic-Tac along the wooden footbridge, so I could take a photograph of the two of them. It was a priceless moment as I looked out to the mountains and Beas below, and to my friends nearing the end of the bridge. I couldn't believe I was here. As we emerged into the grounds of the party, I noticed that the large fenced off area where we danced last night was in fact a set of tennis courts.

A spectacled middle-aged man stepped out from a house adjacent to the courts and greeted us. He was Dutch and the owner of the tennis club, who occasionally rented the grounds to party organisers. We were invited to stay and have coffee. He gestured for us to take a seat at a modest wooden table and went into the house returning a minute later with a bowl of water for Tic-Tac. After making a fuss of him he commented on what a lovely dog he was and sat down at the table with us. We had just learned that he spent six months a year here with his wife as she appeared, carrying a tray of cups and a pot of freshly brewed coffee. It tasted amazing. I was so grateful for a decent cup of coffee at last.

With Tic-Tac still in tow Kurt and I decided to climb the hill that stood in front of the nearest mountain, hoping it would provide a great vantage point. An hour passed uneventfully, but we then heard something coming our way. And fast. We panicked at the loud growl ahead of us, not knowing which way to turn. Kurt was concerned it might be a brown bear and unsure of what to do he tried to see if he could find an alternative escape route, 'If we run, it could take chase,' he said. 'We must stand our ground, shout at the top of voices and wave our arms above our heads in hope of scaring it.'

'Are you crazy?' I said with my heart pounding as the creature fast approached.

Tic-Tac rose on his haunches, growling and barking. Suddenly the beast emerged and we screamed and waved our arms. A local man yelped and fell back upon seeing us, clutching the long, felled tree he was dragging on the ground behind him. We halted the commotion instantly, and Kurt and I looked at each other and burst into hysterical laughter at our mistake. We assisted the poor man to his feet and apologised for thinking he was a bear. He had no idea what we were saying and quite puzzled, was quick to continue down the hill, leaving us chuckling behind him.

It was another hour before we reached the top, but the climb was worth the effort. The opposite mountain was even more magnificent up close. Curvy lanes of snow led down from the rugged frozen peaks and coursed around the pine trees that shot up from a carpet of emerald. We spent a couple of hours laying back, appreciating the enchanting view and pure fresh air.

The trail back down to the tennis club proved hard going. We slid on our backs for the most part, but eventually reached the courts in half the time it took us to go up. On route back to Vashisht, the territorial dogs had amassed again, this time in greater numbers. I carried Tic-Tac as we cautiously bypassed them and crossed the main road, placing him down safely on the other side. As we approached the carved temple door at the entrance to Vashisht village Tic-Tac wagged his tail and left us where he had found us. I knew I would miss the brave little guy and his smile for a long time to come. Kurt and I indulged in a long, well-earned soak in the sulphur baths before our evening meal with the others at the house.

Tomorrow would be our last day in Manali, having decided to leave our house in the orchards and embark on the next stage of our journey, to Leh. The bus station was busy when we arrived and so we had a long wait in line for our tickets. At the booth, we were met with the disappointing news that the opening of the road to Leh had been delayed due to extreme weather conditions. With our plans unexpectedly forced to change we had to quickly plan our next move. I asked Kurt if he would like to travel to Agra and Jaipur – I was itching to see the Taj Mahal and Palace of Winds. He had no interest in Jaipur; he had been before and didn't like it there, but he did have some things he could do in Delhi and friends he would like to visit in Agra. We agreed to buy some tickets for Delhi leaving tomorrow, with the intention of returning in seven days.

Back at the house our guests began to arrive for the farewell gathering Neria and Sophie had organised. Fabian was first, the Australian who'd played the bongos at the last full moon party and a friend of his, Damika from Sri Lanka. I learnt from Fabian that he was wanted on drugs charges in Australia and didn't know what to do when his Indian visa ran out, which was a matter of days away. If he returned to Sydney, he would be arrested and probably face a prison sentence. I couldn't imagine what it must be like to have been in his shoes.

Rutger and Floyd appeared, followed surprisingly by Daniella and Harper, who I first met in Dehra Dun. The atmosphere instantly became livelier and the evening passed joyously as we all shared stories and laughed at silly jokes.

When I awoke, the house was empty. I walked to the Green Forest Café to enjoy one last set of their delicious momos. While I was there I spoke with a local man called Girish, who I found out also performed massage. He asked if I would like to come along to his premises to watch as he had a client booked in soon. From a small corrugated shack about ten-foot-long and six feet wide he conducted a successful business. Inside was a mattress on the floor, three blankets hung on a wall and a portable kerosene stove and cutlery sat in the corner. His client arrived on time and I watched him chopping heavily into his back with his hands and roughly massaging him. The customer was fully appreciative of his services and paid Girish generously before leaving.

With business out of the way, Girish invited me to stay and share a chillum or two and discuss the differences between eastern and western massage. I discovered that the shack also doubled up as his permanent home.

He seemed happy with his lot in life, 'Appreciation is the path to happiness. I look upon those who have less and consider myself blessed, while most in the west look at those who have more and live unsatisfied wishing they were them, never finding real contentment.'

I left contemplating what he'd said, concluding that you need little else in life other than inner happiness and the few basics to live, everything else seeming to complicate things the more one accumulates.

Around a bend at the top of a hill, a man stood with old soiled bandages loosely wrapped around his partially exposed hands and feet. Bone protruded through the rotting flesh of his extremities. I took a guess at severe leprosy. It was sad to see him suffering so much. Why did people have to still live like this in such a modern age, and with so much money in the world? I gave him the last of the notes I had on me and counted them into a cup on the ground as he groaned in pain.

I was confronted by another deeply upsetting sight as I continued on my way. Every now and then on my travels around the town I'd seen a donkey standing in the same place on the way to Old Manali, his front hoof raised from the ground. It looked as if his ankle was broken. Sometimes there was another donkey standing by his side as if shielding him from the passing traffic. This healthier donkey was strapped with reins, and like many donkeys and horses in Manali, he was a working animal. It appeared as if the injured one had been discarded. Lame and malnourished, he was no use to anyone. His short grey fur had bad mange and his large sad eyes looked infected, where flies buzzed a merry dance about them. I could take most things India threw at me, but when it came to the hardship and suffering of humans and animals, my helplessness felt like a punch in the stomach. Here, now, my heart shattered as I looked at the sweet disabled donkey, that had been thrown to one side and left to fend for himself, lying dead under a tree, his eyes wide open, glassy and vacant; not a trace of his spirit left.

That night I lay awake for some time recalling instances from my past that had led me to withdraw into myself and often lose hope. I had felt alone and abandoned on so many occasions; my time in Manali had been like a holiday in more ways than one. It had offered relief from what I'd come to expect and given me a multitude of warm memories to cherish. I hadn't left yet, but already I missed the good friends I had made, the evenings spent laughing and chatting until we were all so tired we collapsed into our beds. I was scared as to what the next leg of my journey would hold. In just a few hours Kurt and I would be on our way to Delhi, away from the security of this magical place I had come to call home.

21

I wasn't sure at first if I was dreaming until I heard it again – a knocking on the door followed by Kurt's barely audible voice, 'Sam, what time is it?'

It was dark so I guessed quite early. I looked over to the clock, 'A ten to four.'

'Okay, pack light. We can leave the remainder of our things here until we get back.'

I pulled back the sheet, grateful for another half hour and gazed at the clock again, 'Shit, it's ten to five!'

'What? Really? Get ready, we have to move quick or we will miss the bus.'

I was with him at the front door within minutes, 'We'll go down through the orchards, it has to be the quickest route,' I said.

The soil beneath our feet was damp from the evening rains, making our descent that much clumsier as we worked our way through the twisting labyrinthine orchards. My mind and body were sluggish. The weight on my back was enough to anchor me where I stood. I had to take a breather, 'It usually takes thirty to forty minutes to get to town, we'll never make it,' I panted.

'It is India, the bus will probably be late. We must try, Sam.'

Kurt took off, too fast for me to keep up. The trails were becoming more evident as my eyes adjusted to the light, but I realised I was hopelessly lost as I arrived at the courtyard of somebody's house where an elderly man with a straggly beard stood barefoot in dried cow dung. At first, I thought it was Pete, 'Sir, the Mall?' I asked.

He looked as puzzled by my appearance as I was by his, 'Mall that way,' he pointed. I took the path shouting my thanks. It was four minutes past five. This was crazy. Memories of Shimla came to mind and I had visions of chasing a bus with Kurt coaxing me from the doorway.

The Rajasthani refugee camp, the Buddhist Gompas, the Post Office, the Moc Restaurant, out into the Mall – Kurt was nowhere to be seen. I located the bus and strapped my pack to the roof as he came bursting around a corner, 'Hold the bus,' he shouted. 'I'm just coming.' Luckily the driver was patient and laughed as Kurt clambered on board, sweating and ridiculously out of breath.

With the Beas to accompany us, we wound down through the Kullu Valley leaving the snow caps behind. At a dhaba that had seen better days we stopped for breakfast. Kurt slurped his way through his second helping of dhal and I signalled to the waiter for two more chais.

'I'm looking forward to seeing the Taj Mahal,' I began, 'I'd also really like to see the Palace of Winds in Jaipur while we're heading down that way too.'

'Yes, you will like the Taj, it is very beautiful. I cannot say I liked Jaipur much.'

'How would you feel if I went there by myself for a few days and then we meet up again in Agra?'

'Good idea. We can meet in say, five days from when we split in Delhi if you like. Give me your journal, I will write the name and address of a hotel where my friend works. We can meet there.'

'Great, thanks, I appreciate that.'

I was surprised at his casual acceptance of my suggestion, but perhaps he had secretly hoped for some time to himself.

The hills gradually sloped into stretches of reddening farmland as the sun descended in a subtle pink haze. The cool air of the Himalayas was sucked into the sultry plains and windows were opened. We'd been travelling for more than twelve hours with at least five more to go. I was looking forward to a half decent meal, a shower and a period of unbroken sleep.

Night crept in and with it light rain. The windscreen wipers swept back and forth revealing the city lights of Delhi shimmering on the road. A little after eighteen hours from leaving Manali and two auto-rickshaw rides later we were at last in familiar territory, but at Harish's hotel there was a less than cheerful reception and Ashoka was quick to declare that there were no rooms available. We made our way through the Main Bazaar looking for somewhere else until Kurt dived into a hotel and a minute later came out smiling, 'Sixty rupees.'

The room resembled a jail cell – cold concrete walls, barred windows that let in rain and insects, and an absence of furniture except for the most basic of beds. The fan didn't work and the filthy showers and toilets were communal. It was evident you got what you paid for but we were past caring.

It wasn't raining in the morning, but it must have been all night. Our beds and luggage were soaked. Some sections of the Main Bazaar were flooded, reeking of raw sewage where people waded shin deep in the murky brown water. A car or two drove through, but autos didn't stand a chance. It was the cycle-rickshaw wallahs that the gods smiled on the most as they merrily peddled by, seats filled with paying customers.

At the top of the road we flagged down an auto to Connaught Place for breakfast and split up afterwards, agreeing to meet later at the hotel. I changed some money and went back to the Main Bazaar to see Harish and the guys. By this time the flood water had receded. Sandbags were removed, shutters were up and it was business as usual. I passed along the Bazaar without a worry in the world, confident in my step, handling each tout and every stare without a problem. I thought how intimidated I was when I first arrived in India, how scared this area had made me feel. Now I loved Delhi and revelled in its chaos. I felt at one with the crowds and moved with ease around the rickshaws and cart pullers, arriving at Harish's hotel in no time at all. My upbeat mood was met by a sullen Ashoka.

'Good morning Ashoka, you're looking very dapper today. How are you?' I tested with a beaming grin. I was beginning to find the challenge of his grumpiness more and more enjoyable. He ignored me and turned away. 'Is Harish around?'

'Harish is away for one month on business,' he grumbled.

'Oh, okay, thanks.' I looked down the hallway in hope I might catch a glimpse of any of the others but saw no one.

I turned the first corner into the alley and collided with Harish. 'Mr Sam, haha, you are being back, what luck I am having today. First rain come and now I am seeing you. Please, are you having time to spend with me? Let me be making you good lunch.'

'Ashoka told me you were away on business.' Ashoka was quick to leave as we crossed the threshold.

'No,' Harish said with a frown, 'I am here, as you can see.'

I followed him up the stairs to the rooftop and sat by the refrigerator. 'I came along last night, but there were no rooms available.'

'No rooms? We have at least five rooms available. I think you are talking with Ashoka, no? He is being such menace to my hotel, letting only Indian guest stay. Much trouble for me. Because I am having to cook, I am not seeing what is happening downstair.'

From under the shelter he poured the chai as heavy rain began to fall. Within seconds the stairwell door flung open. Nitin and Anil ran out dressed only in their shorts. Nitin sprinted over, nearly slipped and gave me a wet hug. He ran out from under the shelter, laid down with Anil and the pair pretended to swim on the ground.

'Have they lost their minds?' I shouted above the din of the downpour.

'Haha, maybe, Mr Sam. We are having this fun because monsoon has finally come. They are enjoying rain very much. I think I would be joining them too if I have not lunch to make.'

Nitin and Anil danced, splashed their feet and sang until Harish cut them off in mid verse for lunch. We sat in a circle as the two boys dried off.

'I am now running tour business from hotel,' said Harish. 'I am arranging good bus journeys for tourist. I am hoping it will bring much western traveller to hotel, but I am most concerned about Ashoka. What to do?'

'I'm looking to get to Jaipur as soon as possible. Can you help?' I asked.

'Yes, of course, why not? I will be giving you very best price. In fact, there is one bus leaving at five thirty this afternoon if you are liking to go.'

'That'd be great. This food is delicious by the way, what is it?' I asked, cheeks filled like a hamster.

'Ah, this is special dog curry,' he replied. 'I am very glad you are liking.'

I stopped chewing. My face dropped as did the rice from my fingers. 'Dog curry, really?'

'Yes, why, are you not liking?' He appeared upset, wounded eyes paining his face, but then he raised a reassuring grin, 'Of course not, my friend. This is murg makkai; made with good chicken. No dog. We have two room of Punjabi guest this week, so I am making Punjabi food for them.' Harish translated the dog curry story to the boys, who in turn exploded into laughter and slapped me on the back for my gullibility.

I confirmed my return for the bus at five and made my way back to the hotel. Standing at the door to our room I searched my pockets for the padlock key only to realise I'd been stupid enough to leave it in the room. I pinned a note on the door for Kurt to meet me on the roof of Harish's. He did so an hour later. Borrowing a screwdriver, I prised the lock from the door and packed my things saying farewell to Kurt for five days. Insecurity trickled through me at the prospect of travelling alone again, but I was also excited by the future unknown.

Harish accompanied me to the top of the Main Bazaar and said goodbye as we reached a crowd of Indian holidaymakers. I found my seat at the back of the coach and glanced out of the window, noticing an Indian girl in her late teens talking to a white girl of the same age who had her back to me. They hugged and the westerner turned to board the bus. For a moment, everything seemed to blur around her as she made her way slowly along the aisle. Her walnut coloured hair, straight to her shoulders, shone in the half light of the interior, framing her face and her Mediterranean blue eyes. She stopped by the empty seat beside me. 'Is this taken?'

'No, all yours,' I answered, and she settled in, placing her holdall on her lap. After a minute or so of silence I extended my hand, 'Hi, I'm Sam.'

She shook it gently and smiled, 'Kate.'

'So, you're off to Jaipur then?'

'It would seem so. I'm doing the whole Golden Triangle thing; you know, Delhi, Jaipur, Agra. Have you been to Jaipur before?'

'No, first time for me. And you?'

'No. This is only my second day in India.'

'How are you finding it all?'

'India? It's all been a bit overwhelming so far.' I glanced away briefly as she smiled, too timid to retain eye contact. 'I'm supposed to be travelling with my friend who is visiting her family in Delhi, but her father became ill just before I arrived. So, I thought I'd give them some time to themselves. How long have you been in India?'

The bus juddered to life and bullied its way into the rush-hour traffic and I told her my story so far.

'So, Kate, where are you from? You're English, right?'

'Canterbury. In Kent.'

'No way, really? I live about twenty miles away from there.'

'Haha, I bet you say that to all the girls.'

I laughed, 'No, honestly, I know Canterbury really well. Let's face it, it's the only decent place for shopping for miles.'

'Absolutely,' she smiled.

She was nineteen and about to commence a Business Management degree at Kent University when she went home. We spoke about our favourite books, music and films, having most in common – it was as if we'd known each other our entire lives, finding it effortless to converse.

'Have you sorted out your accommodation in Jaipur yet?' I asked.

'Sort of. My friend recommended a hotel. I just need to find it.

And you?'

'No, I just turn up and hope for the best.'

'Well maybe you can come with me to my hotel and see if there's a room there for you too. To be honest, I'm quite worried about what to do when I get off the bus.'

I was relieved she asked. I didn't fancy scurrying around all night looking for a place to stay myself. 'Yeah, no worries,' I replied casually.

The driver overtook on a blind bend and a set of headlights careered towards us, missing us at the last second. I shut my eyes tight and clutched the railing of the seat in front. When I opened them again I turned to see her looking at me, smiling and calm, almost oblivious to the dangers of the road, as if she were sitting in her living room.

'Aren't you worried?' I asked.

'The driving? No, not really. There's nothing I can do about it. Besides, when it's your time to go, it's your time to go.'

Just before ten we arrived in Jaipur. Climbing down from the coach into the dry evening heat we grabbed our luggage and negotiated one of the many auto-rickshaws in wait. We were taken to our hotel without quibble and the driver asked if his services would be required the next day. I asked him to come back at nine the next morning.

There were two rooms available: one with air conditioning, television, double bed and en-suite bathroom; the other with a ceiling fan, single bed and a keyhole latrine. I requested the lesser of the two.

'I wouldn't have minded your room, you know,' she said at her doorway.

'I've got no problems with mine, honestly,' I replied. 'Well it was nice to have met you.'

'You too', she said and unlocked the door.

'Do you have any plans tomorrow?' I chanced.

'I was going to see some of the sights I guess. I'm here for maybe two or three nights.'

My blood began to race, my mouth became dry, 'Well, um, if

you're at a loose end, maybe we could meet up at some point?' I bumbled.

'How about we see Jaipur together? Maybe we could hire that rickshaw guy for the day. You seem to know your stuff. I have no idea what I'd be looking for anyway.'

'Cool, yeah, right, okay. I'll have a think where we can go and give you a knock at about ten to nine?'

'OK, great.' She smiled and then closed the door.

For a moment, I stood lingering in her perfume before making my way a little light headed to my room.

22

Double checking the last of my notes, I placed the folded pieces of paper in my pocket and checked myself in the mirror. I didn't have my best clothes with me but had opted for the smartest trousers and shirt I could find. My hair was a mess, in desperate need of a cut and my futile attempt at styling it was interrupted by a light tap at the door. Kate stood in the hallway, a turquoise salwar kameez complimenting her pearl skin. 'Hi Sam, are you ready to go?'

'Yep, all set. You look amazing by the way.'

'Thanks, that's very sweet of you.'

Our rickshaw wallah was studying his offside mirror, pressing his thin moustache into place with a finger as we approached. 'So, where's a good place for breakfast?' I asked, catching him a little by surprise. Immediately he turned and smiled.

'Ah, good morning, sir. Breakfast? Yes, I will take you.' Just two minutes along the same road he came to a stop outside a busy café. I agreed a reasonable price for the day and asked his name. 'Jameel,' he replied. 'I will wait for you here. You will recognise my rickshaw, I am sure.' His English was good and his rickshaw was unmistakable; striking yellow and black with an Islamic crescent and star either side of the seating area.

I took the lead and found us a table, a waiter in tow.

Kate ran her finger down the menu, 'Um, banana pancakes and a cup of Earl Grey tea please.'

I let out a short laugh.

'What?' she laughed back.

'I don't know; it was the whole "a cup of Earl Grey tea" thing. It was sweet. Your pronunciation of the English language is lovely, perfect in fact. I wish everyone spoke as well as you do in England.'

'Uh okay, thank you?'

The waiter bounced gently on his tip-toes.

'Oh sorry, I'll have...' I glanced at the menu, 'The same as my friend here please.'

'Very good, sir,' he said and pitter-pattered away to the kitchen.

'So, where are we going today?' she asked.

'I thought we could start off with a tour of Amber Fort, get some lunch and then this afternoon maybe a visit to City Palace?'

'Sounds good to me.'

As she looked out to life on the street, I found it difficult to take my eyes from her. I couldn't remember ever being so struck by a girl. She turned and broke my gaze, 'Sam?'

'Huh?' The waiter hovered behind me arms balancing our breakfast. 'Oh sorry, thank you,' I said, and moved aside, allowing him room to place our food down. He squeezed back and responded to a raised hand in a sea of heads.

'I'm sure you'd love Manali,' I said. 'Especially around breakfast time; eating honey porridge and drinking fresh apple juice all the while breathing in the fresh air of the mountains.' I suddenly realised how much I sounded like Ruben or Jack.

'Sounds idyllic. I'm kind of using this as a trial for the possibility of a longer trip next year, maybe two months or so in the summer holidays. We'll see how it goes though.'

'India again?'

'I was hoping so, maybe a trip to Manali and on to, um where did you say you were going? Leh was it?'

'Yeah, the road up there is meant to be amazing.'

'Leh, yes. But I'm not sure I'll do the whole thing alone, maybe with a friend trustworthy and willing enough.'

She caught the waiter's attention, 'Could we have the bill, please?' I reached for my wallet to pay, but she held her palm up,

'No, allow me, please, it's the least I can do.'

'Are you sure?'

'Of course.'

Sharp eyed Jameel started his engine as we rose from the table. I asked if he'd take us to Amber Fort. 'Yes, of course. But maybe first I take you to Jal Mahal. It is on the way. Very romantic,' he assured us with a cheeky grin. 'Jal Mahal was built in 1734. It was once a hunting lodge, but now it is flooded by Man Sagar Lake exposing top floors only.'

Set against a backdrop of rugged hills the elegant palace appeared to float on the dark water of the lake, displaying a near perfect mirror image of the cream coloured walls lined with archways, each corner marked by an octagonal tower and elegant cupola.

'It's such a shame it's been abandoned like this,' Kate said as she adjusted her hair slightly.

I tilted my head, 'I don't know, I quite like it. It looks haunted, as if the walls long for the return of idle court gossip or the brag of a recent hunt.'

'It does feel ghostly; I imagine more so on a misty morning. It's very beautiful.'

The city dwindled into the simple village life of Amber. A slower pace, people milled about the muddy streets as if the outside world ceased to exist. Nearing the top of a steep slope, Jameel brought the auto to a stop. I got out and pretended to tie my shoelace and memorised the notes I wrote earlier hoping to impress Kate. I met her at an arched gateway where we left Jameel.

Walking through, I quoted what I'd rehearsed, 'The town of Amber was the capital of the Rajput Kingdom from 1037 until 1727 when it shifted to Jaipur. Amber Fort was constructed in 1592 by Raja Man Singh.'

'Wow, you know your history. Very impressive,' she remarked.

'Thanks,' I said, picking up confidence in my step.

'Did you know it all before you wrote it on those pieces of paper?'

I looked away, flushed, 'I, uh, kind of researched it from the guidebook last night.'

'It's very sweet you went to all that effort. Thank you.'

Hand-painted elephants were ferrying tourists to a higher level of the fort. 'Would you like to take one?' I asked.

'An elephant ride? Not for me thanks. I'm quite happy to walk, unless you want to?'

The tourists swayed from side to side, looking more anxious than happy. 'The expression on those passengers' faces says it all. I think I'll give it a miss,' I chuckled.

We wandered the luxurious courtyards and audience halls in comfortable silence except for the occasional comment on the geometrical patterned archways or elaborate ceilings. From a cool pavilion, we stepped into the blazing sunshine of a courtyard where a group of restless langurs were squabbling and the scent of fresh flowers whispered the dry breeze.

'Have you travelled anywhere like India before?' she enquired.

'I nearly did a couple of years ago. I knew a South African guy who worked a few months at a time in the UK just to save enough money to go backpacking. He asked me if I wanted to go with him on his next adventure; he was planning to spend six months in an Israeli Kibbutz and after that I'm not sure.'

'Sounds exciting!'

'I told him I'd think about it, but inside the thought terrified me. What if things went wrong and we were miles from anywhere? Or we ran out of money? He was very much the kind of guy that lived for the moment, whereas I was quite the opposite.'

'So, you just decided not to go?'

I gazed below to an island in the waters of Maota Lake, 'I met a girl and that was that. The decision was kind of taken out of my hands.' We retraced our steps through the complex to the exit. 'I regretted it for a while. A few months later I was browsing a copy of National Geographic in a doctor's waiting room. There was an article about what people had compared to others. Photos showed average families sitting outside their homes, possessions displayed out before them. I was particularly struck by the Bhutanese family who lived in a primitive tree house and had next to nothing. I wished then I was with my friend seeing a world like that for myself.'

'But you're doing it now? Look how much you've seen and done already.'

'I know and I haven't regretted a second.' I smiled, 'I'm hungry, are you ready for lunch?'

Jameel was snoring, slouched in the front seat of his rickshaw. I tapped gently on the side. He swatted an invisible fly and murmured, 'Taken, not free.' I tapped again. This time he woke with a start, 'Oh my God, I have fallen asleep. I am so very sorry sir, madam.'

'No worries, Jameel. I'm Kate and this is Sam. Please, none of this sir, madam, nonsense.'

'Thank you most kindly, Miss Kate. It is so hot. It is making me a little tired.'

'Can you take us into the city for lunch? Somewhere we can get a pizza maybe?'

He knew the perfect place – a newly opened chain restaurant, 'Very good air-cool,' he said.

Halfway through sharing a pizza with all the trimmings, Kate asked, 'So, the girl you met after your friend left for Israel, did it last long?'

'About eighteen months. We broke up at the beginning of this year. It ran its natural course and we went our separate ways. Another reason I came to India I guess.' I was in a state of bliss and wasn't in the mood for Saskia's doom and gloom. I could count the serious relationships I'd had on one hand, and all had ended badly. I turned the focus and question back to her. 'Is there anyone special waiting for you at home?'

Just then a thumping bhangra song began to play and the four waiters serving stopped what they were doing, lined up and danced in perfect time to the music. Kate and I looked at each other and laughed. A couple of minutes went by, the music stopped and the waiters returned to their duties, applause aplenty from entertained customers.

Baffled and none the wiser, we resumed eating. 'Those monkeys in the fort were naughty,' said Kate. 'It was so funny when they ran off with that girl's banana, though she was asking for it holding it out like that.' I laughed and agreed, but didn't pursue my question, the moment had passed.

I couldn't help thinking there was something very 'first date' about all of this. Maybe I was imagining it, but it felt exciting, as if I had a school boy crush. Aside from us getting on so well, I was captivated by how her face lit up every time she smiled, which she did frequently, and by the way she played with her hair as she talked. She was sincere and I wholeheartedly believed that the girl sat before me was the real Kate.

The wide roads were as manic as any other Indian city with the usual anarchy of dogs, cows and people and the competitive clamour of rickshaws, cars, buses and trucks, but Jaipur had the addition of camel drawn carts and working elephants to slow progress further. Parts of the city were painted pink in honour of a visit from Prince Edward of Wales and to this day the colour of most of the buildings were the same, although somewhat bleached by the sun.

Outside City Palace, a heavily bearded man closed-in on Kate's side of the rickshaw. He gently wagged his head and held out his blistered hand. His disfigurements shocked her for a moment. The hand and foot on his right side were missing and he leant heavy on a crutch. She placed her index finger up to suggest he wait for a second as she pulled out some notes.

'I feel awful when I see people living like this,' I said as he limped on. 'There I am travelling around without a care in the world while so many have no choice but to scratch around for the slightest of a living.'

'It certainly does put some of the trivialities that preoccupy us into perspective,' she responded. 'But that said, you shouldn't feel too bad, Sam. If that man was in your position, I'm sure he would be making the most of his life like you are. Have empathy for others and appreciate what you have also.'

'Hello, I am sorry to interrupt. Maybe I tell you about City Palace?' Jameel asked.

'Thank you that would be nice,' Kate replied.

'City Palace built in early 1700s. Inside are two largest silver urns in the world at one and half metres high. They are made from fourteen thousand melted silver coins. Also, you will see Chandra Mahal where family of former rulers of Jaipur still reside. Okay, I will come back for you in forty-five minutes.'

A man dressed in a long white coat and with a red turban upon his head greeted us at the gates and guided us into a courtyard at the foot of the Mubarak Mahal. Blended of Rajput, Moghul and European styles it now housed a museum. Inside, the laughter of school children echoed throughout the hall as we browsed embroidered shawls, silk saris and other costumes of the former royals.

Kate paused to study the detail of a Kashmiri pashmina, 'Nathaniel would hate this sort of thing. In fact, I think he'd hate India altogether.'

'Nathaniel?'

'My boyfriend. Well, sort of.'

My heart dropped. I hadn't realised until that moment just how much I liked her. I followed her into another courtyard; the scarlet Diwan-i-Khas commanding the centre. We went inside to look at the silver urns Jameel spoke of.

'Oh, is it serious?' I asked.

'It's early days yet. He wasn't too keen on me going away to India, which is a kind of ironic as he's applied to the University of York, so we wouldn't be seeing much of each other anyway. We'll just have to see how it goes I guess.'

In the shadow of the Chandra Mahal, a seven-storey domed pavilion, I watched her photograph a set of lavishly designed doors said to represent the four seasons. I wondered if I was pursuing a lost cause and should put my heart in check.

By the side of the road as we left, I spotted a soft drinks stall. 'Pani?' I asked the young guy perched on the refrigerator. He nodded, pushed himself up, lifted the lid and retrieved a bottle of water. I held up three fingers, 'Kitna hai?'

'Tees,' he replied. I didn't haggle and gave him a reasonable thirty rupees.

With our water, the three of us took shade on a bench beneath a tree and watched two young men eyeing up the ladies as they walked by. They laughed and teased each other oblivious to the entertainment they were providing us.

'Thank you so much for today, Sam. I've had a wonderful time,' Kate said.

'No, thank you, it's been amazing. I hope you weren't too bored.'

'It was a bit touristy, but to be expected I guess. I'm not into history so much, but it's all been ever so romantic,' she stumbled for a moment. 'I mean, you know, the buildings like the palace in the lake and the fort with those lovely views over the hills.'

Something amazing was happening and I liked to think Kate felt it too. Meeting a girl had been the farthest intention in my mind and the happiness was tinged with uncertainty, but the more I compared Kate to Saskia the more differences that became apparent. In Kate's company, I felt at ease, even when a little nervous to impress. Her beauty came from inner kindness and she was smart; not in a pretentious or condescending way, simply that conversation could go in so many directions.

Later that evening after Jameel had taken us back to the hotel, she asked if I played Blackjack. 'The card game? Yes, but I'm not very good.'

'Me neither, it's just a bit of fun. I brought a pack of cards along just in case I was at a loose end.'

She was good, thrashing me five games out of seven. I reached over to tidy the pile of cards and she did the same. Our fingers touched a little longer than necessary. We glanced at each other before I moved my hand away. 'I suppose we should probably get some sleep so we can make the most of the day tomorrow,' I said.

She saw me to the door and then leant forward to kiss me on the cheek, 'Thanks for a nice evening.'

My guard was now a crumpled heap on the floor.

A section of the Palace of Winds appeared on the cover of my Lonely Planet and I'd dreamt of seeing it ever since Kurt gave me the guidebook. Pyramidal shaped and built from orange and pink sandstone, the fifty-foot-high honeycombed façade consisted of fine latticed windows, carved grills, majestic domes and finials.

Jameel gazed up from the roadside, 'Hawa Mahal or Palace of Winds was built in late eighteenth century and was designed to resemble the crown of Krishna. The tiny windows you see were meant for royal ladies to look out on the street below and not be seen by passers-by.'

It was a cloudless sunrise, excellent weather for photography. While I was loading a film into my camera, a man came over from across the street and asked if I'd like to photograph the palace from his rooftop opposite. Of course, there was a small fee, but the view was worth every rupee I was assured. He invited us up and it was just that. From where we stood we could see the building and street below in all its glory.

'I take it from all the pictures you've taken you like this place?' Kate asked as we descended the stairwell.

'Definitely! It's just how I imagined India to be. I can't believe I'm seeing it for real.'

Squatting nearby on the roadside were two men with a pair of round wicker baskets at their feet. They wore vibrant orange turbans, matching shirts and baggy white trousers and both sported dashing handlebar moustaches. As soon as they saw us they lifted the lids to the baskets and began playing a strangulated tune through their flutes. Within seconds a cobra in each basket rose and swayed, hypnotised by the sound. Kate paid the snake charmers for the performance and said to me, 'This is how I imagined India to be.'

Inside the Hawa Mahal, climbing the stone staircase to the upper palace, we paused occasionally to look through the windows and to imagine what it must have been like for the ladies of the royal harem.

During lunch in the old city, she asked if I would like to accompany her to Agra. 'Of course,' I replied, elated. 'It'd be my pleasure. Maybe we'll bump into Kurt.' Honestly, I didn't want to meet up with Kurt until I had to; I was keen to spend as much time alone with her as possible.

With two bus tickets bought for eight in the morning, we returned to the hotel and played cards as the sweltering afternoon spilt into a warm evening. I asked her what her plans were after university, 'I was hoping to work for a cat welfare charity to learn as much as I can with the view of maybe starting my own one day.'

'Cats, huh? I've never really given them a second look; they don't seem to do much but sit around.'

'I think you share that view with Nathaniel. He's not an animal lover. He thinks the knowledge I gain at university would be wasted on such a venture, and that I should be pursuing a career elsewhere that receives a wealthy income. Money has never interested me though, but I care very much about animals.' She was passionate and focused about what she wanted to do, that much was clear. When she spoke about Nathaniel, it seemed to irritate her. I wasn't surprised, he irritated me too.

'You've got to do what makes you happy. Don't get me wrong though, I do love animals, I've just never had much to do with cats. I've always been a dog person, been around them all of my life.'

'I've never had a dog, though I used to walk the neighbour's Jack Russell when I was younger. He was a sweet little chap called Ben.'

'The dog or the neighbour?'

'The dog, silly.'

We thanked Jameel for his services and paid him well. He'd been an excellent driver and his upbeat demeanour as well as his local knowledge had added to the joy of our sightseeing. While we waited for our bus I noticed a group of Indian men staring at Kate. I asked her if it made her feel uncomfortable.

'Sometimes, but I'm getting used to it. A few guys got a little too friendly when I first arrived in Delhi, but I was quite firm with them, which seemed to work. My friend Rani told me what to wear and how to handle the men, but it can still get a little scary. I'm so glad you're with me though.' She placed her hand on my arm and smiled.

23

The journey east along the baseline of the golden triangle was bumpy and I'd noticed an increase in roadside carnage. Recent accidents were more frequent than ever before. My nerves frayed every time we were thrown from one side of the road to the other in what felt like an intense game of 'chicken'. And I think Kate even had a look of worry about her.

After two hours, we came to a stop, the road ahead blocked by an annihilated tractor with a goods carrier crumpled into its rear. We weren't going anywhere any time soon and as the stationary bus became an oven, we took refuge from the sun in the limited shade of a pathetic looking tree. A couple of metres away four vultures squawked and fought over the rotting flesh of a buffalo carcass, while around the accident site three men stood arguing.

It was fast approaching midday and our water was running low. The other passengers were looking as clueless about our future progress as we were, but they took it all in their stride as if this was an everyday occurrence of travelling this road, which it probably was.

A young man leant over us, 'Hello, you must come, we leave now,' he said. We followed behind as he whistled to himself. He pointed to a rumbling green jeep, 'In back please.' Four men were crammed in the back. Before we had time to think about what we were doing, we were politely coaxed in and on the road again.

The jeep made the bus ride feel like travelling on a cushion of air. A bar pressed into my lower back, which I was sure was going to result in a colourful bruise and I lost count how many times I whacked my head against the metal frame above me. Kate gripped the seat just as tightly and we forced a smile at each other.

An hour or so later we were reconnected with a bus that took us the rest of the way to Agra and alighted in the shadow of the imposing Agra Fort. A group of cycle-rickshaw wallahs huddled around us, pulling us this way and that. With a little haggling, we chose one and hoped for the best.

We were taken to a hotel that Kurt recommended to me. Supposedly it commanded the best view of the Taj Mahal, and although busy all year round, Kurt told me to drop his name to the manager which I did. As if by magic the fully booked hotel suddenly had two vacancies.

The rickshaw wallah hovered in the reception area and as we collected the keys he tapped me on the arm, 'My name is Brima, I am very good rickshaw wallah. Maybe you would like to be hiring me for city tour also.'

'You know the city and its history well?' I asked.

'Oh yes. Very good knowledge I am having, sir.'

'Okay then. Can you come back for us at five o'clock?'

'Yes, no problem. Nothing is problem for Brima.'

I assisted Kate upstairs with her backpack. She walked into her room and quickly turned around to exit.

'What's wrong?'

'I know I'm being stupid, but can you get rid of those bug things on the bed and the wall?'

I investigated the room. Three cricket-like insects resided. They sat motionless: one on the bed, one above the bed on the wall and one on the teak bureau next to a glass and compliment slip. I trapped the first one, slipping the paper underneath the glass and at arm's length, disposed of it outside the door. The next was livelier and had me chasing it around the room. I came in close, leant over and it leapt, landing on my cheek. I screamed and brushed my face frantically as Kate looked on, peaking in from around the doorway. I flicked it off and it landed at her feet which in turn had her jumping around on the spot shrieking.

We must have made quite a racket as a member of staff came running up the stairs and to our rescue. 'Yes, yes, please do not be worrying. Very unharmful,' he grinned and collected the remainder of the insects by hand. So much for my heroics! The assistant left me red faced and looking for a hole to crawl into. Kate laughed as she settled in, 'We're as bad as each other.'

Brima arrived all smartened up and on time. His hair – side-parted – was shiny and flattened to his head and he looked to have trimmed his moustache. His bright open-necked shirt complimented his smart trousers and his worn leather sandals. He enthusiastically ushered us to his rickshaw and then rode us through the dimming streets.

'Sunset very good time for Taj,' he called back whilst snaking in and out of the heaving traffic. 'Shah Jahan build Taj Mahal for love of favourite wife who die giving birth to fourteenth child in 1631. It take twenty thousand men from all over Asia to construct Taj which is being finished in 1643.'

Catching a glimpse every so often of the huge dome, we sauntered through a set of immaculate gardens and as we drew closer, the mausoleum appeared in its entirety through a shaded archway. It suddenly looked so small, yet so perfectly formed. The immensity and beauty of the structure was revealed when we passed through and for a moment we were motionless. Nothing I had ever seen could compare. The sheer size alone held me in awe.

With an occasional ripple from a gentle breeze, the bevelled edges, ivory dome and brass spire reflected in a long pool leading up to the structure. We climbed the stairway to the base and stepped inside the inner chamber that housed the cenotaphs of Shah Jahan and Mumtaz, who lay side by side. Escaping the loud echoes of chatter from other visitors, we went outside again and stood below one of the four soaring minarets to look out to the setting sun turning the Yamuna river scarlet with its reflection.

My head filled with a million thoughts, each one connected to Kate. I wanted to know everything about her, to hear her speak and hold on to every word so I could remember her voice once she was gone. For a moment, we stood in silence, unified by the splendour of the scene before us and by the emotion of simply being here, together. She surprised me by discreetly placing her hand in mine and squeezing it tight. With what looked to be tears in her eyes she turned to me and said, 'Sam, I have to book my train ticket to Delhi tomorrow. I'm really going to miss you.'

'I'll miss you too.' Whatever I tried to do to stop this from happening, I was helplessly falling in love with her. 'We can still keep in touch when I get back, right?'

'I hope so,' she said as we descended the steps and walked the charbagh in shadow, taking in a final view of the Taj, now tinted crimson in sunset.

Brima wiped imaginary dust from the back seat when he saw us. As he manoeuvred through the heavy traffic I asked if he knew where I could hire a car and driver for tomorrow morning. Agreeing a reasonable rate, he assured me that one would be waiting outside our hotel first thing. I was steadily discovering that Brima could make just about anything happen. He told us he could also arrange flights and porter services, personalised shopping experiences, accommodation, sightseeing tours and luckily for us, train tickets. He said to leave it with him and he would acquire a ticket. He may have made a little commission, but it took the sting out of arranging things ourselves.

Joining Kate in her room, we commenced a long game of cards before falling asleep on the sofa. I awoke with her head resting on my chest. She stirred as I freed my legs from the pins and needles that had gripped my legs. As I stood I stumbled, allowing the wall to support me as I circled each foot to resume circulation.

'What time is it?' she asked in a half yawn.

'Um,' I checked my watch, 'late, just after one.'

We were both thirsty. I told her I would be back in a minute and went downstairs to see if I could get some drinks. Half expecting to trawl the streets, I was surprised to find a member of staff at the desk, wide awake and with a little too much energy for the hour. Ordering a couple Cokes and two bottles of water, I went to pay and asked, 'Is the rooftop open?'

'Oh no sir, much too late,' he replied.

I slid a fifty note across the counter, 'If my friend and I are very quiet, could we go up there for half an hour?'

He paused for a moment to deliberate and then replied, 'Okay sir, but much like mice. Please step quietly and speak softly as I may be getting into trouble.'

'Of course, you have my word.'

He passed me a key, 'Please be locking door when you leave and return key to reception.'

The drinks were waiting for us on a table when Kate and I tiptoed out onto the roof. In addition, a plate of cold samosas was at the centre, which we were both grateful for as we hadn't eaten since lunch. Hardly a sound was to be heard, as if we had the whole city to ourselves. The Taj, a deep blue and glinting ever so slightly silver by the pale moonlight, was made prominent by the lighter shade of sky. Everything was said in the silence that hung between us as we stared out over the rooftops to the mysterious silhouette. When we weren't eating, our fingers were interlocked over the table and we gazed into each other's eyes.

At her door, I leant in to kiss her. She stood on tip-toe reciprocating and I brought her in closer, my arm around her back. I held her hands for a moment longer before wishing her goodnight.

'Sleep well, Sam,' she said and clicked the door closed.

I hoped it wasn't all a dream or she'd got carried away with the moment, but when we met for breakfast on the roof and watched the sun warm the Taj, nothing had changed. Brima met us a little later and peddled us along the waking streets to Agra Fort where we met Ali, our driver for the day. The curves of a brilliant white Ambassador gleamed in the sunlight and we took our places in the back. A small fan hung precariously from the ceiling but did little to lift the stifling heat.

Ali didn't say much on the way to Fatehpur Sikri, but instead focused his attention on his driving. Every now and then a pair of thick rimmed spectacles and a neat moustache would glance into the interior mirror and he'd ask if we were okay which we returned with a smile and nod. When he brought the car to a stop, he leant over and told us we were in the village of Sikandra and asked if we would like to visit the Tomb of Akbar the Great before we went to Fatehpur. Kate and I got out and entered through a red sandstone gateway with a white marble minaret on each corner. The grand mausoleum itself was also of sandstone with arched colonnades either side of a pishtaq – the entrance to the tomb.

'Do you have any cats yourself?' I asked, short of anything else to say.

'Two, at my parent's house. Mickey and Holly. They're getting on a bit now though. Mickey stays in my room quite a bit while I study.'

'That's sweet,' I smiled. 'There's quite a bond there then?'

'Yeah, they're real treasures. Cats are quite magical. They often appear when you think about them or when you need a friend the most.'

I wasn't sure if my eyes were deceiving me, but from behind an elliptical banyan tree, a skinny tortoiseshell cat appeared. Kate saw it too and looked at me, just as surprised as I was.

'See, I told you so,' she laughed, and then leant over and tutted. The cat trotted over and brushed up against her leg. We spent twenty minutes stroking her and playing with a stick. It was the first cat I'd seen in India or had noticed.

'I'm sold on the idea of cats now, she was adorable,' I said, as we got into the car.

'Excellent, another one converted.'

She closed her hand around mine and a sense of euphoria filled me, as if my world was utterly perfected by her being in it. I tried not to think of tomorrow, but grasped every second of today, holding her tightly, reminding myself this moment was real and soon to be a memory.

Ali gave us the low down on Fatehpur Sikri as we arrived outside, 'The ghost city of Fatehpur Sikri was the capital of Moghul power between 1571 and 1585. It is one of the finest preserved examples of Moghul architecture in India. We do not know why city was abandoned, some say maybe bad water supply, but likely it was due to troubles in the Punjab where Akbar moved his capital to Lahore.' He cleared his throat, 'Your entrance fee has been paid for and I will meet you at the Buland Darwaza gate in one and half hours.'

I had the guidebook with me and consulted the map, walking us through Agra Gate and past the triple-tiered Naubat Khana where the Emperor's arrival was often announced by musicians. Kate was upbeat and playful, deliberately bumping into me a few times as we walked. On the third time, I bumped into her back. She bumped me again and walked faster, flashing a smile over her shoulder. I sped up and so did she, through a courtyard and in and out of the Diwan-i-Am's elaborate pavilions.

I caught up with her in a passageway leading into the inner citadel. 'Got you,' I said laughing and tagging her arm. We came out breathless into the Turkish Sultana's House – the fine dado panels and sculpted walls giving the appearance it was made of wood rather than sandstone.

'Phew it's hot,' she said, wiping her brow.

'We can take a little shelter over there in the Diwan-i-Khas,' I said and pointed to a square building.

Inside was cooler, but not much. At the centre of the small room was a circular platform intricately carved and supported by serpentine brackets. It was connected to each corner by four stone pathways where we stood underneath sipping from our water bottles.

'Representatives of different religions would discuss their faith and stoop forward along one of those pathways to talk in private to the emperor who sat comfortably at the centre on a throne of cushions,' I explained, craning our necks. 'Maybe court staff would take notes on the discussions where we're standing. It's strange when you think about it, how this was such an important place and how it would have been a great privilege to be in the Emperor's presence.'

Kate walked ahead of me into the next courtyard, 'So where are we now?'

I opened the Lonely Planet at a bookmarked page, 'Um, I think this is the Pachisi Court, named after the traditional game of pachisi, where people – often beautiful ladies – would serve as playing pieces.'

'How the other half live,' she said and walked ahead into the Harem complex where I lost sight of her.

I looked around, wondering if she was watching me looking clueless from the shadows somewhere. Just then I heard a shriek to my right. I scanned the archways and caught a glimpse of two men with their backs to me, and then Kate in front of them with her back to the wall. I ran over, threw one of them aside, got hold of the other and pinned him by his throat against a pillar with the length of my forearm. I was consumed with rage, white heat coursing through my veins. I stared into the man's eyes baiting for his blood.

'Kate, are you alright?' I shouted.

'I'm fine, Sam. Let him go, he's done nothing wrong,' she said from behind me.

'What do you mean? I saw them right on top of you. I heard you scream.' I still held him fast, his anxious face inches from mine.

'No, everything's fine, honestly. I got a little lost, turned around and ran into these gentlemen by mistake. It was my own silly fault. I broke this poor man's glasses.' He waggled his head and smiled nervously. 'Please, let go of him.' I softened my grip and released him.

'Are you sure? They didn't hurt you?'

'Of course, I'm sure.'

I apologised to the men, offering to cover the cost of the glasses. 'That will not be necessary, please, they are very old. I have a new pair at home. No harm is done. It was our stupidity for not looking where we were going.'

I thanked them again and apologised to Kate as we made our way under a gateway leading to the courtyard of the Jama Masjid. 'I don't know what came over me, I guess I panicked. I was so worried something had happened to you. I would never have forgiven myself if it had. I'm sorry I got angry.'

'It's okay to get angry. What scared me was how terrified you looked when you held him against the pillar.' She put her hand on my arm in reassurance, 'Let's not worry about it too much. Thank you for coming to help me, that was incredibly gallant of you.'

'Ah, you have arrived, very good,' a voice spoke from behind us. We turned to find Ali. We were grateful for the distraction. I was still shaken and could tell Kate was too. He walked us out, pausing at a tomb clad in white marble and adorned with delicate jali screens on all sides. 'In 16th century, Fatehpur Sikri was only small place of pilgrimage,' he said. 'Salim Chishti, a Sufi saint, live in village and would welcome visitors seeking advice. Despite his many wives, twenty-six-year-old Akbar, still he have no son as heir to throne. He seek words of comfort from Salim Chishti and saint tell him he would have three sons. And three sons he is having, over three years, fulfilling saint's prophesy.

'In honour of saint, Akbar shift capital from Agra to Fatehpur Sikri.' Ali pointed at the different coloured threads fluttering from the screens, 'To this day Tomb of Sheikh Salim Chishti attract childless women from all over who tie small cotton thread to jali screen and make wish in hope of miracle.'

Kate and I held each other's hand tightly all the way back to Agra. From time to time, by the side of the road, we caught sight of several performing bears, stood on their hind legs with their front paws out as if they were about to clap. Their owners had a tight hold of a chain that was connected to a ring through their nose. Ali told us the parade was for the benefit of passers-by who might stop and pay good money to be entertained by a dance from the poor creature. It was a very sad sight.

Brima was waiting for us at the Fort. He handed Kate her ticket to Delhi as we transferred from the Ambassador to the rickshaw. The train was scheduled to leave first thing the following morning. We looked at each other and back to the ticket again, both wishing the sands of time would re-tip in our favour.

Brima was keen to take us to a couple of businesses for him to earn a little extra money. He assured us we wouldn't have to buy anything and we wouldn't have to stay long, so we agreed. The first stop was a jeweller. From a side street, we followed Brima through a doorway into a small room where a stout man sat behind a glass counter filled with sparkling stones on cushioned velvet. He got up, greeted us, went into a sales spiel and insisted on showing us his workshop behind the counter.

Ten boys, of primary school age, worked hard in silence on a dusty floor polishing stones at spinning wheels. With no intention of making a purchase, we politely made our excuses and left.

The next business was a carpet warehouse. Again, some of the workers were young men who busied themselves sweeping soapy water from large carpets while older gentlemen mumbled memorised patterns at hand-worked looms. We cracked through the hard sell from the owner and met Brima outside, who at last took us back to the hotel where we enjoyed a late lunch.

'Would you do me a favour, Brima?' I asked as we approached his rickshaw. He tilted his head. 'Could you take us somewhere where we can get a nice view of the Taj Mahal from the opposite riverbank?'

'I know very good place and on way is fine gift shop.' Kate and I looked at each other and chuckled. We had to admire his spirit.

The gift shop displayed a vast collection of items, from large stone statues of gods such as the elephant headed Ganesh and the monkey god Hanuman, to gruesome paintings of Kali adorned with a necklace of skulls and holding a severed head in one hand and a bowl to collect the blood in another. I bought a miniature marble Taj Mahal and as it was being boxed I turned to Kate and said, 'Something to remember me by.'

Brima peddled us across a busy bridge over the Yamuna. 'I will take you to Mehtab Bagh,' he called out over his shoulder. 'Mehtab Bagh mean Moonlight Garden. This Moghul garden perfectly aligned with Taj Mahal on opposite bank. Shah Jahan come here to collect thoughts and look out to River, wishing he were still with his beloved Mumtaz. Some say Shah Jahan want to build black marble mausoleum for himself in garden, as a twin to Taj Mahal, but this could not be as he was imprisoned by son.'

The area was all fenced off, overgrown and deserted, but Brima assured us all would be well and to wait for a moment. He strolled over to a dishevelled shack, tapped on the roof's plastic sheeting and a hunched up elderly lady appeared from within. He returned with her at his side. She grinned and said, 'Come.'

We looked at Brima. 'Yes, go, it is okay,' he said. 'I have given her twenty rupees. I can collect from you at end of day, no problems.'

Dismounting our carriage, we trailed behind her for a while until she came to a section of the fence. A small crudely cut-out door flapped open when she pushed it. She nodded and waved us through, 'Straight ahead,' she croaked.

Kate let me go first as she held my shirt for guidance behind. We followed a trail flanked by sand banks and tangled shrubs. The fire of the sun flickered around tall swaying reeds as we approached the water's edge. There was nothing but the river, and for a moment we thought we'd been duped, but our eyes followed a man walking his camel along a shallow ledge, and as he disappeared from view, we realised we were the wrong side of a large twisted tree. We squeezed round and there, the camel drank on his master's tether from the rippling golden reflection of the Taj.

I held Kate's hand, helping her under some barbed wire and we sat upon a wall. With an arm around each other, listening to the echo of city life, we watched the sun melt into the Yamuna, transforming the Taj from a merlot to the arrival of evening indigo.

She looked up at me, 'Thank you, for everything. It's all been so amazing.'

I leaned in and kissed her softly on her lips before we left the secret garden to the shadows of the moonlight, and carefully made our way back to our rickshaw wallah.

24

I waited for her on the roof for breakfast. The bells and buzzes of rickshaws and the motorised traffic below interrupted the peaceful swell of the Taj Mahal. Morning light had not long broken and dark monsoon clouds threatened the sky. Over coffee I contemplated last night; the Mehtab Bagh, laughter over our evening meal, black jack and Limca back at her room, her falling asleep in my arms once again with me following soon after. I fell in love with her the moment she boarded the coach in Delhi and now time was inches away from piercing my heart.

She surprised me, placing her hand on my shoulder and leaning in to kiss my neck. She hung her woven shoulder bag over the back of her chair and ordered an apple porridge and an orange juice. I ordered another coffee. 'Sam, you need to eat and look after yourself,' she said.

'Thanks, but I'm not that hungry.'

'Two apple porridges and two orange juices please,' she said to the waiter.

The food arrived as Kate was reaching into her bag. She retrieved a pen and her journal and opening it in the middle she began writing. 'I can't believe we're here already. Here's my telephone number.' She ripped out the page and passed it to me, 'I hope we can continue this when you get back.'

'I hope so too, but what about Nathaniel?'

'To be honest, I never saw it lasting anyway,' she smiled.

I folded the paper and carefully tore it in two, placing the piece with Kate's number safely into my wallet. I was about to write my number down on the remaining half when I heard a faint siren coming from downstairs, followed by a member of staff bursting through the doors. 'Please be vacating your seats immediately. There has been a very small fire in kitchen, nothing to worry about, it is all under control, but you must all come now.'

There was only one other guy, a young European, who joined us as we made our way outside with the other guests. After a little commotion, we were told we could return to our rooms. There was hardly any time left for us to grab our things before Brima whisked us away to the railway station.

I could have only wished the train was late, but it rolled into the platform five minutes early. She boarded and waited for as long as she could at the doorway. Not knowing if we were ever going to see each other again, tears welled in both our eyes, 'I'll wait for you, I promise,' she said. Then her eyes widened with sudden realisation, 'Your number?'

'Oh yeah, of course,' I desperately rummaged my bag and found some paper and a pen. The train jolted forward and moved away. I scribbled frantically, walking at first in time and then into a jog.

'Take care, Sam,' she said, but then I lost her and all I could do was call out, 'I love you,' as she disappeared in a metallic blur. When I could see the train no more, I looked in my wallet to check if I still had her number. I stared at the gentle swirls of her childlike handwriting, then tucked all that I had left of her safely away.

I was brought back to earth by a boy of maybe nine or ten blocking my path. His dusty feet and legs were swollen like balloons and for a moment I stood shocked. I recognised his condition as elephantiasis and wondered how he coped, he could hardly walk. I withdrew some money from my wallet and placed it in his outstretched hand and then walked on to meet Brima in the foyer.

Kurt answered the door to his hotel room dressed in only his shorts,

'This better be good,' he grumbled, squinting in the sunlight and rubbing his eyes. 'Sam!' he laughed, 'You are early, how great to see you. Come in, come in, put your things down. I will get dressed and we will go out and get an early lunch at my friend's restaurant. I was getting a little bored to be honest. I have seen the Taj five times since I arrived.'

'But you've been okay, yeah?'

'Yes, yes, I caught up with a few people and took it easy,' he shouted from the bathroom. 'You enjoyed Jaipur?' I filled him in of my encounter with Kate. 'You are very lucky to have met her,' he said. 'Do you have her contact details?'

'Yes, but she hasn't got mine.'

'My friend, if it is written in the stars it will be. If not, it is better to have known her than not at all, yes?'

'Of course, but you know?'

'Oh yes, I know, as much as any other man that has loved and lost. Have you been to Agra fort yet?' I said no. 'Then after lunch we shall go and then catch the train back to Delhi.'

I introduced Kurt to Brima downstairs, 'Here is Agra's finest rickshaw wallah.'

Brima went all coy and blushed, 'Oh thank you, sir, I am trying my best.'

He listened to Kurt intently, one foot on the spoked wheel of his carriage, elbow on knee, hand under chin, 'No problems, we will be finding this place, this much I am sure.'

Amid brickwork and concrete, the Taj Mahal flickered past, replaying vivid yesterdays of Kate and me. The momentum of the tricycle lolled me into a personal silence – images, inner voices, sewing echoes of recent lives I'd left behind. I could feel her still with me. I could turn at any moment and she'd be there. But I dare not look, knowing the reality. Inside I clasped seeping memories to call upon should I need her; to talk with her, hold her, to smell her perfume. I was incomplete without her.

'Yes, this is the road,' Kurt called out to Brima. 'Take a right, past the guy carrying the table on his head.' The traffic swerved around us as we made the turn. 'Here, this is Aamir's place.'

'Here, Mr Kurt, sir? Are you sure?' Brima asked.

An old timber framed building, peeling paintwork, cracked wooden door, no windows and no name. I looked over to Brima and laughed, 'I think Kurt might have got us lost again and won't admit it.'

'Yes, yes, you laugh, but not so soon,' Kurt retorted and got down from the rickshaw and knocked at the door.

'Here we go,' I chuckled to Brima.

Apart from the cawing of a crow nearby, only silence. And then the door opened and a young Indian appeared: smart, short beard, laced red topi upon his head and a white robe tied at the centre with a red silk sash. 'Ah Kurt,' he said, smiling warmly. He bowed slightly, palm to his chest, and said, 'Assalamu Alaikum, my brother, good to see you again. I have that book I spoke of the other day, I found it my kitchen under some pots and pans, what it was doing down there I'll never know.' He looked over Kurt's shoulder and saw Brima and me. 'Friends welcome, Assalamu Alaikum,' he said, passing Kurt and shaking my hand as I stepped down. He then put his hands together in Namaste to Brima and invited us inside. Brima stayed put and waggled his head. 'No, my friend, please come, join us, I insist,' Aamir said. 'There is safety for your rickshaw around the back.'

'Wa Alaikum Salaam, Aamir. They did not believe there would be anybody here,' Kurt looked over his shoulder with a wink and a smug grin.

'Then, my friends, I humbly welcome you,' Aamir smiled and gestured us inside. We walked forward through the stooped doorway and along a sloping hallway wafting of cinnamon and ginger. Down a stone staircase lit only by candles, we were brought to a standstill in the pitch black of a room. 'Please, one moment,' Aamir said and was consumed by the darkness, reappearing in low atmospheric lighting behind a counter at the end of a cellar with around twenty low wooden tables surrounded by tangerine and maroon soft furnishings.

He invited us to make ourselves comfortable, but Brima held back. Aamir beckoned him over. 'My friend, are you not hungry?

All those hours of hard riding? Come, as my guest, as a friend.'
Brima glanced to Kurt and me in further confirmation and joined
us at a table while Aamir shuffled away barefoot across the jade
floor into a room, I presumed the kitchen, and soft Arabian music
began to play.

He returned to the table several times, arms balancing dishes,
steam rising and fogging the patterns Moroccan lanterns glittered
upon the walls. 'Please, enjoy,' he said and finally sat down with us.

Platters of mouth-watering houmous and falafel, stuffed vine
leaves, tagine chicken and grilled merguez couscous were offered
up by the plenty. I enquired more about his restaurant, at how it
had no sign outside. How did anybody know about this well-kept
secret?

'This is not so much a restaurant as it is a place of debate,' he
replied. 'I open on Wednesdays, Fridays and Saturdays to a few
friends and colleagues, invited from different backgrounds and
trades. I never charge for my services; I enjoy the evenings far too
much.'

While Aamir, Brima and Kurt were engrossed in conversation, I
excused myself for the wash rooms. On my return, I noticed a sitar
leaning in a corner, 'Do you play, Aamir?'

'Yes, my friend, and you?'

'No, just the guitar.'

He got up and retrieved the instrument, asked me to sit cross
legged and balanced the sitar between my left foot and right knee
and instructed me to pull the plectrum over the bottom set of
strings with my right hand and fret my left fingers on the high
strings. Although what I was producing was a far cry from
spectacular, I surprised myself, finding it a lot easier to play than I
imagined. I passed it over to Aamir. His fingers moved effortlessly
across the strings emitting enchanting sounds that I associated
strongly with India. But it was Brima who impressed us the most.
We were left speechless by his fiddly runs and expert chord
changes. He handed the sitar back to Aamir, oblivious to our
surprised faces.

We applauded. He blushed and said, 'Thank you, but not

necessary.'

'Where did you learn how to play like that Brima?' Kurt asked.

'When I was boy, Uncle Deepak, he visit our village many time in Rampur. Every evening he teach me to play a little more each time. Before he die, he give me sitar. It is still at family home in Bihar. Very nice to be playing again, very good memories.'

'How long have you been a rickshaw wallah?' I asked.

'Um, maybe twenty-two years now I think.'

He made a meagre living. His rickshaw was hired which left very little for him and his family at the end of each day. That's why he tried to make a little extra from business owners by ferrying customers to their doors. Like so many other cycle-rickshaw wallahs, he found life tough, working long hours carrying all sorts of customers and their heavy baggage come rain or shine. He liked tourists the most as they tipped well and found they were generally very courteous to him, unlike some of the richer Indian people, who treated him more like an animal; insulting him and quite a lot of the time underpaying him. But he thanked the divine goddess Lakshmi, grateful of the opportunity of earning an income, however small; rather that, than live life begging on the street not knowing where the next meal might come from.

It was easy to slip in and out of each other's conversation, relaxed enough to enquire about something and not feel like you were being rude or stupid. Aamir encouraged honest and open dialogue in his establishment. Though debate might sometimes get heated, it never reached boiling point. He carefully selected his guests in good faith and of good character. Evenings could run into the early hours of the morning, guests moving from table to table, listening in, deciding if they have something useful to add with the freedom to interject should they wish.

Aamir kept our contact details in a leather-bound book and hoped our paths would cross again one day. The three of us thanked him for his hospitality and mounted the rickshaw bound for Agra Fort.

'I'm going to grab a quick shave,' I said, spying a street barber. I stepped into the shadow of the amaranth fort walls and took a seat.

Every so often I glanced over and caught sight of Kurt in a discussion with a mahout beside an elephant. When my face was smooth, I walked over to them.

'I am trying to make a deal with this man to hire his elephant for two days, but he is driving too hard a bargain,' Kurt said. The mahout stood by, hand on hip awaiting an answer.

I laughed, 'Why on earth would you want to hire an elephant? I mean who would drive it?'

'I would. Last time I was in India I went to the elephant fair in Sonepur and was taught how to control and ride an elephant. It is no problem for me if the elephant is tame.' I conjured a mental image of Laurel and Hardy trudging the streets of Agra, getting lost in narrow alleyways and wedged between buildings. 'I thought it might cheer you up after Kate.'

'Thanks Kurt, that was really nice of you to think of me,' I said, guiding him away from the frustrated mahout. 'I think it might be best if we just carry on as planned, eh? Remember what I was like on the back of the Enfield. I think an elephant might be pushing our luck a bit too far.'

'You have a good point.'

I wasn't really in the mood for site-seeing. Despite Kurt's best efforts at cheering me up, nothing was going to pull me out of this quiet solitude without Kate for a while. I kept up a happy façade as best as I could, but inside I was empty.

Agra Fort's exquisite Moti Masjid and luxurious audience halls of the palatial complex were mostly a blur. I couldn't take any of it in until I came out to a balcony overlooking a length of the sandstone walls and the Taj Mahal further down on the river's edge.

Kurt stared out with me, 'Shah Jahan's hair and beard were said to have turned white overnight when Mumtaz died,' he said. 'He never fully recovered from his loss and weak with illness, his power slipped and he was overthrown by his son, Aurangzeb. Along with his first daughter, Shah Jahan was imprisoned, doomed to spend the remaining eight years of his life looking out to the Taj Mahal, a crushed man.'

I thought, 'Thanks Kurt, that's just what I needed,' but didn't say it. Instead I tried a smile and let him lead the way out and find us somewhere to eat.

At the railway station, we tipped Brima well and said a sad goodbye. I took one last look at him as he became anonymous with the crowds and said one last goodnight to Agra.

Coming home to Delhi, I hoped I might catch a glimpse of Kate, but I had no such luck. It was nice not to find Ashoka on reception, but a cheery Nitin and his puppy dog ways. Kurt was beat and wanted to hit the sack early, which I was happy with. Once I'd caught up with Harish on the rooftop, I took some time out alone on the higher level. I looked out to the sky above Paharganj, Kurt's words tinkling in mind, 'If it is written in the stars, it will be.'

I was up early, back on the roof for an omelette breakfast – no dog, nor monkeys just cheese – I hoped. A long haired American guy came up and asked Nitin for some tea. Nitin tilted his head this way and that, the two getting nowhere. I called over to Nitin, waggled my head, 'Berigybillywahbindah, chai, ya?' I emphasised with my eyes.

Nitin could hardly contain his laughter, 'Hallylahhallylah.' He turned and chuckled quietly to himself as he made the tea.

'Hey man, that's some damn fine Hindi you speak there,' the American said.

'Oh, thanks,' I replied without setting him straight.

I wanted to change some more money for the week and arranged to meet Kurt at the Laxmi Narayan Temple not far from the bank. He was late; something about a puncture on an auto. We spent twenty minutes wandering the gardens of the temple – all around us the candy coloured cream and red shikharas that housed the many shrines.

Stuck in traffic at the top of Arakashan Road on the return, I paid the driver and we got out to walk the rest of the way to the Main Bazaar. At the opening to the bridge before the station, we stopped, held back by shock. An old man was being beaten half to death by a policeman armed with a lathi in the middle of the road.

'Hey. Leave him alone. He's had enough,' Kurt yelled.

The cop's shoulders rose up and down, heavy with his breathing. He lowered his baton and turned. My stomach dropped as I saw it was the same policeman who dealt with my missing traveller's cheques, and who I assumed still thought I owed him money.

'You,' he said, and raised the bamboo cane in my direction.

'Run,' I said to Kurt under my breath.

He immediately took chase, tailing us through the Main Bazaar as we fought our way through the crowds. Kurt darted a sharp right down an alley. The cop slid and fell trying to take the corner. We took a left and then another right and he hobbled past as we stood in silence against a wall in somebody's back yard. After ten minutes of not uttering a word to each other, we broke cover and came out on the Main Bazaar again, keeping a close eye around us.

'What was that about?' Kurt asked as we entered the hotel.

'I'll tell you about it later. Right now, we need to get out of here, just in case. He's got my passport number, so it wouldn't be difficult for him to find us.' Maybe I was being paranoid, but I didn't want to hang around just in case.

The streets leading up to the bus terminal in Old Delhi were crammed and the stuffy auto was hardly moving. The seconds ticking away, the heat and the symphony of horns was driving Kurt crazy, 'I have to get out of here. We will run, we will get there faster,' he said, and reached for his wallet to pay the driver.

I put a firm hand on his arm, 'We will not run, Kurt. We left early, we still have time. Let's see if the traffic will ease.' And it did. With five minutes to spare, we were on a bus bound for Manali.

25

Mandi verged an outward bend of the Beas and embraced the Kullu hills behind. While sipping morning chai, I looked out to the small, dense town and allowed the calm and cool atmosphere to dissolve the heat and overwhelming sounds of the Golden Triangle. Tilting my head to the sky I let the fine spray of rain rinse away the film that had coated my skin since I left Delhi.

'I like it when it is raining like this,' a soft voice said to my left. I glanced to see a young Indian man, in his late teens if I had to guess. 'It reminds me of my childhood when I would find shelter in an old stable and make figures from straw. My name is Jay. You are here on vacation?'

Was it a vacation? It felt more like a way of life now. 'Sam,' I returned. 'Yes, I suppose, an extended one you could say. And you?'

'I am a student on leave with my friends over there.' He turned his back to the valley and pointed to a group of teenagers sitting on a wall. 'I think you might want to wake your friend.' Kurt had been dozing near the chai stall and was blissfully unaware the engine had started and passengers were heading back to their seats. I woke him with a gentle nudge, only long enough for him to resume his position on the bus, resting his head on a scarf placed against the window.

To pass the time Jay and I spoke about India, every now and

then glimpsing out at the mountain snow sparkling against a broken sapphire sky. In just a couple of hours we would be in Manali.

'How would you like to feel really alive?' He opened the window next to his seat and pulled himself out using the ladder attached to the side of the bus. I leant my head out and looked up at his feet on the rungs. 'Follow me if you are brave enough,' he called out.

'Are you crazy?' I shouted back. His friends followed him, legs dangling from the windows. I put my head out again to see Jay's face smiling down at me from the roof, 'Come on Sam, you only live once.'

Apart from a handful of people, Kurt and I were the only ones left and he hadn't moved an inch since we'd left Mandi, so I left him in peace and pulled myself up to sit on the rim of the window frame. As the bus hurtled along I questioned the sanity of what I was doing. One wrong move and I'd be taking a one-way trip, hundreds of feet down a mountainside.

I heaved myself over to the ladder and clumsily found my footing. Jay laughed, encouraging me with an outstretched arm. I clambered to his position, adrenaline surging, and slumped down beside him.

'Put your feet under the metal bar for safety,' he said, pointing at his feet to demonstrate. He threw his arms out to mimic an aeroplane. I did the same and we burst out laughing.

Jay insisted on taking a photo of me. With one hand clutching the railing, I fished around my bag and handed him my camera. I positioned myself so I had the guys beside me and tried my best to smile and keep my eyes open despite the wind nipping at my face.

'A great picture, I am sure. I even got the mountains in the background,' Jay said as he returned the camera. I made sure it was tightly stowed away and the flap of my bag was secured over the top.

Once the initial excitement had died down, we were left to our own thoughts, each of us staring out to the endless snow-tipped ridges. My mind drifted in and out of the past few days, little rushes of excitement pulsing through me at the slightest breeze of Kate. I looked over to my roof-rack companions every now and then, reciprocating a smile when I'd catch an eye, and return to my musings as did they. Even with these people, who'd I'd only known a short time, I found myself at ease. I realised how long I had shunned the outside world, never allowing anybody in. In India, my defences had weakened, and thus, life had got that much easier, that much happier. I'd spent too long by myself in an empty room and had found so much security in that way of life. The emptiness of a cold room I hated as a child, had become a sanctuary as an adult.

'Duck, Sam!' Jay shouted, and just in time. A low branch skimmed the top of my head as I leant forward. We laughed together as I stole a glance behind watching the tree as it disappeared around a bend.

On arrival in Manali, Kurt and I said goodbye to Jay and his friends and we found a trusty old auto to climb the hills to our Dhungri home. The rooms that Neria, Sophie and Tyler occupied were now empty but for the fond memories that lingered. I unlocked the padlock to my door and inhaled the familiarity of my room that would soon be gone forever. My thoughts again drifted to Kate. For all the rewards travel has, its share of heartbreak is equalled.

'Somehow, with the absence of Tyler, Sophie and Neria, Manali feels as if it is missing a certain spirit,' said Kurt, who had appeared at the door. 'Even if we were all to meet here again, it would never be the same. It is time to move on and for you, another destination to be uncovered.'

This was the house where I had recognised my strengths and realised my weaknesses; the house where I first felt part of a family. The man that stood before me, through simple kindness and patience, had taught me how to believe in myself and reap the rewards that life had to offer. I would always hold the deepest respect and gratitude towards him and be forever in his debt, although he would never ask a single thing from me.

My room was now as empty as when I first found it. Before pulling the bolt across I took one last look at the mountains. The sound of laughing in the living area, the smells of cooking from the kitchen, the early morning voices of the locals collecting apples merged into one as we left.

For the next two days, we would be taken along some of the highest mountain passes in the world. Extreme weather conditions rendered the route impassable for all but a couple of months each year and even while open it was known to be treacherous. During this window, local people reunited with loved ones or took advantage of trade, whilst a handful of travellers like us were drawn north, intrigued by the mystery of the unique Buddhist town that for many years had been kept hidden.

At the bus station, we met a guy called Eli. Cropped black hair and goatee beard, he was roughly the same age as us, enjoying some freedom after two years' national service in Israel. His neatly pressed clothes, structure and organisation about his kit certainly gave the impression he'd experienced a form of military life.

'Ah you are travelling to Leh also?' Kurt asked as he strapped our luggage to the roof.

Eli checked the last of his things, clipped his pack shut and hoisted it up to him, 'Yes. I plan to do some trekking while I'm there. You are trekking too?'

'No. We are just visiting, taking it easy, you know?'

'How long do you plan to stay?'

'Two months maybe.' Dismay dawned as he said this. Leh would be the last new place in India I would see.

Eli bagged a window next to Kurt. I got the window opposite, the seat next to mine empty. The remainder of the bus was occupied by Kullu and Ladakhi folk.

The first hour was relatively plain sailing. From Manali we climbed a land of giants, corkscrewing higher around every bend leaving villages tiny below us, pine forests dwindling away. The roads became more unforgiving and we were thankful our driver knew what he was doing. Aside from recent rock fall and glacial streams sluicing down the slopes taking with them broken sections of tarmac, the weather was taking a turn for the worse and a thick fog was closing in fast, bringing traffic to a sudden standstill.

For what seemed forever we edged along, bumper to bumper, heavy snow setting in, blizzard state, hitting the bus at all angles and blotting out any remaining views. Soon, black triangles emerged up ahead and we came into a clearing surrounded by mountains, a handful of battered tents clinging on for dear life.

'We are at Rohtang La,' Kurt shouted as we stepped into the thick of it. Against the wind and stinging snow, we made it to the nearest tent and stooped inside.

'Come, make yourself comfortable,' said an old Kullu man. He adjusted his pillbox cap to a tilt, got up and attended to a kettle on a stove, leaving two young Indian men sat beside him huddled in thick yak fur coats. 'Tea for all, yes?' We nodded. 'Good, sit,' he said and pointed to a log against the wall of the tent. The men opposite nodded, said they were on vacation and asked the usual questions.

'Not much of a holiday for you guys, huh?' I said.

'Oh, no sir, it is being quite the reverse. We are loving this mountain adventure. We have never felt cold such as this or seen snow before for that matter.' They grinned, immense pleasure written upon their faces. 'You see we are from the golden city of Jaisalmer, deep in the Thar Desert. All year round, very hot.'

Halfway through our chai, I took a peak outside. The snow was lessening, but still intent on grounding us for a while. The old man trickled more tea into our glasses while the wind rippled the leather sheets at our backs.

'This is why Rohtang Pass is known as the Pile of Bodies,' Eli remarked. 'Many lives have been lost over the years trying to cross. It is good to wait a little longer. It looks like it will soon pass.'

An hour slipped by before the thick curtain of cloud drew back to reveal a clear sky. A blinding white sun shone down upon the Pir Panjal Range, causing the ice lanes trailing its slopes to glitter. We gave our thanks for the tea for which the old man refused payment and boarded the bus, moving away from the predominantly Hindu region of Kullu and ascending towards the Buddhist Lahaul and Spiti valleys. From the southern side of the pass, the Beas began its descent into Manali, while on the northern side the Chandra River flowed westward. Slow going over several miles of recent snowfall, we advanced carefully through the thick slush, walled in by ice either side until eventually the land levelled out, the white attenuated and elongated shadows raced over a vast semi-arid desert against a horizon of sandy snow streaked peaks. The three of us checked in our passports briefly with a bored looking police officer who sat behind a desk outside his brown tent noting down our details should we have an accident or go missing, before moving on again through a dusty grey of scree and boulder strewn slopes.

Kurt was lost in thought. I was beginning to think there was more behind this than just leaving Manali, but there was no prising any further information from him. Eli was taking nearly as many pictures as me and every now and then he would look around, as if to confirm what he was seeing was for real. Kurt didn't have a camera with him. He believed that if he took pictures, it would be the photographs he would remember and not the events of his trip. I understood where he was coming from, but I couldn't lay that much trust in my memory.

From the tiny village of Keylong we travelled onwards and upwards to Jispa; the mountains more rugged, the road more treacherous. It was being rebuilt in places by a huddle of hooded ghosts; road workers from the east of the country who made their money working through months of harsh conditions.

Late afternoon handed over to early evening by the time we arrived in Darcha. Eli, Kurt and I registered our passports again at a checkpoint and rented a two-man tent for the night, while the other passengers chose their seats on the bus as a bed. We got our heads down swiftly so we would be ready for the early rise. Bitterly cold, I was the only one without a sleeping bag – Aiden locking the one I had away with my backpack in Delhi somewhere.

Despite searching for sleep, it wasn't to be found. The two-man accommodation may have been the cheapest option, but it left very little room for breathing. Condensation was dripping on my face which froze if I didn't wipe it away. There was next to no room to move and I was on the verge of wetting myself having tried to hold it until sunrise. At just gone 3am, I unzipped the tent and stepped out. I was in full flow, smiling at the relief that overcame me, when I stopped to the sound of rustling ahead. My eyes were still unaccustomed to the darkness, but I could just about make out the figure of something the size of a dog heading my way, grunting or maybe snarling at my presence. It was enough for me to move cautiously back into the tent and keep as still as possible as I listened for the slightest sound of movement from outside.

26

I awoke to the sound of rustling and nearly jumped out of my skin at the thought of the animal inside our tent.

'Beast! Beast!'

Confused and a little scared by all the shouting, Eli was the first to respond, 'What the hell are you going on about?'

I tried to explain what had happened this morning.

'Probably a red fox,' Kurt suggested. He dropped his voice to a lower, sinister tone, 'Or maybe a snow leopard sniffing out fresh meat.'

'That's just great,' I replied and headed to the unsavoury mud brick toilet, leaving behind laughter in the distance.

The morning's journey was broken only once by an overturned goods carrier in the road. As the bus shunted back and forth to pass, the incident was complicated by another bus trying to manoeuvre past at the same time. It had mounted the side of the road and tipped to one side on top of our bus, causing major problems.

Kurt interrupted the sound of heaving gear changes, 'We should be at the town of Zingzingbar soon. It is about 4300 metres so you may experience signs of altitude sickness.'

When we reached Zingzingbar, the interior of the bus was silent. People were either sleeping or staring longingly from the window for the journey to end. Apart from a dull headache and a little shortness of breath, I was enjoying every second. Now and then, isolated Buddhist monasteries appeared, built into the slopes. I wondered how on earth anybody could reside there and how they survived the severely cold winters. As it was, the inside of the bus was like a refrigerator and this was the best time of year.

Gradually the landscape continued to alter as we circled the mountains. The high snow walls either side of the highway were a dirty grey from passing exhausts and spray from the road. Through the mighty Zanskar Range and the crisp sweeping folds of Baralacha La, we steadily descended into Sarchu Plains where spectacular ochre rock formations rose from a stark desert in the sky.

At a little brick hut by the side of the road in Sarchu we stopped for a while over a lunch of fried momos. Eli joined me for a cigarette as we looked out to the mountains.

'Are you trekking with others, Eli?'

'Maybe I will find a party once I arrive, but I hope to do it alone.'

An icy wind rippled through a line of multi-coloured Tibetan prayer flags sending thoughts and prayers to the heavens above. 'That's brave of you. It's a bit barren out there.'

Ahead lay an empty expanse stretching for miles, no sign of life to be seen. 'I will be kitted up well and my route is planned to coincide with villages along the way for a night's rest. And even places like this; there is life if you look hard enough. You see, there on the wall of that mountain.' He pointed but I saw nothing but rock.

I turned to him, 'What am I looking for?'

'Look there, you see, the goats.'

Again, I saw nothing and wondered what was in that cigarette of his when something shuffled on the rock face. It was an adult goat and two unsure kids making their way down the crag.

'Mother teaching them,' he laughed. 'If you know where to look you can find food and shelter.' They disappeared into an opening, maybe a cave or another path through the mountain.

'I wouldn't have a clue what I was looking for. I guess your army training helps.'

'That and my father's knowledge of the land. We enjoyed many camping trips when I was young. He taught me how to hunt and build shelter, much like the goats, yes?'

It was strange to hear of a normal relationship between father and son. It was hard to picture such a permanent secure world as this. To me this was the stuff of fairy tales. I pondered in quiet thought as we made our way back to the bus bound for the Gata Loops – twenty-one hairpin bends fringed by the Zanskar Range.

Feeling somewhat detached from my friends, I sat in silence gazing out at the changing landscape, gently unravelling something new and fresh to my eyes. I thought about the early morning hours in the back of the car travelling to Blackpool or Devon; mum in the passenger seat, dad driving; music from the eight-track filling gaps in their conversation – Glen Campbell or some love song sung by Eric Carmen or Bobby Goldsboro. A rare week once a year, I was allowed a reprieve in his regime. The only time he lifted some of the weight, allowing me the light air of freedom, almost treating me like a real son. But the end of the week would always be clouded by the thought of returning home, back to the prison of my sparse room.

Behind a slow-moving convoy of coaches and goods carriers that created a thin pencil line trailing in the distance ahead, we traversed through Nakee La and Lachulung La coming out into the Morey Plains; a dramatic landscape of naturally chiselled formations created by the elements. It was as if we were on another planet – scene after scene unfolding from a sci-fi movie.

The bus revved its gears, struggling to ascend a table top mountain where we reached the highest point of the journey, Tanglang La – a sweeping panorama of snow-capped peaks and a captivating view of the Morey plains in the distance. Near a small shrine, Tibetan prayer flags fluttered behind a square yellow stone inscribed with the words:

TANGLANGLA
ALTITUDE:
17582 FT

5328 MT
YOU ARE PASSING THROUGH
SECOND HIGHEST PASS
OF THE WORLD
UNBELIEVABLE IS IT NOT?

Stretching our legs, we took in what little air there was before recommencing, crossing the Indus River and sweeping past the desolate Buddhist gompas of Shey and Stok constructed seamlessly into the forgotten landscape. White memorial chortens and simple Tibetan-styled homes steadily furnished a landscape of fading green and gold. The fat sun fell lazily behind a ridge, the road smoothed out and we gathered up speed to our destination.

'The Last Shangri la', 'Moonland' and 'Little Tibet' were among the appellations given to Leh over the years. As we came to the end of our long journey it was easy to see how the capital of the kingdom of Ladakh lived up to all of them. The sleepy town hugged by crumbly, biscuit beige ridges sprawled out to introduce the chocolate velvet Zanskar Valley. On a hillock to the north, Leh Palace overlooked the town. Once the highest building in the world and modelled on the Potala Palace in Tibet, the 17th century former royal residence was now partially in ruins.

Kurt used the palace to navigate us through the laid back main bazaar, but at the end he looked about hopelessly, 'I cannot remember which road leads to the house I stayed in last time. We will find somewhere else for now and I will search again after dinner.'

With that, we climbed a steep hill and wandered into a guest house within the residential district of Karzoo. There was only one room available so the three of us opted to share. Eli and I each took one of the two steel framed beds, while Kurt volunteered to sleep on the foam mattress that was rolled up and strapped to his pack. The room was cold, the stone walls icy to the touch. In a square alcove on the left wall were three worn shelves and at the end of the room, a window, held in place by a feeble old frame. Despite the low temperature there was something quite cosy about it.

We found somewhere to eat in the main bazaar, then Kurt and I went in search of the house he had previously stayed in. Walking was hazardous at times, the darkening pathways marred by potholes leading down to rushing water below. After a few dead ends and a little head scratching, Kurt finally found what he was looking for. At the entrance to a white timber-framed house, a Tibetan lady attended to some yellow flowers in her porch under a lamp hung beside the door. She immediately recognised Kurt and with a surprised squeal gave him a hug.

'Julay, Julay,' she said, turning to me and beaming from ear-to-ear.

'Do you have three rooms vacant?' Kurt asked as we were led into her immaculate home.

'Oh, I am sorry. We only have one room for next two month.'

'That's no problem,' I replied, 'I'll see if I can stay on at the guest house.' I took a sip of the odd tasting tea I was presented with, which was bitter and greasy.

'Are you sure, Sam?'

'Of course.'

'OK, good.' Kurt turned back to the lady, 'I will pick up my things and be back later. Sam, we will meet for breakfast, yes?'

'Sounds like a plan.'

Sitting opposite each other in the dimming light Eli and I talked about plans for my future in India. With the way my finances were looking, I was unsure exactly what the future held. I'd previously spoken to Eli about the possibility of offering a massage service and he was keen to remind me of the earning potential from travellers around Leh.

'It would be great for trekkers returning from a big hike,' he said. 'I will find another room in the morning, that way you can use the spare bed in here to work from.' Would it work? I had no idea, but it had to be worth a try. The thought of leaving India so early was unsettling. I estimated that I had enough money to last me only two more weeks. As Eli slept, I went about creating a poster, stating my services, appointment times and costs.

27

On the pavements of the main bazaar, people sat selling vegetables and spices from boxes and sacks, all the while smiling at one another, appearing happy and without a sense of urgency in their lives. It was a far cry from the chaos of the big cities. I met Kurt and Eli for breakfast who each shared contentment with their new lodgings. My room was ready for any potential customers so I just needed to find a place that could photocopy my poster, and then hope some local businesses would find a space to display it. This proved to be quite easy and soon my advert was posted in over a dozen shops and restaurants around the town. I had allocated three appointment times: 10am, 1pm and 4pm, with the plan being to hang around for fifteen minutes to see if anyone would show and if not, continue with my day.

Eli bid us farewell to go in search of a trekking expedition, then as we walked away from the main bazaar, Kurt said, 'I would like you to meet a friend of mine if you have time. Her name is Ciri.'

Leading the way, he took us up a steep hill and within ten minutes we'd arrived at a house. 'I am hoping she still rents her regular room.' At the top of a flight of stairs and along a narrow hallway was a dark varnished door. Kurt knocked and it was answered by an attractive lady in her late forties. She held her thumb between the pages of a red leather-bound book and laughed in surprise as she recognised her old friend.

'Wow! Kurt, come in, come in,' she said in a broad Italian accent. 'It's been, what, two years since we last saw each other?' She turned to me, 'My apologies, my name is Ciri.' I leant forward, shook her hand and introduced myself. 'Lovely to meet you Sam, please take a seat. I will prepare some tea for us.' Once more the tea was strangely bitter and greasy, but I did my best to show a face of appreciation out of politeness.

'Sam does massage. He is very good.' Kurt explained. 'I thought about your back, Ciri, how is it?'

'Oh, very stiff, it hurts most days.' Ciri's hand reached around to her back and frowned as if it troubled her as she spoke.

'How long have you had a problem?' I asked, placing the quarter of a cup of tea left on the table.

'Five years ago, I was travelling in a cycle-rickshaw that was hit by a goods carrier. I broke my back and am lucky I can still walk. Sadly, the rickshaw driver did not survive.'

'That's awful.' My imagination worked overtime picturing the macabre scene. With her permission, I ran my hands along her shoulders and down her back. 'I believe with a little work, I can help to improve your posture and reduce the pain you currently feel. It would also relieve some of the pressure on your internal organs, in turn aiding your digestion and breathing.'

'That sounds wonderful, Sam. How about I book you in for two hours a day? I will pay five hundred rupees a time, if that's okay with you.'

'Thank you, only if you're sure though. Maybe you should see if I'm any good first.'

'I am a good judge of character and if Kurt says you are good, then you must be. I trust him with my life. Come by tomorrow morning, you can start then.'

I couldn't believe my luck and thanked Kurt profusely as we walked into town, much to his eventual irritation. Before I returned to the guest house to check in on my 1pm and 4pm appointments, I crossed off the 10am from all the posters in town. With my afternoon empty, I joined Kurt and Eli for a few games of black jack. At the turn of dusk, Kurt took us to a small restaurant called the

Tibetan Friend's Corner Café. He knew the owner well, an elegant middle aged Tibetan lady called Dolma and like everyone else he'd reunited with she was over the moon to see him. We ordered a portion of fried momos and thukpa; a delicious Tibetan noodle and vegetable dish. It was accompanied by that strange tea once again. Tibetan butter tea I was told was great for high altitude and warming in cold climates and provided lots of caloric energy. Made from yak butter, tea leaves and salt, it was presented to us in a clay tea pot with small wooden cups. I had a feeling I would have to get used to drinking it.

A little later Ciri came in and joined us at our table, and just like I did in Manali, I felt a happiness and security that I'd never felt in England. Before I retired to bed, I opened my wallet and took out Kate's telephone number. Her words whispered around my head, 'I'll wait for you, Sam, I promise.'

The sun rose slowly above the peaked horizon. Outside with my breakfast of steaming jam muffins, I heated my hands around a coffee flask. It was my favourite time of day. My mind was at peace and my spirits were high. It felt comfortable here, safe. People were relaxed and greeted each other with smiles. There had been a few touts, but otherwise I was left alone to go about my day. Locked away from the prying eyes of the rest of the world, Leh was unscathed by negativity and interruptions of modern life.

I headed out for my morning appointment with Ciri, with only the essentials I needed for my morning's work: a bottle of massage and essential oils, a small wooden bowl, a towel, soap and a bottle of water. I followed narrow trails fringing the riverbank and passed men and women washing their clothes in the water and laying them out to dry on the grass. Avoiding the holes in the road, I climbed the hill and stepped into the house where Ciri rented her studio apartment.

I entered to the heady scent of sandalwood. 'Good morning, Sam. Can I get you some tea?'

'Is it normal?' I asked.

'Normal? How do you mean?'

'Every cup of tea I have had in Leh has not tasted so good.'

'You do not like the butter tea?' she chuckled. 'It's an acquired taste, but the more you drink, the more you will get used to it. I was the same when I first arrived in Leh, but now I couldn't go a day without it. It is very beneficial.'

I removed the items from my bag and placed them on the table as Ciri poured. She removed her blouse and laid on her front as I prepared the oil in the mixing bowl. I went about slowly kneading her neck, 'How many times have you been to India?'

'Once a year for nine years now. I always stay in Leh for a couple of months. In Milan, I have three beauty salons. Six months a year I leave them in the capable hands of others and travel this wonderful country. I'm fifty-two now and with each year I appreciate the time away from work more and more. What are your plans Sam?'

'In life or India?'

'Both.'

'To be honest, I haven't thought about what I'm going to do when I return home. I met a lovely girl in Delhi called Kate and we travelled to Jaipur and Agra together. She doesn't live too far from me in England and I'm hoping to see her when I get back. As for India, I'm not too sure. Kurt is here and he is a good friend and now I have work, so it seems I might stay in Leh until it's time for me to go home.'

'Yes, Kurt is a good man. We have been friends for a long time. How much time do you have left in India?'

'Just under six weeks.' In my head, it sounded like a long time, but when I said it aloud it dawned on me how little time was really left.

Ciri sat up with her back to me. She rolled her shoulders and exhaled deeply, 'That was wonderful Sam, thank you.' Picking up her blouse, she redressed.

I looked at my watch, not realising how much time had elapsed, 'I should get going. I'll catch up with you at the Tibetan Friend's Café this evening maybe, if not tomorrow for our appointment?'

'I will look forward to seeing you again,' she said, paying me as I left.

I checked in at the guest house for my next appointment, but nobody was there. I wasn't disappointed. The regular slot from Ciri was enough to keep my finances ticking along nicely. Instead I decided to visit the main bazaar and browse the shops. Traditional curios and artwork filled glass cabinets and shelves; silver jewellery mounted with turquoise stones, golden hand-held prayer wheels and wooden masks detailed with large eyes and long sharp teeth. At one shop, I gave in to the seductive sales patter of a sweet old lady who sold me a cream woollen jacket, candles for my room and a blanket.

A large percentage of Leh's population was made up of the Ladakhi people who traditionally wore long woollen robes – charcoal or tan in colour – tied under the arms and around the waist by a sash. Some of the women wore a colourful shawl on their back to carry goods or maybe an infant; their hair was worn in pigtails, sometimes also by the men. Occasionally I'd see people with a black top hat, pointed brims to the left and right, and beads worn around their necks. From time to time a small hand-held prayer wheel was spun amongst mutters of 'Om Mani Padme Hum.'

Although the region of Ladakh was predominantly Buddhist, a small percentage of the population was from Islamic Kashmir. The Jama Masjid – a small, but beautiful white mosque was tucked away under the shadow of Leh Palace. Several times a day I would hear the hypnotic tones of the call to prayer from a loud speaker perched at the top of the single domed minaret.

Returning for my four o'clock appointment, which again went unfilled, I found Kurt waiting for me at one of the tables outside. We shared a flask of coffee and were joined by Eli.

'I have rented a room here,' he said. 'I wasn't too keen on the other place and luckily one became available here this morning.'

'Any luck finding an expedition?' I asked.

'Some possibilities, but nothing that has struck me. I think I will go alone as planned.'

Making an early start the next day, I walked into town to explore Leh Palace. The sky was white without a single beam of sunlight, but this didn't dampen my spirits. I'd found such tranquillity in Leh that it would have been difficult to find anything to diminish my positivity. Since meeting Kurt and Tyler all those weeks ago in Dehra Dun, my mind was clear and illuminated by sunshine. The thoughts that usually darkened and dirtied the water lay dormant and I could almost forget they were there at all. In this little town, a smile was guaranteed around every corner. People here had next to nothing by way of possessions, but they appreciated what they did have and that included family, which had a far higher value than any amount of wealth or material objects. Girish once told me in Manali, 'The more you have, the more you have to worry about,' and then gave me an all-knowing smile. He knew the secret to happiness and it seemed so did the majority of people in Leh.

I approached the summit of a hillock, which allowed a stunning view of the town stretching out to the mighty Zanskar range. Behind me, the palace loomed high above like a guardian of the town. It was built from reinforced sand coloured walls and overhanging balconies with window frames of rust red. To one side of the building an ornate wooden porch at the top of a flight of stairs, which I presumed was the entrance, had a hand-written sign that read, 'UNDER REPARE – PALACE CLOSE FRO ONE MONTH' dated yesterday's date.

Retracing my steps, I was met by a young monk no more than ten years of age who was dressed in a tan robe and wore white trainers. 'Sorry palace close,' he said with a smile.

'Thank you,' I replied, 'It's a shame, I imagine it's very interesting inside. What an incredible view of Leh though.' He tilted his head, seemingly unaware of what I'd said. Instead he replied with the same as before, 'Sorry, palace close,' and sat on a crumbled wall alongside a white stupa, gold pinnacle pointing to the sky.

With time to spare before my appointment with Ciri, I went back to the guest house for breakfast. I was at the door to my room, about to enter, when a fellow traveller approached me. His hair was long, dark and curly, his skin tanned and he wore loose fitting clothes;

baggy fractal trousers and a Metallica t-shirt. 'Hey, how you doing? I'm in the room above you. I booked a car to go to Tikse Monastery tomorrow afternoon. The French couple next door to you were meant to be coming with me but they had an argument and cancelled, so there's a free place if you want to come instead? It's all paid for.'

I paused and checked my mental diary, 'Ah yeah, sure. I'm Sam,' I said, reaching out my hand.

'Connor,' he said, shaking it. 'Okay man, do you know the Kashmiri restaurant near the mosque at the top of the Bazaar? Say we meet there at five this afternoon and we'll grab something to eat and discuss details.'

'Cool,' I said. He replied the same and disappeared up the stairs.

It was at Ciri's, after the massage and over a cup of sweet black tea, that we discussed Kurt. She'd noticed that he hadn't been himself and was unusually quiet in her company. She had quizzed him and discovered he was missing his ex-girlfriend a great deal. He'd never mentioned any previous relationship to me. I decided to find him to see if he wanted to talk. He'd never faltered in his friendship and it was my turn to be there for him. I went to where he was staying, but there was no sign of his whereabouts. I stopped off at the Tibetan Friend's Café, but they hadn't seen him since last night. It was at my guest house I finally found him in Eli's room laying on the spare bed.

'Hey guys, do you want to grab some lunch?' I asked.

'You two go, I will stay here,' Kurt mumbled.

Eli looked up from sorting through his rucksack with a cocked eyebrow, 'No, you two go. I need the extra bed space to pack.'

We made our way into town with Kurt's head down most of the way. I'd never seen him so lifeless. 'How are you Kurt? I haven't seen much of you lately.'

'I am okay, I guess.'

'It may not be my place to say this, but Ciri mentioned you might be missing someone from back home, a girl maybe? She's worried about you.'

He stopped for a moment and managed a smile, 'I am sorry,

Sam. Yes, I have been thinking of a good friend. We were very much in love, but life has a habit of getting in the way. Too much work leading to too little time for the important things. I miss her a great deal. It has been so long now since we last spoke.'

'You should have spoken to me sooner. You know I know how you feel, right?' We'd arrived outside the Tibetan Friend's Corner Café, 'Shall we go in?' I said, placing my hand on his shoulder.

Inside the simple space, the air was filled with Ladakhi chatter, laughter and wafts of enticing food. Kurt sat and I went to the counter. A Tibetan girl in her early twenties greeted me with an amiable smile that complemented her pretty face. She wrote our order down on a notepad and a few moments later served our drinks.

'Julay Kurt,' she said placing the pots of tea on the table.

'Julay Tsering, it is good to see you again,' he replied warmly.

'It is lovely to see you too. Your food will arrive soon.' She whistled her way into the kitchen as Kurt and I resumed our conversation.

'What about Saskia? You do not speak of her much either. What happened between you two?' he asked.

It was still a wound that wouldn't completely heal, despite the time spent with Kate. I stared into my cup, 'I was hooked from the very start. She was smart, confident and focused. We had fun and I loved her get-up-and-go attitude. I never thought in a million years she'd accept when I asked her out on a date, I was simply chancing my luck. Her interest in me caught me off-guard. It didn't take long for things to sour but it was already too late. We were together for eighteen months; the majority of which I was miserable, but somehow always believed it was because I was doing something wrong. If I could do a better job of making her happy then everything would be great. I finally came to my senses and we split in January.'

'Sounds like you made a good decision.'

'Yeah. I know it was the right thing to do, but sometimes I find it hard to let go. When you spend that much time with someone, I don't know, I guess you just feel lost, like you don't know where you're going anymore.'

'Yes, this is how I feel too, very lost at the moment,' Kurt's eyes searched his tea for the reflection of memories.

I sat back and sighed, 'I miss the whole idea of being in a relationship I think.'

'You may have a chance at happiness with Kate when you get home. Surely that's worth staying positive for. You cannot dwell on the past indefinitely. It is no good.'

'Maybe it is time for us both to look ahead towards a brighter future.'

'To a brighter future then,' he said and raised his cup.

The Kashmiri restaurant wasn't where I expected it to be and I had to squeeze by a shaggy, black yak in a narrow alleyway to get to the entrance. Connor was already sitting inside drinking a Coke and waved me over, 'Hey man, I'm having Kashmiri chicken and rice, you want the same?'

'Is it safe?' I asked, cautious of not falling ill again.

'You mean is the chicken an escaped convict?' he laughed.

'No, I mean...'

'Hey dude, it's all cool. I've eaten here a lot and haven't got ill yet.' He signalled to the waiter, 'Two Kashmiri murghs, one pulao and two Cokes.'

'Are you from Israel?' I asked at a guess, considering the high volume of Israeli travellers I'd seen in the north.

'Ha? No man, I'm from Bombay.'

'Oh, so you moved to India?'

He laughed, 'Moved? From where? Na, I was born in India. I'm an Indian, yaar.'

'Oh, it's just that I don't see many Indian backpackers. In fact, you're the first. You dress, well, like a foreign backpacker.' I seemed to be digging a larger hole for myself by the second.

He laughed again, 'I get that a lot. I've been backpacking the north for a month now, just came up from Manali a week ago.'

Connor was very likeable and as we tucked into the food we chatted fluidly about all kinds of subjects. He was funny and smiley but could be serious when appropriate. He talked about the poverty in India with sincerity and empathy and I found out that he lived with his family of two sisters, one brother, mother and grandmother in Bombay and was a successful studio technician. His long-term girlfriend Radhika was due to arrive in Leh in a few days' time and we agreed we'd meet up again later in the week.

We headed back to the guest house and arranged to meet outside the entrance the following day for the ride into Tikse. It had been a long day and I was happy to see the inside of my room. I said goodnight to Connor and after a short time pottering I went to bed falling asleep almost before my head even hit the pillow.

28

The journey to Tikse was without drama. The roads were clear and the occasional drivers we encountered seemed relaxed. Not far from the monastery, a small hut selling refreshments caught my eye and I asked the driver to stop. I'd skipped lunch in a rush to get ready and was now feeling gnawing in my stomach. It was a quaint little place; tiny window frames, splintered paint and dusty windows, chequered red and white table cloths covered the old wooden tables and from one corner, the proprietors – an elderly man and woman – smiled a greeting of Julay as we entered.

We settled down to a bowl of mokthuk each, a delicious Tibetan soup consisting of momos and vegetables. Connor addressed the owners, who spoke little English, but enough for a comfortable conversation. They were husband and wife and ran this little café for the benefit of travellers to and from Tikse. In 1960 the couple had made a gruelling sixteen-day journey on foot from the Tibetan capital, Lhasa, over the Himalayan Mountains into India on the trail of the Dalai Lama to escape the cruelties of Chinese occupation in Tibet.

I asked more about Connor, about his hobbies. He loved music, playing instruments and working in recording studios, but his real passion was bass guitar. He'd been practising since he was a boy and rarely missed a day without fretting strings. I went on to ask how he was finding Leh, 'It's so chilled here man,' he said, slurping the last of his soup. 'I mean it's a small place, and there's not much to do, but I can't seem to bring myself to leave. It's as if I could spend forever here, like a strange spell has been cast. I felt the same in Manali. When you're in the city, you get so used to the pollution, the noise and people rushing around, you don't stop to think that there might be an alternative. This is the first time I have experienced so much peace, space and such fresh air. I didn't know what to do with myself for the first couple of days when I got to Manali, it was kind of unsettling. I felt so small in such a huge world.'

Tikse Gompa was situated at the top of a craggy hill and stood at 3600 metres in the Indus valley, commanding impressive views of the mountains. The 15th century monastery of red, white and ochre was topped by golden finials, and the surrounding area was beautifully fringed with stone walls of whitewashed chorten. Similar in style to Leh Palace, it reminded me once again of Potala Palace in Tibet and I could see why it had earned the nickname, 'Mini Potala'.

We left the car and climbed the terraces of monk's quarters until we reached the entrance. The hallways echoed chanting voices in prayer and the shuffling of feet of young devotees draped in brilliant red robes who giggled at the sight of us as we passed by. The stone rooms were filled with Buddhist statues and murals exploding with colour, and within one room we were brought to a halt at the sight of the fifteen-metre-high Maitreya Buddha, exceptionally detailed and painted blue and red with a huge gold face.

Passing a row of prayer wheels, we ascended the steps to the roof terrace and were both left in wonder. Multi-coloured prayer flags lined the walls, flapping in the icy wind, introducing the expanse of fertile fields that led to the dark desert mountains.

An invisible weight had been lifted as a result of our visit. Connor and I agreed our spell in Ladakh was immensely relaxing, yet somehow the time spent within the walls and halls of Tikse awarded us a new depth to our inner peace. We said little to each other as we returned to Leh, mutually in awe of the monastery and aware of the gift we had left with.

Ciri had kindly recommended me to a friend of hers who was staying nearby; a French lady called Mrs Lebert. Despite a few wrong turns, I was fast learning the quickest way to get around Leh and found her apartment with relative ease. It had an excellent view of the Buddhist Shanti Stupa tucked away under the shadows of the jagged peaks. Mrs Lebert was immediately sociable and invited me to stop for tea and have a chat. She was a little overweight, had short dark hair and I would say she was heading towards sixty. The conversation was somewhat stunted as she spoke little English and I no French. We did however manage to come to an arrangement, booking my one o'clock slot – Monday to Friday – for the next week or so. Things were looking up. The trickle of travellers that graced my door would never have been enough to fund my journey onwards. Hopefully with Ciri's and Mrs Lebert's regular income, I would earn enough to stay in India after all.

Tsering was looking as radiant as ever, smiling infectiously, 'You are joking me?' she said, reading my order back, 'One bottle water, six veg momo, and bowl of chocolate custard?' She giggled. 'I know custard, I know chocolate, but chocolate custard? Haha, whatever next, chicken lassi? Wait, I will ask Dolma.' Her head reappeared from between the kitchen curtain and said, 'Haha, chocolate custard we will try.'

I was eating the last momo when Tsering carefully replaced my empty plate with a bowl of custard, grey rather than the chocolate brown I was expecting. She hovered in anticipation. I chewed the momo faster, swallowed and took a deep breath and a spoonful of the dessert. Velvet, rich and sweet, but not sickly, I dived in again, burning my tongue.

Fanning my mouth, I looked up, 'Tsering, this is the best chocolate custard in the whole world.'

She let out a squeal of delight, clapped her hands, her voice raised a pitch higher, 'Thank you, thank you, I will tell Dolma. Now maybe we can add to menu, "Sam Special Chocolate Custard".'

I'd been in my room for about twenty minutes when Connor showed up, tapping at the door. 'Hey man, bong? Upstairs at Ali's.'

Ali was from Israel and had previously invited me to his room a few times for a smoke, but I hadn't taken him up on his offer. Connor affectionately nicknamed him 'Ali Baba and the Forty Flutes' and upon entering his room it all became clear. It looked like some sort of Aladdin's cave; silk scarves covered the walls, warm lighting gently touched the interior from behind soft furnishings: beanbags, comfy cushions and folded blankets. A breeze of traditional Middle Eastern music accompanied the smoke of a hookah and incense.

'Ah my friends, come, sit, sit,' he spluttered from smoking the pipe. 'I will play some flute.' He handed Connor a plastic bottle half filled with water, a small metal pipe stuck out from one side. 'Please, fill your lungs with hashish and your hearts with joy.'

Connor got straight to work, lit up and bubbled away. He inhaled, screwed his eyes and blew a plume of smoke from left to right, swinging his curly locks. 'Yeah dude,' he said and passed it on. Like the first time I smoked a chillum, it hit me hard. I had to take a moment to compose myself.

Ali turned off the stereo, picked up a bamboo flute, 'Please, help yourself to hookah. This is a piece I compose about crossing from Middle East into Asia,' and began to play.

Embers still burnt in the dish of the hookah. Connor and I took a pipe each. It had a strange woody taste, a little bitter, but sweet with a hint of apple. It hit the pair of us straight away and we fell back, floating on a sea of blue and gold cushions, while Ali continued to play his flute like a mythical god.

I couldn't move and I didn't want to. I was in a place way beyond calm, as if every nerve ending was still and at peace. The music sped up and the incense and hookah smoke whirled around the room like a dust storm. The room started spinning in time to the song. I felt a sudden bout of nausea with the rush.

Ali and Connor leant over me some time later, 'You are not used to hookah my friend,' Ali said, helping me into a more comfortable position.

'Are you okay dude?' Connor passed me a bottle of water, 'You were out for a while; we were getting worried.'

'Yeah, I think so.' I looked up to the window. It was dark outside. 'What was in the hookah?' My head was still see-sawing.

'A little hashish and a little opium, my friend. But I think it was the enchanting notes of my flute that were responsible.' Ali smiled warmly, 'I will make us some tea.'

'Oh dear, you do not look good,' Ciri remarked as I unpacked my things for the morning session. 'Was it a late night?' I smiled in affirmation as she made fresh coffee for us both. 'You know Sam? My back and neck are feeling so much better since we started. I feel a vast improvement already.'

'I'm pleased to hear it, you definitely feel more supple,' I replied, working my fingers and thumbs across her shoulders.

'Before you leave today, I will give you a book on meditation. Maybe you can relax your mind. You say that you feel at peace in Leh, yet I cannot help feel there is something troubling you. I think you'll find what you are looking for if you search deep enough.'

I left her, book in hand and took a light lunch at Tibetan Friends, before making my way to my afternoon appointment with Mrs Lebert. The majority of the time was spent in silence, broken occasionally by bird song from outside. I stared out at the Shanti Stupa and was overcome by the thought that my adventure would soon be coming to an end. I wasn't ready yet for that to happen.

Just out of town I sat on a wall and updated my journal, looking up every so often at passers-by; two school boys in red shirts and navy trousers sword fighting with sticks, laughing as one outmanoeuvred the other; a toothless grandmother carrying an equally happy baby on her back in a basket, and an old man who stood with his yak, staring on as I wrote.

There was a set of postcards hanging from the door of a shop in the bazaar. Most were of Leh, but my eyes were drawn to the images of barren mountains and snow-capped peaks, which I

238

learned were from the road west to Srinagar and the valley of Kashmir.

Life in Leh was good and I couldn't have asked for more. I had been blessed with good friends and the money I was earning from massaging would allow me to see out this wonderful trip in full. I felt happy; at least I thought I did. Despite all the positives a dark cloak still enveloped my soul and I struggled to make sense of it. I had had months to relive the unpleasant memories of my time spent with Saskia so I didn't believe it was that. I wondered if the fact that I was missing Kate was bringing me down, but I only met her just a short time ago and this undefined force had been casting its shadow long before then.

I walked over to Kurt's place and found him sitting on the porch reading a book about the life of Osho, an Indian mystic, guru and spiritual teacher. He seemed happier within himself, his bright blue eyes showed as much as he smiled, 'I think our talk the other day may have done some good. The more I think of our conversation, the more I feel positive about the future,' he said as I sat beside him. The house was surrounded by mountains on all sides and I looked out to a wild meadow where yellow flowers peeked through the tall grasses. The owner of the house had a little brown dog who was taking a nap at Kurt's feet.

'You do look more at peace, Kurt. I noticed as much as soon as I saw you.'

He stretched and got up, 'Thank you, Sam, I am. Are you hungry? Let's say we eat.'

Inside Tibetan Friends' Ciri was talking to Dolma and we were all invited to the back room where a long table was already laid, apparently reserved for special friends and family. Dolma sat with us and ate then later handed the three of us a beaded necklace each made from wood and threaded with orange string, 'It is Tibetan Mala,' she said. 'It help with meditation and prayers. Roll one bead at a time and say, Om Mani Padme Hum.'

'Thank you', I said. 'I think this will be very useful', and I began practising the chant, much to Dolma's delight. Smiling, she got up to go to the kitchen.

Kurt stretched his back and sighed, 'So what do I have to do to get one of your massages? My shoulders are aching too much; I think it is due to the weight of my backpack.'

'I'm not surprised. I struggle to even lift it off the ground. How about now?'

'Yes, thank you, I would appreciate that'.

We bid thanks and goodbye to Dolma and Ciri and headed back to the guest house, chatting along the way. Kurt lay almost in silence as I massaged his back and shoulders for about forty-five minutes. I left him to enjoy some much-needed sleep and knocked on Connor's door hoping he'd be around. He invited me in and offered to share some of his meal.

'Where are you heading to after Leh?' he asked.

'Nowhere, this is it for me until I go home. I have work here so I can afford to stay and it's a nice town.' I broke away some naan bread and soaked up some sauce.

'You should come to Bombay. The south is so different from the north. You could stay at my place.'

I laughed, thinking he was joking, 'Bombay, that's a bit of a stretch, isn't it?'

'Listen, I'm leaving here in a few days. I have to pick up some things I left in Manali. We could get a train from Delhi.'

'Nice idea, but I'm not sure I'll have the time to get to yours and back again.'

'Okay, but have a think about it, yaar?'

Later when I returned to my room Kurt had gone. He'd left a note thanking me. I thought about the idea of going to Bombay and studied my guidebook and map. If I went back to Delhi with Connor, I would only be retracing my route, but I preferred the idea of adding a few more lines on my map. After flicking back and forth through the pages of my Lonely Planet, I found that I could travel west to Srinagar, south to Jammu and catch a train to Bombay from there. I went straight up to Connor to seek his opinion.

'Sure, you can go that way if you want, but you probably won't make it to Bombay. It's all-out war in Kashmir. I can't say I would be brave enough to do it.' He grabbed my guidebook off me and flicked to the Jammu and Kashmir section. 'Here, read this. It's your choice at the end of the day, but just be prepared for what you'd be heading into.'

Connor handed back the book and I read the paragraph he had marked with his finger.

'Srinagar now has the feel of an occupied city and there's a strictly enforced curfew after dark. There are road blocks everywhere and soldiers in bunkers on all street corners. Most of the fighting takes place in the old city, usually during the night. This part of town looks like Beirut at the height of troubles and should be avoided if you value your life.'

The warning these words carried was clear and enough to cancel out any thoughts I had of pursuing an adventure west.

29

Since I arrived in Leh I'd been putting off visiting the Shanti Stupa. Feeling a little under par I thought the fresh morning air and a good walk might do me some good. I found my way to the foot of a stone stairway and looked up to contemplate the five hundred steps that Ciri told me there were to the top. Despite a lack of confidence that I would make it the whole way I started to climb anyway. Halfway I stopped to catch my breath and laughed to myself that no doubt Kurt would have taken these at a sprint two at a time.

Built by Japanese Buddhists and inaugurated by the 14th Dalai Lama in 1991, the Shanti Stupa commemorated two and half thousand years of Buddhism. The domed stupa topped by a tall spire was a brilliance of white against the craggy bronze hills and zaffre sky. Reaching the courtyard, I stopped for a moment to take in the view over the valley. Clusters of aspen trees shot up from patches of green, filtering into the sparse cream desert that led to the colossal mountains. It felt like I was on heaven's doorstep. I approached the monument and strolled around the circumference of two levels, stopping on occasion to photograph the bright and colourful reliefs; images of Buddha's life encircling the dome.

When I arrived in the courtyard again, an old monk threw a stick for a small dog to chase and retrieve. Each time the dog faithfully came back, stick between clenched teeth. The monk giggled and patted his friend on the head as the animal's tail wagged a cloud of dust behind. The monk and I said 'Julay' to one another and exchanged smiles before I descended the long walk down into town for my morning massage appointment.

Ciri was insistent that I spend half an hour a day meditating with her before our session. She seemed quite fond of mothering me and it felt nice to be cared for. The usual smell of sandalwood greeted me as I stepped into her apartment and she was already pouring black tea and sweetening my cup as I sat down.

'Please, sit beside me. Cross your legs and rest your palms in your lap, back straight, eyes slightly closed, but not all the way. Circulate your breathing slowly and deeply and free your mind of the past; it is gone. The future is a blank canvas, so we can only truly find happiness in the present. Try to ignore the outside world and any grudges or past regrets. Wish all those you have ever encountered, bad or good, happiness. Now, focus your thoughts only on your breathing, maybe from your nose, mouth or abdomen, whichever part of your body you feel comfortable with. If your mind wanders, then bring it back to your breathing. Breathe positivity in and negativity out. Let us begin.'

My mind had always been easily distracted and today was no different. I tried to stay focused on what Ciri had said and imagined inhaling bright colours and exhaling dark shades. As the time passed it became easier for me to hone my concentration and I started to relax. I felt an element of control over any negativity and anger passing through my body. When she lifted me from what felt like a trance, I gave her my deepest thanks. She smiled, pleased that she had helped. It was as if she wanted to do all that was in her power to heal me.

I asked if she knew anything about Kashmir, 'Please Sam, tell me you are not thinking of going? Over fifty people a week are killed there and there are no discriminations on who is targeted. It may be one of the most beautiful places in the world, but it is also one of the most dangerous.

'Last year six western tourists were kidnapped: two British, two Americans, a German and a Norwegian. One of the American men managed to escape, but due to negotiation breakdowns over the release of Pakistani militants, the young Norwegian man was beheaded. His body was found in a forest clearing with the words 'Al Faran' carved into his chest. The others were never found.' She stopped eating and sipped her tea as I looked on in shock, 'Only last week, six Indian tourists were dragged from their houseboats on Dal Lake and murdered too. The chances of something bad happening to you are very high.'

Later I caught up with Kurt at the Tibetan Friends' Corner Café. I asked him what he knew about Kashmir and he echoed Ciri's warning. Feeling slightly unwell I sat back and tried to relax. Kurt left and Connor came in a few minutes later with a beautiful Indian girl of about the same age with a radiant smile upon her face. It was Radhika. I asked her what she did for a living and she told me she worked in the television and film industry in Bombay. According to Connor, her talents were in high demand to which she blushed.

I left them at the restaurant to go and call my mother. I'd lost track of how long it had been since I last phoned, so it was overdue. She was pleased to hear from me, though I detected something was wrong, 'Darling, I've got something to tell you.' She paused, as if preparing the words in her head, 'Your grandfather has had a bad stroke and the hospital has discovered severe cancer of his pancreas. He's in a bad way. I'm going over to Ostend tomorrow to see him.'

Following a brief pause, I asked, 'How are you, mum? Are you going to be okay?'

'I'll be fine, sweetheart. I'm more concerned about your gran.' She hesitated then followed with, 'He's asked to see you.'

Walking back to the guest house, my mind worked overtime. My grandfather was once the best a boy could ask for. A wonderful man I not only loved but looked up to and respected. As I replayed the time spent with him I felt sickened by the cruel twist of circumstance that had changed everything and taken this stable figure from me.

I had been so preoccupied I'd not realised I had taken a wrong turn. Hoping to find a familiar path back into town I turned back on myself. As I did so I was hawked by a shopkeeper, 'Come my friend, you want to live in luxury? Very good houseboat on most beautiful lake.' I looked up and saw a grinning Indian man with a large eagle beak of a nose, reddish hair and beard, 'Yes, my friend, Kashmir is perfect for you, you will like, come.' He beckoned me into his shop and I took a seat at his counter. He talked and talked, but none of it really went in, I just stared down at the counter and photos underneath the glass of wooden houseboats and mountainous landscapes, lush meadows filled with flowers and smiling parents playing with their children or enjoying a boat ride.

'How much?' I interrupted.

'Three nights on houseboat, very good price. You will not find better.'

'I'll book it.' I paid him without a hint of a haggle.

He looked surprised as if expecting a long series of negotiations but was quick to supply a bus ticket leaving in three days' time in case I changed my mind. 'Okay, very good sir. You stay on houseboat on Nagin Lake in Srinagar. I will make all arrangement for you. No problem, sir.'

Early the next morning I was shaken out of a deep sleep by rapid banging at the door. I opened it to find Connor distraught, 'It's Radhika, she's not waking up. There's alcohol and pills all over the place.'

'What! I mean how, why, what happened?' I struggled to make sense of what he was saying.

'We split up last night. I want to be free, find out more about me and see the world.'

'Um, okay. That was a bit sudden, wasn't it?'

'I guess so, but hey man we can talk later. I need your help!'

We ran to the hotel and burst through the door. There, laying on the bed unconscious was Radhika, and like Connor had described, pills were scattered all over the floor and a half empty bottle of vodka lay on its side on the bedside cabinet.

'Radhika,' I shook her gently to try and rouse her. 'Radhika?'

Connor stood by helpless. She lifted her eye lids, 'Uh? What?'

'Radhika, have you taken the pills on the floor?'

'Pills, what pills?' she murmured. Her eyes closed again.

'Radhika?' I shook her again, 'You need to keep awake. The pills, did you take any?'

'No, I threw them at the wall.'

'And the vodka?'

'Yes, I drank the vodka.' She closed her tear drenched eyes once more, kohl staining her cheeks.

'I need you to keep awake for me, okay?'

Connor was beside himself, 'Oh my God, Sam. What have I done?'

'I need you to try and keep calm, mate. Give me a hand and help me sit her up.' He came over and rested her upright against the wall.

'I want him gone. Get him out!'

'I think you should wait outside for a while.' He agreed and left, closing the door behind him.

'I'm going to be sick,' she said.

I quickly helped her to the bathroom and held her hair back as she threw up. When we returned to the room we sat together until she was well enough to talk.

'Maybe he needs a little space,' I said in reassurance. 'It might not be permanent. I think he's had a taste of travel and is feeling a sense of freedom and adventure. Once he gets it out of his system and returns home, he might reconsider his decision.' I gave her a bottle of water to drink.

'I love him so much, Sam. We've been through so much together. How could he do this to me?' She sobbed.

'Just try and think of getting yourself better for the moment.'

'You know he said we could go to Manali together? Did he tell you that? The pig!'

'He did, but it might not be a bad idea. It could give you time to talk things through.'

I found Connor outside sitting on a wall smoking a cigarette. I suggested he should take her back to his place and keep an eye on her. It was probably best she wasn't left by herself.

'Is she okay with that?' he asked.

'She finally came around to my way of thinking and has agreed to travel back to Bombay with you. You need to look after her for a while. Hey, you can pay me back by looking after me when I see you in a week's time.'

Connor's eyes lit up, 'You're coming to Bombay? That's awesome, dude!'

'Yeah, somebody's got to keep an eye on you guys, right?' I didn't mention the route I would be taking.

After leaving them as they prepared for the journey back to Manali, I took the two-mile walk from the bus station to Ciri's where today, freshly baked bread was waiting on the table accompanied by orange juice. As I massaged her, I thought about our insightful conversations. Her words were always filled with meaning and depth and there was never a day when I hadn't walked away with something new to think about. She had taught me how to channel my negative energy and turn it into happiness. But right at that moment, not even meditation could help how I was feeling.

It was Mrs Lebert's last day in Leh. She thanked me over and over for the work I had done and tipped me five hundred rupees in appreciation. I took one last look from the window – a view of the Shanti Stupa I knew I would hold dear forever.

Later I found Kurt lying on his bed reading in a flood of sunlight from his room window, 'Hey, how are you?'

'Sam, come and sit beside me. Yes, I am very good, very happy these days. What is going on in your world?'

'You know, this and that, keeping busy.'

'I am very pleased it has worked out so well for you here. Yesterday I meet a new friend. His name is Paul and like you, he is from England. I would like you to meet him.'

'That would be nice. Have you eaten yet?'

'No, but I am getting hungry.'

'How about we share some steamed momos for old time's sake?'

'Yes, why not? And you can pay now as you are a rich man,' he laughed.

At Tibetan Friends' we shared twelve vegetable momos and spoke in detail of our time together; recalling memories of getting lost countless times, running for buses and avoiding deadly snakes. We laughed so much as I reminded him of the time we thought a bear was coming down the mountainside and when we fell from the Enfield. We talked of the long nights in our little house in the orchards with our other friends and where it all began, our first meeting in Dehra Dun. My heart filled with sorrow at the thought of never seeing him again.

My voice was shaking, 'It's been brilliant, hasn't it?'

'Sam, it has been the best time of my life. You look so sad. We still have so much time left.'

'Yes, you're right, my friend. I was just being sentimental.'

On my way back to the guest house I removed the massage posters from the shop windows. In my room I mulled over my impulsive decision. It was time for me to leave Leh and I was ready to be on my own again for a while. In that there was no doubt. After some contemplation, I came to realise I felt the same about my choice of onward route. I didn't feel excited nor did I feel scared. There was simply an overwhelming acceptance of the journey ahead.

I heard voices coming from outside my door. One of them was Ali's and there were also two girls that sounded familiar. I opened up to find Ali talking with Sophie and Neria. I couldn't believe my eyes, and it appeared neither could they. They screamed with delight as they saw me and hugged me until I thought I was going to faint.

'What are you doing here?' asked Sophie.

'I could ask the same of you. Have you seen Kurt yet?'

'No, we've only just arrived. We're not staying here; we are in a hotel in town. Have you met Ali?'

Ali put his arm around my shoulder and pulled me in, 'Ah Sam and I are very good friends. We shared some bong and played some flute.'

'Hey, maybe we can all catch up tomorrow night at the Tibetan

Friends' Corner Café, at say seven? Ali knows where it is,' I said, and stepped back into my room.

'We'll be there,' Sophie replied with affection in her eyes.

The smell of baked muffins and fresh coffee in the morning was something I was sure to miss. That and my morning visits to see Ciri. I asked her to walk in a straight line along the length of the room. The difference in her posture was unbelievable.

'I was all bent over and could not turn my head when you first came to Leh. Now I can walk with back straight, turn my head and I have had no pain for over a week now. Thank you so much,' she said.

I asked if she would join me for dinner at Tibetan Friends'. She said she would, then leant over to a drawer and pulled out a thin brown parcel and handed it to me, 'Do not open this until you leave Leh. Promise me.'

'Thank you Ciri, that's so sweet of you. I promise.'

On my last visit to the beautiful house with the yellow flowers, I found Kurt and Eli.

'Hey, when did you get back?'

'This morning,' replied Eli. 'Good to see you, my friend.'

'Yeah, you too. You'll have to tell me all about your trip. Are you both free to come along to Tibetan Friends' at 7pm? I'm arranging a bit of a gathering, including a couple of surprise guests.'

Kurt was quick to accept for the both of them.

'Bring your friend Paul along, it'll be great to meet him,' I said.

At 6pm I looked around my room, taking one final check that all my things were packed and ready for my 6am departure. I felt apprehensive. I would be leaving one of the most peaceful places on earth to go to one of the most dangerous. About me was only silence, aside from the occasional bird song and Ladakhi voices coming from outside. There were a lot of friends waiting for me, people that would disappear from my life tomorrow.

With the haunting voice of the muezzin calling to prayer from the Jama Masjid, I took a deep breath, pulled myself together and stepped inside the Tibetan Friends' Corner Café.

30

I lay awake in cold silence cradling the memories of last night; my friends' faces suspended in the dim light, radiating warmth and security. Everything I could have ever asked for was right here in Leh and I was on the verge of leaving it all behind. A part of me felt I was making a mistake, that I was about to go looking for something I already had, but there was a stronger urge for me to go. It was like something had taken control, an inexplicable force was guiding me onwards. Despite the knot in my stomach and the nerves that were now pulsating through my whole body, there was no undoing my decision. I was going to Kashmir.

Throwing my backpack over my shoulder, I gripped the handle of my guitar case and walked determinedly out of the room. The owner of the guest house was leafing through paperwork as I approached. I asked if it was too early for breakfast, and in that gentle Ladakhi way, she smiled and said, 'Okay, take seat.'

The morning air nipped the back of my neck and ran its cold fingers through my damp hair. I savoured the peace and serenity of my morning ritual as much as the jam muffins and coffee. Reaching into my backpack I took out Ciri's gift and unfolded the brown paper wrapping to reveal two postcards; one of Lord Ganesh, the other, the smiling face of the Dalai Lama. In between was a frail envelope with italic Tibetan handwriting. I opened it carefully and withdrew a letter.

'Dear Sam,

Thank you so much for all the lovely chats we had. I will remember our time together forever. Thank you also for all you have done with my posture, it feels as if the accident in Agra never happened. I am forever grateful. I hope it stays this way.

I have a feeling you will not be taking anyone's advice about travelling to Kashmir and although I think you are being extremely reckless with your decision, I understand and respect your need to continue your exploration of India and your inner self.

With this letter you will find 5000 rupees. I ask that you enjoy the rest of your time in India and find happiness in your life wherever you go. Also, there are two cards enclosed. One is Ganesha and one is of the 14th Dalai Lama to help remove any obstacles and protection for when you need it most.

The writing on the envelope says, 'You will be in my heart and prayers always'.

Ciao,

Ciri'

The coach departure point was a lot further than I anticipated. When it finally came into sight I stopped, spun a roadside prayer wheel for luck and took one final look at Leh. Of the other passengers on board, most were a mix of Ladakhi and Kashmiri folk. The Kashmiri men wore long woollen tunics covering their bodies below the knees. I saw no Kashmiri women. Behind me, sat in the corner, was the young French guy from the room next door at the guest house. He appeared to be on his own and was watching two dogs lazing in the rising hue of dawn blue. There was no sign anywhere of the girl he was staying with. I turned back as the engine started.

Spitok Monastery drifted by and the rugged Ladakhi Range smoothed, turning dark coffee under an irritated sky. At the village of Nimmu, the Zanskar River converged with the Indus and flowed into the Zanskar Gorge. Twisting around the serpentine bends of the Hangro Loops, the sparse landscape graduated into dusty scree with the occasional Buddhist gompa grasping a mountainside. A far cry from the joyous journey from Manali to Leh, a silence consumed not only the desolate world outside, but the interior of the bus.

Traffic consisted mainly of military vehicles, the odd jeep or a bus trying to manoeuvre past in the opposite direction. Not far from the town of Khalsi we stopped at a checkpoint and the French backpacker and I were required to present our passports to a weathered faced man sitting behind his desk under a tent. He looked at us with suspicion, mumbled something and questioned us about the purpose of our visit and intentions once we reached our destination. Satisfied by our answers he handed our documents back to us and we continued the journey for a while until the bus stopped again in the town of Lamayuru for minor repairs. Perched upon a hillock stood a tenth century Buddhist monastery, one of the oldest in Ladakh. The French guy and I sipped tea as we stared at the mountainous moonscape.

'You know this area was once a lake they say? It dried up, hence all this eroded rock. I am Pierre. Are you travelling to Kargil?'

'Yes, I think the bus stops for a night there. I'll then go on to Srinagar. Are you on your way to Srinagar too?' I was hoping he would say yes.

'I will leave the bus just before Kargil. I want to find alternative transport into Padum. Cigarette?'

'Thanks.' I pulled one from the packet he held out, 'What's in Padum?'

'It has nice scenery and is good for trekking. There are no direct buses, so I will try and hitch a ride from a goods carrier if I can. Do you want to come?'

'Thanks, but I don't think I'm really equipped for a trek. Maybe you could travel to Srinagar with me instead?' I quipped in the vain hope he would.

He laughed it off, 'No, I enjoy life too much, my friend.'

'It's really that bad, huh?'

'Yes, really bad. You can get carried away with all the beautiful scenery on this road, but it is flooded with tears once you pass Kargil.'

I didn't want to think what was past Kargil until I was past Kargil. I steered the subject to his girlfriend, 'You were in the room next to me in Leh. Weren't you staying there with a girl?'

'Ah yes, we shared a room and have the sex, you know? But she was impossible. She whine about so many things of India. It drive me crazy. When I leave this morning, I was very happy.' He took a lungful of fresh air.

I chuckled, 'Fair enough.'

The Ladakhi lady who was sat next to me departed, leaving an empty place for Pierre to fill. We conversed as we corkscrewed the slopes, the wheels gripping the cliff edge. Every now and then, the conductor leant from the doorway and yelled instructions to the driver, assisting him with other vehicles as they attempted to get past. The road cut through the lunar landscape, rugged hills wrinkled like the back of a giant rhinoceros, and was free flowing for an hour until we tailed a military convoy. Light rain fell and we slugged along the muddy road, while passengers nodded their heads in sleep. Outside, road workers cleared and rebuilt the crumbling road in a fog of thick tar smoke.

Irrigated valleys and patches of flora appeared as we followed the Wakha River to the monastery village of Mulbekh. Pierre called out to the driver to stop, 'I am going to see if I can get a ride to Padum from here,' he said to me. 'Good luck, my friend. I think you will need it, au revoir.'

With his departure came insecurity. I looked about the bus and felt hostility hanging in the air. There was a hardened, sad look in the eyes of the Kashmiris and whenever I tried smiling at someone I was met only with a frown; except for one teenage boy who kept looking over at me. When he caught my eye, he grinned and waggled his head as if to say hello. There were three other Kashmiris grouped together who also threw looks over their shoulders every now and then, though there were no smiles, only sneaky looks which I put down to western interest.

It had been thirteen hours since we'd left Leh, but it felt much longer. The vehicle came to a stop; we had reached Kargil, the gateway between Buddhist Ladakh and Islamic Kashmir. While most of the passengers stayed close to the bus, I went off in search of a bed for the night. An uncomfortable atmosphere shrouded the town, making me feel alien and unwelcome. I neared a bend in the road and heard a horn and engine from behind, but it was too late to get out of the way. The wing mirror of a goods carrier clipped the top of my guitar and sent me off balance, knocking me to the ground. I wasn't injured, but my guitar had taken a slight chip from the headstock. Shaken up, I kept to the edge of the road, holding my wits about me as I continued looking for a hotel.

Children with flies about their faces stood in doorways, while bearded men with woolly hats and waistcoats sat talking, glaring up as I passed. I asked around, but the few hotels were either closed or had no vacancies. My patience was thinning. I ventured off the main thoroughfare hoping one of the side streets would have something to offer me and at last I was in luck. The owner of a small hotel was poised ready for my arrival, his friendliness uplifting my mood.

'Welcome, sir,' he said. His face was old yet he had a young twinkle in his eyes. 'You are looking for room?'

'Please, do you have any?'

'Yes, many room,' he replied.

I was guided up a staircase and shown a room on the corner of an L-shaped hallway facing the stairs. It wasn't bad, I'd certainly stayed in worse. I pulled the window closed, keeping the cold out and muting the sound of the river below. The thought of traipsing the streets of Kargil again was not a desirable prospect, but I needed to eat so I set out.

Though it wasn't evident from the outside, the featureless mud brick building I found appeared to serve food. Looking through the windows I saw a large room clouded with smoke and local men sitting around tables eating or sucking away on gurgling hookahs. Eyes raised and chatter ceased as I entered. There was no menu, only a stubble-faced man behind the counter who nodded, I assumed to take my order.

'Chocolate custard please,' I uttered. It was the only thing I could manage.

'Uh?' he quizzed.

I repeated myself, but was still met with the same response. The food the locals were eating didn't appeal. One man to the right of me pulled at what looked to be nothing more than mutton fat with his teeth. He paused to speak to the guy behind the counter who then pointed at an empty table and ordered me to sit. Like an obedient dog, I promptly did as he asked. All around I was met with stares, accompanied by murmuring and laughter. The three men who continuously glanced at me on the bus sat in a corner, watching me with more intent than the others. Even after everybody had gone back to their own business, the novelty of my presence worn thin, they never once took their eyes off me. I was used to people staring at me in India, but this felt different.

My attention was snapped away as a bowl of lumpy custard was placed on the table. It wasn't the best I'd tasted, but it was enough to line my stomach and I bolted it down as quickly as I could, keen to be out of there. All the way back to the hotel I kept my eyes over my shoulder, my paranoia getting the better of me. With my back to the door of my room, I stood for a few moments, allowing my heartbeat to settle. A double knock sent it racing again. 'Sam,' I heard. 'It is I, Pierre.'

'Pierre?' I said. What was he doing here? More so, how on earth had he found me?

'Oui, it is me. May I come in?' His whimsical French accent was a pleasure to hear. I wasted no more time in opening the door to his beaming face.

'Am I glad to see you,' I said, and hugged him much to his surprise.

'Ah yes, it is good to see you also,' he said. 'I have no luck finding transport to Padum. I hitch lift here with Tata truck. I will try again later this evening.'

'How did you find me?' I asked.

'Ah, it is not difficult. You and I are the only westerners here. I ask around and I find you. Do you have cigarette?' I pointed to the packet on the table, 'Merci. I am very hungry, have you eaten?'

'Yes, well sort of. I've just come back from town.'

'Ah, then you must take me to where you eat. I find it difficult to find good place here. What did you eat?'

'Chocolate custard.'

'Coostard? Ha ha, you find coostard in Kargil?'

'Yeah, it was a bit lumpy, but not so bad.'

'Ha, then I must get chocolate coostard.'

The adhan from the local mosque echoed across the town as we made our way through the back streets. I felt at ease in his company and we laughed our way into the restaurant. He paused for a moment and looked around the room and then walked boldly up to the counter, 'Okay, I know what we will eat. You let me choose for you, Sam?' I nodded and looked for the men that made me feel uneasy, but they were gone.

Pierre asked for two dishes of something called rista, some baked bread and two bowls of chocolate custard for afterwards. With some sweetened black tea, our meal shortly arrived. The rista was mutton meatballs in rich red gravy and Pierre assured me it would be safe to eat, 'Look about you, my friend. You see, three people eat the same, so I think it will be okay.' It was and I was pleased to have something more substantial.

'Ah yes, this coostard is very good, I enjoy,' Pierre said as he lapped up the last of it with a wooden spoon.

We navigated our way through the dark streets back to the hotel, stopping off to pick up some cigarettes from a man sitting in a shop alcove. He puffed away at a large hookah and offered us a smoke. Pierre, the first to try, inhaled a deep breath and blew a plume of tobacco smoke into the star filled sky. 'You try,' he said and passed me the pipe.

I tried to identify the familiar taste, 'Peach,' I said upon realisation.

'Yes, peach,' the shopkeeper confirmed with a smile.

Pierre bid me farewell at my room, 'I will now try to get transport to Padum,' he said. 'There are night vehicles travelling from Kargil apparently. Goodbye, my friend. Here is my address should you visit Paris one day.'

Alone again, I made sure I was packed and ready to leave. I set the alarm for 3.30am for my 4am departure and got my head down for some sleep.

31

BANG, BANG, BANG.

Pierre? I checked the time, it was 2.36am.

BANG, BANG, BANG.

This wasn't the light friendly tap of Pierre's knuckles. The metal door handle turned repeatedly. I kept silent, fear freezing me to the bed. The commotion stopped. I could hear voices, but the words were foreign. Footsteps marched along the corridor and the banging started again, this time on other doors. I listened, trying to make sense of what was going on.

'Sir, please, you must leave.' The distinctive voice of the hotel keeper whispered through the door. He sounded panicked.

I got up and spoke quietly back, 'What's going on?'

'Very bad men, sir, here to take you away. No time, please you must leave now.'

Already dressed, I rushed over to my backpack and guitar and put my hand on the key in the door, 'Are you sure it is safe?'

'Yes, but not for long, they will be back once they not find you. I tell them you leave for Padum earlier with friend.' The voices increased as the banging continued.

In the dark hallway, the hotel manager gently grabbed my arm and locked the door behind me. He rushed me down the stairs and instructed me to hide behind some hedges outside the hotel entrance, 'Wait there, I will tell you when they go.' I didn't need to be told twice as I heard the thundering marches from the landing above heading towards the stairwell. 'Go!' he said as he turned to face the oncoming force.

I darted behind an apricot tree amongst thick bushes. My heart thumped against my rib cage and my breathing sounded like a violent ocean in my head. I did everything I could to control it and quieten myself as the sound of shouting echoed from the reception area. From where I was situated I couldn't see inside the building, but only ahead and to the right-hand side. I crouched low into the darkest shadows and moved my backpack over my torso. I dared not move. I took up steady breathing exercises that Ciri taught me to calm my mind, but it wasn't doing much good.

Stepping out from the hotel to my eye line, three men appeared quizzing the manager with intent. I recognised them instantly from the bus and the restaurant. They wore identical phirans with shalwar-kurtas underneath. One had a green camouflaged jacket and beneath, the muzzle of an automatic rifle glinted in the light from the hotel interior.

My backpack tipped forward against the bush in front of me. I pulled it back, but it snagged a branch and rustled the leaves. The men stopped talking and tuned the air for the source of the noise. The man with the gun walked to my position, stopped half a metre away and scanned the darkness. I could now see him more clearly – his cold eyes, his full beard, his flat felt hat and the Kalashnikov that hung from his shoulder within his jacket.

Suddenly the manager dropped to his knees and started wailing. Their attention snapped over to him. They pushed him face down into the gravel and started yelling at him. Agitated, the man with the gun stuck the barrel to the back of his neck and shouted something. The manager's wails quickly became whimpers. After he was questioned some more they promptly left, storming into the blackness of the night.

Too terrified to move or utter a word to each other, the hotel keeper and I remained silent and motionless. This was a scenario I knew only too well. While the circumstance of being dragged into the mountains to be murdered provided a new variant, the fear of harassment entwined with imminent violence and harm was familiar territory. I glanced at my watch. It was approaching 3am. I needed to move soon, but stayed in position for a few more minutes.

I looked over at the manager who lay still, like me, petrified of their return, 'Are you okay?' I whispered. He was quiet for a moment and then nodded his head. 'Is there a way to avoid the bazaar?'

'Behind hotel, upside and right. Follow road, keep out of light,' he whispered back.

'Thank you. I'm so sorry.'

I stood, looked around and followed his directions away from the hotel. Around the back of the building, I skimmed a wall with my heart fit to burst, turned right as directed and walked slowly down a slope, careful to keep my eye out for any movement. From a distance, I heard a vehicle approaching. I dived into an alleyway and a goods carrier passed. Out of the shadows and into the dim silver light of the moon I walked on, all the while sticking to the shaded edges of the roadside.

At the end of the street, I saw my destination. As I drew closer I heard voices and paused to deliberate my next move. Were they here? Questioning the passengers on the bus? If I stayed hidden, the bus would leave without me. If I moved forward, I could walk straight into the hands of the potential kidnappers. I advanced slowly while trying to analyse the environment. The teenager who was looking and smiling yesterday was walking directly towards me. I stayed still, hoping I wasn't seen.

'I bring Kashmiri salt tea. You like? Please come and join us.' He placed a stainless-steel beaker on a segment of wall next to me and walked back to where the light was shining. My paranoia was in overdrive. I put the hot cup under my nose and sniffed with suspicion, my eyes alert for the slightest flicker of danger. I wasn't going to take anything for granted and poured the drink into the dirt.

A few minutes later I summoned the courage to approach the bus. A group of six men, plus the boy who brought me the tea, were crowded around a torch pointing upwards from the ground. I thanked the teenager as I returned the beaker and boarded the bus, which was almost full with the other Kashmiris, except for three vacant seats. In the relative safety of my own seat I leaned forward and pretended my shoe laces needed retying in hope I wouldn't be seen by anybody outside.

Relief only came when the bus began to move away. I became aware I was shivering and tucked my hands into my pockets. Over and over I played the scenes of the morning in my head, recalling flashes of what had happened, feeling guilt for the hotel manager and fear of what might have happened had he not helped me. I kept looking around, paranoia in overdrive that they were still on the bus. I even questioned the authenticity of the shopkeeper who sold me the bus ticket. Was he part of this? What would be waiting for me on the houseboat? Occasionally I looked up and found the young man smiling at me. I smiled back and nodded as I had done since the beginning of the trip.

A commotion ahead brought our bus to a standstill. Tyres were burning on the road, sending black smoke spiralling into the morning sky, while a group of about thirty teenaged boys shouted and hurled stones at any vehicles that dared to pass. Our driver opted to pull over, but the bus behind us tried to push through the melting rubber barricade. It was immediately pelted with rocks, one of them smashing the windscreen. The driver brought the bus to a halt and stepped down, hands cradling his bloody head. The group of boys immediately set on him, crowding him and shouting. Luckily his passengers were quick to drag him to safety.

Three hours passed and I watched the chaos play out until it finally subsided. We were given passage forward, but were drawn to a halt again only twenty minutes later, this time by the military. Our driver was instructed to pull over and we were told to alight. Nobody was travelling any further today. An army convoy was on its way from Srinagar and the road was too narrow in places to pass other vehicles either side. My passport was checked and I was told to await further instructions.

We were situated in the town of Drass, noted to be the second coldest place on earth after Siberia, with recorded winter temperatures of -60^{0}C. It was nowhere near as cold as that now, but it was still very chilly. I looked around the handful of hotels in the village, but all were fully accommodated. Hardly surprising as we weren't the only ones stranded – there were also two other buses and a lot of army vehicles. Unsure what to do from here, I took a seat on some steps alongside two Sikh gentlemen.

'Welcome to India, my friend. May I ask what you are doing in remote Drass?'

'Hoping to get to Srinagar.' I cupped my hands, blew into them and rubbed them together to keep warm.

'India has a way of slowing us all down wouldn't you say? Have you eaten yet?'

I turned to meet their faces, both with bushy beards and navy turbans, 'No, like the lack of accommodation, there seems to be a shortage of places to eat too.'

'Then I insist you join us. We have plenty to go around.' He produced a cylindrical tiffin tin from a holdall, sectioned off into different compartments holding separate meals of rice, curries, pickles and chapatis. The variety of spicy smells ignited my rumbling stomach. 'Please, help yourself to as much as you like.'

Although somewhat dubious, I saw they were eating the same too, so I tucked in. It tasted as good as it smelled. 'I hope you are enjoying the food,' said the other who wore a pair of dark shades. 'We pride ourselves on our cooking. We have restaurants in Delhi and Leh.'

'What brings you here?' I asked.

'For the next few weeks we are on a holy pilgrimage to the Hindu shrine at Amarnath Cave. The pilgrimage was banned for many years due to threats from militants, but this year, the route is open. Many people from all religions are attending. This is why you find no hotels available here.' He brushed his hands free of crumbs and leant forward, 'Where are our manners? My name is Jumeet and this is my dear friend and business partner Adesh.' We exchanged greetings. 'If you are ever in Leh or Delhi, please look up our establishments. You will always be welcome.'

'I will do, thanks. Do you know anything about the protesters this morning?'

'The school children? Ah yes, they are upset as their teacher has been missing for over a week now, feared to be kidnapped or killed. They are seeking answers from the authorities, who do not seem to care. Kidnapping and murder is commonplace in these parts.'

I told them about the incident at the hotel in Kargil. 'Then you are extremely lucky to have escaped unhurt,' Adesh said. 'Count your blessings you sit and eat this meal with us. As for Drass, I think we could be stuck here for some time to come. I spoke to one of the officers earlier, but he was very vague as to when we would start moving again.' Adesh's words concerned me. Not just for the lack of hotels and restaurants, I was worried my stay on the houseboat would be cancelled if I did not arrive on time. Plus, hanging around in the middle of nowhere with a western target pinned to my back did nothing for my sinking morale.

'You should not worry too much,' Jumeet said, as if reading my mind. 'It would not be wise for an attempt on your life to take place with such a heavy military presence. I do not think it would be in the militants' best interests. Kargil is a much easier spot for abduction I think, maybe your houseboat in Srinagar also. You must be on your highest alert in these parts.'

I thanked them for the meal and wandered off for a cigarette. I wasn't alone long before the young man from the bus joined me. He was between sixteen and eighteen I guessed. Like his companions, there was a hardened look in his eyes. 'Hello, my name, Feroz. What is your name please?' he asked gently.

'Sam. Thanks again for the tea this morning. Do you live in Srinagar?'

'Yes, in Srinagar,' he replied. He asked me the usual questions of what I did for a living and where I was from and finished by asking, 'And you have guitar? Do you play?'

'Yes, and you?'

'Oh no, I cannot afford guitar.'

'Wait here a minute, I'll go and get it.' I went to the bus and unhooked it from the roof-rack. I handed it to him and he unzipped the case and removed it. He strummed the open strings and cocked his head to the sound hole, intrigued by what he heard.

'Please, you show me.' He returned it and I fretted a few notes. 'Very good Sam, I like, please show me how to do.'

He took a short lesson and picked it up quickly, showing real talent for a first timer. At the end of the tutorial he handed the guitar back to me. I declined, 'You keep it, Feroz.'

'Okay, I will return it later to you.'

'No, you keep it. It's yours.'

'To own? What? I cannot take your guitar, what will you do without it?'

I laughed, 'I'm sure I'll be fine. In fact, you'd be doing me a favour, it's only weighing me down. I'll write down some scales and chords later to get you started.'

He was delighted, unable to believe his luck, 'Thank you, thank you,' he beamed. 'I am liking to do you favour by receiving this gift.' He began peeling away the Hindu Om sticker I'd stuck on the base. He looked up and saw my surprise, 'Please, I am very sorry, but I do not wish to have this on guitar. I am proud Kashmiri, not Indian; Muslim not Hindu.'

'No problem Feroz, it's yours to do what you will with it. So, I take it you're not fond of Indian people?' I was slightly confused. After all, wasn't Kashmir part of India, thus making him Indian?

'Indian military and police are very bad to Kashmiri people,' he explained. 'It makes me dislike them. Not hate, dislike. They take many innocent Kashmiri to prison for no reason and torture and kill also.' He paused for a moment, looked around as if he'd said too much already and lowered his voice, 'India fights for Kashmir and so does Pakistan, but we Kashmiris are caught in middle and suffer a great deal. We are just wanting to live our lives in peace.' His eyes surveyed the group of military uniforms kicking the dust and smoking cigarettes nearby. He changed the subject and pointed to a crowd of excited men shouting near the bus, 'Come and join in our game and share some Kashmiri salt tea. All my good friends.'

Feroz explained the rules, 'It is quite simple. Here you throw coin at rock, nearest coin to rock win all coins.' He invited me in and gave me four one paise coins. I was pitted against the chubby moustached driver of our bus, but I failed miserably, throwing a coin too wide on the fourth attempt. The driver scooped the pennies from the floor and did a little dance as his friends cheered him on. I reached in my pocket so I could check my wallet for more coins, but it wasn't there. I excused myself to look in my backpack. Mentally I retraced my moves back to Kargil and the commotion at the hotel. And then it dawned on me. In my haste to leave, I had left it on the dresser. I didn't care for the money, there wouldn't have been much in there anyway. It was the thought of losing Kate's telephone number that troubled me the most. I looked through all my things again, only to be met with disappointment. I double checked my journal in case I had written her number in there, but I hadn't. She was gone.

Feroz brought me the tea and asked if I was okay. 'Yeah, I'm fine thanks,' I lied and drank the lukewarm liquid, tasting of sea water. I gave him the empty cup, smiled and told him I was going for a walk, leaving him by the bus as I trailed off into the mountains.

Tenebrous clouds quilted the peaks with a threat of imminent rain. As I walked I rolled random combinations of digits in my head hoping one would click into place as her number, but none seemed correct. I could have kicked myself for being so careless. I was looking forward to meeting up with her again when I got home, but now there was no chance of that happening. To say she meant so much to me after knowing her just a few days could seem premature, but time is only relative and to some degree it felt as if I had known her forever.

It was getting colder by the minute and I started to shiver. Drops of water fell from the sky, biting hard at my face. A vicious wind was racing up behind too, tearing at my muscles and causing agonising cramps. I decided to turn back, but I must have strayed from the main path. Everywhere looked so different. Wrapped up in my own self-pity, I hadn't been keeping an eye on the scenery behind me to assist my route back to the bus.

I walked, hopefully the way I'd come, but was stumped when I came to a fork leading off in two separate directions. I prayed for divine intervention and somebody up there must have taken pity on me because after a half hour of walking along the path I chose, I heard talking and laughing, and then from around a large boulder, I came into a clearing of army vehicles and goods carriers.

'I see you have been introduced to the climate of Drass. It is rather challenging weather wouldn't you say?' Jumeet joined me in the doorway of a hut to escape the force of the wind.

'I thought British winters were cold, but this makes those feel like a spring day in Delhi.'

'Quite the contrast from Delhi. You wouldn't believe we were in the same country. We have the best of both worlds. When it is too hot in Delhi, we employ others to manage our restaurant while we take pleasant summers in Leh. When too cold in Leh, we return to Delhi.'

'Sounds like you've got it all worked out, Jumeet.'

'May we tempt you to join us for dinner in one hour? We will take food in the shelter and warmth of our room.'

'Are you sure you don't mind?' It was difficult to say no considering the lack of alternative options I was presented with.

'A guest is a gift from God. It would be our pleasure. One hour then, it is settled.'

India had again shown me that the generosity of its people had no bounds. Over dinner, the two gentlemen explained to me what it was to be Sikh. 'The Sikh who wears all five Kakaars is considered a true Sikh,' began Adesh. 'Kes: untrimmed hair; Kangha: the wooden comb – usually holding the hair in place; Kirpan: the curved sword – placed at the waistline; Kara: the iron wristlet, and Kachera: baggy under shorts. Sikhism is a simple way of gaining salvation attained by performing duties to society and family through honest labour, sharing food with others, meditation, charity and selfless deeds.'

Jumeet poured some coffee and spoke where his friend left off, 'Like Kashmir, the state of Punjab also suffers with problems at the hands of the Indian government. A secessionist movement was sought to create a separate Sikh country called Khalistan from the region of Punjab. But India is just as defiant as it is with Kashmir. I will give India one thing, when she digs her heels in, she digs in firm and protects what she believes is rightfully hers. If she gave away Kashmir and the Punjab, what would be next? Every state in India would demand independence.

'I feel something big awaits India on the horizon. A new India will be born from its continued strength. We may be looked upon by the rest of the world as one of the poorest countries, but one day we will be seen as one of the wealthiest. As for Kashmir, I see no solution any time soon. I fear that life for its people is getting worse by the day. A violent storm is brewing in these mountains, one that will take many more lives.'

Adesh and Jumeet's conversation was insightful and I looked forward to taking them up on their offer of a meal in their restaurant when I returned to Delhi. I could sleep in the bus which I was thankful for. Before I settled in, I sat outside with my back to the rear of the vehicle and smoked a cigarette.

'Some people are liking five-star hotel, but I am preferring our five-million-star hotel,' Feroz said, squatting down beside me and staring out to the infinite space above us. A shooting star sped across the sky and disappeared out of sight. My thoughts returned to Kate.

32

The man lying in front woke me with his snoring. Considering the hard seat that was my bed, I'd slept relatively well. It had just gone 4am. Outside I stretched my stiff arms and legs and felt the chill of the morning seep into my clothes. I could just make out the black silhouettes of the mountains and a dark figure approaching me. Feroz's face came into view, 'I have made traditional Indian chai for you this morning, Sam. I hope you like. Please come and sit with us.' I sat with him and his father and uncle around a circle of stones that held a small fire beneath a boiling pan of tea. I was offered flat bread and dried salted meat which I chewed while Feroz spoke of his love of Michael Jackson and Manchester United Football Club.

'Thank you for your gift,' Feroz's father said as Feroz went off to find a place to wash the cups. 'He has been hurting our ears for most of last evening, but it is good to see my son happy again. He has been much troubled of late since his brother was taken away by the Indian authorities.'

'He never said anything to me, what happened?'

'Feroz is a proud boy and very strong, but I see the hurt when his mother weeps for his brother's return. We do not know what happened to Ahmed. One morning, two officers broke into our house and took him away. That was three months ago. We try desperately to get more information about what he has done and where he is, but we are told that if we continue our pursuit of information, we will meet the same fate. Ahmed was a good boy and would do nothing to dishonour his family. We cannot believe he has done anything wrong.' A look of sorrow scarred his eyes as he recounted the memory.

Feroz returned and asked if I would talk to one of the officers and find out when we would be moving, 'Maybe you will have more luck than we do. You are westerner; they will respect you more than us Kashmiris.' The officers I was pointed to showed little interest in me. Their awkward attitude reminded me of the policeman I had dealings with in Paharganj. It was difficult to get any attention and when I did, they swatted me away like an annoying fly.

At 11am, much to everyone's relief, a line of green, dust stained military vehicles appeared on the horizon. It was the convoy that everyone had been waiting for. Lorries thundered past and the passengers of the awaiting buses let out a triumphant cheer. I joined in, but my clapping slowed to a stop as I witnessed war weary soldiers crammed into the back of trucks, heads down and clutching firearms. Tanks on trailers and ammunition carriers sped past. Ski-goggled men gripped heavy artillery from the back of Jeeps. What was merely talk and fantasy was now reality. The cold stone of war fell into place with a heavy thud. Carrier after carrier rushed by throwing dust into the air until the last was seen heading around a bend. Half an hour later we were granted permission to travel and commenced our slow journey towards Zoji La.

The road became a dirt track and the tyres struggled to keep a grip on the slippery mud from recent rains. The bus splashed through sludge and slid towards the edge with terrifying views below. There were moments when anxiety shot through me and had me clinging to my seat as if it were my last second on earth, but the driver, as so many of these skilled drivers do, took complete control with the assistance of his guide calling out corrections to him.

The Kashmiris on board had warmed to me with the friendship I'd gained from Feroz, though at times I felt they were becoming a little too friendly. Some of them took to exploring my shoulder bag and the driver was handed my sunglasses to wear. But it all seemed to be in good humour and they were returned sometime later.

I was listening to my music, trying to take my mind from the road when we were brought to a halt again. Along with some of the other passengers, I stepped down from the bus and saw a group of soldiers squatting and peering over the cliff edge. I walked over to them and followed their eyes down to where an upturned goods carrier had fallen from the road; its front end crumpled by the impact; axle lying to one side. Despite being fully equipped to assist the situation the soldiers did nothing but laugh and make jokes. I grew irritated and asked if there was nothing they could do. 'Not our problem,' was the answer I received with another round of laughter. There was no movement from the smashed cab, only an eerie silence. I looked again at the officers, frustrated and appalled. I tried again to appeal to their good nature, but there was none to be found. Instead I was ordered back to the bus where I sat looking on hopelessly until we moved away from the scene.

Within an hour, we'd stopped yet again, this time for a rest break. The only place available for something to eat was crowded by road workers, their bodies and clothes blackened from endless hours of hard graft. Squeezing my way through to the front, I was dismayed by what was on offer. Workers pushed and shoved to order portions of fried strands of batter. When I received my turn, I could see why it was so popular. It was incredibly cheap, fifty paise to be precise. As I crunched the greasy mess, I looked about me and saw how quickly the workers were consuming it. I had no doubt this was the first thing they'd eaten for a long while. By the looks on their faces, they were overjoyed by the measly portions. I was humbled once more.

My mood sank as we moved off – an amalgamation of the last few days and tiredness. Although the other passengers were friendly enough, I was unable to escape certain memories of late, dark shards cutting into my thoughts and tormenting me. I suddenly felt very alone. Hoping to shake off the visions in my head I switched on my music again. The landscape blended from sparse rock faces to a world of brilliant green. Stunning meadows filled with long grass and flowers, silver ribbons of water weaved through the countryside and tall pines rose to soaring heights to meet the pure snow of the Karakoram and Pir Panjal mountains.

The bus stopped, once again delayed by the convoy. I stepped down to the fresh air of the valley and looked upon the most beautiful land I'd ever seen. Accompanied by a soundtrack of atmospheric drums and the haunting voice of Enya, tears fell without warning. I'd travelled so far to reach this point. My past was gaining on me and I was struggling to leave it behind. I hadn't cried since I was eleven years old. 'Be a man,' my father would say.

Although he never hit me, my father filled my life with terror and military routine. He never wanted children, but loved my mother and so accepted the package; except that the extra baggage was locked away in a room upstairs. In India, I had experienced freedom beyond what I could possibly imagine. This left me feeling torn. I was lucky to be alive and able to travel this amazing land. I was not one of the unfortunates like the beggars and the poor I had seen so many times. Their struggle continues day in and day out where mine was seemingly over. Yet it was becoming increasingly hard to forget the constant oppression I was once so accustomed to. Over the years, I accepted it as a way of life and when it finally ended I was too preoccupied with working hard and involving myself in relationships, that only with the benefit of hindsight, I know were destined to fail.

I took a few deep breaths and wiped my face dry before returning to the bus. The convoy broke away at various points and travel became swift. The driver suggested that I should not register my passport at the various checkpoints, but lay down in the aisle out of view. His reasoning was enough for me to comply; he said there were militants posing as police and army to deceive travellers to kidnap them. We passed through Sonamarg, 'the Meadow of Gold', just as the sun was setting. A deep red, it had transformed a lake into a gigantic pool of blood, which reflected the dark mountains and an avenue of tall chinar trees. At last we'd reached Srinagar.

It had gone eight by the time we stopped outside a moored houseboat. Feroz handed my luggage down from the roof and before we exchanged addresses, he presented me with two gifts.

'This is phiran,' he said. 'It will keep you warm during cold nights and Kashmiri sweater, mine, to remember me by.' I took the grey phiran, the same loose tunic the other Kashmiri men wore, and pulled it over my head. 'Now you are real Kashmir man,' he laughed and embraced me tightly. 'Insha Allah my brother, you are in my heart always.' I was thankful to Feroz for his friendship. His humour and the warmth of his family and the eventual acceptance from the other passengers had made the trip that much more bearable. Feroz returned to the bus and waved from his seat until the night consumed him.

I was hurried inside the ornate wooden houseboat by a clean-shaven man in his early twenties, 'Please, come inside. It is curfew, not safe for you out here.' I had little time to admire the grand reception area. He was terribly flustered, 'Please sir, can you help me, I am in big trouble with police?'

'What's the matter?' I asked, becoming somewhat flustered myself.

'I am being accused of stealing from police officer, but I have been in houseboat all day. Please, will you be writing letter to say you know me to be of good character and that I would never do such a thing?'

He awaited my answer, hands held together in prayer, begging almost. I was taken aback by his request, 'I don't know you, and I've only just met you. I would be lying to say I did.'

'My name is Bashir, this Nabi,' he pointed to a skull capped elderly gentlemen in the corner behind me. 'Now you know me, please can you help? If I get arrested, I will be sent to jail or maybe I get tortured. I would never steal from policeman; I am not crazy.'

I was in a real quandary. I wasn't in the habit of lying and was conscious of my personal safety whilst in Srinagar. But what kind of reception would I have staying here for three nights if I didn't carry out his request? 'Okay, I'll do it, but I'll keep it brief. Do you have a pen and paper?'

'Of course, thank you so much.' He searched a chestnut drawer and gave me the items.

'Dear Sir,' I wrote. 'I have stayed with Bashir on his houseboat before and have always found him to be polite, conscientious and above all, honest. In my opinion I do not believe he is capable of the crime he has been accused of.' I signed off at the end and ripped the page from the jotter.

He thanked me again and headed out of the door. I was left with Nabi who showed me along a narrow corridor to my bedroom. 'Dinner in half hour,' he mumbled and slid the door shut behind me.

I kicked off my shoes and sat on the bed to unwind, running my hand along the embroidered bedspread. The room had an en-suite bathroom with a proper bathtub – a luxury I'd long forgotten about. I ran the bath only to find brown murky water and the occasional leaf float to the surface. Deciding against a bath which was evidently drawn from the lake, I washed from the sink instead where the water was marginally clearer.

Along the hallway of carved cedar panelling were two other bedrooms, both like mine, a kitchen and a storeroom, an open dining room and beyond that, a lounge and reception. Each room was laid out with patterned Kashmir rugs and comfortable Victorian chairs were complimented by a range of elegant walnut cabinets and tables. It was the most luxurious accommodation I'd stayed in; a palace fit for royalty.

'Please sit,' Nabi said and presented me with my evening meal. Each serving of food was pointed out on the plate, 'Aab gosht – milk curry lamb; dum aloo – yoghurt gravy potato; nadir palak – lotus stem and spinach.' Lastly, he placed a steaming glass of creamy liquid before me, 'Kewah – almond and cardamom tea.' He waggled his head and left me alone to eat. The food was a comfort and tasted amazing. With my plate empty, I retired to my room and updated my journal, content with my decision of staying in Srinagar after all. My thoughts were interrupted when Nabi popped his head around the door, 'Please sir, be keeping shutters on windows closed at night because of kidnapping problem.'

Somewhere across the lake, distant explosions and rapid gunfire were occasionally heard, but soon the noise drifted and disappeared into my dreams.

33

I awoke to the sounds of creaking wood, the splashing of oars and bird song as light danced through the branches of a tree and the slightly open slats of the shutters, casting flickering patterns across the bed. I looked out over Nagin Lake at the pretty lotus flowers and water lilies resting on the sparkling water. Canoe shaped shikara boats glided past, some with coloured tarpaulins taxiing locals, others packed with goods for sale; bright flowers, handicrafts, vegetables or textiles. On the far side of the lake, dark shadows lined the folds of the Zabarwan range as the sun rose, warming the rock a deep maroon. Perched upon the top of a hill opposite was the Hari Parbat Fort, first constructed by the Moghul emperor Akbar. It was hard to believe so much trouble existed in such tranquillity.

Breakfast was simple; an omelette, toast and black tea.

'Ah good morning, you are enjoying your stay on houseboat?' Bashir asked as he walked in with two brown paper bags filled with groceries.

'It's lovely, thanks. How did you get on with the police last night?'

'I did not need letter. Police catch suspect and I am free from trouble. But thank you for help.'

'I need to get a bus ticket to Jammu and a first-class train ticket from Jammu to Bombay. Could you tell me where the best place to get them from is?'

'I will get them for you. You must stay on houseboat; it is very unsafe in city.'

'Okay, what about cigarettes?'

'Ask Nabi, he will get for you.'

I handed over a thousand rupees for the bus and train ticket and Bashir disappeared out of the door again. I was about to sit on the veranda when I was stopped by Nabi. Apparently, it was too unsafe to even step outside. I asked him if he could get me some cigarettes, but he tilted his head unable to understand. 'Cigarettes? Smoke?' I said placing my pinched fingers to my lips.

'Ah, smoke, yes,' he said and put his hand out. What usually cost no more than 50 rupees for a pack, suddenly turned into 300 by the time I finished leafing out the notes.

The thought of not being able to leave the boat at all during my stay was disappointing and instantly made me feel claustrophobic. Sitting at the table, I looked out to the lake and wondered how to pass the hours. It wasn't long before my thoughts were answered by a papier-mâché salesman who seemed well acquainted with Nabi. On the table, one by one, the salesman displayed his wares: delicate elephants, mice, apples, trinket boxes and the like; all finely painted and crafted by hand to perfection. I heard his pitch but had to tell him that sadly anything so fragile would be destroyed in my luggage by the time I made it home. He left disappointed and I returned to my musings. Just twenty minutes passed before another salesman came on board, this time offering a selection of freshly cut flowers. I declined again and he paddled away in hope of another customer.

Salesman after salesman arrived and departed throughout the day. Nabi told me times were hard with the lack of tourists and earning money was a rare opportunity, one that must be seized. Although my finances were comfortable, I still had to keep a close eye on my pocket, knowing that if I was frivolous, I would soon run out of cash again. After lunch a tailor arrived and I agreed to have a lining stitched into a jacket I had bought in Manali. I negotiated for him to tell me more information about the city as part of the deal, to which he was very obliging.

'Srinagar is the summer capital of Jammu and Kashmir,' he said. 'It is situated in the Kashmir Valley and lies on the banks of the Jhelum River, a tributary of the great Indus. The city is famous for its glorious Moghul gardens, beautiful lakes and canals and exquisite houseboats. Also, Srinagar is famed for its Kashmiri carpets, handicrafts, woollen clothing and dry fruit. Nagin Lake is split by the road outside of your houseboat by Dal Lake. One of the highlights of Dal Lake is the vegetable market, where tradesmen sit in their shikaras crammed together competing for business. You must come and see for yourself if you get a chance.' I looked over to Nabi who shook his head in disapproval.

The salesman offered me a cigarette. I accepted and as I placed the tip in my mouth he struck a match and held the flame towards me, before extinguishing it with a flick of the wrist. 'Due to the dislike of British in Victorian times,' he continued, 'The Maharaja would not allow the British to build upon the land of Srinagar. Instead, they took to the water, building houseboats as a retreat from the sweltering plains.'

'When did all the trouble begin in the city?' I asked.

He was reluctant to answer at first, but when Nabi left the room and was out of earshot, he explained, 'After the partition of British India in 1947, India and Pakistan both laid claim to Kashmir and invasions by Pakistan lead to war. The government of India sent troops into Srinagar to defend the city and they have been here ever since. In 1987 the Indian government rigged state elections, arresting opposition candidates and supporters. The resentment of Indian rule and bad treatment of Kashmiris led to an eruption of violence that continues to this day.'

He paused to take a sip of Kewah, and then continued, 'The majority of the main fighting takes place in Srinagar's old city, but also spreads out over a two-hundred-kilometre-wide radius. These are very dangerous times with the up and coming elections in September. As a Kashmiri and citizen of Srinagar, there is no escape from the trouble. People get dragged from their homes in broad daylight and shot dead. School children are forced by militants to carry hand grenades in their school bags with instructions to throw them at Indian army posts. Once upon a time, Srinagar was the perfect place to holiday; houseboats and the city flourished with tourists from across India and the rest of the world. Now, the houseboats are all but empty and the streets run with blood.'

Nabi returned and cleared away the cups and ushered the salesman to the door. He didn't seem to want him to tell me more. The salesman bid me farewell and left with my jacket under his arm with a promise to return it in three hours.

Seven salesmen later, the tailor returned with my coat, professionally stitched with a black lining. He was followed on board by a man who sold colourfully embroidered wallets. I bought one to replace the wallet I left behind in Kargil.

Cabin fever was getting the better of me, so I asked Nabi if I could take a ride with him in his shikara. Refusing at first, he told me it was far too dangerous, but after offering him fifty rupees he quickly changed his mind. He paddled me out a short distance, nervously glancing in all directions, with our rectangular houseboat always in sight. Stretching my legs out I began to relax, catching a fleeting glimpse of a kingfisher or two and listening to the single oar ripple the water. We made our way back after twenty minutes and were nearing the houseboat when the shikara came to a stop. The boat was grounded on some thick lake weeds. Nabi became tense, desperately trying to free us from the tangle as another shikara was seen approaching from the rear. He stabbed the weeds with the oar while keeping a close eye on the teenager in the oncoming boat. The boy came up level with us, held out a beautiful water lily and offered it to me. I took it and he simply glided away, just as Nabi managed to free us from the lake's clutches and docked us at the houseboat.

That night, the sporadic gunfire and explosions sounded nearer than yesterday and I lay awake unable to find peace. Since leaving Leh I had felt uneasy, not only because I was on a fool's trail where so few travellers feared to tread, but the news of my grandfather had awakened a corner of my soul, which had laid dormant for so long. Scars itched, yearning to be reopened. I remembered seeing him collapsed one early morning, lying in the darkness on the hall floor. I offered to help him, but his pride refused me and he implored me not to tell anyone. Not that I would have done, I never did. Every knock and tumble, each sore head and injury, were our little secret.

34

His face said it all without him muttering a single word; a lightning switch from a cheery good morning smile to an uneasy frown. All it took was one question to induce the panic of Bashir's blurted excuses. 'Could you drive me into the city today please?' I asked. Each justification was brushed away with answers of my own self responsibility, but it wasn't enough to sway him. I had one more trick up my sleeve. The sight of one thousand rupees snapped his frown into a confused head tilt, eyes of wonder at the illusion before him. His objections became lost, his mouth numbed as he considered the offer. He looked left and right for the disapproving face of Nabi, reached out to the notes, paused and drew them from my grip.

'Please, we will not stay too long, maybe one hour,' he said as he stuffed the money in his shirt pocket.

'Come on Bashir, until lunchtime at least,' I countered.

'Okay, until twelve o'clock only.'

I glanced at my wristwatch. It'd just gone eight. By the time I got ready and had breakfast we could leave by nine. I washed in front of the mirror and caught the nervousness in my eyes. 'The war takes place during the night,' I said to myself, but my half-cocked smile did little to convince my diminishing confidence.

It was a bright, crisp morning and the sun warmed the back of my neck as we made our way to a white Maruti hatchback. Bashir ushered me into the back seat and quickly took his place behind the wheel. He was clearly agitated. We drove along the road, which separated the two lakes and was flanked either side by tall poplar trees and lines of moored houseboats. In the distance the city rose on the horizon and traffic thickened as transportation was stopped before a bridge. Soldiers were checking the contents of vehicles and drivers were heavily scrutinised. When our turn came, two armed uniformed officers approached our car. One pointed a lathi at Bashir and ordered him to get out while the other circled the vehicle with suspicion. Bashir looked over the seat to me and then back to the soldier who was tapping the windscreen. He stayed calm, but nervous tension was evident in his eyes. The soldiers became irate, 'Get out!' one of them shouted to Bashir. Bashir stayed motionless with a look of increasing frustration. The officer slammed the stick on the roof and demanded he step out immediately. The other officer fell behind his colleague and raised an automatic rifle at the car.

With the uncertainty of what might happen next, I urged Bashir to do as they said. He clicked the door open and was pulled out, hauled across the bonnet, questioned and searched for any weapons or suspicious contraband. I was told to stay put. With the window rolled down and a gun in my face, question after question was fired at me, 'How do you know this man?', 'What is your country?', 'What is the purpose of your visit to Srinagar?' 'Where is your passport?' I answered him as fast as my rattled brain could calculate the questions. I was ordered to join Bashir by the front of the car and we were told not to speak to each other as they searched the vehicle. I was terrified that the two of us might become another statistic. What had I done convincing Bashir to take me into town?

We were finally given clearance and told to move on. Bashir apologised as we crossed the bridge over the Jhelum River. I tried to reassure him that I understood it was not his fault, and that it was I that was sorry for putting him in the predicament in the first place. 'I did not move at first because I was scared they arrest me for being nothing but Kashmiri,' he said. 'Please do not be sorry, it is a daily occurrence of Srinagar life.'

After a while we turned from the main road into a narrow street of bullet peppered buildings and businesses with their shutters closed. Apart from just a few civilians, only soldiers walked the streets, some of which wore camouflaged flak jackets, cricket shin pads and toughened metal helmets with caged face guards. We slowed to allow a horse and cart to pass. I looked out of the window to my left and it was as if a news report was playing out before me. Lying on the ground were two bodies covered by white sheets, crowded by a scattering of people. Voices were raised, some sobbing. Another body was carried out and placed alongside the other two. A young man, no older than me, lay motionless, with a swollen face, bruised and spattered with dried blood. The side of his head was partially missing, exposing a dark red mass and fragments of bone. An elderly woman knelt at his feet, tears streaming down her face. She raised her hands and yelled to the sky.

I observed the scene in stunned silence. I had only ever seen one dead person before and that was my father. He collapsed from a heart attack in front of me one Sunday morning when I was eighteen. It was early Spring and the weather was not too dissimilar to what it was now. There was coolness in the air, but the sun was strong. Colours were vibrant, birds sang and families were out and about enjoying their weekend. The scene was filled with life; except for my father in the middle of it all lying on the ground dying. He no longer belonged; nature dictated that. This wasn't the case here though. People's lives were being taken prematurely and my reaction to what I had just witnessed was very different. Sweat poured from my face and nausea tied a knot in my stomach that grew bigger and tighter as each minute passed. Bashir saw my distress in the interior mirror. He manoeuvred the car around the cart and drove along the bunkered streets until he found a place to stop alongside a reel of circular barbed wire blocking a road.

'Are you okay, Sam?'

I took a sip of water and wiped my face clean of moisture, taking deep breaths as I tried to gain focus, 'Do you know what happened to those men?'

'Maybe caught in fighting from night time. Many die in city, very dangerous time after dark.' There was no element of surprise in his voice, 'Like Phil Collin sing, just another day in paradise.'

'Cello!' a soldier shouted as he whacked the roof of the car. Bashir quickly moved on.

Everybody was on edge here. As we drove we passed tired, burnt out buildings: businesses, people's homes; some nothing more than rubble. 'Where Are Our Children?', 'Bring Back The Disappeared', 'Kashmir: Paradise Tortured', 'Stop Rape Of Kashmiri Women', 'Indians Go Home' and 'Give Us Back Our Homeland' were just some of the slogans that were seen either hanging from walls on banners or spray painted around the city. Men, women and children were being killed here daily, yet I'd never once seen anything on the news about Kashmir back home. This was no Hollywood blockbuster where Superman came to save the day. The ongoing struggle and suffering of the people here went on almost in secret as far as the rest of the world was concerned; all for a piece of land.

Bashir turned into a busying bazaar and pulled up in a side road. He leant over his seat, 'We will visit Jama Masjid, one of the oldest mosques in Kashmir. I think this is maybe what you look for in Srinagar.' We got out of the car and before me stood a large square building. Unlike other mosques I'd seen there was no dome, but a pagoda style roof. There was no denying the magnificence of the structure. Merchants lined the paths leading up to the entrance selling their various goods. A young boy whose arm was missing at the elbow and who had two stumps where his legs once were cried out, 'One-rupee sir, one rupee,' but Bashir had already ushered me past before I could donate. I removed my shoes and followed him through a high archway into a courtyard flourished with lawns, shrubs and small trees. The fawn stone walls were broken by grand entrances, topped in the centre by wooden minarets with a view of Hari Parbat Fort in the distance.

Bashir strolled alongside me into a spacious carpeted hallway of shiny deodar pillars that projected long lines of shadow from sunlight that pierced the arched windows. Beneath one of these windows a teenage boy and an old man knelt side by side reciting lines from the Qur'an.

'Look around, you will be safe here,' Bashir said. 'I will pray now.'

I left him to his prayers and wandered the quiet mosque, trying to shift the unease that resided within. My mind was cast back to the men laid upon the ground who yesterday, were alive, feeling, breathing and seeing the world around them. I couldn't understand how people could cause such harm to one another.

Bashir finished his prayers and stood next to me eager to leave. I followed him from the courtyard into the street and bent down to the beggar boy and gave him ten rupees. I asked Bashir if he could ask him what happened. They spoke in Urdu and Bashir translated, 'Boy was playing with brother last year near broken bricks. Brother pick up piece of metal from ground and explosion kill brother and badly hurt this boy. There are many mines planted all around Kashmir, many people hurt each year.' I looked at the boy and pictured the scene, my stomach turning at the vision.

Undeterred by our presence, two starving dogs fought with each other over a dying raven by our car. Bashir laughed and got into the driver's seat. This time I sat beside him. He appeared relaxed, maybe because of his time in the mosque. 'Now we go to Roza Bal, Tomb of Jesus Christ.'

I wasn't sure if I heard correctly, 'Did you just say the tomb of Jesus Christ?'

'Yes, tomb of Jesus Christ. Buddhist, Arabic, Sanskrit, Persian and Kashmiri historical texts say Yuz Asaf, which was Jesus real name, did not die on cross, but was healed from his wounds and he migrate to Kashmir to continue word of God. He marry Kashmiri girl and they live in Pahalgam until he die of old age.' If this were the truth, was I about to enter the final resting place of Jesus?

Amongst old brick buildings was an unimpressive white building with two sloped roofs. We removed our shoes and walked into a secluded area overpowered by the scent of burning jasmine incense. Behind the glass of a wooden framed cabinet was a shrouded coffin and nearby, a stone cast of footprints said to be those of Yuz Asaf, showing imprints of crucifixion wounds. Bashir pointed out that the wooden sarcophagus was merely a façade, the real tomb was in an underground chamber below us. The tomb laid in an east-westerly direction – the Jewish direction of burial. 'It is not a Muslim tomb,' he whispered. 'Muslims bury their dead in south-westerly direction.' Whether the story held true or not, it was nothing short of captivating. I felt very lucky to have been brought here.

The drive back took us along wide avenues with sandbagged bunkers. Nervous soldiers peered out from behind protective mesh, guns pointing ready for any signs of trouble. It was not long before we stumbled upon our own set of problems. We turned a corner and in the centre of the road was a white buckled van, alight with roaring flames. Thirty or more young men dressed in t-shirts and jeans were shouting, throwing rocks and pieces of timber at a line of khaki clad officers armed with truncheons and riot shields. Bashir was quick to reverse in search of an alternative route. I gripped the seat as we swung from street to street, passing over bridge after bridge. All the while the medieval backdrop of the old city lined the banks of the Jhelum. Bashir increased his speed. 'I do not like driving. Grenades can be thrown or we could hit mine at any time.'

I'd been incredibly stupid and selfish. It was one thing not to consider my own safety, but I had ignored Bashir's also. He had been so good to me all morning. I sat quietly. The only thing that came from my mouth was an apology, but to this he said, 'Please do not apologise. It is good you have seen for yourself what we Kashmiris must suffer. Do not forget us when you leave. I have one more place I would like to show you.' We arrived at a clump of chinar trees and got out to the haunting sound of the adhan. Across the water was a large white mosque with a single minaret and huge dome with the mountains behind, mirrored in the glass of Dal Lake.

'This is Hazratbal Shrine,' Bashir said. 'The subedar of Moghul Emperor Shah Jahan construct Ishrat Mahal along with garden at site of mosque in 1623. During visit, Shah Jahan order building to be converted into prayer house. Inside is Holy Relic, Moi-e-

Muqaddas, the sacred hair from beard of Prophet Muhammad.'

Just then there was an explosion somewhere nearby and we sought cover under the chinars. This was followed by the blunt sounds of automatic gunfire. I was grounded with fear, but Bashir grabbed me, 'We must go now, Mujahideen maybe near.' We ran to the car with our backs low and he hurtled us back to the safety of the houseboat.

That evening I asked Bashir and Nabi if they would join me for my meal. They had previously eaten in separate quarters, but tonight, my last, I insisted they spend it with me. We spoke more about Kashmir and of that morning and after dinner, as the sun set gold upon the lake, Nabi sat with a one hundred stringed instrument – a walnut box known as a santoor. He hammered out the strings emitting soothing strains as the golden shimmer on the lake turned a deep blue and night fell.

35

It was early when Nabi entered my room to wake me, 'Time, Mr Sam.' The sun had not yet risen. Colours of dawn melted across the sky releasing the shadows slowly from the mountains. When a simple breakfast of eggs and toast was served, Nabi retired to the porch and the comfort of his hookah. Trails of smoke fogged the glow of the lantern perched beside him. In my room, I packed. I held the sweater Feroz gave me, hoping he would be kept safe in the dangerous city he called home. Placing the garment over my head I slipped my arms through the sleeves and felt the soft wool glide across my skin. I packed his phiran and folded my newly lined jacket. 'Smoking jacket,' Nabi said at the bedroom doorway.

'Huh? Oh, a smoking jacket, is that what it looks like?'

'Smoking jacket,' he repeated and cocked his head with a grin.

I walked the corridor and ran my hands along the wood, my fingertips collecting memories of my time on this floating palace. Nabi bowed as I walked out on to the veranda and said goodbye. I reached the humming hatchback with Bashir at the wheel and took one last look back. We left the princely home and picked up momentum under the maturing sky. The bridge we were previously stopped at was free of soldiers, however, the city was packed with twitching troops and armoured vehicles. It was 6.57; my bus was due to leave at eight. Bashir handed me an envelope with my tickets for onward travel, and once goodbyes were exchanged, he was quick to depart.

The street was deathly silent. In front of me, on the corner of a windowless burnt-out building was a bunker; to my right a bullet riddled car and to my left, a chai wallah starting his morning shift. I bought a glass of tea and waited patiently for the bus to arrive. It was chilly so I pulled out my newly lined jacket and put it on. I began to wonder if Bashir had dropped me at the right place, but by 8.20 I heard the rumble of a nearing bus. I handed my ticket to the bearded conductor and boarded, finding a window seat midway down. It was just under three hundred kilometres south to Jammu – I was in for another long mountainous journey. The bus drove off, but was then halted by sudden banging. My pulse raced. I was half expecting bullets or bricks to shatter the windows. But the doors opened to a flustered Sikh gentleman who came aboard and sat beside me. 'Phew, I am just making it. Good morning sir, I am Mastaan.'

'Good to meet you, Mastaan.'

'So, are you a little bit crazy?' he enquired.

'Pardon?'

'You are extremely brave visiting Srinagar as a westerner, either that or you are completely insane,' he laughed.

His jolly manner was quite contagious and put me at ease immediately, 'I could say the same to you.'

'You are so right, but I am here on pharmaceutical business. Please, I mean no disrespect, but your attire tells me you are here discovering our fine country, rather than making money from it.' He withdrew a pile of paperwork from a leather briefcase and began to skim read, write and sign sheet after sheet as he chatted to me.

We rolled along the waking streets of Srinagar, past protest banners, the army and police, a blur of grey phirans and a rush of brown timber and red brick buildings, over canal bridges with views of moored barges and gliding shikaras. The road widened and a group of young men, faces and identities covered by bandannas marched with arms high in the air and chanting in unison. From a side street, a swarm of police, canes aloft, rushed towards the unarmed men, trapping some against shuttered shop fronts and administering beatings across their arms, legs, torso and head. Disgusted, I turned away and to Mastaan who looked on, 'It is hard to witness. I wish all these problems would end, but I fear it will only increase.' He returned to his paperwork as if he was quite used to what he saw. The coach drove over the last bridge and the city of martyrs faded away.

I removed the envelope Bashir gave me and withdrew the train ticket only to find the destination was wrong. It read Jammu to Mumbai. I opened the guidebook and scanned the index for this Mumbai place but found nothing. Skipping from page to page I became quite flustered. Mastaan must have noticed, as he put his pen down, 'Is there something the matter?' he asked. I explained and a grin lit his face, 'Ah do not worry, my friend. Mumbai is Bombay. The name of the city changed earlier this year. Nationalist Shiv Sena party wished to reassert Marathi identity. Bombay was too much of a reminder of British oppression I think.' He looked again at the ticket, 'You must wait on the train for a seat to become available I am afraid. It seems you are booked in unreserved second class.'

The snow on the mountains had thinned. Rugged peaks revealed themselves with stunning plateaus below. We stopped at a village for a break. Here Mastaan departed with a firm handshake, 'We are now in the town of Qazigund, also known as 'The Gateway to Kashmir.' I have business here, so I say goodbye and wish you the very best of luck.'

When the bus set off again it did so at breakneck speed. I tried to keep my attention pinned to the views of the Pir Panjal, abundant with foliage, rather than stare down at the colossal descents. To pass the time I wrote in my journal, jotting down the warning signs on the roadside such as, 'If Married, Divorce Speed', 'Life Is Short, Don't Make It Shorter', and my favourite, 'Life Is A Journey, Complete It.' It was a shame the driver seemed to completely ignore them. The next sign was a yellow stone at the side of the road overlooking a valley of mountains graduating into a field of greens.

It read, 'Last View of the Kashmir Valley.' Not only was I leaving Kashmir, but I was climbing down from the land of giants. My time in the Himalayas was close to an end.

Ahead were two huge black holes bored into the mountainside marking the entrance and exit to the 2.5 kilometre Jawahar Tunnel that connected Jammu to Kashmir. We were one of the random vehicles being stopped and searched by the police. Three uniformed officers wearing green berets spoke outside the window. The one who seemed to hold the upper rank said to his colleague, 'I wish I was away from here and with my family in Shimla.' A smile rose on my face as I thought back to Kurt and Tyler.

Each passenger was asked to vacate one by one. I put my journal away and my pen in my jacket pocket and felt a flat disc wrapped in paper. 'Smoking jacket,' I whispered to myself. 'Smoke in jacket!' The words slammed into place like a hammer to the back of my skull. No wonder Nabi had needed so much money for cigarettes, he'd bought me hashish. Adrenaline consumed me. I tried to stay calm and stuffed the soft disc in the cupped ashtray below the window, praying it wouldn't be detected. As I got up from my seat, the leading officer approached me, 'Sir, I will need to check your passport. Come with me please.'

I followed him from the bus. He looked through my documents and up at my averting eyes. He checked my luggage, jacket and trouser pockets thoroughly and then said I could return to my seat. I was about to breathe a sigh of relief when I noticed he was following behind. I had to think quick. I turned and he nearly bumped into me, 'I couldn't help overhearing your conversation earlier,' I said. 'Did you say your family was from Shimla?'

'Yes, why are you asking?'

'Oh, no reason really, it's just that it's one of my favourite places in India. The scenery is so beautiful and the town, so elegant. I especially like the Mall with the Gaiety Theatre and the stunning Christchurch. Oh, and those cheeky little monkeys.'

His eyes widened and his face relaxed with a broad smile as his mind was sent back to the place he loved the most, 'Ah, you have been to Shimla? Yes, I am from there also. I miss my home town very much, so peaceful. Not like here where there is so much trouble.' He leant on the seat in front of mine. I leant back to block his view of the ashtray, 'Did you take a ride on the train from hilltop station?'

'Unfortunately, not,' I said. 'I didn't have enough time. But I very much wish to go there again soon.'

'Ah, then you must come and visit my family and me. I will be retiring in one month.' He withdrew a pen from his top pocket and wrote his address on his notepad. 'Please stop by, it would be a delight to have you as a guest. I would love to show you around.' He ripped away the sheet and handed it to me. I folded it and thanked him. He was about to say something else but was interrupted by one of the other officers tapping at the window. 'Ah there seems to be problem. Please excuse me. It has been a pleasure meeting you.' He about turned and walked away, chuckling to himself saying, 'Yes, those cheeky little monkeys, always up to no good.'

The coach entered the tunnel and the interior was sent into darkness. I prised the charas from the ashtray and threw it from the window. With a huge overdue sigh, I closed my eyes, the alternatives of what could have happened running through my head. The penalty for carrying even a small amount could lead to a lengthy prison sentence. The thought made me sick to my stomach. With the Jawahar Tunnel behind us, the sun shone bright on the mountains. Alone with my thoughts, I stared out of the window for hours until we finally reached the humid city of Jammu.

36

The creeping heat of the plains was evident. No sooner had I stepped from a cold shower I was sweating again. Leaving the claustrophobia of my room I walked the wet streets that shone from the emerging sun. Shutters were down on the cluster of buildings fringing the pavement. Shattered glass, rocks and wood were strewn about the street. Some sections of the road were barred off with wooden poles and melted tyres blackened the road surface. Something bad had happened here overnight. Like Srinagar, Jammu was suffering its own set of problems. Nevertheless, shopkeepers swept the front of their properties and began to open for business as usual.

Before catching the train, I went in search of Raghunath Temple, said to be one of the largest Hindu temple complexes in India. The white and golden peaks of the shikharas came into view and I entered to the smell of damp and the perfume of burnt-out incense. Dedicated to Lord Rama, the 19th century temple consisted of seven shrines, each with a tower of its own. I didn't have time to explore the complex in full, but sought a little solace before the long journey ahead. I padded the wet marble floors passing vibrant deities lining the golden walls until I came to a tall statue of the monkey god, Hanuman. Deep in silent prayer a man stood before it as if hypnotised by its presence. I had to admire such devotion, wondering if I would ever find the peace of mind this man seemed to emanate. It was as if he read my thoughts and turned to face me with a smile. 'I like to free my mind of clutter once a day,' he said. 'So much to do and so little time, yet a minute here feels like a lifetime.'

On the railway platform groups of passengers spoke over hot chai, young men scrubbed pots and pans readying them for train kitchens, an elderly woman on the tracks was losing a tug of war with a cow over a piece of plastic, and amongst the huddled homeless, a girl of no more than ten approached me, pitching her fingers forward and giving me a cheek to cheek grin. I lined her hand with a few rupees before she ran off laughing back to her friends.

At 9.30am the train arrived. I hoped a seat would become available sooner rather than later as I didn't fancy spending the next thirty-three hours standing. Pacing the aisles wasn't as bad as I thought it might be. It was an experience seeing the many colours and hearing the different languages spoken. People of varying religions sat side by side harmoniously, getting along with each other regardless of their beliefs. Occasionally I stood by an open doorway, allowing the breeze to cool my skin, gazing out to a panorama of dwindling pine forests and increasing parched, irrigated fields.

We skirted the Pakistani border and made a course in a south-easterly direction towards Delhi. Finally, I found a seat by the window and watched the last of the Shivalik Hills drift out of view as we sped through the state of Punjab, making a half hour stop at the city of Jalandhar. Passengers piled out of the train to buy snacks and stretch their legs whilst chai wallahs and water sellers offered goods through the barred windows to the remainder of the people on board. I bought a small disposable clay cup of tea for two rupees. Once drained, it seemed a shame to throw away, but it was far too delicate to sit in my backpack.

Men, women and children strolled the gangway selling their wares; from soft drinks, newspapers and cigarettes to handicrafts, novelty musical instruments and balloons. With perfect timing, just as the train departed, they jumped to the platform and scuttled over the tracks in wait of the next train. The handful of passengers that were late getting back on made a run for it, clinging to the doorway railings to hoist themselves in without a second to spare.

To my left, a lady in a blue sari hemmed with gold talked to her son whose feet dangled above the floor. In front of me, two overweight middle aged men played cards. One wore jeans, the other perfectly pressed trousers; both had shiny black shoes and white open necked shirts with vests beneath. From the Punjab, we passed Ludhiana and crossed over into the state of Haryana with a brief stop at Ambala. The lady next to me was kind enough to mind my seat while I went for a cigarette. I lit up by a doorway in a connecting carriage with a rushing blur of pastures and rivers at my back. The area was shared by an old man who sat on the floor. 'Gold Flake, baba? You are smoking Gold Flake, Indian Brand, no?' I looked over to where the croaky voice came from, but the man continued to stare forward.

'Would you like one?' I asked.

'Okay, sit with me. We will pretend we are old friends.' I slouched opposite him and offered him the pack. His hand circled the air and came to rest on the extended cigarette. His eyes were as white as his hair and stubble. Beside him was a crutch and a cane. I lit his cigarette and he leant back, blowing the smoke past me. 'You are wealthy British man.' He put his hand on my boot and ran his fingers across the leather, 'Hmm, but not as wealthy as some. Maybe you are a traveller, why else would you be on train?' he laughed. 'We are all travellers through life, my friend. Your name, sir?' I told him and asked his, 'Janardan,' he returned, and coughed and wheezed. 'You are looking at my eyes. Hello, I can see you.'

I gazed a moment longer at the milky orbs before looking away, embarrassed that he saw me studying him. 'You are not blind? But your eyes...' I said, glaring back. 'I'm sorry if I offended you.'

'You have not offended me and yes, I am very blind. One might say as blind as a bat,' he chuckled and coughed again. 'I always know when someone look at me though. Maybe I is wrong, but it is very funny to tell people I can see them.' With a giggle, he slapped his good leg.

I flicked my cigarette to the wind, 'Have you got far to go?'

'I never have far to go these days. Life is short for me.' He pulled himself up to the swaying wall, exposing his right leg. His calf muscle was almost missing to the bone. 'Now you see my leg. Difficult life, but we all suffer in different ways, don't we Mr Sam?'

'I've never seen so much suffering as I have in India. At times, it's been too much to bear.'

'You have suffered, yet I hear light in your voice,' Janardan paused, cocked his head and raised his hand, 'I am poor. Some say I have nothing. All time I feel pain in leg and in back or in head, but I smile because God give life to do best with and I am truly grateful.'

I stood to stretch. The middle-aged man who sat opposite my seat joined us for a cigarette, 'You are from which country?' he asked me in a confident, but strange American-Indian accent. I answered and he nodded his head, 'I am from the US of A. I moved to California six years ago, after selling my fifth company.' He told us of his successful life without pause, and about his trip to see his family in Jammu and Delhi. He repeatedly swept his hair back with a flick of his hands and rattled a gold watch on one wrist and a thick gold bracelet on the other. He pointed to Janardan with his nose in the air, 'You should think about moving away from him, you never know what you might catch from a dalit.'

'I'm sorry, a dalit?'

'Dalit, untouchable, just like his mother and father. He is the lowest of the low in the Hindu caste system. Hardly worthy of being alive, except to beg, clean latrines and pollute this train.' He swept his hair for what seemed the hundredth time showing off his gold.

'I don't believe anyone is lower than anybody else,' I said. 'Everybody has their own talents. One man can be great at one thing, but fail at another. We're all the same. We all have our strengths and weaknesses.'

He seemed to ignore me and continued his insults, 'India is great and it is great because we do not allow slum dwellers like him to step above their mark.'

Janardan listened in silence.

'I agree,' I replied. 'India is great, but I don't believe it is for the reason you've given.'

'You are from the west and have very little understanding of our culture.' He took a packet of macaroons from his pocket and opened them, 'After these I am fasting for twenty-four hours. I prove to God I am of good character and strength.' He offered me the packet and I took one.

Steadying myself from the motion of the train, I returned to the floor with Janardan. I found my friend's hands and gave him the biscuit. He accepted and leant forward with a moan and placed it against the wall I leant upon. His good leg pulled back and with a mighty thrust, the macaroon was obliterated to dust. 'You see, I am very good at pinball, not all useless,' he chuckled. Our fellow passenger was outraged, his cheeks filled a rosy crimson and he stomped back along the aisle without a word said.

'Many man like him,' said Janardan. 'I am used to it. Anyway, he not the man he like to think he is. He not American or rich as he say. He liar. Fake and over confident with insecurity beneath. And he suffer with worst diseases of all: arrogance and ignorance. He is blinder than me.

'Once I was wealthy. I had many acre of farmland, but I have accident and lose use of my leg, and with it my livelihood. My son die of cholera, so there was nobody to continue business. This is life; sometime good, sometime bad. What to do but live.'

We spoke a while longer until I excused myself to go to the toilet. I told him I would be back soon. Waiting a few minutes for the cubicle to become vacant, I found a relatively clean room. The tracks rushed past beneath the hole in the floor in the centre of two steel footsteps. When I returned, Janardan was gone.

Staring from the window at the dying sun I looked back upon my trip, linking the chain of events to this moment. I realised then, that despite my darkest hours, I'd always had an inner voice reassuring me everything would be fine. It was impossible to believe at times, but somehow it had always been right. There seemed to be a reason for everything, something to value and pull strength from for the future.

Slowly declining below the horizon, the sun bid goodnight to the parched red earth. It was ten past eight when we reached Panipat and just over an hour later the train arrived at New Delhi where it stayed for a while. The men opposite departed and were replaced by a quiet Sikh man and his wife. I decided to get some air and smiled to myself as I waited in line at a chai stall. It seemed so long ago since I walked here with Aiden, Don and Ruben. So much had happened since. The night brought with it a still calm. The world around was quieter, talk was low and people dozed by their belongings. My shirt was once again damp with sweat, but my smile widened at the thought of how cold I was just a few days ago in Drass.

In my carriage people bunked up in the single beds above their seats and some on the lower tiers too. I pulled my legs to my chest and rested my head against the window. Small dwellings of corrugated iron lined the track for a distance until the city lights disappeared and the night sky cloaked the landscape into complete darkness. My view was exchanged for the sleeping interior. Entering the state of Uttar Pradesh, and not far from Agra, we swung south west at Mathura.

37

Ca clack ca clack, ca clack ca clack, ca clack ca clack... 'Hello stranger.' Soft muffled words bounced lightly away from me. I opened my eyes, my vision misty, my head weighted with sleep. Long brown hair shone in the light of the overhead bulb.

I rubbed my eyes from the drowsy blur, but could hardly believe the clarity, 'Kate?' My heart skipped, 'I thought I'd lost you forever.'

'I couldn't believe it when I saw you. You looked so sweet fast asleep there.' Her beautiful eyes reflected happiness as she tightened her hands gently around mine.

'I knew the moment I first saw you that I loved you. I've missed you so much,' I said without thinking.

Ca clack ca clack, ca clack ca clack, ca clack ca clack. The train slowed and let out a deep sigh as it halted at a barely lit station. She rose and turned to leave, 'I love you too, Sam.' Her eyes brimmed with tears. 'I have to get off here. Come with me,' she whispered and held out her hand.

The train jolted me awake as it gripped the tracks. The Sikh gentleman and his wife were asleep. The man in the bunk above them snored softly. She seemed so real. I took a deep breath and closed my eyes in hope she might return, but she didn't.

Carrying his toothpaste, toothbrush and soap, the Sikh man opposite exchanged places with me in the bathroom. The toilet had quite a few hours of use since I last visited and the floor was now covered in faeces. I was surprised considering the hole in the floor seemed more than adequate. I held my breath, washed and cleaned my teeth.

After a brief stop at Kota in Rajasthan, the train came to a rest for a short while at Ratlam in Madhya Pradesh – the central province between northern and southern India. Some passengers including myself bought a light lunch from the on-board kitchens. What I chose wasn't so good; a spicy vegetable burger covered in soggy breadcrumbs. Nonetheless it was enough to fill a small gap.

The train swept across high iron bridges, wide rivers gleaming below from the afternoon sun; past shanty villages, where people washed themselves next to the tracks as their children played dangerously close nearby. Cities built up and faded away amid an endless land of arid earth, sparse of vegetation and life.

I asked the Sikh gentleman if he would take my photograph. He held up the camera, the lens pointing to his face. I motioned to him with my finger to turn it around the correct way and he laughed at his mistake, 'I have never used camera before,' he said and clicked. We travelled onwards through the fertile green plains of Gujarat and soon arrived at the city of Vadodara. Two masculine looking women dressed in saris held out their hands for donations. The man in the seat next to me, suggested that to avoid a curse, I should pay the Hijras. I didn't want to risk any more bad luck and as I handed over some money and was granted a closer look, I realised they were men convincingly dressed as women.

A young girl on the platform of Surat Station tapped away at the bars of the window, holding out her hand to me and then to her mouth. I handed her five rupees, the only change I had left. She was joined swiftly by at least eight other girls, all holding their hands out too. They became agitated and more aggressive with their demands and boarded the train when I gestured I had no more money spare. Quick to my rescue, the Sikh gentleman shooed them away as the train moved off.

Stop after stop we stayed anywhere between five and fifty minutes at stations. Familiar faces left, fresh faces arrived. The dry heat gradually turned humid and a white sky stretched out over a dull jade countryside. Masses of corrugated dwellings emerged. Small tropical islands surrounded by large expanses of water were frequent. We were nearing Mumbai.

At 6.35pm, the train squealed into Mumbai Central Railway Station. In the hectic rush hour, I had to locate a local train to an area called Dadar situated in the heart of the city. I trawled through the crowds in desperation until a sympathetic lady assisted me by pointing out the correct platform heaving with commuters. When the train arrived, it was every man for himself. I scrambled to find my place, but was shoved aside and left wondering what had just happened as the train left, throngs of commuters hanging from the doorways. The empty platform soon filled again, but this time I was ready and at the edge. I wasn't going to be caught out again and looked around me at the competition who were as eager as I was to get where they were going. When the train arrived ten minutes later, I wasted no time getting on. I hurled myself in and stumbled to find a seat. One stop later, getting off proved to be as much of an art as getting on. Joining the crowds, I was carried up the stairs by the crush of people and I didn't really have a choice but to exit on to the soaking streets of Dadar.

Once the crowd dispersed I could breathe freely again. I looked about in the pouring rain in hope I could find somewhere to make a phone call. Through the downpour, I saw a yellow sign advertising telephone services and made a dash through the ankle-deep water. The rain spattered the ink of my journal as I tried to read Connor's number. I dialled and waited for a response. The voice of a young man interrupted the ringing, 'Hello?'

'Hi, can I speak to Connor please?'

'He is not here. Can I take a message?'

'Um, my name is Sam. I'm meant to be meeting with him. We are friends from Leh.'

'I am sorry, Connor is in Manali and will not be back for at least a week.'

I went silent as I wondered what to do next, 'Thank you, ah, I'll try and find a hotel.'

The other end went quiet and I thought the receiver had been put down. As I was about to place the phone down I heard a tinny voice through the hard pelt, 'Do you have our address?'

'Yes.'

'Please come over. My mother will be home soon. She will know what to do.'

Walking the streets, I asked people if they knew where Connor's road was. A few wrong directions later I arrived at his door completely drenched. The house was very grand, Victorian in age I guessed, with wooden steps leading up to where I stood. I knocked and waited. A boy of mid-teens answered and studied the drenched, plastered haired westerner before him, 'Are you Sam?'

'Yes.'

'I am Louis, Connor's brother. Please, come in. It is such awful weather out there.'

I shook my shoes free of excess water and placed them inside the door.

Connor's grandmother was next to greet me and offered the use of a shower and Connor's room to change into dry clothes. I came out refreshed to the living room which comprised of a large seating area and equally large dining room. On a red couch were Connor's sisters, Patrice and Titiana; two beautiful girls in their late teens, and on a red matching chair sat Connor's grandmother and Louis at the dining table where he invited me to sit opposite. The younger members of the family threw question after question with great enthusiasm about my life and my travels in India. It was all a little overwhelming, but I welcomed the friendly interrogation and answered as many of the questions as I could.

Connor's mother returned home within the hour, 'I know absolutely nothing about your visit,' she said. Mrs Reveredo was an elegant woman, in her late forties. There was an air about her that told me immediately she was the boss of this home. She studied me well, weighing up the odds of trust, 'I cannot telephone Connor to confirm your story. I am afraid you cannot stay here as I do not know you.' She paused for a moment, 'You may have a meal here and then I will take you to Connor's apartment where you can stay for the night.'

The meal was God sent, especially after what I'd eaten in the last three days. Fresh homemade fish curry, fluffy rice, warm chapatis and a cup of cardamom tea were presented. Later, Mrs Reveredo took me along to Connor's apartment one road up from the family home. As I thanked her for her generosity, she gave me the key and said she would return in the morning to check on me. It couldn't have been a more perfect end to my long day. Of course, it would have been nice to see Connor, but the apartment was kitted out with all the mod cons and even had an electric guitar in the corner of the living room. I relaxed, made myself comfortable and watched music videos on *Channel V*.

A ringing telephone woke me, but I had no idea where it was coming from. Disorientated, I fumbled around until at last I found the source behind a side table. It was Connor's mother wishing me good morning and inviting me over for breakfast. Outside, pregnant clouds rolled steadily over the monsoon sky giving birth to bouts of heavy rain. Connor's apartment was situated on the corner of a crossroads. For the most part, the view was of flat rooftops and long avenues of dense palm trees. Directly below the living room window was a taxi rank. Under limited shelter the drivers talked and read newspapers by a line of yellow roofed black Ambassadors.

I cleaned my teeth in front of the mirror and slowed the brushing to a stop, taking a long, hard look at myself. When I arrived in India I was pure white and clean shaven with a neat short back and sides haircut. Since then I'd lost a lot of weight, my hair was nearing shoulder length and I had a short beard. The fear that had always been present behind my eyes was diminishing and I could see a more confident version of my reflected self. Despite my scruffiness, I was proud of the person staring back, of all I had achieved in India.

Still uneasy, my stomach revolted at the thought of breakfast, but as I stepped over the threshold of the Reveredo's, that all changed. Sweet and savoury aromas filled the room and had me drifting like a puppet on invisible strings to the dining table. A young lady spotted me from a doorway and disappeared, returning moments later with a wooden trolley filled with various dishes. I thanked her and she shyly looked away with a smile.

'Good morning, Sam,' Mrs Reveredo said as she walked into the room and opened the French doors to the balcony. She sat down as the girl began placing the food on the table: toast, jams, marmalades, cereals, fruit, sponge cakes, chapatis and eggs: fried, scrambled and rolled omelettes. Silverware filled with coffee, tea and juices: mango, orange and apple. The young lady bowed and left us alone. 'Please help yourself,' Mrs Reveredo said from behind the Times of India.

'Thanks so much for everything. Breakfast looks amazing, I hope I haven't put you to too much trouble.' I reached forward and took a chapatti and fried egg, filled a delicate china tea cup with hot coffee and a sparkling crystal glass with orange juice.

She peered over the newspaper, 'What are you saying? I am having trouble understanding you. Are you speaking English? If so, you are mumbling or talking too fast. Please articulate and speak up.' I couldn't help but grin as I apologised and repeated myself clearly. 'That is better. It is no trouble, thank you for being polite.' She glanced down at the paper and then folded it away. 'You have travelled from Kashmir Louis tells me. Please, refrain from filling his head with your stay there. I do not wish to encourage him to see for himself what you speak of. He has been talking of nothing else since you arrived.'

'Of course, I'm very sorry,' I said, sipping my coffee meekly.

'And please, stop apologising, it is starting to become quite irritating don't you know?' She buttered a slice of toast and added marmalade, 'I have booked you on a tour of the city tomorrow, but first we must make you presentable. You will come with me this morning and shave that thing from your face and get an overdue haircut.'

I chuckled nervously. Maybe I wasn't as confident as I thought after all. 'Have you heard anything from Connor?' I asked.

'No. I will let you know if he telephones.' She got up and called to the maid, 'Lajni, we are finished here, thank you.' The maid came along and began clearing the table. Mrs Reveredo looked over to me, 'You are ready then, no?'

I was taken along to a posh barber shop and instructed to memorise the route back to Connor's apartment. She took me inside and spoke to one of the barbers and said she would meet me back at the house for lunch.

My hair was cut to a smart crop and I received a traditional Indian shave, declining a moustache and a head massage. I was about to pay, but was told that Mrs Reveredo had already taken care of it. I walked back to Connor's apartment and stayed there until midday when I set out to the family home. Mrs Reveredo was pulling some weeds at the foot of the steps. 'Thank you for the haircut and shave. Please, allow me to reimburse you, and for tomorrow's tour too.' I took out my wallet.

By the look on her face, she didn't recognise me at first, 'Ah, that is much better. Now you are beginning to look like a proper gentleman. Thank you for the offer, but please put your money away.' She turned and walked up the stairs, 'Now we will have lunch.'

'Could you tell me the nearest place I could make a telephone call from? I need to call my mother,' I asked as I was sat down at the table.

'Yes. You may telephone from here after lunch. There is a telephone in Connor's old room.'

Lajni served an incredible dhal; rich and full with fiery spice. There were additions of soft saffron rice, chutneys and rotis, and lassi to die for. 'Lajni is an excellent cook, Mrs Reveredo,' I remarked.

'I am afraid I have no experience of her cooking,' she replied. I cocked my head. 'The food you eat here is cooked by me. Lajni is only the home help. She does not cook, only assists me from time to time with the preparation.'

'In that case, you're an excellent cook, Mrs Reveredo. It's the best food I've tasted since I arrived in India.'

'Flattery is not necessary, but nonetheless appreciated.'

'Hi mum.' Titiana came in with a spring in her step. She put her rucksack down and kissed her mother on the cheek. 'Hey Sam, how are you? Wow, you look so different, very handsome.'

'Oh thanks,' I replied, rubbing my hand across my smooth face. 'A bit of a difference, huh? Have you had a good morning?'

She sat down next to her mother and helped herself to lunch, 'Yes, a very good morning. I have been to college. I am studying law,' she said with pride.

After lunch, I went into Connor's room to make the phone call I'd been dreading. I dialled my mother's number and took a deep breath.

'Mum, it's Sam.'

'Hello darling, I can hardly hear you.'

'I didn't think I'd catch you, I thought you'd still be in Belgium.'

'I only came back this morning to collect some things. I'm going back this evening.' She hesitated, 'Your grandfather is in a terrible state. He's in intensive care and we've been advised to expect the worst.'

'How are you coping?'

'I'm okay. Don't worry about me. I will take care of things here, just try not to think too much about it.'

'Thank you.'

'Hello? I can't hear you Ste...' The line went dead. I tried to call back, but it just rang and fell silent again. Patrice was on the sofa playing a pair of small tabla drums when I came out. I made my excuses and took my sombre mood back to Connor's apartment, where I sat and recalled memories of my grandfather until sleep took hold.

38

I opened my eyes to darkness. A heavy weight bore down on my chest and there was a sheet covering my face. It felt like it had been pinned down either side. I wriggled and let out a yelp, prompting a hard knock to the side of my head. Then the sheet loosened and I could grab a few breaths of warm air before it was tight across my nose and mouth again, secured around my ears. Consumed by fear I lay still, praying for the ordeal to be over, questioning what was happening.

The burden on my body shifted and next I heard a muffled whisper, 'Keep quiet or I'll kill you, you little bastard.'

As the perpetrator moved again I screwed up my face and bit my lip to stop myself emitting any sound. At the same time, I was desperate for air and wasn't sure how much longer I'd last. I was given the freedom to breathe again, but only briefly before the sheet felt tighter than ever and the weight became more concentrated around my torso and face. Death felt imminent.

Elbows and knees seemed to be digging in all over my body. It was excruciating. I then felt a hard punch in the top of my arm. All I could do was let out a whimper, I had nothing else to give. After that everything started to feel lighter and I found a gap for air.

My eyes shot open, my breath still short. I was drenched in sweat, clinging to the bed sheet below me, realising the cruel trickery my mind had performed. How could a dream feel so real? To recall in such clarity an all-too-familiar moment so long ago departed. I tried to stay alert, but the darkness took hold once again.

39

My soul still bruised, I said little to Mrs Reveredo as she guided me to the tour bus departure point outside Dadar Railway Station. The coach was already filled with Indian tourists as I boarded and we joined the endless congestion of taxis, rickshaws, cars, trucks, bicycles, and faded double decker buses – the first I'd seen in India. Our guide was in his early twenties, short curly hair and introduced himself as Chinmay. He spoke in Hindi then translated into English.

'Mumbai is capital of Maharashtra and home to thirteen million people. It is the most populous city in India and the most industrialised. The city was once seven islands of mangrove swamps and mud flats that were home only to Koli fishing communities. In 1862, the British merged the islands into a single land mass with a harbour and causeways to mainland India.'

The tour commenced at Colaba Causeway in South Mumbai where there was a striking view of the Arabian Sea, light flirting with the water's surface in the morning sun. We were then introduced to The Gateway of India, an archway built from concrete and discoloured yellow basalt with four prominent turrets on each corner.

'Gateway of India was built during British rule in 1924,' Chinmay explained. 'The structure is twenty-six metres in height and is known as the Taj Mahal of Mumbai.' He pointed opposite the gateway to two buildings: one large hotel with pink domes on four corners and a tall building with arched windows, 'To the left are the Taj Mahal Palace Hotels. The first opened its doors to guests in 1903 and due to its popularity, the palace needed extra room and so the twenty-storey tower alongside was added in 1973. Guests have included royalty, presidents, performers and religious figures; such names as Margaret Thatcher, Prince Charles, Mick Jagger and The Beatles. Please take twenty minutes to enjoy the area and then return to bus.'

Stepping down we were approached by salesmen and chai wallahs alike. I ploughed my way through, bought some tea and stood alone watching the small boats bobbing in the harbour. I was tapped on the arm by a toothless man with one arm, the other missing at the shoulder. He tilted his head to the side and held out a gnarled hand which I filled before returning my glass and heading back to the bus.

'We will shortly be stopping at the Ferozeshah Mehta Gardens. These magnificent grounds are known as the Hanging Gardens due to their location on the western side and top of Malabar Hill.'

I strolled for a short while, looking at trimmed hedges shaped like animals and people, but found the heat a little overbearing. Beneath the shade of a bougainvillea tree, I drank a Limca and watched two green parrots hopping from one branch to another. Chinmay came over and asked if he could join me.

'How are you liking the tour?' he said, sipping from a bottle of Coke.

'Yeah, it's okay. I wouldn't usually go for something like this, but somebody else booked it for me. I guess it's a good way to take in all the main sights.'

'I'm glad you like. Sometimes I find it tedious; the same thing day in and day out,' he laughed.

'How long have you been a guide?'

'Just over a year now. It is a good job, so no real complaints. I better round up the rest of the passengers; that is a job in itself. We will catch up later, yaar?'

By a heavily wooded area at the roadside, we pulled over so

Chinmay could provide us with information about the next place on our itinerary: The Towers of Silence.

'We are situated outside the fifty-seven acres of forest that house the Parsi Dakhma or Towers of Silence. Parsis are followers of the Iranian prophet Zoroaster. In Parsi tradition, Zoroastrians believe that as soon as a person dies, the body becomes impure. The earth and all that is good is the work of God, and death is evil. A corpse is said to contaminate the elements, so huge towers were constructed where bodies are laid out, exposed to the sun and pecked away by vultures.'

He paced the aisle slowly as everyone hung on his words, 'It is considered an individual's final gift to provide the birds with what would otherwise be destroyed and so the bodies are arranged onto rings that surround a central pit. The outer ring is for men and the inner ring is for the women and children. Remains of the dead are left for one year before the skeletons are swept away into the pit underneath.' He lightened his tone and smiled, 'Now we will go to Mahalakshmi Temple.'

A sprinkling of rain fell as we skirted along Marine Drive before coming to a stop. 'This temple is dedicated to Lakshmi, the Hindu Goddess of wealth, health, fortune and prosperity. Please enjoy and return to the bus in thirty minutes' time.' Chinmay sat down and put his feet up as we piled off.

I followed the other passengers along a teeming avenue flanked either side by stalls selling orange garlands and other offerings to the deities. A single shikhara pointed to the sky to the right of the entrance and I walked inside to find vibrant idols of the goddesses Mahakali, Mahalakshmi, and Mahasaraswati adorned with nose rings, gold bangles, necklaces and flowers. The ornamented halls were filled with worshippers deep in prayer as the wisp of incense floated above their heads. Outside, a sadhu approached me and blessed me by painting a red stripe in the centre of my forehead – for a small fee naturally.

Next on route was Taraporewala Aquarium, housing over one hundred species of marine and fresh water fish from the Arabian Sea and Indian Ocean. We were to stop here for an hour for lunch.

I had no interest in the aquarium really. There were three other coaches and I expected it to be busy. The thought of all the noise, the mass of people and wall to wall fish staring at me made me feel claustrophobic. I wanted a cigarette. I lit up on a wall opposite looking at the high-rises curving away either side as if a bite had been taken out of the city. A shuffle beside me broke my gaze from a dark stretch of cloud menacing two fishing boats on the horizon. Sitting down, a white guy with long retiring blond hair in a pony-tail, said nothing at first, but just stared at me. I drew on the last of my cigarette, stubbed it out, lit another and looked out to the sea again.

'So, you're new here kid, huh?' he eventually rasped in an Australian accent.

I glanced over, 'Yeah, arrived a couple of days ago.'

Maybe in his early thirties, he looked a lot older. His face was withdrawn, with rat like features and his body was undernourished. 'You going to give me one of those or not?' he said, pointing at my cigarette.

'Sure.' I flipped the lid and slid one up from the centre.

He took it, handed it back to me and grabbed the packet for himself, 'You can't be too careful, kid. You can't trust anyone.' He looked around suspiciously, as if he was being watched and lowered his voice, 'I may have a lot of connections, but I have a lot of enemies too.'

'Oh right,' I murmured back.

'You better watch yourself, I'm high up in the biggest criminal organisation in Bombay.'

He accepted my lighter, 'I hear it's Mumbai now?'

'Huh?' His sunken eyes disconnected and glazed through me. Judging by the grey lines and needle marks in his arms, he was high up in something, but I wasn't sure if it was a criminal organisation.

'Wait for it...' he suddenly whispered.

I sat rigid in anticipation.

'Bam!' he hollered and shot out his arm.

I flew to my feet and span to face him, 'For Christ's sake, mate.'

Slowly unrolling his fingers, he revealed a lump of charas in the palm of his hand, 'You need hashish or girls? I can hook you up with the right people you know.'

'Thanks, but I'm good.'

'Then maybe you need protection? I can protect you. India can be a tough place, kid.'

'Honestly, I'm fine thanks.'

'Then maybe you can spare a little money for food?'

'Food, eh?' I gave him twenty rupees, if only for him to leave, and got up as Chinmay came from across the road. He moved off, keeping watch around him, should the enemy be on his tail ready to attack.

'So, how were the fish?' Chinmay asked.

'I didn't go in. We have quite a few of these places in England, so I've kind of seen it all before. Is there much more of the tour left?'

'Not much, no. We will go through Bollywood and then onto Juhu. There I finish my day. You will then be returned to your drop off points via a few temples, a race course and the airport by the driver only.' I asked what his plans were for the future. He said he hoped to save enough money so one day he could see the world, 'It is extremely difficult for an Indian to obtain a passport. Like everything, you have to have money.' Again, I was reminded how lucky I was to have the freedom granted by living in the west. A passport was something I took for granted.

Re-joining the bus, we drove off as Chinmay continued his commentary, 'We are now passing Chota Kashmir, a pleasant picnic spot with beautiful gardens and boating lakes. Chota Kashmir is famous for being the location of many Hindi movies and music videos. Any Bollywood fans on the bus?' The crowd erupted with surprising excitement, 'Then you will enjoy the next section of our tour. We will pass by some of the most famous Bollywood studios on route to Juhu Beach.'

As we travelled past the various studios, the bus filled with enthusiastic chatter and the sound of clicking cameras. This seemed to be the highlight of the tour; everyone had a sharp eye out for the slightest glimpse of the Indian version of Mel Gibson or Goldie Hawn. For me, they were merely buildings of no real interest.

Arriving at Juhu Beach, the afternoon sun split the clouds and illuminated the littered sands. I strolled with Chinmay, watching others enjoy the water; children taking donkey rides and trained monkeys performing tricks. 'Have you tried panipuri?' he asked.

'Can't say I have.'

'Then you must, come.' He directed me to a stall with a man frying small crisp balls and serving them onto paper plates.

Chinmay put four fingers up and the man nodded, 'What are they?' I enquired.

'The hollow puri is fried and filled with water, then mixed with chutney, chilli, masala, chopped potato, onions and chickpeas. You are in for a real treat, my friend.'

He instructed me to place the whole ball in my mouth and bite down. I did, and the crisp puri burst with savoury flavours. A second later a fiery spice kicked in and had me fanning my mouth. We did one more each and laughed at my watering eyes as we walked the soft sand a little further.

'Chinmay, Chinmay,' a voice called and we turned to see a young man running towards us. 'Chinmay, how's it going man?'

'Hey Diwan, yeah cool. Diwan, this is Sam, he's from England. Sam, this is Diwan, he's from Mumbai.'

'Hey, do you guys want to join us for cricket?' Diwan asked.

Chinmay looked to me, 'It's up to you, Sam. You can go back to the tour or you can hang with us.'

'I'm up for a spot of cricket. Though I must warn you, I haven't really got a clue how to play.'

They looked at each other as if I'd said the strangest of things and Chinmay smiled, put his arm around my shoulder and said, 'No problems brother, we will look after you. It's only for fun anyway.'

We were joined by two other friends along the way and I was handed a bat. I missed two shots, but on the third I whacked the ball so hard it went into the sea. Diwan ran into the water laughing and retrieved the floating tennis ball. Play continued for an hour until exhausted, the five of us tumbled to a sand bank and listened to a Bollywood soundtrack on a portable cassette player.

'Shall we grab a bite?' Chinmay asked. The two others declined due to work commitments. Chinmay and Diwan invited me to their favourite restaurant. I accepted, but first I gave a quick call to Mrs Reveredo and apologised for not being able to attend the evening supper. She was fine and told me to enjoy myself, but to be careful.

Not far from the beach, we strolled into a small, but busy restaurant with cooling fans swaying overhead. Sitting at a long table with other diners, Diwan ordered for the three of us. 'You like fish, right?' Chinmay shouted at me above the din. I nodded. 'Then you will love the surmai curry here, it is sooo good! Oh, yeah, sorry, surmai is kingfish, the king of all fishes, haha.'

Served with white rice, the curry smelt out of this world, and although the sauce was a little hot for my tastes, it was amazing nonetheless– the fish tender and fresh, the rice so soft, and the serving so large I was left hardly able to move when I'd finished. I insisted on paying, but my money was refused. The two guys told me I was their guest.

'Thanks so much for everything, I've had a great time,' I said, as we went outside.

'You are going?' Chinmay asked.

'I don't want to outstay my welcome.'

Chinmay tilted his head, 'What are you talking about, man? You said you are having a great time, yaar? How would you like to see a city within a city?'

'What do you mean?'

'Hang out with us more and you will see,' Diwan answered. 'It's about eleven kilometres from here though.'

The thought of walking another step feeling so full was enough to insist on me paying for a taxi. It was the least I could do. The guys hailed one and negotiated a price and we travelled the jammed streets of worn grey buildings until we stopped at some newly built high-rise apartments. The ground was lined with flattened garbage and a sweet and sour smell of decaying waste assaulted my senses.

'Do you guys live in one of these apartments?'

'No, my friend,' Diwan said. 'We live in a city of dreams.'

315

Walking behind the tall buildings we emerged into an astonishing sight. Thousands of tiny shacks crammed together and mounds of trash serving as both a children's playground and feeding spot for stray dogs and cattle. People milled about the squalor. Some worked, beating wet clothes on the ground or carrying impossibly heavy loads on their backs. The roar of low flying aircraft and whipping of overhead railway electricity cables were heard nearby. 'Welcome to Dharavi,' Chinmay said as I stood trying to take it all in.

Taking a bridge over a stinking garbage-strewn river we entered one of many lanes leading into the slum. The alleyways were a shallow stream of monsoon water. We splashed through, passing homes, food houses and businesses. It really was a city within a city, though every shack looked as if it might topple at any given moment. Chinmay alerted me to what I was already noticing, 'You do not get many tourists around here, Sam. You may find people looking at you, but they are only wondering what you are doing here. You will be okay, you are with us.' From each dwelling, eyes followed. Many doors were open and inside the homes families cooked or watched television, talked or argued, and children laughed and cried. Some shacks had two levels, and most had raw sewage running in ditches underneath. It was overwhelming to say the least.

They led me to a small building and unlocked the door. Diwan leant forward and hugged me, 'I must be going now, Sam. I am working late nights at the airport and now it is time for my sleep. It has been wonderful to meet you.'

He turned a corner whistling as he walked, kicking a flattened football, returning it to the boy who owned it. Chinmay opened the rusty door, 'Welcome to my home. This is where I live with my mother, father and younger sister. They are away visiting my aunt who is very ill. Please come inside and make yourself comfortable. I will make us some tea.'

I sat on a rug laid across the warm concrete floor and looked around the immaculate room. There was a wooden double bed with two thin rolled mattresses beneath. Three shelves held tins and pots, utensils and a small statue of Ganesh. Hung upon the walls were black and white family photos in frames. A portable gas stove and a television set rested upon a dented refrigerator and a cassette player sat next to a small, but surprisingly strong fan at the end of the bed. The room for four people was the size of my bedroom back in England, yet it contained everything of a fully functioning home.

'How long have you lived here?' I asked.

'All of my life. I was born in this very room.'

'Do you like it here? I mean, are you happy?'

'I like it here and yes, I am happy I guess.' He looked over his shoulder and smiled, 'We all want more in life, but I am content because I love my family and they love me. That is all that matters, no?' He switched on the TV and surfed the channels with a taped up remote control. 'You see, we are a tight community here. In the evenings, we sit outside our homes and talk with our neighbours and mostly get along. Sometimes there is quarrel, but usually it is sorted out soon enough. We help each other in times of trouble and pull together when in need. We are all in the same boat and to an extent, accept our fate, although we all have our dreams. But it can be very hard at times, especially when friends get ill or die. There is too much disease here and not enough medical attention, plus, it is hard not knowing where the next meal might come from.'

He poured the tea and passed me a glass and found something to watch. His eyes lit up as he realised what it was. 'Kabhi Haan Kabhi Naa, I love this film, it has only just begun. It stars Shahrukh Khan, a very good actor, have you heard of him?'

'No. In fact, I've never watched an Indian film before,' I replied, not understanding a word that was coming from the box.

'Ah, okay. I will tell you what is happening as it goes along. It is such a great film with very good soundtrack.'

It was a romantic comedy, and although a little hard to keep up with, it made me happy to see Chinmay enjoying himself so much. As each song played he'd get up and dance, at some points showing me some steps. We laughed a lot and as the credits rolled he asked if I would like to stay the night, 'You could tell me of your travels in India. I have never left Mumbai and would love to hear more.'

'That's very kind of you Chinmay.'

'First I must use the toilet. Do you need to?'

I nodded and he grabbed a bar of soap and two plastic jugs. It was heart wrenching to see so many people living this life, but there were so many smiles and a great deal of spirit. They worked hard doing jobs others would never contemplate. I stopped to look in one building and saw five children no older than ten on a mound of plastics sorting through for what could be used again. Around their bare feet were old hypodermic needles, the casings of which would be used for recycling. Next door, a baby cried alongside a pile of rotting animal innards leaning against a wall. The fetid stench was hideous. I peeked through the doorway to find an old man stirring a large boiling pot. 'He is producing animal fat for cosmetics to the rich around the world,' Chinmay informed me. 'He is not very popular here. Many people complain about the smell.

'Dharavi has over five hundred thousand residents and over five hundred businesses. Many things are made here for companies all over the globe: textiles and pottery and as you have seen for yourself, cosmetics and recycled goods. Dharavi has everything a city has; doctors, schools, temples and shops.'

I was beginning to forget the rest of Mumbai existed outside of this fascinating, almost medieval labyrinth. Reaching a long line of people – all looking over their shoulders at me – we stood in the queue for over twenty minutes waiting to fill our jugs from a communal tap. When our turn came Chinmay asked if I would like to go to the shared toilet huts or relieve myself at the side of the railway. As I was only in need of a wee, I chose the latter option. Working our way back the way we came and up a side alley we proceeded out to the railway line where trains shot past inches from where children played and others squatted to go to the toilet. 'It is okay,' Chinmay said, spotting my nervousness of where to go, and in front of so many people. 'Everybody has to go. It is life.'

I waited and waited, but couldn't go and then a dribble turned into a torrent and I let out a sigh. 'Ah, good, you managed,' Chinmay smiled a few feet away from where he squatted. We washed our hands and face and he took the jug from me and pocketed the soap. Nearby was a hillock; even that had residences perched upon the sides. We climbed to the top and watched the sun melt over the thousands of endless grey metallic rooftops.

Some streets were pitch black, others illuminated by the barest of light and if it were not for my friend, I'd be completely lost. He guided us back to his home with ease where we stayed for the rest of the evening. I told him of my travels and he told me of his life growing up in the slums. It was the early hours of the morning by the time we bedded down on the foam mattresses and within a matter of seconds, I was fast asleep.

40

Something brushed my feet. I looked over my toes and saw a rat the size of a small cat. It met my stare, twitched its whiskers and scuttled out, squeezing through the gap under the door that streamed daylight onto the ground. I looked around in case there were others, but saw only Chinmay asleep and oblivious. I closed my eyes, but only for a few minutes. An alarm sounded and Chinmay rose with a yawn, 'Good morning Sam,' he said in a sluggish voice. He rubbed his eyes and smiled, 'Did you sleep okay?

'Apart from the raised voices next door, I haven't slept that well in ages.'

'That is good. My neighbours they argue very much, but you get used to it after a while.' He stood, stretched and touched the ceiling with his fingers, 'I will make us some breakfast. I can get you back to Dadar as tour bus driver will collect us nearby for my shift.'

After the toilet run, Chinmay cracked some eggs into a pan and prepared some rotis his father had left him. He spoke of what the future held for the slums, 'I fear for our city. It may be a disgusting slum to most, but it is our home and we treasure it. More and more of those apartment blocks are rising and more areas are destroyed for new developments for the rich. Some of the residents of the slum are given the opportunity to rent an apartment, but rents are high and the spirit of the community is lost; people live behind closed doors and become strangers to each other and crime rates increase. Some who cannot afford the rents have their homes and possessions destroyed by the builders and end up living off the streets as beggars. What to do? Only the rich have the answers, but they seem to only care for themselves. There are over three hundred people a day coming into Mumbai from other states looking for hope where there is no hope to speak of.'

I looked back over Dharavi as we waited for the bus. The several emerging skyscrapers under construction towered above, throwing dark shadows across the slum. I wondered what the dawn of this new India had in wait for the city of dreams.

It was a little after nine when the bus arrived at Dadar packed with more holiday makers. Outside, Chinmay gripped me in a hug and asked me to keep in touch. 'Of course, my friend. Take care of yourself,' I said and waved the coach goodbye. I walked the short distance to Connor's apartment, had a shower and crashed until the telephone rang at lunchtime. Mrs Reveredo was on the other end panicked, asking if I was all right. I told a small lie and said that I'd spent half the night in the bathroom ill to save her the worry of where I'd really been. She invited me for lunch and said she would prepare a remedy for my stomach.

Mrs Reveredo didn't stay long, so I was kept company by Patrice who told me about the college where she studied medicine in hope of becoming a doctor. Tatiana came around later and the three of us went to a fifties style American restaurant where we ate masala dosa. It was lovely, not only the food, but the company the girls provided. They were always so polite, positive and eager to find out more about my life, and I theirs in Mumbai. On the way back to the family home, we stopped off at a street stall and drank a sweet bottle of masala milk with chopped almonds. Mumbai was certainly sizing up to be the most delicious of cities.

Arriving back at the house I was elated to see Connor.

'I'm so sorry, dude,' he said as he emptied his pack. 'I got caught up in Manali, and to be honest, I wasn't sure you'd actually come, but I'm so glad you did. What's been happening with you since you left Leh?'

I told him about Kargil and Kashmir and the unexpected charas on route to Jammu, the train journey and even about Dharavi. Lastly, I told him how fantastic his family had been. In exchange, he told me that Radhika had mislaid her backpack and thus they were delayed. They were slowly patching things up, but it was going to take time. The spark of travel was still in his eyes as he spoke of how much he missed the north and how he wanted to visit Nepal soon. 'I'm glad to be home,' he said, 'but I miss the adventure and freedom so much. It was so amazing up there.'

His mood lightened throughout the evening once we got back to his apartment. With Megadeth in the background we spoke some more about the Himalayas and laughed over tales of Ali and his forty flutes. Later, deciding on an evening walk, we ambled along the streets slated silver by the moonlight and an occasional haunting glow of a street lamp. A scattering of people slept on the pavements; the lucky on charpoys. In an upper class Parsi colony, Connor and I found a bench in a public garden surrounded by three-storey Victorian homes. He advised me to keep my voice down to discourage any unwanted attention from the police who patrolled the streets at night.

'They'll find any reason to bust someone,' he said with a look of fear in his eyes. 'They treat some people so badly, yaar, especially the street kids. They beat and arrest them for no reason at all. Six months ago, I came back from work late with my cousin and we were chased by a drunk cop. He managed to catch my cousin and hit him so hard with his lathi that he couldn't walk for a week. We'd done nothing wrong, man.' Through my experience with the police in Paharganj, I could well believe it.

Lajni served us brunch at the family home. When she walked back to the kitchen, I enquired with Connor how she came into service for the Reveredos. 'My mother found her living under the stairs leading up to the house with her husband and young daughter. They hadn't been there long. They were in a such a poor state of health and were very thin. My mother employed Lajni as a maid and cleaner, and her husband was employed as a handyman and gardener. He now has several other jobs with neighbours too. Mum found them a small apartment not far from mine and a good school for their daughter.'

'Where's your father, if you don't mind me asking?'

'He expired five years ago. He had a large pharmaceutical business and the house and all the money was left to my mother. She has raised us really well and only ever wanted the best for us. She does a great deal for the poor. She works tirelessly for the homeless children of Mumbai and tries to support their education and wellbeing.' He stretched back from the filling meal, 'She came from nothing herself, yaar – a poor village girl from outside Bangalore. My father met her when he was on business and they fell in love instantly. They were amazing together.' His eyes reflected the loss of his father and he changed the subject, 'Did you bring your washing with you?'

'Yes, is it still okay to use the washing machine here?'

'Of course. Hand your clothes to Lajni, she'll take care of them.'

It was the 15th August and the celebration of forty-nine years of independence from British rule in India. Everybody on the streets was in high spirits: some singing the national anthem, Jana Gana Mana, at the top of their voices; others holding aloft the national flag: a horizontal tricolor of saffron, white and green with a navy spoked wheel representing the chakra at the centre. Connor and I boarded a train to Victoria Terminus Railway Station. A fusion of Victorian Italianate Gothic Revival and Indian architecture and centrally crowned with an octagonal ribbed dome, it looked more like a palace than any train station I'd seen before. It was renamed to Chhatrapati Shivaji Terminus earlier in the year.

A little on from Churchgate we departed a local train and walked the rest of the way to a rock concert to mark Independence Day. With the amount of people ahead of us in the queue as we arrived it didn't look like we had any chance of getting in. Connor came up with a plan, 'Go to the front and tell security you're a British journalist covering the show and I'm your translator.'

I wasn't so sure, 'You think they'll fall for it?'

With a gentle nudge, I left the line with Connor in my shadow. I reached one of the stocky guards expecting rejection, but miraculously we were waved through without question. Connor gave me a hearty slap on the back and laughed, 'See dude, you get nothing in this life unless you try.'

Of the three bands that played us into the night, it was the last I liked the most, covering music I knew; Pearl Jam, Alice in Chains and Nirvana. I was so impressed by the guitarist that I never took my eyes away from his fingers, trying to pick up some ideas for myself. He must have noticed and beckoned me on to the stage. Looking around I saw that I was the only white face in the crowd. Were the band aware of my so-called journalist status? A security guard guided me up to the side of the stage where I began to take photographs. I felt like a real VIP.

After the penultimate number, the lead singer made a speech in Hindi, I'm guessing something to do with Independence, which sent the crowd into a frenzy for the final song, also in Hindi. As they left the stage to deafening cheers, the guitarist shook my hand and gave me his plectrum, 'Hey man,' he said. 'I take it you play guitar. Maybe some of today can rub off on your playing.'

'Bloody hell, that was awesome,' I shouted above the roar as I returned to Connor.

'What?' he yelled back, laughing. 'I think I've gone deaf, yaar.'

Connor was finishing up writing some music at his flat for an up and coming charity benefit. 'Hey dude,' he said, placing his pen down. 'How did lunch go?'

'Yeah, great.' I had spent the morning with Radhika and we then went to lunch at a classy restaurant overlooking the sea.

'Cool. I want you to meet a really good friend of mine tonight, you'll like him a lot.'

An hour or so later we arrived at Buzz's apartment. From the outside, the building looked on the verge of demolition, but I was surprised to find the opposite as we were invited into a beautiful home that was deceivingly spacious. Marbled flooring and newly decorated hallways and rooms with modern furniture and fittings, we made ourselves comfortable in the lounge whilst Buzz prepared a cold mango juice for us. He reminded me of Connor, but older, with shoulder length dreadlocks. He had a look about him that told me he'd seen a lot in life, and that was indeed the case as I looked around at photos in silver frames of him with various musicians. Some I didn't recognise, but I caught a glimpse of him standing alongside Maxi Priest and on stage playing guitar with Bob Marley's Wailers who he toured with for years. Clearly this guy had done well in life.

'Wow, that's pretty impressive,' I said.

He smiled and said thanks as if this wasn't the first time he'd been asked about it.

He shouted down the hallway to his wife that we were going out and to not wait up. He drove us in his white hatchback to a bar overlooking the moonlit sands of Chowpatty Beach. Inside a drunk girl was participating in karaoke, attempting to sing Mariah Carey's Hero. Connor called over with a frown, 'Hey, let's go to the dressing rooms. One of Mumbai's best jazz bands haven't long finished, they should still be hanging around.'

It was clear that Buzz and Connor were good friends with the band. I stood in the smoke congested room as the guys briefly caught up with each other. Lucas, the guitarist must have been in his late thirties as was Henry the singer. I warmed to them straight away as they welcomed me into the fold as if I was an old friend. 'Joint?' Lucas said, passing over the half smoked spliff in his hand. 'Whiskey?' laughed Henry offering up a half-filled tumbler.

'I'll relieve you of the joint, but pass on the whiskey, cheers.'

Out into the night, the five of us piled into Buzz's car, hitting the streets at speed, stopping off at a few late opening liqueur houses along the way. I'd never laughed as much as I did that night; my stomach ached and tears streamed down my face. It had just gone 5am by the time we came to a stop. Buzz leant over from the steering wheel to face me, 'I think you're gonna like this.'

'Huh?' I said, my eyes heavy with the dope.

'You'll see,' Connor replied.

I waited patiently, intrigued to find out what an earth they were going on about. And then, just as the light gradually made an appearance, with it brought one of those unforgettable moments. The silhouette of an enormous rusted cargo ship emerged grounded on the rocks.

Connor saw the awe in my face, my mouth open, my eyes wide wonder-struck. I could hardly believe what I was seeing, enhanced no doubt by the smoking. 'Haha, yeah dude. It was wrecked a few years back and hasn't been pulled free yet,' he said, finishing his last beer as the light shed further detail across the hulk.

Transfixed, I nearly jumped out of my seat to a knock on the window and a street cleaner who smiled with his hand open, a delicate white and yellow flower in his palm. He handed it to me, 'Frangipani, smell, smell,' he said. His grin widened as my eyes lit with the fruitiness of the most beautiful perfume. If heaven had an aroma, this was it. He waggled his head and continued sweeping as Buzz started the engine.

Buzz, Lucas and Henry left us at Dadar station. Connor put his arm around my shoulder, 'Great night, yaar. Breakfast?'

We grabbed some omelettes and some chai in a small café. There was chatter and laughter coming from some local guys in the seat behind. I paid it no attention, but Connor swung round and barked something in Marathi which altered their faces into stunned silence. He turned around and resumed eating.

'What was that about?'

'They were making fun of us. They thought we both tourists, but I put them straight.'

Whilst Connor slept I sat in his living room going over the same old ground I'd travelled so many times before. Despite one of the best nights of my life, my past was still present and the future for my grandfather hung in the balance. It was in a way a blessing Connor had to work as I wanted to be alone again and see a bit more of India before I went home.

Radhika was waiting in a running taxi outside. I managed to get maybe four hours' sleep, but felt surprisingly awake.

'Bit of a late night yaar?' she said as we pulled away.

'You heard then?' I laughed.

She remained impassive, 'I worry for him, Sam. I guess I want him to settle down you know, take our relationship more seriously.' The driver began humming and beating out a rhythm on his horn. She looked sideways at him irritated.

'I'm so sorry. You guys are trying to patch things up and I go and spend a crazy night out with him.'

'It has nothing to do with you, he is like this all the time. I'm hanging on to thin air don't you think?'

'Maybe, but maybe not. He genuinely does love and respect you. His eyes light up whenever he talks about you.' Hers illuminated as I said this. 'The problem with Connor is his head is filled with a million and one things he wants to do with his life. I've got to admire him for that, but I can see how you may feel somewhat left out. It's so difficult. But I do think there's a future for you guys and if anyone can pin him down, it will be you and you only.'

Her eyes welled, silent tears fell. She held my hand and squeezed, 'Thank you.'

Checking her compact, she recomposed herself and spoke to the driver. We came to a stop along a main road near Juhu. 'Come,' she said.

An aroma of sandalwood guided us through the lanes, moving us with a tide of faces, drawing us into a chamber of waxwork deities, flickering shadows behind. Chanting held me mesmerized. Orange robed devotees rocked back and forth in homage to a lifelike statue of Lord Krishna draped in gold. A priest held out an aarti lamp, offering it to worshippers. Radhika ran her cupped hands over the naked flame and raised them to her forehead in blessing.

'To remove the darkness from our lives,' she said as we left.

She stopped at a pharmacist. Next door was a travel agent. I said I'd be back in five minutes. Within three I was back outside, a ticket for a bus to Goa in my hand.

'You are leaving?' she asked.

'For a short while. I need to lift a little darkness myself.'

'Ahhhh, babaaa.' I nearly walked straight into him. He was naked. The skinniest person I'd ever seen. I took a step back as he lunged towards me, his legs barely able to carry him. I gave him some money, Radhika the same. He took the notes, lurched past us, eyes vacant, bones jutting out from shrink wrapped skin.

Sipping our drinks in a café in Colaba, normal conversation felt awkward and out of place. 'I don't know how to be,' I said, my thoughts spilling over the silence. I looked up, saved her the trouble before she questioned me, 'I know I have to live my life and all that, but that guy, he was what our age, maybe younger? Where are these gods to allow that to happen? Don't worry, I don't expect answers; reincarnation, fate, blah, blah. Someone will always have an answer, but there doesn't seem to be many solutions.'

'I think you need to speak with Mrs Reveredo. Maybe she will help you with what you seek.'

I never saw Mrs Reveredo before I left. In the headlights of the bus the rain fell. Connor, Radhika and I stood soaked. He leant forward, arm out and we embraced. 'Seven days then, yaar?'
'Seven days.'

41

The rumble of tyres brought me to with a start. Bowing palms, fields jade under a slate sky, the occasional white church standing as a reminder of Portuguese rule. The rain hadn't let up all night, the land ever wet with the pressing monsoon. This road was known to be notorious but I'd slept through for the most part without giving it a second thought.

Sitting up I adjusted myself, briefly exchanging eye contact with the lady in red next to me, moment enough to notice her elaborate gold earring attached to a chain and draped to a piercing in her nose. On her lap lay an empty silver vase which she held with hands far too old for her age. Between her sandalled feet, a jute sack; stuffed full and tied with a frayed cord.

I never knew when I was going to arrive anywhere in India by bus, but given how long the journey was supposed to take and the length of time we'd already been travelling, I guessed my departure point of Mapusa would be soon. My backpack had been with me all night. Picking it up, I lifted my leg over the jute sack, hopped forward and caught the top of my foot on a crate of chickens in the aisle. I pulled free but slipped the catch, sending the birds screeching from the cage, fluttering feathers about the crowd.

Women screamed, children laughed, the owner of the fowl ran ragged in a bid to round up each bird. I tried to assist, but my herding skills were useless. Instead I was politely, but firmly told to get out of the way and sent to the front of the bus as it pulled over. Keeping my head down, I mumbled apologies as I eased past two men obstructing the exit. I leapt from the doorway, hitting the ground ungracefully and rolling into the bushes as the bus pulled away.

My intentions weren't to stay in Mapusa, only long enough to find a place to eat and source transport to Anjuna. Although it was like most Indian towns, it didn't have the intensity or bustle I expected. Despite the downpour, goods were being set out on the roadside in market fashion: fruit and vegetables, sacks of pulses, herbs and spices in neat rows all under the protection of umbrella stands. Apart from the traders and a few locals the streets were deserted. Maybe because of the early hour, the weather or the fact that it was out of season and the thousands of holidaymakers from around the globe were yet to swarm through the town. Whatever the reason I was grateful of the space and lack of attention to my presence.

I negotiated a rate with a taxi driver who took me straight to a hotel in Anjuna. The room was far from perfect, but I was in no need of luxury. The leaves of a palm tree blocked most of the light from the window and cast elongated finger-like shadows along the wall. I sat on the bed, which was positioned beneath the window and browsed my guide book.

I awoke sometime later to find the rain had cleared. The palm swayed in a light breeze, allowing a swinging fan of light into the room. Taking the Lonely Planet from my chest I placed it in my bag and went out.

The hotel was situated within a stone's throwing distance of the beach lined with tall rocking palms gracing the base of the hills. The deserted sands were a dull beige under the white sky, the sea a dirty green. Most of the food shacks were closed apart from one, which sat upon a slight ridge. A man leant on the bar, head tilted in sleep. Speckled black and white dreadlocks hung loose to his shoulders, his goatee beard rested upon his chest. I cleared my throat and he awoke, focused in on my face, yawned and rubbed his eyes, 'Ah man, I'm so sorry. This weather can really drain you. Welcome to

Royston's. Take a seat and I'll bring over a menu.'

By the open front I watched the tide curl white as it licked the shore.

'There you go,' he said, holding out a lime green menu with little palm trees in the corners. Although his complexion was Indian, he spoke with a London accent. 'My name's Royston and this is my bar. What can I get you to drink?'

'I'll have, um...' I browsed the list of drinks, 'A sweet lassi please.'

'No problems, back in two shakes of a lamb's tail.'

He disappeared through a set of saloon style doors. I was too preoccupied watching a cow on the beach scratching its ear with its hind leg to notice him come back until he placed a glass down with a lime green straw bobbing out. 'Have you decided on any food?'

'Cows on a beach, you don't see that in Blackpool.'

He laughed, 'Blackpool? Man, I haven't thought of that place since I was a kid. So, you're from England?'

'Yeah, the south.' I put my cigarette in my mouth and extended my hand, 'Sam.'

He shook it, 'Good to meet you. Yeah, we get cows, pigs, dogs and if you're lucky the occasional monkey.'

'What do you recommend, Royston?' I asked, returning to the menu.

'Swordfish and fries, caught first thing this morning. That's cool.'

'I've never had swordfish before, so go on, I'll give it a try.'

He poked his head over the kitchen doors and called out my order. Walking behind the bar he uncapped a bottle of Coke, 'First day in Goa?'

'Arrived from Mumbai this morning. Pardon me for saying, but you don't sound very Indian.'

'Ha ha, I am and I'm not. I was raised in London until I was fifteen and then my parents moved out here. That was about twenty-five years ago. My dad's English and my mum's Indian. They met while he was on holiday in Goa. My mother was born in Anjuna. I think she missed Goan life a bit too much.'

'Can't say I blame them, it's idyllic.'

'Oh, it's peaceful now, but when the tourist season comes, it's the complete opposite. Non-stop partying around the clock and non-stop work for me, which I'm not complaining about. I'd rather be busy if you know what I mean.' He took a swig of his drink, 'When the season finishes I stay open, but hardly anyone turns up. But it's cool, gives me time to unwind until it all kicks off again.'

He'd been in the kitchen for a while by the time I finished my meal, so I left some folded notes under my cup and took a slow walk along the beach in the fine rain. Hearing faint footsteps closing in behind me I turned only to find a couple of pi dogs combing the sand in the distance. Minutes later the drizzle turned into a downpour and the breeze gathered momentum. The dogs scarpered with their ears down, tails between their legs and I made a desperate dash back to my room.

The bad weather persisted into the evening leaving me nothing to do but read, listen to music and stare at the wall. I thought about my grandfather in hospital, how he had asked to see me. What could he want? He must know how difficult it would be. It wasn't a simple case of a ferry ride across the North Sea. Besides, we'd already gone through the motions of a last goodbye on my most recent visit to Ostend. There was nothing more to be said and me seeing him in a debilitated state would surely be as distressing for him as it would for me. I decided to get an early night with the intention of catching sunrise.

A fiery warmth torched the sky, painting the shore the sparkling saffron I'd hoped to see. Royston was sweeping away the night's sand from his porch.

'Are you serving food?' I asked.

'Hey man. Yeah, give me ten minutes. How's bacon and eggs?'

Over breakfast I asked how long he'd owned the bar. 'About ten years now, since my father retired and passed it on to me. He called it Paradise Place, but I renamed it and gave it a bit of a facelift. How's breakfast?'

'Yeah good, thanks. Reminds me of my nan's...' I stumbled for a moment then quickly changed direction. 'Have you got any recommendations on what to see in Goa?'

'There's loads to see in Goa. Arambol is my favourite of all the beaches. I'm heading out there tomorrow to help out a friend if you want to come along.'

'Yeah sure, what time?'

'Early, around eight. Meet me here, we'll have breakfast and go after that.'

I soaked the last corner of toast in egg yolk, 'I'll catch up with you again this evening if you're around. I'm off to Vagator this morning.'

'Cool. Try and climb up to Chapora Fort if you can, you'll get great views over Morjim beach, Chapora River and across Vagator and Ozran beaches.'

Near the hotel, the owners of a group of taxis congregated. I haggled the fare to Vagator with one of them and within twenty minutes I was at my destination. 'On left side, Little Vagator,' he said, as we pulled into an empty car park. 'Right side, Big Vagator.' I asked if he could pick me up in an hour or so. 'Yes, I will be here.'

I'd only taken a few steps when an Indian lady came over; maybe early twenties, tight green top and skirt to match. Both forearms were covered in black bangles; on one wrist hung a cloth bag from which she produced a handful of marble ornaments. I smiled, said no thanks and walked on. She followed, pursuing me with her pitch. The faster I walked, the more she kept up until I stopped, and said no thanks again.

'Then maybe I can show you good time instead,' she said, putting her hands on her hips and slowly gyrating.

'No, that's fine, thank you.'

'But much special time, very nice, you and me.'

'If I buy one of these,' I pointed at the ornaments, 'will you leave me alone?'

'Yes, yes, of course, sir. Now which one you like?' I went to choose but she interjected, 'You cannot decide? Why not buy one and then you are getting second one at half of price.'

'Okay, how much?' I sighed.

'I am giving you for three hundred rupees only.'

'Okay, so I've only got two hundred rupees spare. How about I take just the green elephant.'

'Very good sir. As you are very nice man, I give you marble flower for fifty rupees only if buying both.'

'Two fifty and we're sold, right?'

She waggled, 'Very good, sir.'

On giving her the money, she began another sales spiel, but I was quick to leave, heading off in the direction of Little Vagator. I heard her catching up with me, but when I turned around, prepared for battle in round two, she wasn't there. From the corner of my eye I saw something move, but when I looked, again there was no one there. All I saw was a copse of palm trees swaying in the wind.

It was reminiscent of walking through a forest late at night, with the devil hounding my back, making me pick up pace and run as if my life depended on it. Occasionally glancing over my shoulder, I made my way across to the larger beach. Rain fell heavily, a forceful wind lashed at my back. I stopped at the base of the hill leading up to the fort. As I climbed, I could hear laboured breathing. Several steps later, wheezing and coughing swept into my ears and with it came a familiar sour smell overlain with a faint sweetness.

A series of octagonal battlements interrupted what was left of the ruined laterite walls of the bastion. The view might have been great on a clear day, but a veil of thick sea mist cloaked all but the tip of Morjim Beach ahead.

Eyes fixed forward, I fought to hold back the tears. I eventually found the courage to turn around. He was a lot further away than I thought. All I could make out was an oversized surgical gown draped over a wasted frame, bare feet except for the weeds entangling the toes. I'd seen enough and started heading along a trail leading to the beach. My clothes were covered in mud, the skin on my hands raw from climbing. With each step, my feet sunk deeper into the black sand until at last I found solid ground. I took one last look up at the fort. Although I could only make out his shadow, I knew his eyes were on me, in me, scrutinizing my soul.

I found shelter in an abandoned hut near the car park and sat shivering, trying to comprehend the sick games my head was playing. By the time my taxi appeared I'd gathered up what little of me was left and hauled myself in the back saying nothing to the driver.

However much I tried to push the morning to the back of my mind, it distracted me from whatever I did. I flicked through the guidebook, remembering what Tyler had said about Hampi. I marked it off next on my route.

The last thing I wanted was to be holed up in my room all night. Instead I went to Royston's where I had my evening meal, a simple tomato curry. He sat down with me and poured a small glass of clear liquid with a slight froth, 'Here my friend, cashew apple feni. My brother-in-law makes a whole batch of the stuff.'

I drained it quickly and immediately felt like I'd swallowed paint stripper. My eyes welled as he filled the glass again. I loved cashews and I loved apple juice, but this took on a whole new level. I guessed it was in its rawest form and didn't wish to offend my host by turning it away. I drank the next glass more cautiously, forcing a smile, but I started to feel sick and heady. My mouth numbed, my tongue found it hard to tackle each word, 'Is feni alcoholic by any chance?' I slurred.

'Of course. This is about forty percent.'

'Oh.' He went on to ask if I was okay. 'Yeah, it's just that I don't drink.'

'Oh.'

I smiled, told him it was fine and excused myself, arranging to meet him in the morning as planned. Staggering back to the hotel I made it to the bathroom just in time, drowning a cockroach on the toilet seat in tomato curry feni. I collapsed on the bed, the room swaying, the palm tree tap, tap, tapping. Despite my stomach wanting to erupt at any second, I closed my eyes in hope it would die down.

The sound of shuffling brought me out of my slumber. I couldn't make out who was there at first, but as my eyes adjusted I zoned in on my grandfather's face, tinged with a yellow hue and collapsed on one side. The vision was so real, but I knew it couldn't be. He was hooked up on drips, dying in a hospital bed in Belgium. I said nothing, my mind in turmoil, my mouth finding it hard to form a single word.

I got up and headed towards the door. He put his arm out to prevent my exit, but I whacked it away and he lost his balance, falling to the floor. Cursing the door handle for not being where it should have been, I struggled my way to freedom. Wobbly sitar music played out of tune somewhere down the hallway. I wasn't sure if I was imagining it, but it faded the further I got from the hotel. Wind and rain against me, I pushed through until I reached the beach where I fell face down in the sodden sand. I moved my head to one side, but could do no more. Thunder cracked overhead. The sky, beach and palm trees lit a brief silver with lightening as the rain hit me like a million pellets.

42

'Jesus, what happened to you?' a man's voice asked. 'Are you okay?'

I opened one eye, the one not buried in the sand and then closed it again, 'Uh?' I groaned as I was turned over.

A blurred face I thought I knew loomed over me, joined by another; an Indian lady, very attractive with shining eyes, 'Should we call a doctor?' she said.

'I'm okay,' I replied. 'Just need a few minutes.'

'Let's get you inside,' the man said, who when I looked again I recognised as Royston.

Slumped in a chair with a glass of coffee and a bottle of water on the table, I heard voices coming from behind the kitchen doors.

'How was I supposed to know he didn't drink?'

'Well, you might have asked him? How much did he have?'

'Two glasses, maybe three shots in each.'

'So, he's had six shots of my brother's feni and he doesn't drink. Thank god I didn't marry you for your intelligence.'

'Ah come on babe, we both know it's because of these stunning good looks.'

'Nice you're taking it so seriously. What if he choked or was robbed or something?'

They both reappeared, the lady smiling sympathetically. She placed a couple of headache pills down, 'How are you feeling?'

'Better now, thanks. Sam, by the way.'

'Aashi. Sorry we had to meet like this. My apologies for my husband's stupidity, he rarely thinks before he acts.'

'He wasn't to know. I should have picked up on it after the first glass. If anything, it's my fault.' I swallowed the pills and light heartedly laughed, 'I'll be fine, I've been through a lot worse.' I looked to Royston who looked to the floor, 'Hey, I'd still really like to go to Arambol with you today if the offer's still there. It's my last day in Goa and I'd like to make the most of it.'

'Well at least let him cook you breakfast, you need something to eat,' Aashi said.

When the eggs and bacon arrived, I could barely look at them, but ate what I could. Royston sat opposite. Embarrassment washed over me, 'I'm really sorry, mate. I didn't mean to cause you so much hassle.'

'You haven't, I'm just glad you're okay. You had us worried there. How did you end up on the beach?'

'I'm not sure. I think I was trying to make my way back here.'

He chuckled, 'Hey man, you're not the first to be washed up on the beach from a crazy night in Anjuna. How about you get yourself a change of clothes and I'll pick you up from your hotel in an hour?'

The door to my room was locked and I didn't have a key.

'Ah good morning sir,' said the young man on reception. 'I was shutting your door last night as you were leaving it open and had not returned. Here, take spare key.'

I opened the door and was relieved to see the only thing laying on the floor was my open journal. My mind still heavy from the feni, I stood under the shower and inspected a mass of tiny bumps on my arms and legs. I glanced in the mirror, they were on my neck and face too.

I slid on my sunglasses and found Royston outside in a white open backed Jeep. 'Feeling better?' he asked as we drove away.

'The headache's died down a bit, but I've got these little bumps all over me.' I held my arm out to show him.

'Sand fleas by the looks of it. They're a real bitch. Try not to scratch, we'll get some antiseptic cream in town.'

The weather was in our favour; a flawless blue sky

complementing the rich green landscape and brilliance of the 16th century churches. Pulling into a driveway of a secluded summer house, we found a man with his head under the bonnet of a black hatchback. 'Still no luck with the car, Lopes?' Royston called over as we came nearer.

'Na man. I've been at it again this morning and it still won't start. I'm hoping it just needs a set of new sparks.'

Lopes looked roughly the same age as Royston, with close cropped hair and a warm smile. 'Go down to the beach and I'll bring some coffee out,' he said. We walked down a slight hill until we came out onto the pearl white sands and crystal blue waters of Arambol where Lopes joined us shortly after with a tray of cups.

I left the pair talking and took some pictures. Fishermen maintained large nets alongside hollowed-out canoes, others sorted through the morning's catch; final moments of life flapping around the plastic sheets. I stared down, watching the fish gasp the air, the very thing that was killing them. Something brushed my shoulder and I turned, half expecting to come face to face with my granddad again, but it was only two boys asking for school pens. Rummaging through my shoulder bag I found two ballpoint pens I'd bought specifically for moments like this. I asked for a photo. One stood with a dead silver fish between his teeth, both grinned with their thumbs up. Re-joining my friends, I welcomed the idle chit chat, the sound of the breaking waves and wind swishing through the palm trees.

We drove into Panaji, the capital of Goa, passing the Baroque-style church, Our Lady of the Immaculate Conception. Criss-crossing staircases led to the foot of the building that was topped with two grand balconies either side of a silver bell overlooking the city. More European than Indian, colourful villas and cobbled streets echoed the ambiance of the long-departed Portuguese settlers.

Whilst Lopes and Royston picked up some spark plugs, I bought a tube of antiseptic cream and a bus ticket for Hospet, the nearest town to Hampi. I was surprised to find Lopes's wife Sophia had dinner waiting for us when we got back. The table was filled with a spectrum of colour: green chicken cafreal and five spiced masala chicken, spiced pork, mackerel curry and coconut curry; bhajis, samosas, hot breads and a generous green leaf salad. She stood back, looking proud of what she'd achieved and justifiably so; everything was amazing.

Hazy light shone through the open patio doors, and with the sound of the sea, I slowly unburdened myself from recent worries. Outside, to a whoop of delight, Lopes finally got his car running again.

That evening, while the sun melted a liquid gold into the sea, Royston prepared a small fire on Anjuna beach, skewering some chicken pieces for our evening meal. We were the only ones, blessed to have the honey baked sands to ourselves, save for a solitary figure in the distance I'm sure only I could see, sitting, staring, waiting for me.

43

I'd been travelling for at least five hours by the time I arrived in Hubli, 155 kilometres west of Hospet. The bus took an unusually long break at the terminal and when I enquired with the driver as to what the delay was, he informed me tensions were high between a group of Hindus and Muslims nearby. By all accounts a gunfight had broken out and certain roads were closed off. With my journal leant on my knee, I wrote with one hand and cracked monkey nuts from a bag with the other.

Occasionally I looked out to the bus station, to people drinking chai, waiting for buses. A group of teenagers flicked small stones at passers-by and feigned innocence when they turned to see what was happening. They caught my eye and congregated around the window, calling out for money. I told them I didn't have any spare. It was the truth. I would've had to dip into my money belt, and judging by their healthy appearance, they weren't in dire need.

I was the only person on the bus. The other passengers were milling about stretching their legs. Hoping the teenagers would lose interest in me, I put my head down and carried on writing, but this only seemed to ignite their aggravation further. The one with the most confidence – the tallest of the gang, who came across as the leader – started banging on the side of the bus. When he had my attention again, he gave a forlorn expression and insisted he was starving whilst his comrades sniggered behind his back.

'Here have these if you're hungry,' I said, holding out the bag of nuts through the top of the window.

'Are you calling us monkeys?' he shouted.

'Of course not, don't be stupid.'

'Oh, so we're stupid monkeys?'

With that he began rocking the bus impersonating the sound of a monkey. His friends found this hilarious and all joined in. There was an almighty shout from behind them as the driver came storming into view. They yelled something to him and ran off laughing.

'These boys see trouble in city and think they can behave like anarchists,' the driver said as he boarded the bus. 'We will be leaving now; road is open again.'

The terracotta earth drew day into night, swallowing up cities into towns, the towns into smouldering villages until the last cinders of the sun were no longer seen. Bumpier by the minute, the driver tackled the roads with care. The same couldn't be said for a motorcyclist whose recklessness saw a nasty end to his day. Speeding past us he hit a pothole, flew over the handlebars and smashed into the ground. The bus narrowly avoided him. From the back window, I saw blood pumping from a deep wound to his head. Our driver carried on regardless with his own agenda.

By nine we finally reached Hospet and despite constant searching, I couldn't find a hotel with any vacancies. A religious festival was taking place nearby the next day and by ten I'd given up hope when I was refused even the floor of a hotel reception. I moved on and decided to look for somewhere to eat instead, but my path was blocked by a middle-aged man begging for money. I still didn't have any spare change and wasn't prepared to fish around in my money belt at that time of night. He moved closer, invading my personal space. Each time I attempted to walk on, he blocked my path.

'Yes, my friend, very good rooms, very good food, come,' said a young voice behind me. The man, seeing we were not alone, shuffled away, leaving me with the boy. 'No good man try to take advantage of traveller, very sorry for bad welcome to Hospet.

Please, my name is Tariq, come inside. I will ask father if we find room for you if like.' I followed my little saviour across the street to a restaurant and ordered a masala dosa while I awaited his return.

He came back having persuaded his father to let me stay in the last available room. I followed him up a staircase attached to the side of the building and along a hallway of doors. He showed me into a room in the centre, 'Please, be making yourself comfortable. You would like coffee or tea in morning? I will bring.'

'Thank you, Tariq, that'd be great.'

'Okay, pay bill tomorrow.' He cocked his head to one side and grinned so wide I thought his lips would meet his ears, 'You are big flim star, yes?'

I laughed, 'Flim star? No, just a regular tourist.'

'Ah, you are looking like flim star. You are most welcome. In morning, I will see you again. You are sleeping well I hope.' With that he clanged the metal door shut behind him.

I slung my backpack down and fell to the bed in the dim light. The room was tiny; no shower or toilet. I guessed the communal wash rooms were down the hall somewhere, but for now I was too tired to care. Without undressing I went straight to sleep.

It was still dark when I awoke, needing to use the toilet. I stumbled around until I found the door, opening it to a sickly yellow light illuminating the corridor. Not knowing where the bathroom was I took a guess and turned left. The hallway twisted in different directions and the further I walked the more the interior deteriorated; cracks appeared in the plaster and peeling paint hung limply from the walls and doors. Some rooms were open, unoccupied with rusted bed frames inside. I saw a faded sign on the wall signalling the direction of the showers and toilets. I followed the arrow.

A set of shower cubicles were on the left with heavily stained curtains. Opposite was a row of sinks and to the right were toilets; a row of heavily soiled latrines. There was a closed off room which I hoped might have another toilet and allow a little privacy. Instead, on opening the door I saw a bed with an IV drip on a stand close by and a wheelchair in the corner. A gut-wrenching smell of warm death brought sour vomit to my throat. I turned away, but something yanked my neck to the pillow and I came face to face with my grandfather laying there, rasping. I tried to scream but nothing came. I couldn't move. He pulled me closer so his cracked lips were at my ear, the overwhelming smell of rotting flesh, alcohol and disinfectant at my nose. His tortured voice bubbled with phlegm as he strained to speak, dribble drooling down his stubbly chin, 'She concocts the poison we so easily consume.'

44

BANG BANG BANG, 'Your coffee, sir.'

I sat shaking, trying to catch my breath, staring at the barred windows, not knowing what was a dream and what was reality. The door banged again. This time I got up and slowly opened the door. Tariq stood with a steaming plastic cup in his hand and a reassuring grin on his face, 'Ah hello, sir, I am bringing coffee for you.' I asked him the time, 'It is five o'clock,' he replied.

'In the morning?'

'Yes, morning time.'

I took the cup, thanked him and returned to bed.

The room was like an oven; there was no fan or air-conditioning to alleviate the heat. Stepping out into the corridor I saw the separate shower room and toilets immediately, clean and newly decorated. The cold water from the shower went some way to clearing my head, but I couldn't shake the previous night's dream. As soon as I was dressed and presentable I went downstairs, had breakfast and brought my bill up to date.

I found the bus station with relative ease but I wasn't sure which bus was going where. There were no signs in English, nor could I find anyone who could help. I sat on a bench and hoped I'd hear a call for Hampi.

My attention was distracted from the bus lanes by a tug at my shirt. On all fours was a teenager squinted up at me. His back dipped low and raised high to his waist which protruded in an unnatural angle. His arms and legs were just bone covered grey with dust. He took hold of my hand and squeezed tightly, but said nothing. I asked if he was okay, but was met with silence. I tried the word, 'Hampi?' and shrugged my shoulders. He let go and turned his palm upwards, I assumed to cover it with rupees. I unfolded twenty from my pocket and gave them to him. He nodded his head to one side, took a firm hold of my hand again and guided me to the correct lane and a bus ready to leave.

The flat countryside gently gave way to a terrain of bizarre gigantic boulders, precariously balanced – the lower black in colour, the higher grey or fawn and heaped together to make up a range of breath-taking mountains. I'd never seen anything quite like it.

In a street flanked with stone pavilions, some empty, others occupied by shopkeepers selling various wares, the bus terminated. I alighted by a scattering of simple mud brick homes where locals attended to domestic duties – hanging their washing or bathing children in the weak afternoon sun. The far end of the bazaar was dominated by an imposing Hindu temple, soaring upwards and touching the sky.

'Hello sir, I am Vijay, best tour guide in Hampi,' A smart skinny boy, thirteen or fourteen maybe, stood with his hand on his chest for sincerity, 'I will show all important monuments and tell you good history of kingdom of Vijayanagar. Hampi very big place, you are most probably getting lost by yourself.'

'Thanks, Vijay was it? To be honest, I wanted to take in the atmosphere in my own time.' After my recent episodes with my grandfather, what I really wanted was to be on my own. My mind was far from recounts of history and storytelling.

'But sir, you can still breathe in atmosphere with me. I can show many monument, tell you what things are or how else will you know?'

'I have a guidebook.'

'What guidebook, let me see.' I showed him the Lonely Planet.

'Ah, this very good book, but not good enough for Hampi. Too many things to see, not enough information.'

I thanked him again and walked away, but he followed. I had to admire his spirit.

'But don't you think too much information might spoil things? While I'm trying to soak up what it might have been like all those years ago, my imagination would be interrupted by you telling me about everything.'

He eyes looked up to one side while he racked his brain for a quick response. One came, 'Ah, but sir, I can be quiet and you can call on me for information when needed. Plus, it is not safe for travellers. Many person is being robbed of their things.'

I had a feeling as I was the only tourist about, he'd shadow me around wherever I went anyway, 'Okay, how much?'

His eyes lit up, 'Ah, for you, sir, I am giving out of season price of only one hundred rupees.'

'Right, we'll see how it goes then.'

'Thank you, you will not regret, I am sure. Uh, your name sir?'

'Sam.'

He cleared his throat and spoke as we walked, 'Hampi was last capital of great Hindu Kingdom of Vijayanagar. Settlements in Hampi date back as far as one CE. Also, royalty of Vijayanagara Empire build temples and palaces between 1336 to 1565. But Muslim group pillaged city in 1565 and then city was abandoned.'

We came to a stop at the foot of the temple at the end of the bazaar, 'This is 7th century Virupaksha Temple. Virupaksha is incarnation of Lord Shiva. As you see, there are many sculptures of Virupaksha rising to top of fifty-metre-high structure.'

He guided me under the gopura into an empty courtyard surrounded by a stone colonnade where small macaque monkeys scuttled to and fro screeching and playing. 'We are now going to sacred Tungabhadra River,' he said, and after passing between two giant oblong stones leaning against each other we stood on the banks of a muddy river roping away into the rocky hills. Ladies in saris washed their laundry at the water's edge, children played harmoniously alongside buffalo cooling from the heat. Small bowl shaped boats woven from reeds and wrapped in animal hide sailed past, ferrying locals up and down the river. 'We take Coracle,' Vijay said, pointing to a man pulling one of these boats into shore.

We sat down cross legged and were pushed out onto the water. The boatman jumped on and after a few moments of spinning in circles, he righted us, keeping us on course around the curves of the banks. Vijay neatened his hair and adjusted the two pens in his shirt pocket. He looked up and smiled, 'We are now arrive at Vitalla Temple, be leaving boat please.'

I paid the ferryman a few rupees and Vijay and I went on foot for a while in silence until we reached a courtyard. A granite chariot, wheels nearly as tall as myself, stood guarding the temple. He told me the main mandapa was completed in 1565 and dedicated to Lord Vishnu. Slender outer pillars supporting the structure were said to emit different musical notes. He was pointing out the details of the floral designs and animal carvings, but my mind was wandering, my vision blurring in and out of the last few days.

'Any chance we could end the tour here, Vijay?' I asked.

'Oh no sir, you have paid me.'

'But you can keep the money.'

'Oh no sir, that would not be right. Hampi has some no good people to foreigner. No, I am being here for you.'

'In that case, could you stand behind that far pillar while I take a photograph?'

'Of course.'

As soon as he disappeared, I turned and sprinted along a road and then off on to a pathway with glinting rice paddies either side. The trail led me into a thick banana plantation where I stopped to catch my breath. I looked behind me with a clear view and no sign of Vijay.

I was glad of the space again. I took a box of cigarettes from my bag and withdrew the last one. I was screwing up the packet when I heard a crack in the thicket to my left, followed by another. When I heard another sound, I looked down the nearby lanes, but there were only endless banana leaves leading to lines of dark palm trees in the background.

I started walking. Footsteps followed in the distance. Hard edged tapping, click click click click. Both my father and grandfather wore Blakeys – cast iron protectors for the heels of shoes. My father insisted I wore them to school, making me a laughing stock and giving bullies even more ammunition. Now that noise, not only brought those memories pouring back, but instilled terror in me that was becoming all too familiar. When I stopped, the clicking stopped. I stepped back, sliding clumsily down a bank into a fan of springy banana trunks.

All the years gone by and the thick skin I'd grown amounted to nothing. I was shaking with fear like a child again, waiting for what would inevitably follow. May it be a second or a minute, the punch, jab or kick would always come next; a new agonizing pain to add to my long list of different places to be hurt on my body.

I ran out onto a dirt track, passing temples set on ascending granite banks and dwarfed by the boulder-strewn hills. I caught a glimpse of people living primitive lives within cave entrances; cooking over stone ringed fires, tending to their young and watching me back with keen interest. The escorting steps had died out, but I could still feel my grandfather near, sticking to my skin like burning oil.

I'd covered a mile or so when a group of young sadhus called out for my attention. I walked on, but they left their position and closed in on me. They asked for money and rifled through my shoulder bag. Turning, I found a gap and pushed through. As I cornered a ruin, I bumped into an unsuspecting goat, bleating and lurching forward, but restrained on a rope by a young man. I'd lost the sadhus thankfully, or they had lost interest in me, and the young man, although we couldn't communicate because of the language wall between us, accompanied me with his bicycle and goat until I reached another set of ruins.

According to my map, I was at the grounds of the King's Palace, the Hall of Viceroy, Hazarama Temple and the Lotus Mahal with its high archways on all sides. I walked a main road for a while passing a lady balancing three copper pots on her head, followed by her two daughters, each carrying a single vessel in the same way. A muscular white bull hauled a wagon laden with wood, steered by a tired old man streaming with sweat.

Try as I might, I couldn't find a way back to the bazaar. I wished that I hadn't taken flight from Vijay, or maybe it was better for him that I had. By a paddy field behind another temple I flicked through the guidebook to gain my bearings, all the while in fear of my grandfather's return. A voice called out, 'Rupee, baba, rupee.' I turned to find a middle-aged man dressed in no more than a loin cloth. His useless legs were heaped over each other in uncomfortable looking angles. He stopped before me hand in the air.

I gave him a twenty, all I had spare, but it wasn't enough. When I walked away, he trailed me. The faster I walked the more he propelled himself after me. I swung around, 'Leave me alone!'

I ran, eventually losing him, clambering over the brow of a hill and skidding my way to the bottom. I felt guilty for shouting. He must have been so desperate. He was drastically thin, his face so gaunt. From behind a large statue of Ganesh, I caught a glimpse of Virupaksha Temple and knew the Main Bazaar wouldn't be far behind.

Crossing the road and down another hill I came out into the Main Bazaar and found a distraught Vijay sitting by the roadside. When he saw me he rushed over, 'I am being so glad to see you. I made very big mistake and lose you. I am so very sorry sir. Please do not be writing to guidebook people and telling them what bad guide Vijay is.'

Despite his anxiety, I couldn't help but laugh, 'Hey, calm down, don't worry. It was all my fault; you've been a perfect guide. If I were to write to the guidebook, I would say just that.'

He said that we still had some time before the bus arrived and if I liked, he could show me the sunset from Matunga Hill, the highest point in Hampi. This time I stuck with him. Everywhere he went I was a step behind. After a while of climbing we came out to a clearing where grey langurs played and swung from the branches of a nearby tree and a chai wallah served up tea alongside a small white temple. The setting sun broke below the clouds and the tangerine sky bled scarlet across the earth, draping the endless temples and boulders in its wake.

My fragility had lessened by the time we returned to the bazaar. Where I first met Vijay was where I left him. The stone age land fell away from the horizon into the dusk and swift distance was made to Hospet where I caught a cycle rickshaw back to the hotel.

I intended to spend the evening in the restaurant below, until last orders or when tiredness got the better of me. I needed to be around people. It was when I was on my own that my mind seemed to plague me the most. I needed the clatter and alien voices to drown out any others that wished to trespass.

Tariq was too busy serving customers at first to notice me, but when he saw me at a table, he came over straight away with the same enthusiastic smile, absent of motive or corruption. 'Hello, hello, it is very good to be seeing you again, Mr Sam. Please, I will be on break in just five minutes. Can I come and eat with you and you will be telling me of your day in Hampi?'

'Of course, it would be nice to have some company. Can I have whatever you'll be eating?'

'Of course, I will choose for us.' He then waved his hands in the air and his head side to side, his smile widening, 'Very good break time this evening.'

He returned with dishes of paneer korma and brown rice, warm rotis and two lassis. He hung on every word I said, even after I spoke about Hampi and told him of the other places I'd visited in India. I finished off by telling him about Connor and his family as we cleaned up a plate of sweet gulab jamun balls soaked in syrup.

With a promise of an early morning coffee call, I left him sweeping the emptying restaurant and went back to my room, laying out my map on the bed. Just over two hundred kilometres north was Bijapur, a city of important monuments built during the reign of the Adil Shahi Dynasty.

I only received one visit from my grandfather that evening, or more so, his face in the darkness. I was paralysed, pinned to my bed and could do nothing but listen to his warbling nonsense. It was like he was trying to tell me something, but my mind was too intent on blocking out anything he had to say. Try as I might, I couldn't escape until I awoke on the sweat drenched sheets to Tariq's knocking. Through bleary eyes, I took my coffee, thanked him and returned to bed.

By nine, after handing Tariq a generous tip, I went to the bus station only to see my bus leave just as I arrived. At the ticket kiosk I enquired about the next bus, if there was one. Another was due to leave in an hour, so I caught up with my journal while I waited.

When the hour passed, a man came over and pointed to a windowless rusted old people carrier, 'Bijapur? Please come.'

I looked over to the guy in the ticket office and asked what was going on. 'Last bus to Bijapur involved in very bad accident, many people hurt,' he replied. 'This man will take you some of the way to reconnect with another bus.'

Counting my lucky stars that I had been late, I stood in the heaving aisle as the vehicle pulled away. As crazy as they came, the driver enjoyed the thrill of playing chicken with oncoming traffic as much as possible, seemingly oblivious to what had happened with the earlier bus.

Dusty, shaken and altogether worse for wear, I made it to the town of Hungund. In the thirty minutes I stood waiting for a connection, I was asked the usual questions by an accumulating crowd. I was happy to oblige with answers and now quite used to the attention, I found it a compliment they found my life so interesting. When I gave my answers, people paused to think on what I'd said in preparation for their next question. When I asked them about themselves, they were so pleased I'd done so. It was a real conversation, which I'd learned to appreciate with all my heart.

By mid-afternoon I'd reached Bijapur and found a hotel with relative ease. According to the guidebook map, the hotel was situated equidistant to the two places I wanted to visit, which were approximately a mile in opposite directions. Though the sky was overcast, the heat was intense, and preferring not to walk I hailed a cycle rickshaw.

Aazim was in his mid-fifties and spoke reasonable English. Between his betel-stained teeth he gripped an unlit beedi.

'Do you need a light?' I asked, as we moved away into the traffic.

'Oh, no sir, this is so I do not smoke. I have not smoked now for fifteen years.'

'Good idea, though I'd be tempted too much to light it I think. Have you lived here long, Aazim?'

'In Bijapur? Ah yes, all of my life.'

In between wiping the sweat from his forehead, he told me more about his home town, 'City begin in tenth century and was known as Vijayapura – the city of victory. Vijayapura was invaded by Bahmani Sultanate of Gulbarga and city name become Vijapur and then later, Bijapur. Bijapur is known by many as Agra of the south because of its very fine buildings.'

Laid out at the end of fine lawns, the 17th century Ibrahim Roza was the first of two monuments I wished to visit. A long pathway flanked by shrubs led me to an arched gateway where the two bulbous domed buildings were visible above; the stonework of both had long faded from white to black in most parts. Separated by ornamental ponds and fountains the interconnected structures faced each other. One was a mosque, the other a mausoleum housing the tombs of Ibrahim Adil Shah II and his wife Taj Sultana. Apart from an elderly gentleman who lay snoring on the flagstones of the mosque forecourt, I was on my own – a rare treat for a place such as this.

Peddled in the opposite direction, Aazim relished in telling me more about Bijapur's history, though it was hard to keep up with all what he was saying above the noise of the street, 'After long campaign, the Adil Shah Dynasty fell with Bijapur to Emperor Aurangzeb after Sikandar Adil Shah, the ruler of Bijapur, refused to be vassal of Moghul Empire,' he paused at an intersection and then rode off again, narrowly missing a mule drawn cart. 'The Golgumbaz, which I now take you to is mausoleum of Ibrahim Adil Shah II's son, Mohammed Adil Shah, the seventh Sultan of Bijapur. It has second largest dome in world next to Pantheon in Rome.'

The square monument cornered by octagonal towers rose high

from the garden city, commanding immediate respect. The interior was said to be equally special with its enchanting Whispering Gallery. As I circled the upper levels of the tomb, groups of school kids were testing the acoustics, hearing their voices echoing back ten times over. I tried myself, shouting hello into the inner dome. Much to my amusement, 'Hello,' and 'How are you?' was reverberated back by the laughing children.

Being so high, the descending view of the city was quite incredible as I made my way down to meet my rickshaw wallah. He took me back to my hotel where I paid him a little extra than agreed. Bijapur was laid back and I felt safe. I wished I could have stayed longer, but I was bound for the long journey to Aurangabad via Pune in the morning, my last stop on the way back to Mumbai.

45

'Hello?'

'Hi mum, it's me.'

'Oh, Sam. I'm glad you phoned.'

Her voice was brittle and although I knew what was coming I asked the question anyway, 'How is he?'

'He, er,' she took a moment to collect herself, 'Your grandfather, he died this morning.'

I felt numb. The last time I saw him was a couple of months before I left for my trip. He looked old, frail and ill. The energy he once had in abundance had departed, leaving a pathetic husk of a man with nothing but a history of abuse.

'Are you okay?' Of course she wasn't, but it was the best I could muster in that moment.

'I'm just focusing on your nan right now. She's so upset and feeling overwhelmed by all the arrangements. I better go now, but call again soon if you can.'

'I will. Give my best to nan. Take care, mum.'

That night I didn't sleep, instead the years of my life played like a disjointed movie in my head. With my father's death came a sense of freedom, for a while at least; until I realised I had swapped one prison for another. This was different. Frank's recent appearances made me realise how much I had been walking in the shadow of constant threat and although I put on a brave face, I'd been breaking up inside for far too long.

The chaos around me moved in slow motion as I left the hotel and walked to the bus station. My intention was to take a day trip to the ancient cave temples of Ajanta and Ellora. For the first time since leaving the north of the country I saw some western backpackers. American from what I could make out. They were gathered in the bus lanes and were in a heated discussion. Keeping my distance, I casually observed them while I quietly sat with my thoughts and guidebook. The two guys wanted to go to Manali, the two girls wanted to head to Goa. They'd missed the best time of year for both, but I held on to that information and left them to their debate.

A boy, no older than ten, appeared and hovered around the group. His left foot was missing at the ankle, the other foot bare and blistered. With one arm, he steadied himself on a battered crutch and extended his hand out.

'What?' one of the girls snapped, dismissing him with a turn of her back. He pulled at her shirt hoping she'd reconsider. 'Yeah, see, I've got no shoes either,' she said, pointing to her bare feet. Behind her I noticed a bench that was being used as a temporary resting place for a backpack and what looked like a new and expensive pair of Nike trainers. Carefully balancing, he placed his hands together in hope she might find pity. She didn't. Instead she pushed him, making him stumble and fall. The friends let out a roar of laughter; the girl smirking in the limelight of attention.

The young lad had a nasty graze on his elbow and knee. I ignored the voice of rage in my head seeking justice as so many times I did. I reached into my bag and offered him a bottle of water to remove the grit and my tube of antiseptic cream. While he tended to his cuts, I bought a couple of glasses of chai at a nearby stall and handed one to him. The backpackers were still laughing, jeering the boy even more now he had his "knight in shining armour" to rescue him. I put forty rupees in the boy's shirt pocket just as a chubby man in a pinstripe shirt, neatly pressed trousers and expensive looking shoes came over. He spoke to the boy, then looked up at the group, whose attention was now directed at a lady struggling with her groceries.

'Why would you do such a thing?' he shouted over. 'Can you not see this boy is poor and has a terrible disability?'

'What's it got to do with you exactly?' asked Miss Barefoot.

'It has everything to do with me as a decent human being. You should be ashamed of yourself.'

'Uh... well... I'm not,' she laughed, spurring the others to do the same.

The man turned to me, 'These are very bad people, such disgraceful behaviour.'

'I'm not with them by the way.'

'Yes, I can see you are not with them. It is a very nice thing you have done for this young man.'

The group climbed aboard a bus. 'I was meant to be getting on that myself, but I think I'll give it a miss.'

Placing his hands together the boy thanked me and hobbled away.

'You are from Great Britain?' the man asked.

'Yes, and you're from Aurangabad?'

'Aurangabad, yes. I have known that boy since he was very young. He is an orphan and part of a local begging gang. I am afraid any money you may have given him will probably go to his boss. He will maybe only earn five rupees for his sixteen hours on the street.'

'Five rupees? That's shocking.'

'Yes, very shocking, but this is the way unfortunately. Sometimes he comes by my restaurant and I feed him out the back. He is very thin, no? I tell him to come by any time, but he rarely does. He tells me he has to work hard or he will be in much trouble.'

'So you have a restaurant?'

'Yes, I have two in Aurangabad, three in Mumbai and a hotel and restaurant in Pune. I am also in the process of launching a signature Indian sauce range. Today I am having a day off, a very rare thing these days.'

'Do you have any plans?'

'Yes. Although I have lived in Aurangabad all my life, I have never visited the Ellora Caves. Have you seen them?' He drank the last of his chai, rested his arms on his paunch and stretched his legs out.

'I was on my way there today.'

'Maybe you would like to come with me then? I would be delighted to share my outing with you. My wife and children find the idea very boring.' He returned the glasses and sat back down, 'My name is Shekhar. So, what do you say?'

'That's really good of you, I'm happy to pay towards fuel.'

'That is not necessary. I am going there anyway; your company is payment enough. I must first pick up a package for my wife from the shop over the road there.' He pointed down the street to a window where mannequins modelled elegant saris, 'If you would be kind enough to wait, I will be back shortly and we can begin our journey into the hills.'

He returned holding a sealed cardboard box under his arm and opened his wallet to show me a small photograph, 'My wife Hami, my eldest daughter Naveena and my youngest, sweet Charvi.' He stared at the picture and smiled, lost in their faces. 'My car is parked around the corner.'

'You've got a lovely family, Shekhar.'

'Yes, I am a very lucky man, they are everything I am.' He opened the passenger door of a shiny black Mercedes, 'Shall we go?'

An Arctic breeze filled the car as he started the engine. My shoulders dropped and I let out a sigh. 'Yes, air-cool very good,' he said. 'Sometimes I come to the car only for air-cool. Much better than stuffy bus, no?'

Not only was I thankful for the air-conditioning, but also for his good driving. He was one of the first I'd seen to use his brakes and mirrors at the right time, plus he kept his speed down. We found a lot to talk about in the hour it took us to get to Ellora. For the most part, he took my mind off things. Quite a lot of his family lived in different parts of England. 'Yes, I visit when I can. My family has a chain of restaurants across the UK,' he said. 'Each time my brother says, "Come and work with us," but I love Maharashtra and India too much and I wouldn't want to be anywhere else.'

We neared the dense forests of the Sahyadri hills, looking out across a sheen of silver water caught alive in the sun. Stretching over two kilometres of the Deccan Plateau, amidst the serenity of the jungle, the 5th and 10th century rock cut hollows of Ellora were said to represent the supreme state of being in nirvana. But as we drew up in a busy car park, it was clear it was going to be anything but peaceful. Groups of Indian tourists had gathered in large numbers to take advantage of the solace also.

Shekhar locked the car, and map in hand we made our way towards the entrance of a cave hewn from the rock face and supported by carved pillars. I was happy to let him guide me. We worked our way through the Buddhist section as he shone his torch over the walls revealing glowing circles of events from the Buddha's previous lives. Though some of the sculptures were fragmented by years of decay the painstaking work of the skilled artists undertaken in minimal lighting was evident. In one cave, ribs were carved high into the roof to imitate wooden beams. Atmospheric light shone through an arched window into the grand hall where a nine-metre stone Buddha sat against a stupa.

Through a series of courtyards, we wandered into the Hindu caves showing a distinct change in style to the earlier ones. Carved reliefs of Shiva and Vishnu were featured throughout re-enacting scenes from the epic Ramayana and Mahabharata.

'I am looking forward to cave sixteen the most,' Shekhar commented. 'The Kailasa Temple is named after Mount Kailash – the abode of Lord Shiva. From roof to floor, the temple was mostly cut downwards from a single rock with the simplest of tools such as hammers and chisels. It is estimated that it took over one hundred years to build, and without the aid of scaffolding too. Simply incredible.'

Spanning out before us was one of the most spectacular structures I'd seen. The intricate temple rose from a spacious courtyard and was surrounded by various sculptures including huge stone elephants. I was drawn back to my youth, lost in tales of exploration. The rising towers were like something out of an Indiana Jones film.

The northern part of Ellora caves were Jain and dated back to the 9th century. Shekhar pointed out a statue of Mahavira, the founder of Jainism, 'See how the ivy trails around his outer body. It would suggest he has been standing there for a long time. He is naked also which represents the belief of abstinence and limiting one's personal possessions. Jainism was born around the same time as Buddhism in India. These caves are an excellent demonstration of how people and religion can co-exist peacefully.'

We talked at length about the day on the road back to Aurangabad. When Shekhar asked me about my family, I said very little, just enough so my answers to his questions were politely adequate. When we arrived at my hotel, he invited me for a meal at his restaurant later that evening and gave me directions how to get there. On the off-chance I couldn't make it, I thanked him for a nice day. I still needed time to absorb my grandfather's death and sort my head out.

But after a few hours of chasing my tail I decided to take Shekhar up on his offer and hailed an auto in the pouring rain. I arrived feeling somewhat embarrassed by my shabby appearance. My clothes had definite signs of wear from my travels and the restaurant was a classy establishment to say the least. It was large and well decorated with soft lighting and tasteful furnishings. Fine Indian paintings hung from the walls. A few of the smartly dressed diners glanced up as I walked in and looked at me in a way that I didn't belong. I felt the same when I scanned the menu and saw the prices were way out of my league. Even a starter would have set me back a week. But the interior smelt heavenly, warm with a thousand spices, and as I turned to leave I found it hard to pull my rumbling stomach away.

I was a heartbeat from exiting when a waiter came over and asked if he could help. I told him that I came to see Shekhar. 'Ah, yes, sir. Please, follow me.' He looked me up and down, then led me to a large table laid out with a white muslin cloth, silver cutlery and a reserved sign placed in the middle. As I sat down, I caught sight of other customers whispering behind their hands and throwing me puzzled looks.

Shekhar came in wearing a smart black suit and spoke to one of his staff. I was behind a jali screen and could see him clearly without being seen myself. The waiter nodded in my direction, Shekhar's head followed suit. He breezed over, 'Sam, great you came, I hoped you would.' I rose from the table and shook his hand. 'I am feeling very good this evening. I have had a big deal go through today that sees me taking my sauce range internationally.'

'That's great news, congratulations.' I toasted my glass with his.

'Would you allow me to choose for you, Sam?' He picked up the menu while the waiter hovered, pen in hand scribbling across the pad as Shekhar rolled off the order. 'So, how are you finding Aurangabad?'

I said that I hadn't seen much and was hoping to explore a bit more in the morning. I helped myself to servings of a chicken dish and rice as he spoke. 'I like to keep my food as traditional as possible. The chicken dish you have on your plate is Murg Norrjeha and is Mughlai, garnished with dried fruits and nuts. The rice is Biryani Badshahi, slow-cooked, rich and fragrant with sliced onions and garlic and a variety of spices including saffron which gives the rice that wonderful golden colour.'

We were nearing the end of our meal when he asked about my finances. I told him I hadn't much money left as I was nearing the end of my trip. 'Now that I have expanded my business I will need more trustworthy people like yourself,' he said, lowering his napkin to the table. 'I need somebody to take charge of the security of some of my stock to and from various countries. You would be paid extremely well and would need to start almost immediately. We will sort out any visas and travel arrangements as required. Please don't answer now, have the night to think about it. I am flying to Abu Dhabi tomorrow. If you are interested, come by the restaurant at seven in the morning and we will talk further.'

I left for my hotel in a slight spin. A successful career at my fingertips? It was hard to say no. Apart from my mother, there was nothing left for me in England and the thought of travelling the world was reason enough to seal the deal. I set the alarm for five thirty, giving the decision time to sink in.

46

Looking in the mirror as I shaved I had no idea what lay before me. I imagined myself in an expensive suit, important and respected. Respected? This was it, everything I could have dreamed of. I could turn my back on the past and walk on, head held high. Washing away the last stripes of foam, I smiled, at last glad to be me.

The sun touched the streets and unearthed what the night hid so well. Roadside shacks, darkness warming to light, life emerging from within. Happiness shone in the faces of dusty children, hope and despair in the eyes of the parents. Piece by piece life assembled itself complete.

My auto wallah, Muhamud, was humming throughout the short ride to Shekhar's restaurant. On arrival, we drew to a stop on the opposite side of the road. I didn't get out. Instead, both Muhamud and I looked on at the commotion that was occurring outside. Police were everywhere, mostly surrounding Shekhar's business. I asked Muhamud if he knew what was happening. He shrugged his shoulders, 'Maybe I find out from over there.' A crowd had gathered nearby. He got out and spoke with a couple of onlookers and returned to the rickshaw. 'Police are making early morning search on restaurant. They are arresting and seizing all assets from a Kanwal Shekhar on suspicion of money laundering and drug trafficking.'

Surely there had been an error. I just couldn't believe this of

Shekhar, but as he was escorted from the restaurant, head down and hands cuffed behind his back, it was evident there'd been no mistake. He was thrust into the back of a white van and the doors slammed behind him.

'Sir, are you wanting me to take you to other place?' Muhamud asked.

I invited him to join me for chai. I was too stunned to eat. 'Did you know Shekhar?' I enquired, as we sipped the tea together alongside a quiet chai stall.

'No, but it is much shocking news. From what I am hearing, he was very wealthy and very popular man. People are being most surprise at this.'

It was shocking. He'd had me completely fooled. I thought about the job offer and shuddered to think about the stock I was supposed to be responsible for. An amazing life had been handed to me on a magic carpet and whipped from under my feet in an instant.

Muhamud stopped off at the bus station so I could buy my ticket back to Mumbai. I stared at the bench where Shekhar and I sat only yesterday and wondered about the alternative, relieved I hadn't become a part of his affairs, but disappointed that the chance at an exciting new life had been so fleeting. The next bus journey would take me one step closer to going home and I had no clue as to the direction my life would take once I got back there. I couldn't see anything positive, only a grim reminder of my empty existence.

I arrived back into the breathing belly of Mumbai and took a taxi to Connor's apartment. He was on a high about a party at the Elephanta Caves he'd gone to with his cousin and I had barely got through the door when he started telling me about it.

'You should have been there man. We got a ferry and didn't get back until seven in the morning. Hey, you want some breakfast? I was just about to head over to my mother's.'

'Yeah, that would be nice. I've missed your mum's cooking. It's been so hard to eat over the last few days.' I didn't tell Connor about my grandfather. It was so good to see him again and I didn't want my last days with him marred. At the Reveredo home, Patrice teased Titiana about a boy from college who kept showing up at their door, while I did my best to bypass any questions about Kashmir from Louis.

Mrs Reveredo came in, 'I have taken the liberty of hiring you a suit. I gathered measurements from your clothes so it should fit you. You will go to the barber shop you went to when you first arrived and get a good shave. It has already been paid for. You two must be presentable for this evening, it is very important to me.' She left and we looked at each other and laughed. 'Something funny boys?' she said, reappearing with a frown.

The whole family including grandma were in attendance; the girls in bright glittering saris, the boys in black suits and bow ties. Connor left us to set up on stage with the band as we sat at one of the many round tables. It was a charity function, set up by Mrs Reveredo in aid of Mumbai's disadvantaged and homeless.

'Tonight, everything is taken care of, which leaves me to enjoy the benefit. I have only to make a speech at the end of the evening,' she said. She'd been working for three months in preparation for this night Tatiana told me. Although she was supposed to relax, Mrs Reveredo couldn't help but interrupt a waiter every now and then to comment on a crease in his shirt or a watermark on a glass.

The evening was filled with music and speeches, and Connor joined us once or twice where he could. Mrs Reveredo was surprised to be the recipient of an award for services to the community. She blushed and wiped a tear from her eye as she made heartfelt thanks.

'She's been working so hard to re-home people on the streets for over ten years now,' Radhika said as we finished the last dance.

We sat at a table and waited for Connor to pack away his kit. 'He loves his music, huh? Nearly as much as travel,' I said.

'Oh yes, I've long accepted the package of him and his music,' she laughed. 'He still wants to travel, so I suggested we could go together which he seems fine with. Fingers crossed, we might well be on the road to recovery.'

'I'm so pleased. Are you happy to do more travelling though?'

'I want to be with Connor and I think it will be good for me.

Listen, Connor has to work tomorrow, so how about we have a proper catch-up?'

'I'd like that,' I smiled.

'Me too,' she took my hand and squeezed gently. 'See you tomorrow.'

47

Radhika met me at the station in Thane, north Mumbai and took me along to her apartment where she introduced me to her mother and brother. After lunch laid out on banana leaves, she said, 'There's a nice little place not far from here if you fancy a coffee.'

Settling into a couch in a quiet corner, I stared into my milky coffee.

'Are you okay Sam, you look, how should I say, lost?'

'I'm fine. I should be able to find my way home from here.'

'No, I mean, you look sad, confused. I don't know, I'm probably being silly, but if you need to talk... I owe you that much. You've helped me and Connor a lot, I'm not sure we'd be together without you.'

'You guys are stronger than you think,' I glanced nervously around the room, while considering whether to pour the secrets that had been bottled up for so long. It wasn't an easy decision, but before I could make it, I unconsciously blurted out, 'My granddad died a few days ago.'

'Oh, I'm so sorry. Were you close?'

'Um, once, yes, but that seems like a lifetime ago.' She remained quiet, giving me time to continue at my own pace. 'He drank. I suppose you'd call him an alcoholic. Not that anyone ever openly acknowledged that. I'm sure my grandmother must have known, but she pretended otherwise; went along with the pretense. No good would have come from her challenging him, so she kept quiet and played the unsuspecting wife; turned a blind eye.'

'He drank a lot?'

'You could say that. I'm not sure how much exactly, but he used to hide bottles of wine and spirits around the house and drank them while nan was out or asleep. He'd drink a certain amount in front of her, a couple of glasses of red with dinner, maybe one at lunch. They'd often share a bottle of wine and it would all appear quite normal. Except he then drank a lot more on the quiet. He kept some bottles in my room, the one I used when I was sent to stay with them and he'd creep in to get them in the middle of the night.'

Already I felt like I'd said too much and was apprehensive about laying myself bare to someone I hardly knew. I trusted Radhika, but would I come to regret the hangover of this conversation if I let it continue down this path? I was thinking too much. The need to talk and share this burden with someone far outweighed any negative consequences in the aftermath. I had seen Radhika at one of her lowest points and it had forged a silent bond between us, an understanding that life can take you to some very dark places. If I didn't speak now I couldn't imagine when such an opportunity would present itself again.

I took my chances, 'I used to love going to stay with my nan and granddad, which was mainly at weekends – Friday to Sunday. Some Saturdays Nan would take me to Hamley's on Regent Street in London to see the moving window displays and explore the endless toy shop within. Or we'd meet up with her millionaire friend, Kitty, and share time in the buffet cart of the first-class section of the train. The two of us would usually end up having coffee at Victoria Station or watching a Laurel and Hardy short in the mini cinema booth in the station foyer.

'I remember the day it all changed though. We were at a family get together – my parents, me and my grandparents –at a pub in Sydenham. My grandparents announced they were retiring to Belgium. Towards the end of the meal, my grandfather got up and headed to the toilet. I followed after him. I looked up to him and wanted to grow up to be like him. When I caught up with him he was standing just inside the toilet with a lit cigarette between his fingers. He brought it up to his mouth and inhaled then took a swig from a hip flask. I had no idea he smoked. As soon as he saw me he flicked the cigarette down the urinal and put away the flask. I knew something wasn't right in that instant and I quickly turned away and went back to the others.

'He returned to the table red faced and did his best to resume conversation in the same mood as when he left. In hindsight, I think I should have tried to reassure him somehow, convince him that his covert operations were not under any threat from me. Then again, would it have made any difference? I was the unchosen keeper of a secret he was determined to preserve. A secret so overvalued that it reigned supreme. The next time I saw him was in Ostend; I was sent there for the school holidays. For the first day or so he was fine, but then it started.'

'What started, Sam?' I tried to speak, but began stuttering, as I often did when I fell into my past. I slowed my breathing, which worked a little. 'It's okay, take your time,' she said softly, putting her hand on my arm in reassurance.

'At first it was the odd kick under the table, quick pinch as I walked past him or a flick of the ear. I guess it was his way of showing who was boss, but the more he saw how weak I was, the worse it became.' I sighed, 'He came into my room at night and smothered me under the bed covers until I couldn't breathe, all the while punching me at various points around my body and my head. I daren't scream or make any other noise.

'Once when my nan was out he whacked me so hard with a piece of wood I lost consciousness. It was always when we were alone in the flat or at night when my nan was in bed. He tried to drown me in the bath on several occasions and liked to flush my head down the toilet. He held my head down on a hot stove and dangled me upside down over the balcony. He even held knives up to my throat and threatened to pull my teeth out with a pair of pliers.' I didn't look up to see her face and the expression it held; sympathy, disgust maybe; all the things I dreaded. 'Hey, I'm sorry, you don't want to hear any of this. You've invited me into your home and I've had a wonderful...'

'Sam, it's fine,' she said in a calm, even tone. 'We're good friends, right? And that's what good friends are for, to be there for each other, as you were for me.'

Inside I was bowing to the force of a fierce gale, afraid at any moment my grandfather might reappear and reprimand me, but I continued nonetheless, 'One occasion in particular stands out when I was about twelve. My nan had gone out shopping so I was alone with my grandfather. I was standing at the back door in the kitchen eating a ham and pickle sandwich, looking out to the top of the church steeple that faced the back of their apartment. Suddenly I heard a metal scraping sound and before I even had time to register what it was, I felt an almighty thud to the back of my head, which caused me to hit the window frame. I felt immediate swelling and an agonising ache all around my skull.

'I stood for a moment with my hand on the glass, and through the pulsating pain, I heard my grandfather's voice from behind me telling me to get my hands off the window at once because I was leaving finger marks. I was finding it difficult to retain balance. Fear hadn't registered at this point. I had no time to figure out what was going on before my legs gave way beneath me and I slumped to the floor. The hair on the back of my head was damp and I felt trickling down my neck. I was ordered to get up and stop acting like a wimp or I'd be in big trouble. The headache was excruciating and my brain felt as if it was going to explode from the pressure around it.

'Tears fell and I whimpered. He hit me again, then booted me hard in the back. I managed to gain some sense of composure, adrenaline kicked in I guess and I pulled myself up using the sideboard as support. At this point I was now facing him and witnessed him placing the frying pan down on the cooker. A thousand tiny pins of light were piercing the darkness of my vision; pain whistled through my ears. I felt an overwhelming sense of nausea and all I wanted was to get to the bathroom.

'He walked calmly back into the living room and closed the door behind him. This was my one chance and I grabbed at anything around – the dining table, chairs, a bookshelf– to assist my journey to safety. Inside the bathroom, I closed the door behind me and slid the lock across. For a while at least I would be safe and I fell back and passed out.'

Radhika looked at me in disbelief. Around us was crowded chatter from the other tables, the sounds of people stirring sugar into coffee and resting their spoons on the hard surface of the tables. A child slurped up the last drops of a milkshake and kept sucking on the straw in case more of the chocolate flavoured treat would magically appear at the bottom of the glass. I felt so alienated from the normality around me. I was ready to end the story here, but Radhika urged me to continue.

'I wasn't sure how long I'd been unconscious, but it can't have been that long as I couldn't hear my nan's voice, so she'd not yet returned. The pain in my head was unbearable, I'd never felt anything like it in my life. I tried to investigate the damage with my fingers and felt a cut and large bump on the back of my head. It was then I noticed the wet patch on my trousers and I began to sob uncontrollably. I felt scared and humiliated. Outside I heard shuffling and my grandfather's slurred voice asking me what I was doing. I was running out of time and had to pull myself together or I'd be in even bigger trouble.

'I told him I wouldn't be long and I summoned the determination to clean myself up, in preparation for my nan coming home. Tepid water filled the sink and I began cleaning the back of my head and neck. When I'd finished, the water was dark pink and I drained it satisfied there was no more blood. I patted my hair gently to dry it, then sat wondering what to do next. Was he lurking on the other side of the door to hurt me? I couldn't go through that again, but neither could I stay in the bathroom forever, so I took a deep breath and slid back the lock, then opened the door.

'He wasn't there so I crept out and made my way to my room as quietly and quickly as I could. Tears fell again as I got to my bed and I laid down, curled up and closed my eyes. Sometime later I heard my nan talking to my granddad. She asked where I was, then she came into my room. With my back to her I pretended to be asleep, concealing the rear of my head deep in the pillow. I heard the door close and I breathed a sigh of relief. I'd managed to fool her.'

'What happened for the rest of your time there?' Radhika enquired. 'Didn't your nan notice your injuries?'

'I only had three more days there on that visit and once I had cleaned myself up and the wound was dry, my hair pretty much covered it. I also wore a baseball cap around the house, which I'd bought the previous day. My nan probably thought I was just keen to show it off. Unusually, my grandfather left me alone for the rest of my stay on that occasion, which I was thankful for.'

'Did you ever tell anyone what was happening?'

'I tried. When I got home I told my Mum I didn't want to stay there, that granddad was hurting me, but she didn't pay much attention.' The years were fast catching up with me and I felt the tautness of tears rising in my throat. 'To be honest though, things weren't much better at home. At least in Belgium I had my nan who is an exceptional cook and she'd buy me little presents like comic books and cassette tapes. My father didn't like me having, well, anything really.'

'Growing up's hard at the best of times, but for you it must have been pretty terrible. I never would have imagined any of these things happening to you. It's no wonder you came to India to escape.'

'I've felt an amazing sense of freedom here. It's been hard at times; I don't think I was very well prepared for what India had to throw at me. I cannot believe the wonderful people I have met and the friends I've made. It's incredible. Lately though I have been drifting back to my childhood in my head and I don't know if it's because I knew my grandfather was dying or if it's because I'm going home soon. I really don't want this adventure to end.'

'Did you ever manage to stand up to your grandfather?'

'Yes, once. When I was eighteen. He pushed me down a flight of concrete steps. I landed badly on my shins and elbow. He came down after me and whether it was the pain, or pent up frustration, I don't know, but I shot up and held him against the wall with my arm against his throat. I told him if he ever hurt me again, I would kill him.'

'What happened after that?

'Nothing like how he was before. He'd still make snide comments and kick me under the dinner table, but I could cope with that.' It was never my plan to open up like this, but now it was done, I felt a sense of relief.

When I returned that evening, Connor was asleep on the sofa with Channel V on in the background. I didn't wake him. Instead, I stared into the television set consumed by the traumatic scenes that plagued my memories. Had I deserved the abuse I'd suffered? Could I have done something to stop it? Why did these men hate me so much? I could understand my step-father to a degree; he didn't want to take on somebody else's kid. Even so, it seemed more than that. Looking back, it was as though he thought I had it easy and was unappreciative.

My grandfather was now condemned to the same fate as my father, unable to hurt me anymore, except to haunt me at my lowest ebb. Despite the challenges in India, I could only look back with fondness. I felt proud of what I had achieved here and the person I saw in the mirror. For the first time, I had freedom and space in my head to think clearly. My mind had taken advantage of this by allowing my past to come forward, which although difficult, in hindsight had granted me the opportunity to find a sense of closure. Yet a nagging feeling remained deep within, that the torment was far from over.

48

Rain pockmarked the streets with a million droplets and drooped the palms with its force. I went out early to pick up some headache tablets and stood by the roadside facing a dull grey block of weather stained apartments, watching the traffic and people wade through the floods. Life backwards going forwards.

I planned to spend the day exploring the Kanheri or Elephanta Caves, but when I saw the crowds at the train station, I lost all spirit. Instead I wandered the vibrant flower and vegetable markets of Dadar watching tradesmen and customers weighing up items in their hands, inspecting for any imperfections and cutting a deal. Potatoes, juicy round tomatoes, carrots, peas and other varieties I couldn't identify, haggled and sold. Stall holders at a stand stacked with a pyramid of coconuts were laughing and joking. I strolled over to the flower stalls, where the air was filled with floral scent and the din of voices where vendors fashioned bouquets and garlands. Jasmine petals spilling over the edges of woven baskets; red hibiscus bouquets stacked in rows and ready for workers to heave onto their heads; jute sacks brimming with vivid colours dragged on wooden pallets around the narrow lanes. Beside a stall with bundles of red roses, a boy tied bright orange marigold blossoms. 'Preparing them for temple,' he said.

After a strawberry milkshake and a questionable vegetable burger at the American diner I met Connor. He was keen to show me the cathedral he'd attended since he was young. St. Thomas' Cathedral was an important monument for Christians in Mumbai. Pointing to the tall white clock tower, he relayed a story of when he and his cousin tried to make their way to the top only to be caught by a priest. Reflected colours of the stained glass speckled the varnished oak benches and avenue leading to the altar. We sat for a while in silence and I glanced at my friend, his eyes closed, at one with his surroundings.

I spent the last night in the spare room of the Reveredo home, now considered one of the family. Connor came with me to Mumbai Central and embraced me on the platform, 'It's been awesome, dude.' He handed me a ticket, 'I booked you a sleeper so at least you can get some proper rest this time.'

'Thanks for everything. We'll keep in touch yeah?' I said as I boarded.

'Of course. Write to me when you get back and let me know you're safe.'

I stood, watching him wave until he was nothing more than the size of a pin. The sprawling metropolis melted away into the tropical green countryside and I settled in for at least twenty-two hours back to the capital. This was the beginning of my journey home.

Dark faces of track side slum dwellers stared up at the train as it glided into New Delhi Railway Station at a quarter to seven. It was good to be back in the city I'd learned to love the most. Standing outside of the railway station, I gazed at the early morning accumulating traffic. The continuous buzzing of an auto pulled me from my reverie. A voice called out from under the yellow roof, 'I am the great Rahul, rider of the rickshaw...'

'Guardian of the morning traveller?' I interrupted, completing his pitch with a chuckle.

The driver leant forward revealing from the shadows a neatly trimmed moustache and swept back hair, 'You know me, sir?'

'How could I not?' I replied. 'You are the great Rahul, the best rickshaw wallah in Delhi, maybe all of India.'

He squinted for a moment, then smiled, 'Yes, yes, I remember you now, we shared chai one early morning several months ago.'

'We did. Sam,' I said, extending my hand.

'Mr Sam, you are still in India? How are you? Long time, no?'

'A long time indeed. So, how would you like to be my rickshaw wallah for the next couple of days?'

'It would be an honour, my friend. Come, the great Rahul will take you wherever you wish and keep you safe along the way.'

'First I need to check into my hotel. We'll discuss rates on route, and remember, I'm not new to India.'

'Haha, of course, sir. I will give you only the very best rate.'

We stopped at a tobacconist, where I saw two young boys. Given how similar they looked to each other, I guessed they were brothers, maybe a couple of years apart in age. The younger of the two approached me, 'Please sir, can you spare any rupees?'

There was something about the pair that lent a feeling of loss; the timid advance perhaps, rather than the hard sell of the confident street kid. The older boy pulled on his brother's elbow and muttered something with authority.

'Of course.' I held out some loose change.

'No sir, we cannot take your money, but thank you,' the elder said stepping ahead of his sibling.

'But why Sanjeev? Sir is not minding and I am so hungry.'

'I have told you I will find more work tomorrow,' Sanjeev replied.

'Look it's not a problem. Are you in trouble?' I took my wallet out.

'No sir, just hungry. Our parents died in motor accident and we were sent to live with uncle. He was very bad man, drank too much and beat us. We are running away from home,' the younger said, stepping forward to take the money.

Sanjeev batted his sibling's hand away, 'Please sir, excuse my brother's rudeness. We will not trouble you any further.'

'How have you been surviving?'

'We went hungry for first few days and have been picking through rubbish for waste paper to sell as recyclable material ever since,' Sanjeev said. 'But recently it has been so difficult to earn anything due to the rains.'

Their clothes may have once been respectable, but were now worn and dirty. They sounded educated and spoke good English, which led me to believe they may once have attended a good school. I handed over three hundred rupees, 'Here, I'm sorry I can't help more.'

'Thank you, sir,' Sanjeev said. 'That is most kind of you. I assure you it will be spent on food and shelter.'

'Take care of each other, okay,' I said, and caught up with Rahul. He fired up the engine and I glanced back and saw the pair smiling, unable to believe their luck.

Along the quiet Main Bazaar that would soon be teeming, we came to an alleyway. I asked Rahul to order some chai from the restaurant across the road. I turned right and right again into the reception area where I found Harish with his head buried in some paperwork. I asked how he'd been.

'Mr Sam,' he laughed. 'Ha, it is so good to see you again. Maybe I thought you leave India by now, but here you are in Delhi once again. I am being much good and how are you?' He came from behind the counter and gave me a hug. 'You are staying?'

'Do you have any rooms?'

'Of course, always room for you. Please come.' He showed me to a room beside the entrance on the ground floor. 'Are you wanting a good cup of chai and some breakfast maybe?'

'Thanks, but I've got someone waiting for me outside, but we'll catch up later yeah?'

'Of course, why not?'

When I reappeared after showering and a change of clothes, it was Nitin who greeted me at reception. He slapped me on the back and grinning he said, 'Neerygun debarawah.'

'Beragoo libbydah,' I laughed and waved goodbye, but I'm not sure if he saw me. He was still giggling as I left.

I met up with Rahul again and drank the now lukewarm chai he'd pre-ordered. I wanted to cram in as much as I could before I left and Delhi had a lot to see. The busier I kept myself the less time

I had to think. There was no point agonising over the prospect of going back to England or what had happened in the past. It wouldn't change anything, only spoil the remaining time I had left.

India Gate was first on my itinerary. Inspired by the Arc de Triomphe in Paris, the monument could be seen from all directions. Rahul accompanied me around the arch as we stared up some of the names inscribed upon the bricks of over 80,000 soldiers of the Indian and British army that lost their lives during World War One and the Third Anglo-Afghan War.

'We close to Janpath Market if you are wishing to visit,' Rahul informed me. 'Much jewellery, clothing and paintings.'

I laughed, 'Really, we're near Janpath?'

'Yes, what is being so funny?'

'Ah nothing, just a friend and I got into a spot of bother here once.'

Declining his offer, we squeezed back into the heaving traffic and moved on to an important Sikh house of worship, the Gurudwara Bangla Sahib. The temple was a brilliant white and topped by a central golden dome and known for its association with the Sikh Guru, Har Krishan.

I removed my scarf from my bag, fashioned a turban to cover my head and left my shoes in the shoe-minding room as I came out onto a warm marble floor with the magnificent temple reflecting in a pool of shimmering water surrounded on all sides by archways. On the premises was a kitchen where food was prepared for anyone wishing to eat, regardless of race or religion.

I thought of Jumeet and Adesh in Drass and mentioned their restaurant to Rahul outside. He knew the area well and took me there. But when we arrived, I found it closed. By now, my rumbling stomach was getting the better of me and the stifling heat was leaving me parched. I'd kept enough aside to have a couple of decent meals and asked to be taken to Pizza Hut in Connaught Place instead.

I came out with the take-away box in my hands, but it was instantly snatched away by a young street girl. She looked so raggedy and thin. I had to pity her to go to such lengths. Slightly bemused, I went back inside and ordered another, quick to make a dash to Rahul this time. Tearing away the segments, I offered half to Rahul, but he politely declined. I insisted, telling him I only ordered this size so I could share with him. 'It's no fun eating on my own, Rahul.'

Meekly he reached over and took a slice, 'I am not eating this before, it is tasting very good, very good indeed,' he said, smacking his lips. 'Thank you, Mr Sam, what a treat.'

He drove me to a popular rest stop for rickshaw wallahs and introduced me to his fellow drivers as his good friend. It was nice to sit amongst them drinking chai and listen to them talking about the roads, Indian politics and of course, cricket. Once we finished, he accompanied me to the Bahai House of Worship.

Made of white marble and composed of twenty-seven free standing clad petals clustered to form the shape of a lotus flower, it was surrounded by nine reflecting pools, their open form suggesting the green leaves of the flower. It reminded me of the Sydney Opera House.

'As Bahai House open to all religion, my family and I are coming here from time to time. It is making very nice day out,' Rahul said, smiling.

I'd always wondered what it'd be like to drive a rickshaw. I tested him, asking if he'd let me have a go as we were leaving. I was surprised when he agreed. He looked around to check for any authorities and found a quiet area. Sitting in the passenger seat, he leant over and gave me instructions on how to drive. I managed to steer the little vehicle in figures of eight while Rahul shouted from the back, 'The great Mr Sam, rider of the rickshaw, guardian of the afternoon rickshaw wallah.'

It had gone eight by the time I returned to the hotel from my evening meal in the Main Bazaar. There was nobody at the desk, but I heard laughing from the room the other side of the entrance where Sean had stayed. I wanted to get a cup of tea and noticed Ashoka sat on the bed with a middle-aged Indian man with a white open neck shirt and black trousers. They were both drinking from glasses filled with what appeared to be Gin judging by the half empty bottle on the bureau.

'Hi Ashoka, any chance of some chai please?' I was ignored.

'Please come in, come in,' the gentleman said, much to Ashoka's chagrin.

'Thanks, but I was only after some tea really.'

'I insist,' the man said. I entered and a disgruntled Ashoka left.

Abhishek was a keen environmentalist. As he drank, he spoke with passion about his concerns, 'I have much fear for future generations. The global consumption of oil, coal and gas is at an all-time high. If we continue living the way we do, the consequences to our lives and the environment will be catastrophic.'

After a while he became a little less easy to understand, slurring more Hindi than English. Just after ten there was a knock at the door. By then Abhishek was quite drunk. It was Ashoka. He told me in an aggressive manner to keep my voice down. I didn't think we'd been talking that loudly, but I said I would. Abhishek was outraged, 'You are having the green eyes of envy, Ashoka. You are jealous that my friend here has taken your place in the conversation. Now please, leave us in peace.'

'The moon is high. You will now leave and go to your room,' Ashoka barked at me.

Abhishek wasn't having any of it, 'You are the one who is to leave my room at once, I tell you,' and pointed Ashoka to the hallway.

Ashoka flew behind the reception desk and picked up the phone.

'Maybe it's for the best,' I said. 'Thank you for a nice evening Abhishek, it's been very interesting talking to you.' With that I bid him goodnight and went to my room.

I was unlocking the door when Ashoka crept up behind me and whispered in my ear, 'Foreign scum should not mix with good Indian people. Now I will have you arrested for causing trouble and commotion.'

'What trouble and commotion?'

He turned away. I went into my room and sat worrying for the worse, assuming he'd call the police. Twenty minutes passed when

I heard voices from reception. I opened my door a fraction to see two uniformed policemen. To my relief, neither were the one I feared the most. I was not called upon or questioned. Instead, Abhishek gave a thorough account of what had happened and said that he felt threatened and harassed by Ashoka. Despite Ashoka's objections, he was told to stop wasting police time or it would be he who was arrested. I closed the door and a few minutes later Abhishek knocked. I apologised for any trouble.

'You should not be the one who is sorry. It is Ashoka that should be sorry and he will be.'

49

I awoke late morning and began packing, trying to put last night and the thought of where I would be tomorrow behind me. With no sign of Ashoka at the helm, I walked out into the midday heat and made my way to Arakashan Road. Under the bridge, past the drawn faces of the addicts and the sleeping homeless, I turned left and into the restaurant adjacent to the hotel where Aiden and I regularly ate. I ordered boiled eggs, toast and a coffee, and read the Times of India. The Befriend Strangers banner had long gone, replaced by a framed photograph of the exterior of the hotel. Paying the waiter, I stepped outside and lit a cigarette. Two westerners in their early twenties came over and asked for help.

'We were getting in a bit of a state,' one of the guys said. 'So far this morning, we've had a taxi driver try to rob us of everything, James here nearly got killed trying to cross the road and we've been accosted by a disabled man.'

'First time in India, huh?' I laughed.

'Yeah, just landed this morning. Can you help with a decent hotel?' the other asked.

I offered the solution of the hotel behind me, 'This is a good place to start. It's clean and the staff are good. You're from the UK, right?'

'Yeah, Manchester. Can you give us any advice?' the taller asked.

'Take deep breaths and try to stay calm, and don't take anything for granted. Turn right at the top of this street, go under the bridge and you will find the Main Bazaar on the right-hand side. There's shops, restaurants and hotels. If you want to get out of Delhi, you can take a train from the railway station across the road, but make sure to buy a ticket from the station. Don't be encouraged to leave the building by someone who claims tickets are available elsewhere. If you want to get a bus, agree a price with a rickshaw driver to take you to the Inter State Bus Terminal in Old Delhi. I'd recommend spending a little time in Delhi to acclimatise first though. She really is a wonderful city.'

'Hey, thanks man, that's really helpful.'

Rahul met me outside Harish's hotel as planned. I discussed the previous evening as we pressed through the morning rush, eventually arriving at Safdarjung's Tomb. The tomb was described as 'the last flicker in the lamp of Moghul architecture.' At the end of a shallow canal flanked by palm trees, I looked up at the mausoleum raised on a terrace of arches and felt sudden dismay at leaving this beautiful country. It had become my life and my home, and I was scared of the mundane that was waiting for me on the other side.

Conscious of my rickshaw wallah baking in the sun, I departed, leaving a trail of thoughts behind. Trundling through Old Delhi and along the bustling avenues of Chandni Chowk, the apparitions of Aiden, Jack and the others floated through me as we turned the corner to the commanding walls of the Red Fort, nearby which we stopped for a meal in a small eatery.

'You are going to miss India, my friend?' Rahul asked as I picked at my dhal and stared out longingly at life passing by on the street.

I attempted a smile, suddenly finding it hard to hold back the tears, realising just how much I would. 'I will, Rahul. That I will.'

Scenes of my trip unfolded in my head; all the things I did and didn't do, all the friends I met and would hold forever dear in my heart. The remaining hours were seeping through my fingers and however much I tried to cling on, the end was approaching fast.

The final monument I visited was India's largest mosque, the incredible Jama Masjid – commissioned by Emperor Shah Jahan.

In the paved courtyard, it was almost impossible to see the three massive domes as I stood at the foot of the pishtaq. The minarets, forty metres in height and constructed of alternating vertical strips of red sandstone and white marble, towered above. I climbed the southern minaret and could see the white domes with thin black onyx stripes and the courtyard below, capable of holding 25,000 worshippers. In all directions, rooftops stretched out for miles with the Red Fort to the east, New Delhi to the south and the endless sounds echoing throughout this beloved city. The sun was setting by the time I left. Pigeons took flight from the courtyard and became silhouettes against the elegance of the mosque and the golden sky.

Rahul was waving some way down the street. When I caught up with him he asked if I wanted to have a shave. I looked at the old man who sat at a table with razors and brushes and noticed he was blind. 'This guy?' I asked.

'Yes, he is the best barber in Old Delhi.'

I whispered in Rahul's ear, 'But I think he's blind.'

'But you are trusting what I say, yes?'

I took a seat and hoped for the best as the barber felt his way around my face, shaving away the stubble with impressive speed and accuracy. When he finished, I couldn't believe how smooth my face felt. 'Now that was amazing,' I said as I paid him.

It was a sad moment to say goodbye to Rahul. We exchanged addresses and hugs and after a hearty handshake, he left with a long buzz and a wave from the side of his auto. As I turned right and was about to turn right again, I was shoved aside by a fuming Ashoka. Harish was standing at reception looking flustered.

'Mr Sam, I am so very glad you are coming back. Please accept my apology for Ashoka's terrible behaviour. He is no longer with hotel. I telephone father and say that I am not able to work with him anymore because he is upsetting too many customer.' He placed his arm on my shoulder, 'Please, you will have good meal with us on rooftop. This will make me very happy.'

I spent the evening with Harish and Nitin on the upper rooftop looking out to the twinkling lights of Paharganj. Just after ten, I said my final farewells and popped out into the Main Bazaar to buy some cigarettes.

A young local with kind eyes and a goatee beard walked up beside me, 'Hello sir, I have seen you before.'

'I bet you have,' I laughed, now fully aware of every sales trick in the book.

There was something vaguely familiar about him and I warmed to his smile instantly, but I found it odd he was so overdressed for the muggy evening heat; a beige woolly hat, maroon trousers and matching cardigan. 'What do you believe?' he asked, quickening his pace to match my evasive steps.

'In India? I believe everything and nothing, and that anything is possible. I've got an early start so if you'll excuse me…'

'I have a message for you, Mr Sam.'

He knew my name? 'A message from who?'

'Please come.' He put out his arm to point to an empty stable off a side alley. I was dubious, but curiosity got the better of me.

'I haven't got any money I can give you.'

'I am not wanting your money sir, only your time. I am wishing to deliver to you an important message.'

'Okay, fire away then.'

'This morning I am having very strange dream. As I see you walk past just now, I knew I had to talk you. Everything is happening exactly as it did in dream.'

'Really? So, the message?'

'Beware the ashes in your stomach.'

'What? What does that even mean?'

'A woman has been placing ashes in your stomach for much time.'

'Who?'

'This I am not knowing, but I can tell you she is very close to you and means you harm. Her name is beginning with the letter A.'

'What? Listen mate, you're not really making much sense.'

'You will find it hard to trust people but will discover pure light in one. Although there will be much sadness, you will be rewarded with a happiness that not many man have. The soul never truly dies, my friend, it is merely purified and reborn.' He bowed slightly, placed his hands together in namaste and strolled out into the street. Before I had a chance to question him further, he vanished into the crowds.

I walked back to the hotel, replaying his words over and over. Ashes? A woman beginning with the letter A? The only person I knew whose name began with an 'A' was my mother; her name was Audrey. This was ridiculous. Just because this guy knew my name, didn't mean I should attribute any worth to his apparent message. Everybody agreed how wonderful my mum was. She was amazing; always there when the shit hit the fan.

Despite the far-fetched nature of his words, there was a sense of truth that I couldn't shake. Scenes from my childhood were vivid in my mind. When my dad came home from work, he would often be whistling when he entered the house, only to come storming up the stairs to my room a few minutes later. What happened during that brief time in-between? What had my mum said to him that made him so angry? I could never work out what I'd done.

It wasn't just my father. My grandfather unleashed the most hell after he'd been talking on the phone to her. Various friends of the family looked at me in a disapproving way too as did anyone I encountered; teachers, doctors, neighbours. Trouble trailed me through life and whatever it threw at me there was always one person I ran back to. When all the commotion died down, when my dad was calm in the wake of his destruction, when there was nothing left but ashes, she was there; telling me she'd always be there.

Something came to mind, at first misty, but soon took shape with chilling clarity. I was about five or six, playing in a neighbour's garden. The sun huge in the infinity of blue, the smell of fragrant summer heavy in the air. My mother was talking in the house with Sandy and Tom. I was throwing a tennis ball with Tess, their red setter. The ball splashed into the pond. Tess pawed the reflection making the sky and trees ripple. She looked lost, the puzzle of retrieving it longing in her eyes. I, like most children, thought nothing of it, my innocent hands stretching out as far as they could. I lost my balance and toppled in. Frantically I grasped the stagnant water, trying to find a grip. My lungs filled, and my eyes blurred as I sank below. Before my panic surrendered to the murky depths, I saw my mother staring down, motionless; a glint of a smile upon her face. Suddenly Tom pulled me to the surface, my chest heaving for oxygen. I vomited water and desperately sucked in air. My mother stood laughing as if it was all a big joke to the look of horror on the neighbour's faces.

More memories came crashing through, flooding my senses, revealing the past I'd subconsciously locked away. The same age, five or six, standing in a shop aisle crying my eyes out. She'd disappeared, left me on my own for staff to calm me and call the police. This was one of many occasions she'd conveniently lost me. 'Always running off', she told the authorities when she collected me. But I never ran off, she was all I had. The second my back was turned, she'd be gone.

A sticky substance left on my bedside cabinet that I fingered and put into my mouth to taste what it was. Only later, after agonising stomach pains and being rushed to the hospital, I was told it was ant poison. I was discovered on the grass on a playing field near to where I lived by a passer-by. I never once saw ants in my bedroom. That's the sort of thing a young boy would notice, surely.

I couldn't believe what my mind was summoning up. None of it seemed real, yet the more I searched within myself, the clearer it became. I'd always felt a disconnect, but it seemed irrational, so I had denied that nagging sensation inside warning me that my very worst enemy wasn't just there at my door, but right beside me the whole time. In my darkest hours, when the unfathomable anger, confusion and a slow decay of my soul had got the better of me I often wondered if I was slowly going mad.

It had been happening for so long, with each day a reminder of all the false starts and the results being held back by my own self-torment; question after question, memory after memory. No matter how many times I tried to put it all behind me, to right myself on the correct path with my head held high, I would inevitably tangle myself into another mess, screw myself up just that little bit further. My mind felt like it was no longer mine; a direful combination of incoherent rantings and doubts of self-worth. Inexplicable darkness held me in its clutches and I was no longer sure if I would ever find a way back to the existence of my core before it had all started.

The only time in my life I had been allowed an element of control and an abundance of freedom was here in India and now it was over. All that awaited me was the dead wood of my current being accompanied by the architect of my insanity; my mother. The woman who should have looked after me, protected me, encouraged nothing but the best for me, hid in the wings, allowing everything to play out as it did. She watched me volley from one hell to another, pretending to care.

Though it was always there trying to wake me and deliver the warnings, my intuition resonated more than ever. For years I'd felt a hostility towards her, something I couldn't understand or comprehend. The countless times I'd want to pull away when she'd reach out to hug me, or tell me she loved me, when all I could do was return a false sentiment. As the years of torment amalgamated and manifested within me, enveloping me in the darkness she held so dear, I found no exit, no reprieve, only the weight of her betrayal pushing down heavier than ever. The one that brought me into this world would be the one that would take me from it. I was left with nothing but a last moment of freedom, a breeze to make a final choice. Tears fell silently as I considered my options, of how I was going to end this insanity forever.

Consumed by ghosts and shadows, confusion and loss, I didn't want another second of this helplessness to play out any longer. The years had ground me down to nothing but dust. I'd travelled over 10,000 kilometres throughout this incredible land and seen the most amazing sights, and like life itself, the destination was never certain, until the end. No matter how much I tried to deny her part in all of this, I knew it to be true. The last place I wanted to be now was home.

A knock at the door temporarily lifted the sea of fog. Harish's voice gently called through, 'Mr Sam, are you still awake?' At first, I ignored him, silently begging him to leave, but after the relentless tapping got the better of me I let him in.

'How are you, Mr Sam?'

'A little tired, Harish.'

'Ah yes, late night for you. You are flying at 3am no?'

'Yeah, I guess… maybe.'

'Okay, so I am finding this in your laundry this morning. I am forgetting until just now when I find in drawer. It was in your coat pocket.'

He handed me a piece of blank paper. 'Um, thank you?' I replied.

'Oh no, sorry.' He reached across and turned it over, 'See, numbers. Maybe important, maybe not.'

I could just about make out some figures though they were faded and barely readable. It was Kate's handwriting.

'Do you have a telephone I could use?'

'Of course, all is now catered for international tourist.'

I picked up the phone, put it down again, picked it up, put it down. I wasn't even sure what to say. I picked it up again and dialled.

Thank you for reading Towards the Within.

If you enjoyed the book and have any thoughts that you'd like to share, please leave a review on Amazon to help other readers.

You can find more information about me on my website www.reecewillis.com

I can also be found on Facebook, Twitter and Instagram as well as Goodreads.

Also by Reece Willis

What We Become

She was everything he could have wanted. From the moment she came into his life, she captured his heart and turned his world upside down.

Now that she's gone, he can't live without her.

Desperate for resolution, Ben follows Kirsten to Thailand. He has a plan and now all he needs to do is be patient and wait for his moment to come.

But his pursuit of her only leads him down a darker path. His mind is in turmoil, plagued by memories of happier times, unable to come to terms with what he's lost, secretly wrestling with the feeling that it's his fault she left.

In this exciting new psychological journey from the author of Towards the Within, a story of love, obsession and regret awaits.